LORD DESPAIR

Beastly Lords Book One

SYDNEY JANE BAILY

cat whisker press
Massachusetts

ISBN: 978-1-938732-36-2
Published by cat whisker press
Imprint of JAMES-YORK PRESS

Cover: cat whisker studio
In conjunction with Philip Ré
Book Design: cat whisker studio

DEDICATION

To PTPR

Until I get to you, I'm too far away!

OTHER WORKS
by
SYDNEY JANE BAILY

THE RARE CONFECTIONERY
Series

The Duchess of Chocolate
The Toffee Heiress
My Lady Marzipan

THE DEFIANT HEARTS
Series

An Improper Situation
An Irresistible Temptation
An Inescapable Attraction
An Inconceivable Deception
An Intriguing Proposition
An Impassioned Redemption

THE BEASTLY LORDS
Series

Lord Despair
Lord Anguish
Lord Vile
Lord Darkness
Lord Misery
Lord Wrath
Eleanor

PRESENTING LADY GUS

A Georgian-Era Novella

ACKNOWLEDGMENTS

Thanks to my editor, Violetta Rand, for her warm encouragement. And, as always, thanks to my mom simply for being there.

PROLOGUE

1847, Belton Manor, Sheffield, England

Simon gazed into the darkness and felt a sense of satisfaction. Not a speck of light could he see. That was how he liked it. Day or night made no difference. Nor should it. The agony in his head didn't care about such things as the rising or setting sun. Only his servants entering with a tray of food or, more kindly, French brandy disturbed his routine. A sliver of light would slice into the infinite blackness as ever so gently they pushed open his door and brought in their offering, placing it almost noiselessly onto the table by his chair.

Occasionally, the infernal doctor arrived, if he really was one, with his nonsense about fresh air and walking and taking drops of laudanum to soothe his disposition. Infuriatingly, the man would leave the door open wide in order to better see his 'patient,' as he called Simon, who felt not the least bit sick.

The quack's latest suggestion of some newfangled treatment involving hypnosis had earned him Simon's roar of rage.

1

"Get out!"

The man had rightly fled. Perhaps he would be smart and never return. Thankfully, someone had closed the door, and Simon's world had been plunged once more into coal-blackness.

Sometimes, if he couldn't keep his mind focused on the game of seeing through the dark and past it, then his thoughts strayed to Toby. Dear cousin Tobias. He'd been chopped up and fed to the birds in front of Simon's very eyes.

Not in a torturous way. No, Toby was dead when the slicing began, having bled out in the cell before they dragged his body into the filthy yard and hacked it to pieces. It was not to punish his cousin but to warn the rest of them—Simon and two other hapless prisoners—about their dire fate should they step out of line as Toby had done. He had asked for another sip of water, as Simon recalled. The guard had taken offense and run him through with a saber.

It had shaken Simon to his core. He and his cousin had been through so much together. Grown up as close as brothers, and thus, when Toby announced his intent to fight for queen and country, Simon had felt it his duty to go, too, despite thinking the whole Burmese conflict was more for the teak wood trade and profit than anything patriotic. Still, victory was essential to keep the French from making any inroads into Victoria's imperial holdings.

Weathering dozens of battles, both of them in charge of Indian troops, they'd ended up as prisoners in the same godforsaken Burmese cell. Having had each other's backs for so long, it was unthinkable that the man Simon had known all his life, who was intelligent, kind, and fierce as hell when necessary, was gone. It was all senseless.

There'd been no reason for anything anymore. No point to life. No point to caring. No reason to give a damn. Just wait for death, which was what Simon had done until miraculously—or perhaps wretchedly—his cell door had opened one day.

Rescue, freedom, *eternal damnation!*

How was he expected to return to this life of luxury and gentleness? How was he supposed to drink tea and sit at a table with civilized people when he knew how uncivilized they could be?

How could Simon stop seeing Toby's glassy eyes?

How could he ever close his eyes and sleep?

That was something Simon could not do, at least not willingly. He fought sleep every night. Fought and lost occasionally. He sat in darkness and didn't let his body or mind know if it was time for wakefulness or for slumber.

Yet against his will, sometimes, he drifted off for a few moments, and all hell broke loose. Battles and viciousness and Toby's eyes plagued his sleep. And that rat-infested cell. Always the cell.

Was he even now in the small space in which he couldn't even stand up, dreaming of this house in Sheffield, this room in his family's home? Was he only imagining this life that felt completely unreal and of which he knew he could never again be a part?

Simon Devere, seventh Earl of Lindsey, simply didn't know. However, as long as he kept his eyes open and kept his surroundings dark so he could not look too closely at the details of the room, then he was here in England in Belton Manor.

CHAPTER ONE

❝I don't think I can toil another day for that man.❞ The unexpected remark came from a young woman of marrying age with caramel-colored hair, who wore an unhappy expression upon her lovely face.

Maggie was home.

Jenny was made aware of her sister's arrival by the slamming of the front door and, thus, was well prepared to watch her flounce into the room, toss her gloves onto the desk, and sit on the other side of it.

Trying to keep the exasperation from her voice, Jenny reminded her, "You do not *toil* for any man of whom I'm aware, so what on earth are you talking about?"

Maggie frowned, picking up a few papers lying before her, glancing at them as if they were in a foreign language instead of being merely payroll for their small cottage and land, and then tossed them back onto the burnished walnut surface.

"You know whom I mean. *Lord Despair.*"

Jenny sighed. "That is unkind. Besides, you are not in *his* employ. You help that poor woman who is near out of her mind with grief over her husband's death. Show some sympathy, Mags."

Maggie sat up straighter. "Oh, I do. I do. I sit with those young ones as they try to conjugate French verbs and speak as fluently as their mother. If Lady TobiasDevere comes into the room with her pale face and red-rimmed eyes, I always ask her how she's feeling. Yet it's been nearly two months, hasn't it, since Lord Despair came home and brought news of his cousin's demise? Not to mention, in reality, her husband's been dead for about two years. Still, the lady cries as if she only saw him yesterday and then placed him in his eternity box today."

"Tobias Devere was a good man, by all reports," Jenny offered.

Maggie nodded. "The children sometimes cry, too, even though I doubt they remember him. Nonetheless, it has sunk in that their father is not returning. Not ever."

Jenny heard Maggie's voice catch and knew her sister was not unaffected by the Devere family's tragedy, reminiscent of their own loss of their beloved yet irresponsible Blackwood patriarch.

"I don't belong there," her sister insisted. "I don't want to be in the middle of their grief. I have my own to deal with," she added. "What's more, I certainly don't want to be a French tutor. Why must I do it? Why can't I stay home and help you with these figures you're adding all day?" She gestured at the ledgers and papers on the desk.

Jenny shrugged. "We are all doing what we can to help Mummy. You know that. And you are as unsuited to arithmetic as I am to French."

"What about Eleanor?"

Jenny smiled at the idea of their younger sister employed at anything gainful.

"If I can figure out a way to put a monetary value on daydreaming and occasionally sketching roses, then I'll find some work for her, too."

Reaching across the table, Jenny laid her hand upon her sister's. "Please, stick with it. I know the compensation is a pittance compared to what you're worth, but because of your being a baron's daughter, they pay you more than they would a real tutor or a governess."

Maggie's nostrils flared. "That we should be discussing wages, like . . . merchants!" Standing, she went to the sideboard and began fiddling with the empty brandy decanter.

At eighteen, Jenny's middle sister, stuck in the country and with no beau on the horizon, was keenly aware of her precarious position. Particularly with no dowry, and with Maggie having sadly had her one and only season cut short earlier in the year by the untimely death of their father.

And then the debt collectors had come calling. Jenny's marital prospects had fallen through immediately when her own seemingly upstanding viscount, who had wooed and won her during her second season, abruptly withdrew his offer. If her father had been alive, he would have challenged the breaking of the verbal contract. Of course, if her father had been alive, the viscount wouldn't have broken it.

On Jenny's part, she certainly would have married as her duty and been grateful for the opportunity to help run Lord Alder's estate and raise any children with which she and the viscount were blessed. Yet, she'd felt only a mild interest in the man or in becoming his wife.

At Baron Lucien Blackwood's death, their mother had been ill-equipped to handle anything more than gathering up her household, including her three daughters and as many servants as she could continue to employ, and head for the family's country cottage in Sheffield. Here, they already had many good memories of hot summers and crisp autumns, the seasons when they were not in London.

And for many years when Jenny was younger, the Blackwoods had come from Town to spend the winter holidays. If the Deveres were in residence, they would hold one of their legendary Christmas parties. Jenny recalled going to Belton Park and meeting both the titled Deveres who lived in the grand manor house and their lesser relations at Jonling Hall. Of which Sir Tobias Devere, used to be the happy lord.

The Burmese War had ended all that. Tobias had left three years ago to do his duty with his cousin Simon, the viscount and heir to the earldom. By the time Jenny and her family had arrived from London, both men were already feared dead. Tobias Devere's family had moved from the hall into Belton Manor.

Jenny hoped their relocation had been made to put the widow and her children under the protection of the earl. She feared, however, it was due to financial strain that was plaguing many of the grand families who were finding maintaining land and actually paying servants was no easy task.

"Even when we are having a passing-fair afternoon," Maggie bemoaned, "suddenly, we will hear wretched Lord Despair—"

"Please," Jenny interrupted, "stop calling him that."

About the same time her family arrived back in Sheffield, Simon Devere had returned in a terrible mental state, or so said the rife and quick rumors of the village residents. What's more, he'd confirmed the worst for Lady Devere, his cousin's French-born wife. Sir Tobias was dead, and Simon, whose father had passed away whilst he was in Burma, was no longer a viscount but now the new earl.

An earl whom no one had seen outside of Belton Manor since his return.

"He is Lord Devere and the highest-ranking nobleman in this county," she reminded her sister.

Jenny vaguely remembered the few times her family had gone to the manor for a Christmas party or a late summer fete. The earl had kind eyes and was quite striking. He was older than her, maybe by seven or eight years, thus she'd never shared more than a passing greeting with him.

However, she'd been left with an impression of him being courteous.

"Actually, I suppose now his father has passed, Lord Devere has become Lord Lindsey."

"Fine," Maggie yielded. "All at once, while I'm reading them a story, enunciating clearly so they pick up the new words, we will hear Lord Lindsey cry out or thump about in his room like a wounded boar. The gloom that falls over the children and poor Lady Devere is practically palpable. They would have been better off staying at the hall."

"Maybe they had no choice."

Maggie considered that in silence, then she gestured at the papers on the desk. "How are you doing? Are we in any better situation than last month?"

Jenny looked down at the numbers before her. "Your contribution helps tremendously." That was overstating it, but every little bit counted.

Maggie nodded in acceptance. "As does yours, at a far higher contribution, I'm certain."

Jenny blushed. Yes, her accounting skills certainly had brought in a tidy sum, and she hoped that would continue, as long as no one knew it was she, a mere 20-year-old spinster looking at their ledgers. They would flip their wigs if they knew her identity, a woman with no experience in business. By sending Henry, their father's manservant whom her mother had refused to let go upon Lord Blackwood's death, Jenny had managed to procure the custom of quite a few clients.

She balanced the accounts of local merchants and publicans, as well as a few nobles. Each client sent their ledgers, via Henry, to the mysterious genius who made short work of determining what was owed to the crown and what was a loyal subject's right to keep in his own coffers. If only she'd known her father's dire circumstances . . .

With her growing clientele and frugal ways, she was keeping her mother, sisters, and their household from destitution. Even if Maggie didn't contribute much, it was the notion of not doing it alone that greatly comforted Jenny and kept at bay the considerable burden of her family's survival resting entirely on her shoulders.

What's more, although she hadn't mentioned it to Maggie or Eleanor, they still had some money from the sale of their house in Town. With this and her mother's blessing, Jenny was determined to give each some sort of Season in London, even if it were greatly abbreviated. Anything by way of a dowry, however, would be impossible. Both her sisters were lovely enough, Jenny knew, if only they could be seen in a few ballrooms, they had a chance to make a favorable match.

As for herself, Jenny found she didn't mind the drastic change in lifestyle the way she had feared. To be a spinster in London would have been unbearable; she would have been scorned by her peers and had her social engagements severely limited as she aged. In the country, she had freedom. She already ran a household and oversaw her sisters as if she were a man. She rode when she wanted and read what she wanted, and no one had forced her to play the dreaded pianoforte or sing or do needlepoint since they'd arrived.

In fact, Jenny hated to benefit from the misery of others, especially her mother and sisters, but her life had improved. And she hadn't had to take up the mantle of a viscount's wife, especially as it turned out, a wife who was not really desired. The only black cloud was the unwelcome possibility that she might never marry, never experience the mysteries of the marriage bed, nor have sweet girls and boys of her own.

"Anyway, I cannot go back tomorrow." Maggie's voice penetrated her thoughts.

Jenny stood. "What are you saying? Why ever not?"

"Mummy has ordered me to take Eleanor into town to get a new hat, as she's lost them all, and gloves as she has destroyed her last pair."

A hat and gloves! Jenny wanted to scream at the frivolousness of it.

"You cannot simply abandon your charges for such a matter. Not when you are supposed to be at work."

Maggie held up her hand. "Do not say that word. I do not *work*. I assist the Devere children. I lend them my educational skills. I am recompensed in the manner of a lady."

Jenny sighed. She understood her sister's anathema to having fallen from the higher station they'd enjoyed whilst their father lived, but a spade was a spade.

Maggie wasn't finished however. "You speak as though Lady Devere places coins in my hand!"

Instead, the payment was sent via a servant each week to the Blackwood household. No *filthy lucre* crossed her sister's palm. And when Maggie went into town to the milliner's shop the next day with Eleanor, the woman would simply write the sum on a slip of paper and send it back to Jenny to pay.

No wonder most people did not think about numbers! Or like her father, didn't consider what he owed until it was too late.

"Why don't you handle the French lessons, and I'll take Eleanor?"

"Because I need a day away from that place," Maggie stated.

"It's only Tuesday," Jenny pointed out. How would her sister make it to Friday?

"No. Lord Despair gave me a fright today, and I need a day to recover. That is that!" Maggie was clearly not going to back down, and if Jenny hoped to prevail and get her sister to go back by Thursday, she'd better give in.

"Fine. I will go to the manor in your place."

Maggie's mouth dropped open. "You will? And do what?"

Jenny considered. All she knew was that she didn't want to give anyone at Belton a reason to withhold any payment on Saturday. She suspected it was not Lady Maude Devere who paid, in any case, but someone in charge of the earl's coffers. Obviously, not the earl himself, since he was apparently in no state to do anything since his return except to sit in his room. Or so the servants' gossip indicated.

"Perhaps I will demonstrate to the children the amazing power of algebra."

Maggie didn't look impressed. "You have a passing knowledge of French and your pronunciation is quite good despite not understanding all the words. Why don't you simply read them a story and try not to mangle it too terribly? They have some books in the small parlor where we meet, and somewhere in that manor is a library."

Jenny immediately felt the sting of her family's degradation that had so bothered her sister these past few weeks. For the following day, after leaving her horse and brightly painted gig on the smoothly pebbled drive and walking the flagstone path to the imposing stone steps and up to the massive front doors framed by a carved lintel and flanked by columns, she announced to the liveried servant that she was Miss Blackwood. She was told to go around to Belton's side door. Not exactly the servant's entrance but neither the one reserved for invited guests.

Straightening her shoulders, Jenny made the long trek around the perfectly symmetrical front façade of the yellow-stone manor to the side door.

To her amazement, the same servant appeared at her knock.

The man shrugged. "It is the way we were told it should be, Miss."

"Very well. Where are the young Deveres?"

"This way, Miss." The tall man led her through a hallway, up some back stairs, and along another hall to a small, elegant room, decorated in robin-egg blue with crisp white chair rails and crown molding. Here, in the well-lit chamber, he asked her to wait.

Removing her coat, Jenny placed it over a tufted wingchair along with her reticule, and took a minute to examine her surroundings. It looked as if the space had been a lady's drawing room turned into a makeshift schoolroom with two ladderback chairs pulled up to a plain rectangular table. On it were dip pens and ink, chalk and two slates, an abacus which Jenny immediately picked up, and a stack of thin sheets of paper.

Fiddling with the beads of the abacus, Jenny approached the bookcase, pleased to see a variety of subjects, even novels and some exciting histories. Just then, the door behind her was flung open and in came her charges for the day. A boy and a girl, neither yet in double digits. They stopped short upon seeing her. Apparently, they hadn't been told of the switch in tutors.

"Who are you?" demanded the boy, not unkindly, simply without preamble.

"I am Miss Blackwood."

"No, you're not," said the girl, obviously younger, perhaps all of four years. "Not at all."

"I am the other Miss Blackwood. And there is yet one more of us," Jenny informed her, "as well as a Lady Blackwood, who is my mother. And your names are?"

"I'm Peter," said the boy.

The girl took a step forward. "I'm Alice."

"Do you speak French?" asked Peter.

Jenny nodded, deciding not to say how rusty her command of it was. Then she looked over their shoulders, but no one else was apparently coming. No adult to discuss the afternoon's lessons. Who taught them subjects other than French?

"Do you have other tutors besides Miss Margaret?"

Peter nodded. "Master Cheeseface teaches me mathematics and writing."

"Master Cheeseface?" Jenny repeated.

The boy smiled and nodded, and then Alice laughed, giving it away as a jest.

"Come now. It's not nice to make fun of people's names." She thought of her own sister and the many in the village who had taken up the moniker of 'Lord Despair' for the despondent man who even then resided somewhere in this magnificent house. Had the children heard that cruel name for their blood relation?

"He *does* look like Swiss cheese," said Peter, "but his name is Master Dolbert."

"I see. And when does he put in an appearance?"

"First thing in the morning," said the boy. "Not every day."

Alice only nodded solemnly.

"You've had no lessons today at all?"

Instead of answering, Peter asked, "Why are you holding our abacus?"

Jenny looked down, only then realizing her fingers had been nimbly sliding the beads back and forth on all ten rows. Familiar, comforting, even though her own had twelve rows. Still, at least it wasn't anything like a flowery foreign language with those dreaded, tongue-tying letter *r*'s.

"Would you like me to read you a story in French and see if you can tell me what the words mean?" And hopefully they could tell her what they meant as well!

In answer, they ran to the bookshelf and pulled out a large illustrated book of Perrault's collected fairytales.

Jenny smiled. "*Ah,* my favorites." If only they were in English.

Eschewing the hard chairs at the table, the three of them sat side-by-side on a sofa by a bay window with enormous panes that seemed to stretch upward forever.

In the middle of the two children, Jenny had the book on her lap and opened it. "Is there one in particular?"

"Start from the beginning, please," said Peter.

Oh dear. It was quite a large collection. "We'll read two today. *Histoires ou contes du temps passé,*" Jenny began slowly and added the book's subtitle, "*Les Contes de ma Mère l'Oye.*"

Her pronunciation was not terrible, and neither child laughed.

"Translation, please, Peter," Jenny said.

"*Stories or Fairy Tales from Past Times with Morals,* or *Mother Goose Tales.*"

"*Très bien,*" she told him. "The first story, which I'm sure you've already heard a hundred times, is *Cendrillon.* Alice, please translate."

"*Cinderella,*" chimed the little girl.

"*Bon,*" said Jenny and plunged ahead.

Reading a paragraph at a time, she let the children take turns explaining what was happening and sometimes directly translating a line. At this rate, they passed a pleasurable hour, and then another with the next story, *La Belle au Bois Dormant,* or *The Sleeping Beauty in the Wood.*

"Oh my," Jenny said, when she reached the end and the ogress queen had died in the tub of snakes and toads. "I'm feeling a tad parched. *Je suis soif.*"

"*J'ai soif,*" Peter amended.

Hmm. Corrected by a child.

"Time for tea," Jenny declared, sticking to English as she rose and stretched. "Where do you normally take your refreshments?"

The children looked at each other. "Someone usually brings it in."

"I don't know about you, but I would very much like to take a walk," she told them. In any case, she couldn't see the bell pull anywhere, certainly not an obvious needlepoint or tapestry pull. No doubt it was concealed as one of the decorative brass or bronze items in the room, but she would feel foolish trying to press and turn every one.

"Shall we go to the dining room and pull the bell?"

Jenny was well aware that children delighted in ringing for service. At least her sisters used to when they were young at their home in London.

As expected, they jumped up, running ahead of her, and making enough noise to rival a herd of the queen's best deer rather than merely two children.

Hoping she hadn't caused any problems with protocol, she followed them.

"WHAT IS THAT NOISE?" Simon asked aloud although he was certain he was alone. A riot outside the prison? Guards carousing? Rescue? But no, hadn't he been rescued already? What could cause such a noise in quiet Sheffield? Were they coming to take him back?

His heartbeat started to gallop and a cold sweat broke out down his back.

They were coming closer, or was that simply a play of echoes? He screamed. At least, he thought it was his own voice. Yes, he screamed again and it felt good to do so. He felt his own powerful resistance and screamed in a way he'd never done in the jail for fear of being instantly and permanently silenced.

Then Simon closed his eyes and *saw* Toby lying at his feet and remembered how he had not said a word for a long time after his cousin's brutal murder. How he had watched silently as they'd dragged him out by his feet and began to . . .

"No," he shouted. "No, no, no, no!"

Simon continued until he felt exhausted. When he stopped, the noises had also stopped. All around him was quiet.

Good.

CHAPTER TWO

The hair on the back of Jenny's neck rose and she shivered. What an atrocious racket! First the children, then the dreadful shouting. She knew instantly who it was.

Feeling both pity and a prickle of fear, she held her arms out as Peter and Alice ran to her for safety.

Was Lord Lindsey on the same floor? Or one above? Should they go immediately back to the parlor or—?

"What in the name of the devil is going on here?"

Slowly, Jenny turned toward the sound of the man's voice, not sure what to expect. A tall man, slightly older than her father would have been, stood in the corridor, hands straight down by his sides and a distinct scowl upon his face.

By his demeanor, a commander, but by his clothing, a servant.

"Who are you?" he asked, his bushy eyebrows rising up into his silvered hairline.

Before she could respond, he addressed the children.

"You two know better than to cause such a ruckus."

"Yes, sir," Alice and Peter said in unison.

"What are you doing running in this wing?"

Jenny decided to take responsibility. "The children and I were going to request tea. We've been cooped up for hours."

"And you are?"

This time he waited for her reply.

"Miss Blackwood."

He looked her over with a neutral glance. "Another one," he said.

She nodded. "My sister could not attend her charges today."

"I see. And one Blackwood is as good as the next," he offered.

She nearly took offense but realized he was making a little jest and not speaking seriously. Or so she thought.

"There's another one, too," Peter informed the man.

"How beneficial." The man took a deep breath as if collecting himself, and Jenny began to understand that he had been truly disturbed by their noise and no doubt upset at the resulting effect on the earl.

"I am Mr. Binkley," he offered. "Butler of Belton, and I apologize for the staff being remiss. Tea should have been brought to you. I will send a tray at once. Please return to the blue parlor."

"May we go to the dining room for a change of venue?" Jenny requested, now that Mr. Binkley seemed to have calmed down.

He looked as if he were battling an inner argument.

"I promise there will be no more running or disturbance," she added. "We will go over our French words for common dining items while we are there."

Still, he hesitated. At last, he muttered, "Very well. Follow me."

Nodding to Jenny as he passed her, Mr. Binkley continued along the hallway in the direction the children had been leading her. The three of them went down the main staircase and across a large foyer. Entering a vast dining room with a long table and about two dozen chairs arranged on both sides, Jenny could only stop and stare.

The table stretched on forever with a perfect sheen of polish and neither a speck of dust nor a single fingerprint in sight. A far cry from the Blackwood cottage's oak table with newsprint, flowers, and occasionally crumbs strewn across it. In contrast, the Devere dining room had the distinct air of disuse and even sadness to Jenny's way of thinking, even if it did boast two magnificent crystal chandeliers hanging from the high ceiling.

"Please wait here and do not go anywhere else."

She nodded to Mr. Binkley, and he gave each of the children a stern glance before retreating.

"Well, that nearly spoiled our outing."

Alice giggled at Jenny's words, and Peter wandered around the room as if he'd never seen it. With a start, Jenny realized that perhaps the children had not. Maybe the family, Lady Tobias Devere and her children, ate in a cozy room somewhere rather than in this sterile, vaulted chamber.

"Can you tell me anything about this room?" Jenny asked. "Do you know that man in the painting?"

Peter had stopped to stare at a large portrait hung at one end of the room over the blue *fleur de lis* wallpaper.

"I don't know." His voice had a strange tenor to it, and Jenny approached him.

"He looks like my father, only much older." Peter's voice was tinged with curiosity.

Jenny studied the portrait. A handsome man about twenty years past the prime of life stared down at her.

"Oh," she muttered, recalling gatherings at the manor when she was a child. She had never been in this room, only the great room that she knew was somewhere close by. It had held the largest Christmas tree she'd ever seen. And this man, the previous earl, had been there along with his only son, Simon, who now suffered alone upstairs.

Perhaps present at those holiday gatherings had been Peter and Alice's father, Sir Tobias Devere, although Jenny couldn't remember him. No doubt, he'd been a gangly youth as was his cousin Simon.

"I have met this man. He was Lord Lindsey, the father of the current earl." The elderly man had passed away while his son and nephew were overseas, following his long-dead countess. In fact, Jenny couldn't remember a time when Lady Lindsey had been alive.

Then she patted the boy's shoulder. "And you look like him as well, Peter, because he is *your* grandfather."

"And mine?" asked Alice.

Jenny turned to say yes just as a young woman entered carrying a gleaming silver tray, followed by Mr. Binkley, who paused at seeing them in front of the six-foot painting.

"When you are finished with your refreshment," he said, his tone brooking no argument, "please ring the bell." He pointed to a bronze statue of a lion on its hind legs appearing to be simple figurine set upon the mantle. "Press the front legs, and I'll escort you back to the study."

She would have preferred poking around and perhaps finding the great room of her childhood memories, but apparently, that was not to be.

"Of course," Jenny said, and settled into chairs with the children. Along with a teapot, cups, and saucers, a pile of scones sat jauntily on a platter with two bowls, one with clotted cream and one with raspberry jam.

Alice squealed in delight, and Jenny quickly lost the will to make them name everything in French since she doubted she could tell if they were correct anyway.

WITH HER HEAD RESTING on the back of the sofa, Jenny found she could not move. Her eyes were firmly closed.

"Ha," Maggie's voice crowed, "I knew it. Those children exhausted you."

"Yes," Jenny mumbled, not raising her head. "They did."

Then Eleanor's sweet voice permeated her tired mind. "Jen, look at my new hat."

With effort, Jenny slid open her eyes and peered across the room at her sisters. Maggie was grinning, and Eleanor, also smiling, had on a beautiful straw hat with both feathers and ribbons artfully arranged.

"It looks expensive," Jenny said.

Both girls deflated immediately at her tone.

"But lovely," Jenny added quickly. "Perfect for the country."

Eleanor's broad smile returned. "Isn't it though? The brim will keep the sun out of my eyes and off my nose."

"Perfect," Jenny repeated and closed her eyes once again. She'd promised Mr. Allen at the inn that she would have his accounts balanced by the next morning, or at least their servant, Henry, had made such a promise. She would have to rally soon and make good on their manservant's word.

Feeling someone sit beside her, she knew it was Maggie, for she'd heard Eleanor scamper off at her usual prancing pace.

"They are good children," Maggie began.

"Yes. We read Perrault and then ventured out to find sustenance."

Maggie gasped. "You never! You left the blue room?"

"Yes."

"You're not supposed to."

"As I found out."

"Who discovered you?" Maggie asked, a measure of excitement in her voice.

"Mr. Binkley was his name."

"The admiral!"

Jenny startled. "Is he?"

"No." Maggie laughed. "But I think of him as such."

"I can see why. He was quite forceful."

"He marched you back to the parlor?"

"No, we had a delightful afternoon tea service in the dining room."

Maggie gasped. "You never!"

"Stop saying that."

"Saying what?" her mother's voice accompanied her into the room. "And why are you sleeping at this hour?"

"I am not sleeping, Mummy, merely resting. I had some long hours at the manor."

Her mother sat down on the other side of her and her familiar lavender scent drifted to Jenny's nose, offering comfort.

"Did you remember it? Belton Manor, I mean?"

"Yes, I did, but I didn't get to revisit the great room."

"Pity," her mother mused. "One of the loveliest rooms in all of England, I'd warrant. Always good of them to open it to the children at Christmastime.

"I saw a portrait of the old earl."

Her mother clucked her tongue. "Nice man. He'd be horrified to hear about the fate of his nephew, I'm sure, not to mention his only son."

"I believe I heard *him* today."

Maggie gasped again.

"What can you mean by that?" her mother wanted to know.

"She means she heard Lord Despair moaning and groaning."

Jenny lifted her head at last and shot her sister a glance but didn't bother to correct her.

Then she turned to her mother. "The children became a bit boisterous when we went to take our tea. All at once, I heard a man screaming. It was bloodcurdling, I must say." Jenny recalled what had happened next. "Then he began to shout the word *no*. A bit weakly at first, but then much more firmly. Over and over, as if he were being tormented."

It had been a heartbreaking sound.

"And I have to go back there tomorrow," Maggie protested.

"Does she?" their mother asked Jenny as if she were head of the household.

"Yes, she most certainly does." She looked at Maggie. "Have you heard similar?"

Maggie sighed. "I have, although rarely. Maybe not quite as long an episode as you mention. Just a shout or a groan. And at times, he thumps around, and those noises bother the children. The admiral—"

"Who?" their mother asked.

"The butler," Jenny clarified.

"Mr. Binkley sometimes checks on us after the earl has an incident." Maggie stood suddenly. "I'm going to write to Ada. I sorely miss her."

Jenny was sorry that her sister had to leave all her friends behind. Clearly, the shortcomings of her new life were making her think about her old one. "Why don't you invite her to come stay with us when the season has finished?"

Maggie shot her a look of utter horror.

"Oh no, I couldn't." She put her hands to her cheeks. "Imagine her seeing me festering in the country after she has been waltzing in London? Good Lord, what if she found out I was receiving payment for my time with the Devere children?"

"That would not do," their mother agreed.

Jenny thought them both overly sensitive.

"I understand that missing the Season is an unfortunate thing, but you should feel a sense of pride in—"

"Don't you dare say 'in your work,' or I shall never go back to the manor. I feel nothing but humiliation."

With that, Maggie stormed from the room.

"Oh, dear," their mother murmured.

"Indeed," Jenny agreed.

22

"HIS LORDSHIP, THE EARL of Lindsey, wishes you to conduct a thorough audit of the prior five years' ledgers. Said volumes will be delivered to your office by . . ."

Jenny read the meat of the missive over and then again. It consisted of a single paragraph addressed to Mr. G. Cavendish, the name she'd called herself since beginning the lucrative charade of bookkeeper, using her mother's maiden name.

Clara, the housekeeper, who'd served them since Jenny was a child, stood before the writing desk, waiting until Jenny reached the end of the letter that had been delivered to their door. It was signed "E. Binkley, representing His Lordship Simon Devere, Earl of Lindsey."

"Gracious!" she exclaimed. *The admiral.*

"There is a lad waiting on an answer," Clara reminded her.

Jenny stared a moment at Clara. Her first thought was that she would be found out if she was not extremely careful. Her second thought was that she should charge more to this particular client. Her third thought was that she probably ought to turn down this entreaty altogether.

Still, she picked up her fountain pen and snatched up a plain piece of writing paper, one without the recognizable Blackwood "B" surrounded by holly and underscored with the very proper motto, *Per vias rectas*. By straight ways, indeed!

What would her ancestors think of her decidedly not straight path? She didn't care to ponder that question.

With quick strokes, Jenny responded that she would be glad to assist the earl and would receive his ledgers anon. She signed it with what was becoming a familiarly fake signature.

Waving the paper back and forth for a few moments, she then folded it and handed it to Clara, who offered her a wry smile and hurried from the room.

What an interesting turn of events. Jenny would be privy to the inner workings of Belton Park, including the manor and Jonling Hall, as well as the surrounding lands and holdings. Perhaps she would even find out who had purchased the hall, which remained empty after Lady Devere and her children vacated it over a year earlier. For some reason, they'd been unable to maintain the residence.

A mere forty-eight hours later, Jenny sat at her desk with the Devere ledgers spread before her and cracked open the latest one, deciding to take stock of the current state of things before delving into the past.

Another three hours later, as well as a pot of tea and four lemon biscuits, she knew quite a bit. Maude Devere had not had the disposable income to pay for the upkeep of Jonling Hall, nor to pay her servants. She'd been forced to let them all go and to sell her home to someone who'd gone through a London estate agent and was, unfortunately, unnamed in the proceedings. Obviously, it was someone quite well-heeled.

Jenny's family had avoided the same fate, although they'd had to part with their darling townhouse on Hanover Square. If she did manage to save enough to give either sister a proper Season the following January, where would they reside in London?

Pushing that worrisome thought out of her head, she plunged ahead. While the old earl's holdings had been quite prosperous in the past, they had yielded dwindling profits of late. The downturn had already begun at the earliest ledger, five years past, as someone had noted a quarter decrease in the year's end total; the next year, the profits were down again. Then, about the time the young earl and his cousin went away, the accounting became spotty, and some earnings were not recorded at all. The handwriting changed, too.

Jenny wondered if Simon Devere had been the one keeping the ledgers for his father until he'd left for Burma. Of one thing she was certain, some of the incomes were going missing from the trade and manufacturing accounts.

Perhaps it was simply from a misunderstanding rather than because of any nefarious goings-on.

Over the next few days, Jenny made notes of her findings, outlined the discrepancies she was encountering, and wrapped the whole package up neatly for Henry to return to Mr. Binkley by early evening on the third day. Jenny doubted the earl was in any state to peruse them, but his butler, and hopefully an estate overseer, would have to understand that she couldn't do a proper accounting of the estate with such gaps in the records.

Lastly, she created her bill for the hours worked, tucked it into an envelope, and affixed that to the package via a sturdy piece of string.

Time to reward herself with a glass of Spanish wine before dinner. After telling Clara she would have her aperitif in their small and rather haphazardly tended garden, Jenny made her way onto the back paved terrace, overlooking boxwoods, barberry shrubs, and roses. Taking a seat at the wrought-iron table, she could see the stables and the small paddock and heard the whinnying of their horses.

Accepting the wine from Clara with a nod of gratitude, Jenny admitted to herself she'd nearly forgotten the other pressing issue on her plate. Thunder, as Eleanor had named one of their horses, had taken on the demeanor of its name and become a bad-tempered gelding. They'd sold off another pair of fine ponies in London and brought with them only Thunder and Lucy, a tame mare. Here at their country home, there already resided an old carriage horse, a Cleveland Bay, nameless as far as she knew, who'd been in the family since before she or either of her sisters were born.

Jenny sighed. Horseflesh was expensive to maintain, especially when one had expensive hats to buy one's sisters and a Season to save for. However, no one would buy Thunder in his current state, and none of them could bear to part with Lucy or the old Bay.

At present, all three horses were grazing in the paddock. One would think the two older ones would willingly stay away from Thunder, but Lucy quite often approached her stablemate, resulting in mayhem. The problem had started with a slip in a pesky spring puddle when they were unwillingly fleeing London for the country. The roads were riddled with both shallow and deep crevasses filled with rainwater. Thunder had stepped in a rut disguised by muddy water and twisted his right front leg.

None of the Blackwood women had any special skillfulness with horses, despite having been taught to ride, and Eleanor loved all creatures almost more than she liked people. Clara's son, their young stable boy George, had tended the leg as best he could on the advice of a neighbor, using a poultice and a tight bandage around the cannon. Its leg had healed, but in the meanwhile, the horse had developed a slight limp.

To make matters worse, Thunder had stuck his head in a raspberry bush, probably seeking sweet berries, and, by the way he blinked and shied on that side, had most likely scratched his left eye. Between one thing and the other, he was anxious and skittish.

Jenny sighed again and took a healthy draught of her wine.

"What are you doing?" her mother asked, taking the empty chair beside her.

"Relaxing. And thinking that something will have to be done about Thunder, but for the life of me, I don't know what."

Clara brought out another glass of wine for the mistress of the house, and Jenny lifted hers to tap glasses with her mother.

"Let George worry about the horses," Ann Blackwood said. "You are doing an excellent job with everything else. Have I told you that?"

She smiled at her mother. "Yes, you have."

"I know you would be established in your own home by now if not for your father's death. Are you terribly disappointed?"

Jenny shook her head. "In all honesty, no. I would have gone to an unfamiliar house and lived amongst strangers."

"You would have had a husband," her mother pointed out.

"Another stranger," Jenny said. "Did you love Father when you married him?"

Anne sat back and stared at the fields beyond the paddock, and then she sipped her wine. "I did."

"Would you have married him if you didn't?"

"Circumstances were different. Frankly, I wouldn't have been allowed. As it was, we were nearly forbidden by my father. If I hadn't loved your father and pressed his case, his suit would have been dismissed."

"Because Father was a Scot?"

"Yes, but I begged my mother to help convince my father. If your father hadn't been a baron, she wouldn't have helped me either, but that small nod to nobility gave him the sheen of acceptance. That and the fact that he'd gone to school on this side of the border."

Jenny considered it for a moment. Her parents had always seemed happy.

"I'm sorry that you lost your love, Mummy. Quite apart from the fact that he was my father, I liked him as a person."

Her mother reached over and touched Jenny's arm. "Thank you."

"I am glad you don't cry anymore. Maggie says that Lady Devere is still crying, and, think on it, her husband has been dead for years even though she didn't know it."

"Maybe she cries for other reasons," Anne suggested. "In any case, I had a good marriage and I have you three girls. I can't complain."

Jenny smiled at her mother's practicality. She had inherited it in full. "I didn't feel for the viscount what you felt for Father. How terrible if I had actually had a deep interest in Alder, and he'd thrown me over the way he did."

"I was lucky not to have to rely on the barbaric Season of the *haut ton*," Anne admitted. They both laughed at her characterization of the round of London events to which many young girls looked forward, while equally as many faced it with dread.

"Your father's family were neighbors to my parents' home in Carlisle, and we were quite used to Scots anyway, since we lived so far north."

But Jenny was distracted by talk of the Season, still going strong in London for another few weeks at least.

"Barbaric or not, Mummy, we must find a way to get Maggie to attend next year. It is unlikely she'll find a suitable husband here."

"What about the new earl?" Anne suggested. "He's a bit old for her, but she might find him attractive. What's more, she's there every day. Perhaps—"

"He's confined like a hermit and sounds like a wounded animal."

Her mother pursed her lips. "I suppose then not suitable for our Mags."

"No," Jenny murmured, "I suppose not. There are always the matrimonial adverts, I suppose. If Maggie is willing, we can—"

A shriek brought Jenny to her feet.

CHAPTER THREE

Eleanor came running in, somehow smiling while still shrieking.

"You'll never guess, never ever," Jenny's youngest sister declared, then screamed in excitement once again.

"Cease that infernal noise at once," their mother said, as Jenny returned to her seat, wanting to throttle her youngest sister for giving them both palpitations. "No one will guess anything until you sit down and speak properly. Dear, oh, dear, I don't know where you got those manners or how we shall ever find you a husband. Maggie will be easy in comparison. She has only a somewhat tart tongue, whereas you—"

"Sorry, Mummy," Eleanor interrupted. "But it is so very wonderful, I could not contain myself."

"What is it?" Jenny asked irritably, still feeling her heart thumping uncomfortably and being reminded of the earl's awful shouting.

"I've had a letter from Maisie. She and Uncle Neddy are coming to stay with us."

Jenny and her mother exchanged a quick glance. She thought she saw alarm mirrored in Anne's eyes.

"He's not your uncle," was all her mother said.

"My cousin, then," Eleanor amended.

"Only by marriage," Anne retorted, then sipped her wine. "And he's your second cousin once removed."

It didn't really matter about Ned Darrow's relation to her dead father. Jenny knew Eleanor was simply over the moon at having Ned's sister, Maisie, visit, for they were the same age and had always got along well. No doubt Eleanor was quite lonely in Sheffield, and this was the chance for some companionship beyond her sisters and their mother.

Ned was another matter, the son of their father's cousin-in-law, he had occasionally been their guest in Town. Usually he stayed a night when he brought Maisie, who often remained with them for a month, and again when he came to collect her for the return to their home in Scotland. He would spend time with her father drinking brandy and wine, and making eyes at her during every meal.

Jenny hated to acknowledge it, but he rubbed her the wrong way. A tad too self-absorbed and a tad too interested in her, truth be told. She had been glad to have the proposal from the viscount, if only to stop the attention of Ned. Now, she would be within reach again as far as he was concerned. She supposed she could pretend to still be in the midst of a long engagement, although perhaps he already knew the truth.

"Ned Darrow should have waited to be invited," their mother declared, voicing Jenny's misgivings.

Eleanor blushed. "I did offer an invitation. At least, I did to Maisie."

Anne clucked her tongue. "That was wrong of you to do, but also quite forward of Ned to accept on behalf of his sister without asking me first. And only think of the expense!"

Jenny was doing precisely that. An extra mouth to feed, or maybe more if Ned stayed, too, and who knew for how long!

"Maggie will have to sleep with me," she said, starting to plan for the inevitable. As oldest, she'd enjoyed the luxury of having her own room while her two younger sisters shared the larger one with two beds. "Then Maisie can sleep with Eleanor."

"What will we do with Cousin Ned?" her mother wondered.

What, indeed?

Then her mother added, "I suppose he shall have to have a bed in the parlor."

Jenny started. "How will I carry out my accounting duties? Where will I keep people's ledgers?"

"Perhaps he will only stay overnight," Anne said. "And in the interim, you can set up a table in my room."

Jenny nodded. *So be it.* Eleanor was looking quite grim-faced, and Jenny reached over to clasp her sister's hand.

"Dearest, I'm glad you'll have some company your own age, but please don't invite anyone else or they will have to sleep with the horses."

In fact, if Ned arrived in his rickety, repainted brougham that had seen better days but offered him the air of nobility, instead of driving an open-air carriage himself, then the driver would have to stay in an empty stall. For Cook, George, Henry, and the housemaid took up the two rooms that stretched off the kitchen.

Eleanor giggled, and her expression brightened once more.

"We shall have enough people in the house to play *Puss, Puss in the Corner!*" She jumped up and went running out of the room, screeching Maggie's name in order to tell her about their unwanted houseguests.

Even then, while Jenny watched, Lucy approached Thunder, who stood leaning against the fence, head down, looking miserable—if it was possible for a horse to outwardly appear dejected. As the mare approached, Thunder startled, reared, and then took a nip at Lucy's shoulder. Each horse retreated to opposite sides.

"Shall I send Clara for more wine?" her mother asked. Jenny simply nodded.

THE ARRIVAL OF NED and Maisie Darrow from Dumfries, Scotland, a week later, caused more upheaval than Jenny could have imagined. While Maisie, with her blonde curls and doe-brown eyes, was sweeter than they'd all remembered and gave presents of thistle jam and lavender soap, Ned was exactly as aggravating as Jenny recalled. More so.

Moments after walking through the door, he made it clear he knew about her broken engagement. After removing his surcoat from his reed-thin figure and taking his hat off, revealing his sandy-colored hair, with exceptionally bad manners, her cousin brought up the viscount's callous dismissal. Doing so under the guise of condolences while all the while looking inappropriately gleeful, was classic Ned.

Jenny had a feeling his true visit had more to do with her than with escorting Maisie to visit Eleanor.

Maggie tried to come to Jenny's rescue by pointedly asking if they should make up a bed for him or if he would be heading home immediately, hopefully making him feel as unwanted as he truly was.

Unfortunately, it rolled off his back like water from a duck.

"I hope you're making a fool's joke," Ned said to Maggie, then looked at Jenny, "for I was intending to stay for a goodly visit. I thought that was clear in Maisie's letter."

He nodded toward where his sister had been standing, but Maisie and Eleanor had already disappeared upstairs, whispering and laughing.

"We certainly don't want you to think that any of cousin Lucien's family are abandoning you upon his death," Ned continued.

"We promise, we don't think anything of the sort," Jenny's mother said. "It is merely that you'll have to sleep in the parlor, as we are out of rooms upstairs."

"That's fine," Ned insisted, his gaze still fixed on Jenny. "I don't mind at all."

Pity. She gave him a tight smile, which was the best she could manage. She'd hoped he would go screaming for the hills when he learned he didn't get a bedroom. Perhaps when he felt the hardness of the settee or its narrowness, he would shorten his visit.

Anyway, she had work to finish. And now Jenny had the inconvenience of hiding it and herself in her mother's chamber.

"Well, I will see you at dinnertime," she told her cousin as she followed the path that Eleanor had taken toward the stairs.

A frown appeared on Ned's forehead.

"Oh, dear cousin, I was hoping we could have a cup of tea together or perhaps take a walk around the property. I, for one, could certainly use a stroll to stretch my legs after the journey."

Jenny opened her mouth and then shut it again. What excuse could she give if she couldn't tell him about her bookkeeping practice? She glanced at Maggie, who made a strange face, clearly implying that she would not bail her sister out in this instance. Not when the penalty was a walk with Ned.

Luckily, her mother stepped in. "I would love the chance to walk and converse about Lucien's family. I'm sure Jenny would join us if she could."

Offering no opportunity for argument and without waiting for a response, Anne headed for the door, snatching up her lightweight wrap from a hook on the wall. Ned had no choice but to follow.

"I'll show you our horses, too, shall I? And then we'll come back for a nice cup of tea. Carry on, girls," she called over her shoulder, taking Ned's arm and forcing him out the front door.

The next few days proved a challenge. First, Maggie had to leave before the midday meal was over. Ned was bloviating about some Scottish election. She could dally no longer or be late for her charges. Rising to her feet in the middle of one of his long diatribes, Maggie excused herself and walked out of the room. This caused him to go on for a few long minutes regarding her rudeness.

Jenny listened silently until she nearly exploded.

"Rather uncivilized to say the least," he pointed out for the second time. "Even if I were not to take offense at her leaving precisely when I was about to tell you the most interesting part about the Liberal Unionists, there would be her health to consider. Digestion is as important for young women as for men." He pursed his lips and nodded to the four ladies left at the table.

"Brother, dear," Maisie said, "surely if cousin Margaret is going walking, that will aid her digestion."

"No," Ned said. "I say, no. She should sit for half an hour at least before moving after a meal."

Meanwhile, Jenny was forced to pretend to sleep late and go to bed early to finish each of her customers' accounts while secreting herself in her mother's chamber.

At the end of the week, during dinner, Ned mentioned how Jenny had taken to being quite a countrified lady of leisure.

Unthinkingly defending her sister, Eleanor let the cat out of the bag.

"That is unkind of you to say," Eleanor began as she took a slice of bread and began to butter it generously. "Jenny works harder than anyone I know and with her arithmetic skills, she takes care of us all. Not to say that Maggie doesn't help out, too, with the French lessons."

Jenny closed her eyes in dismay, hearing Maggie gasp slightly and then try to cover it with a cough.

"Oh, dear," said Eleanor, realizing belatedly that she shouldn't have spoken of anything to do with her older sisters' activities.

Anne tried to rescue the situation for her daughters.

"What Eleanor means is that Jenny has inherited the tendency of her father toward numbers, thus she keeps the household books, much to my gratitude, for I do not have a head for accounting at all."

Ned was still frowning slightly.

"And Maggie, she . . . ," their mother trailed off, nonplussed.

"I try to help Eleanor prepare for her first Season by giving her the polish of a good French accent. *N'est-ce-pas?*" Maggie asked her sister, turning to her with flashing eyes.

"*Oui,*" Eleanor said quietly.

Ned blinked. Then he laughed. "While I admire Jenny for trying to get her pretty head around arithmetic, it is not really in her realm of abilities, not by the natural order of things. How can a woman be expected to make heads or tails of numbers?"

Jenny felt her mouth drop open. She nearly set about putting him straight with some choice words about mathematics when he added insult to injury.

"Besides, Lucien was notoriously bad at accounting himself. He told me as much once. Said household accounts were all gibberish to him. I guess it was a pity he didn't get himself a good keeper of his books so that you all wouldn't have found yourselves banished to the country, eh? He can't do anything about that now, can he?"

He sipped his wine in the silence that followed, unmindful of how many insults or hurtful words he'd managed to pile on. Unfortunately, he then had more to add.

"As for Eleanor having a Season, the cost of the gowns will certainly make that impossible, never mind the cost of tickets! Why, she may as well speak Punjabi as French. I'm sure that Maisie will tell her all about it when she has her first Season in a few years' time."

Maisie had the grace to blush at her brother's tactlessness. She even placed her hand over Eleanor's.

Jenny wanted to strangle him. Especially when, with gusto, he tucked into the pork roast that her bookkeeping skills had paid for, oblivious to the discomfort he'd caused.

At least, though, he'd forgotten about Eleanor's remarks.

THE VERY NEXT DAY, another terrible heart-stopping moment befell her. For when Jenny glanced out her mother's bedroom window early in the morning after beginning the baker's ledger, she saw a carriage that was clearly driven by a driver wearing the earl's livery. Sure enough, as it drew to stop in front of their humble cottage, she could clearly see the Lindsey coat of arms emblazoned on the carriage door.

And who should disembark when the door opened? None other than the admiral.

"Christ's wounds," she exclaimed under her breath.

Mr. Binkley's arrival could mean only one thing. He'd come to speak with the fictitious G. Cavendish.

Practically leaping down the stairs to the first landing, Jenny heard Clara opening the door and halted as her mother beat her to the hallway. Taking a step backward, Jenny hid in the shadows of the stairwell.

"Mr. Binkley," Clara announced to Anne, who studied him. "Butler to Lord Lindsey."

"Sorry to intrude, madam," Mr. Binkley began. "I am looking for Mr. Cavendish."

Oh, dear. Jenny grasped her hands together. Did her mother remember what she'd told her about using her family name? Jenny held her breath.

"Mr. Cavendish?" Anne paused. "Lord Lindsey's butler wishes to speak to Mr. Cavendish," she said overly loudly, not knowing Jenny was close at hand but clearly trying to tell her.

If the situation were not so serious, Jenny would have laughed at her mother's strange tone and the sound of the butler taking a startled step backward.

Unfortunately, the door to the parlor opened at that moment, and Ned appeared, looking sleep-worn and grumpy at having been awakened before ten in the morning.

He opened his mouth. "What is this all about?"

"No call to speak loudly," Jenny interrupted, revealing herself by coming down the last few stairs, knowing Ned could ruin it all in an instant. "Cousin," she added, "please return to your room. We have things well in hand."

Ned stared from Jenny to her mother to Binkley.

"I am happy to offer my services by dealing with whatever has come to our doorstep," Ned said, beginning to puff himself up as usual.

An idea formed in Jenny's head.

"Yes, of course, *your* services! Your services will be called upon," she assured him, offering him her brightest smile. He would be Mr. Cavendish. "If you will but return to the parlor, I'll be in shortly to . . . to relay any important information. However, recall that you are in your nightclothes and this is the Earl of Lindsey's butler." She gestured to Mr. Binkley. "We must make a better representation to him than to appear in such a state of undress."

Ned glanced down at his crumpled housecoat over his pajamas. "Yes, of course." And with that, and a warm smile in return for Jenny's apparent friendliness, he disappeared quickly into the parlor, shutting the door firmly behind him.

"Was that Mr. Cavendish?" Mr. Binkley asked after the exchange, his expression doubtful and perhaps a bit disappointed.

Jenny looked down at her feet. Could she say a bald-faced lie, and in front of her mother?

"Why, yes, of course." It was Anne who responded. *Bless her!* "He was working late into the night and must have slept in the parlor. Please, come through to our modest dining area for a cup of tea while he dresses."

Mr. Binkley's eyes widened at being offered tea. And in the dining room, no less. Why, his whole world must seem topsy-turvy! However, he couldn't refuse an offer from someone superior to his station no matter how inappropriate.

Giving Jenny another long look, apparently the admiral was dying to ask her why she, Miss Blackwood, was at the home of Mr. Cavendish. However, that would be forward, presumptuous, and rude, and thus, she knew he would not ask.

Gesturing for him to follow her mother, she said nothing, merely offering him a serene expression.

As soon as his back disappeared down the hallway and into the dining room, Jenny tapped on the parlor door.

"Enter," Ned said as if it truly were his room.

Jenny gritted her teeth and then pasted on her friendly smile once more.

"Cousin," she said, pushing the door open and peering gingerly inside, making sure he was indeed fully dressed before she entered.

"Come in," he said. "Pray, what is going on? Why is the earl's butler calling on your home?"

"I am going to trust you, as my cousin, as the son of my father's cousin, as a friend to this family, as the brother to my sister's dear friend." Still she paused. He could help, or he could ruin everything.

"Yes, yes, I am all that. Tell me. You can trust me. You may not know this, although I believe you do. I have a deep fondness for you and would do nothing to cause you distress."

Jenny took a deep breath before speaking and considered crossing her fingers if only she believed in such foolishness.

"Very well. Lord Lindsey's butler came here asking for Mr. Cavendish. Well," she spread her arms. "I am Mr. Cavendish."

"You? Whatever do you mean?"

"I conduct a bookkeeping service, and I do it as G. Cavendish. My sex is merely assumed by my clients to be male, of course."

He frowned. "That's absurd."

"No," Jenny shook her head. "I assure you, it is the truth."

"But how can you possibly—?"

She held up her hand. "Do not insult my mind, Ned. I am adept in arithmetic, enough to help local merchants balance their ledgers and figure out their tax duty to the crown. If it were not true, would the earl have sent for me?"

For the first time since she'd known Ned Darrow, which was her whole life, he was rendered speechless. She smiled.

"I cannot let Mr. Binkley know that I am a woman. In case he is not as forward-thinking and," Jenny nearly choked, "as open-minded and understanding as you are."

He was silent a moment, considering. Basically, he held their livelihood in his hands, and she didn't like that notion. Not one bit!

"I believe you," Ned said.

She let out the breath she'd been holding and nearly hugged him. Nearly.

"On account of the high regard I feel for you," he added, "and for the sake of our future, I will help you."

Their future! Was he exacting a price for his help? She feared he was, but she couldn't deal with that now. Not with the admiral having his ear talked off by her mother in the next room.

Jenny nodded, not sure if she had agreed to something or not.

By Ned's broad smile, he seemed to think they now had an understanding.

"What do you want me to do?" he asked.

She jumped forward. "Let me bring Mr. Binkley in here. You may tell him of our familial relationship, except you must be a Cavendish, not a Darrow. Tell him I must stay during the meeting as I do clerical work for you because of my excellent penmanship. Then if he asks questions, I can somehow guide you to the correct answer."

Ned paled slightly. "I've never done anything like this before."

She felt sick. She wished she could say the same thing. "Normally, our manservant Henry takes ledgers back and forth to my clients, but this is different. Obviously, Henry can't meet with Mr. Binkley."

"But why is the butler here?"

She frowned. "I have looked over five years of the Belton estate's books and found some abnormalities. Funds have gone missing and—"

A tap at the door silenced her.

"Jen, whatever you're doing, do it quickly."

It was Maggie, whispering through the door. She went to it and yanked it open.

"We're nearly ready. Go get Mr. Binkley and bring him to Mr. Cavendish's parlor."

Maggie frowned. Jenny swallowed and gestured behind her toward Ned, who was even then puffing up his chest and tugging down his coat sleeves. Maggie's eyes widened in horror, but she nodded and darted off.

Jenny waited at the study door. This simply had to work.

CHAPTER FOUR

With Mr. Binkley seated in one of the chairs by the writing desk and Ned on the other side, Jenny hovered by the door waiting for Ned to take charge.

He gave the earl's senior servant a broad smile. And said nothing.

Sweet mother! She glared at him from behind the butler's back.

Ned coughed. "Binkley, is it?"

The butler nodded, then he turned around offering Jenny a quizzical look.

Luckily, Ned drew his attention back. "Miss Blackwood is my cousin, and she . . . assists me."

"We have met," Mr. Binkley said. "She seems to be quite a helpful person, showing up where least expected."

Ned shrugged, having lost the exact thread of his meaning.

Binkley clasped his hands behind his back where Jenny could see them. She had a feeling the admiral was trying to quell his impatience.

"However, this is a rather sensitive situation, as I'm sure you can appreciate after reviewing the ledgers," the butler continued. "I would prefer we speak in private."

Jenny felt cold all over. Ned could say the wrong thing in a heartbeat and the pretense would be shattered. From the look on his face, he knew that.

"With all due respect, Mr. Binkley, Miss Blackwood is already entirely familiar with the earl's account. I often use her to transcribe my rather messy handwriting. Chicken scratch as my mam used to call it."

Bravo! Again, Jenny could have hugged him.

"I see." Binkley turned once more to give Jenny a particularly hard stare. "Perhaps, then, Miss Blackwood, you would mind ceasing to loiter behind my back. It gives me a sense of menace from my days as a foot soldier."

Hmm, he certainly oozed discipline, and now she knew why.

Obligingly, she entered the room and stood beside her desk, trying to look meek.

Binkley addressed Ned once more. "Because of the delicate matter of revenues dwindling or going missing as you discovered, and because of the situation that occurred three years hence, I'm here to request your presence at Belton."

"Why is that necessary?" Ned asked, sounding bored and as if he were now in complete control.

Jenny wanted to throttle him. After all, this could be her most lucrative client, and they served the earl at Mr. Binkley's pleasure. Annoy him and he was likely to decide to find a real bookkeeper in Manchester or London.

"What Mr. Cavendish means is, that he would hate to intrude upon the earl's privacy," she blurted out.

"You will not come into contact with his lordship," Mr. Binkley said, sounding every bit like an admiral in command of his navy. Again, he gave her a hard stare, perhaps reminding her that she had strayed where she oughtn't to the last time she was at the manor.

"Of course," she muttered.

He turned to Ned once again. "I must insist that you come to Belton as there are too great a number of ledgers to easily transport. What's more, I believe you may have questions that could best be answered if I were close by."

"I see," Ned said, then looked to Jenny. She raised her eyebrows and nodded. "In that case, when would you like us to come."

"Us?"

"Well, I must bring Jenny because . . ."

"Because of your *chicken scratch*," the butler supplied helpfully although not in an enthusiastic tone. "If you can come tomorrow, I'll have the library clear for you both to work."

"Tomorrow?"

Jenny decided this had better be the conclusion of their meeting.

"I can certainly clear Mr. Cavendish's schedule for tomorrow. We will see you at half past nine if that suits."

"Yes. Fine."

In another minute, she had the butler out the door and was watching him climb into the earl's carriage.

Leaning against the door jamb, arms crossed, she nearly laughed with relief to see him go. *Good Lord*, she must have just aged a year.

Suddenly, Ned was at her side.

"He didn't even thank us for going tomorrow on such short notice."

Jenny rolled her eyes. "He doesn't have to thank us. We work for him."

"Oh, right."

In the next moment, she felt Ned take hold of her upper arm and with a bit of tugging, uncross it and tuck it under his own, holding it close to his side.

Ah, the price to be paid. It would be costly indeed!

"This is rather exciting," he said. "I've never done such a charade. And to think, we are doing it together." He patted her trapped hand.

"Yes," she said, "think of that."

JENNY WOULD BE NICE to Ned. That was her nature after all. What's more, he was doing her the greatest of favors, but still, did he have to keep reminding her of that? Between Mr. Binkley's departure and breakfast, he'd mentioned his contribution "to her well-being" at least a dozen times.

"What a bind I've got you out of!" he declared, stuffing his mouth with meat pie at dinner the night before.

"What a godsend that I was here with Maisie," he said over porridge and thick bacon rashers at breakfast.

"This is what comes of being deceitful," he'd gloated around a mouthful of toast before slurping down his tea.

As if she'd had a choice, being a woman.

Jenny already wanted to scream, and they'd only just arrived at Belton Manor. Ned had tried to hold her hand numerous times in the seclusion of his carriage, after insisting they take his old brougham with his driver rather than her open-air gig. Having about decided to punch her cousin in the nose, she felt the carriage wheels turn onto the gravel drive.

Besides, she thought grumpily, leading Ned around to the side entrance and knocking, she hadn't truly needed his help. She would have figured something else out if he hadn't been at hand. For the life of her, though, she didn't know what.

The same servant greeted them at the door. Obviously, he'd been told that Jenny wasn't there to tutor Peter and Alice this time for he took a different route through the hallways and stairs before showing them into a beautifully-endowed library, with floor-to-ceiling books that must have cost a pretty penny.

"How marvelous." Jenny had not been in such a room since she'd wandered into the wrong chamber after too much champagne during her first season. Her father had found her sitting in a chair, glass in hand, and perusing a biography of Isaac Newton and his mathematical equations at one of Lord and Lady Jersey's fabulously extravagant balls.

There was a large round table with four comfy leather chairs arranged around it, and Jenny and Ned seated themselves each at one of these. On the table were two stacks of leather tomes, presumably ledgers, as they looked like the ones she'd already studied thoroughly. Pens, ink, blank paper, it had all been thoughtfully laid out for them.

Jenny pulled out her abacus from her satchel. It helped remind her of her abilities while it didn't entirely quell the butterflies fluttering in her stomach.

"Where do we start?" Ned asked, leaning back in his seat as if he had no idea what a book was or how to open one.

"*You* may find something interesting upon these shelves," she told him, "or *you* may take a nap." For all she cared. As long as he stayed quiet and didn't bother her. "*I* will start with the latest ledger and work backward. I find that's the best way not to be led down the wrong path."

She pulled the top book off the stack and found it to be very old indeed.

That wouldn't do. Standing, she began to sort the ledgers by decade, until she finally spread open before her the accounts prior to the ones she'd already viewed, six years ago. Then she fell silent and began to read and figure and add and subtract.

Perhaps an hour had gone by, perhaps more, when the door opened and the admiral entered. At that particular moment, she was hastily writing on a piece of paper while bent over the ledger, her nose nearly pressed to the paper to read the minute scrawling someone had written in the margin.

Glancing up, she took in Mr. Binkley staring at her and then looking at Ned who was splayed across a divan by the window, an open book on his chest, and snoring lightly.

Sweet mother! She should have set him up at least to look the part.

"Ahem," Mr. Binkley cleared his throat. They both looked at Ned who didn't stir.

"He's taking a bit of a break while I transcribe some notes. Can you tell me, Mr. Binkley, did the earl himself, the young one, I mean, the current one, keep the books until the time he went away?"

"No. Why do you ask?"

"Because even though there were already some systemic changes occurring in the ledgers and in the estate's revenues over the last six or seven years, they changed drastically three years ago."

"*Ah,* yes. It was his lordship's cousin who maintained the ledgers."

"Tobias Devere?"

"Yes, starting approximately seven years ago, I would say. Sir Tobias was adept at numbers and asked the earl's father if he could take over the household accounts, and then it grew to be the entire estate that he handled."

Odd, she thought. With an estate as vast and wealthy as the Deveres, they didn't have a professional bookkeeper in their employ.

"And before Sir Tobias, who kept the ledgers?"

"His lordship, the previous earl, had an estate steward who has long since departed."

Ned snuffled in his sleep, and they both looked at him for a second.

"And the current earl has no interest in the accounts, eight years ago or since?"

"I'm afraid he never had a head for it, Miss. Not that he wasn't interested in his family's estates. That would be an incorrect assumption. Lord Devere, now Lord Lindsey, was always a participant in the running of this manor and of his father's vast holdings. He understood its workings and the needs of its people."

Before he became a despondent recluse. *And now?*

She kept that question to herself.

"I see." Jenny flipped a few pages back and forth. "Who handles the accounting now?"

Mr. Binkley clasped his hands behind his back and looked down at her. "Apparently, *you* do."

She felt her cheeks redden and glanced at Ned again. *Useless creature.* The butler had seen through their charade, no doubt. Yet, she shouldn't assume that was what he meant.

"What I meant to ask was who has been handling this since his lordship and his cousin went abroad?"

"I knew what you meant," Mr. Binkley said. "The old earl was alive for two years of his son's absence."

That told her nothing. She smiled encouragingly. *Was there more?*

"Not any *one* person," the butler added.

For the first time, Jenny had the feeling that he was withholding something from her.

"I have made some entries, and the earl's valet has kept some accounts. Even the housekeeper, Mrs. Keithley, whom I don't believe you've met, has been called upon to give a reckoning. She was visiting her sister in Gloucestershire when you were here before. Hence the reason no one brought your tea."

Jenny frowned. What a slipshod method. And the admiral, by his discomfort, knew it.

"I don't quite understand how the heir to the earldom and his cousin, who I suppose was also a potential heir, could both go to war and leave the entire estate without an overseer, no disrespect meant to yourself, of course."

"None taken, Miss, I assure you."

At that moment, Ned snored particularly loudly and awakened himself. He sat up, blinking, recalling where he was and why he was there. Then he saw Mr. Binkley and jumped to his feet.

"Yes, as I was saying, the ledgers show some grave discrepancies."

Jenny nearly laughed but simply sighed, and Mr. Binkley had the grace to keep silent.

"I will continue to delve further," she told the butler, giving up on the pretense entirely. "Now that I have a better understanding, I will look more closely at the recent issues. At least I'll be able to tell you where to go looking for lost income."

"She means that I will, along with her help—" but Ned stopped when she sent him a quelling look.

Only after Mr. Binkley left did Jenny realize she still didn't know why the estate had been left to flounder after the earl's passing without someone truly in charge. It was unconscionable.

JENNY HEARD THE SCREAMS and couldn't ignore them. She wished she could simply creep past the closed door to the earl's chamber, yet her heart would have had to be made of stone. All she wanted was a blasted cup of tea but had got quite lost on her way from the library.

"No," Lord Lindsey yelled, for she was certain it was he.

Glancing down the hallway, she fervently hoped to see some member of the staff, but it was quite deserted. No doubt everyone at the manor was used to his strange torment and ignored it.

Another shout and then deep moaning permeated the door, and almost unthinkingly, Jenny placed her fingers on the handle and turned it. Her heart pounding, she pushed the door slowly open and glanced inside into utter darkness.

Surprised, she hesitated before entering. At that hour of the day, the room should be filled with bright sunlight. Instead, it was as dark as pitch.

Regardless, when she heard Simon Devere moan again, she moved toward him, ignoring the gooseflesh that arose on her arms. Her eyes were quickly becoming accustomed to the minimal light that had followed her in from the corridor.

After a moment, she could make out the shape of a large, four-poster bed to her right, but the earl was not in it. His tragic sounds were coming from directly in front of the heavily draped windows. Under foot was a thick carpet that she crossed as quickly as she dared, not wishing to trip and land at his feet.

Instead, she ended up standing before a man who was fast asleep yet sitting up in a winged chair and obviously having a terrible nightmare.

She could not even make out his features, just overly long hair and a pale face against the darkness. Should she pull back a curtain? Should she touch him to awaken him?

The earl thrashed suddenly, screamed loudly, and awakened, sitting bolt upright. He seemed to be staring right at her but said nothing, showing neither surprise nor alarm at her appearance. Then he looked to his left and right, down at his own lap. Finally, he gripped the arm rests and breathed deeply.

"My lord," Jenny began, and he looked at her again. "I am sorry to intrude upon your privacy, but you were in distress. I sought only to awaken you."

He cocked his head.

At his continued silence, she had a momentary fear that the Earl of Lindsey was indeed out of his mind.

"I will fetch Mr. Binkley."

As she turned, his arm snaked out and he grabbed hold of her. She nearly yelled with surprise, but before she could, he gasped.

"I can touch you," he murmured.

"My lord? Are you well, my lord?"

"You are a well-spoken demon," he said, his voice low and scratchy with misuse.

"I beg your pardon?"

"My nightmares never beg," he told her. "They usually cause me to beg." He looked around his room again, then back at her. "I've never dreamed you before."

"I am no dream, my lord."

He sighed. "For all I know, I am in my cell in Burma, dreaming that I am in my room at home."

"I assure you, sir, you are home."

"You cannot assure me. I have had this dream too many times, though without you, to be sure. I will awaken in a minute and smell the stench of the prison. That's always my first clue as to where I am."

"If you were sleeping in your cell, my lord, don't you think you would smell it even here, in your dream home?"

He nodded. "That makes sense." Then he frowned, his eyebrows drawing together. "Yet nothing really makes sense, does it? I was just there. I know it."

"No, you were here. You were screaming. I heard you. I'm sorry to intrude but you are definitely sitting in a chair in Sheffield, England."

"Is that so?"

"It is."

"Maybe for the moment," he allowed after a pause, "but in a very few minutes from now, I may find myself back in Burma. You, with your soft voice, will disappear. I'll be on a hard, dirty floor with flea-infested vermin crawling over me, skin itching with no relief and I'll be freezing because the sun has gone down, it's monsoon season, and I'm only wearing thin rags. Or I'll be boiling hot because the blazing sun is shining harsh against the prison wall. And I'll be very thirsty."

Jenny was mesmerized by his words, vividly imagining the terrible conditions and wondering how anyone could survive for any length of time. Yet, they say he'd lived in the prison for nearly two years before he was rescued by British soldiers.

"I'm thirsty now by the way."

The earl said it in such a matter-of-fact manner that she nearly missed his words.

"Oh," Jenny exclaimed, glancing around. If only she could see better. But there, by his elbow on a small round table was a pitcher of water and a glass.

"If you release me, I'll get you a drink."

He hesitated. "You will not disappear if I release you?"

"No, my lord. I promise."

"I like the feel of you," he said, still holding on,

Jenny had to admit that his touch was an entirely new sensation and not unpleasurable. For where his hand firmly gripped her wrist without hurting her, she was tingling.

However, instead of releasing her, he drew her closer until she was off-balance, pulled nearly onto his lap. Then he sniffed her. This stranger actually leaned forward and sniffed in the vicinity of the front of her gown.

"Um," she began.

"I like the smell of you, too. Lemons, I believe. That's strange. I've never dreamt such a scent before."

Then he released her.

Taking a shaky step back, very aware that his gaze was trained on her, she reached for the pitcher.

"There is water right here, my lord."

He visibly flinched but said nothing.

"I'll pour you a glass," she offered.

"Just like that?" he asked. "Others have died for the same."

Jenny didn't know what to say. After a pause, she merely repeated her words.

"I'll pour you a glass, and you'll drink it." For surely, he sounded delirious, and perhaps it was due to thirst.

He tilted his head. "If you exist, and if I am here, then I suppose you will. And I'll accept it from you and drink. I'm sure I'll be relieved for a while. The mind can make even air seem like a cool, delicious potable when you are out of your mind with thirst."

Unable to envision such suffering, Jenny hurried to pour him a full glass. As she handed it to him, their fingers brushed and he visibly shuddered.

"I don't recognize you, but you certainly feel real," he said.

"I am, my lord."

She watched him examine the glass and sniff the water and then he gulped it all down, tilting his head back and holding the glass upside down against his lips to get the last drops.

"There is more if you wish."

"No, that's fine. I'm not thirsty anymore, but I know it won't last. When I'm in the cell, I'll wonder how I could have imagined the water so veritably. Yet, if I close my eyes again, you'll disappear and I'll be back there. I know it. I try very hard never to close my eyes."

Poor tormented man.

"If you don't know me," she reasoned, "then how could you imagine me. How could I be only a dream? Don't you only dream of people you know?"

He stared at her, then he looked her up and down and down and up in the very thick gloom. Not insolently, and not with any type of improper insinuation that might make her blush. He simply studied her.

"That makes sense. I have dreamed many people while in my cell. With my eyes open, I swear, I talk to the living and the dead. With my eyes closed, I am often here in this very room or walking the orchard. Sometimes I am even riding one of my favorite horses." He paused and then he reached out, startling her, as he took gentle hold of her forearm once again.

"But it's true, I always know the person or the place. Or the horse, for that matter."

Jenny nodded.

"I don't know you, do I?" he asked, his tone almost pleading.

Oh, dear. She hated to break the logic of her own argument, but she also was unwilling to lie to him.

"You don't know me, my lord, but we have met."

He dropped her arm instantly. "A riddle. And proof that you could be imaginary."

"No," she added quickly, wondering why she felt so desperate to prove to the man that she was real and that he was safe in England.

"You and I met, more than once, when I was but a child and you a mere downy-faced youth. Thus, to be honest, we know *of* each other, but you don't know me. Certainly, you would not envision me as I look today, nearly twelve years later."

"Again, you make sense," he said. "As well as any of this makes sense. How did you come to be in my bedroom if you are real?"

"I was passing by your door and heard you call out."

"Was I very loud?"

"Yes, my lord."

He nodded. "When I am here, I stay quite still and remain quiet in order not wake up and go back there. Do you understand?"

She nodded, fascinated by his thoughts.

"When I am there, I scream and scream, hoping that I am in a terrible nightmare. My voice sometimes awakens me, and I am here again. And if I keep myself in darkness, then I can't see the rats."

Tears sprung to her eyes.

"There are no rats, my lord."

He shook his head.

"No, not now. But later. Unless I stay awake. Or is it that I must keep dreaming of home?"

She was no doctor, but she believed if he remained in this room in the dark, not knowing if he was awake or dreaming, then he would slip into madness. If it was not already too late.

"What if I keep you awake by talking to you?" Jenny wasn't even sure what she was saying or why. She only knew she wanted to help. "You won't go back into the cell while we're having a conversation, will you, my lord?"

He considered. "No, I don't believe I will. Nor while drinking. I will have another glass of water after all."

She poured him one quickly, and he drank half of it before setting it down beside him.

"What about nourishment?"

"What about it?" he asked.

"Someone brings you food, I assume. And you eat it?"

"Yes."

Jenny wondered if only Mr. Binkley came in or if the as-yet unseen housekeeper, or perhaps one of the maids. For beyond a doubt, this man needed company if only to be kept anchored in the here and now.

"Who brings it?"

"Binkley. And others I don't see. I believe they are afraid of me."

"Pish," she said.

"Indeed, but that's what Binkley said when he was forced to play housemaid."

The admiral was probably trying to knock some sense into the young earl. Yet she thought Mr. Binkley had no idea of the extent to which Simon Devere had been traumatized.

And you do? asked a mocking voice in her head.

For some reason, yes, she believed she understood his fear. It was not a fanciful melancholy, although many might think it such. It was more practical than that. He had been taught while in the cell that sleep meant cruel dreams of being home. One and one made two. And now that he was home, how could he be sure he wasn't still in captivity in one of his dreams?

The terror at waking up in the cell would not relinquish its hold on him.

In all likelihood, he needed a doctor to ease his mind back into reality. However, at that moment, she was the only person there.

"The food you eat, is it pies, perhaps, and roast fowl or pork?"

He nodded.

"Do they taste real?"

"Yes."

"Do you think they could be so vivid in a dream if you were in fact still in your cell?"

Jenny thought he smiled until she realized he was actually grimacing.

"You would be surprised at how real my dreams are. I put a particularly delicious morsel in my mouth once, I'll never forget it. It was a spoonful of warm apple Charlotte, and I told myself that if it were a dream, I didn't think I could survive. Then I awakened in hell."

She gasped, disappointment lancing her as if she'd been there.

"However, I did survive. Lack of sponge cake and apples and creamy custard notwithstanding."

Wretched soul.

"Therefore, dear phantom beauty, I eat what is given to me by Binkley. I even bathe four times a week. And of course, there are other calls of nature that are handled quite differently in this world than in my other one."

Jenny didn't want to think about the horror of attending to bodily functions in a small enclosed place. With rats and fleas constantly biting his skin.

How could she help him? What could she——?

Phantom beauty? Did he truly think her beautiful?

Then she remembered the darkness of the room, and how she could barely make him out in the gloom. Likewise, she must be merely a female voice with a feminine shape, rustically styled hair, and an outdated gown that he could not see.

A tap on the door frame made her jump. The earl did likewise, and they looked at each other like children caught doing something naughty.

All at once, Jenny realized she absolutely should not be in the earl's chamber, alone with him.

CHAPTER FIVE

Neither of them spoke, but upon seeing Mr. Binkley standing in the doorway, Jenny relaxed. Thank goodness she'd left the door wide open. That certainly bespoke an entirely innocent situation.

Taking a step backward, she addressed the admiral, who stood staring at her as if she had two heads.

"His lordship was in some distress. I entered to see if I could help him."

The butler nodded. Then he put his hands behind his back in that manner she'd seen in her own parlor.

"This is the third time you've been somewhere unexpected, Miss Blackwood. I'm starting to think you are a fairy creature."

"I thought she was a demon," the earl chimed in.

Jenny couldn't contain the nervous laugh that escaped her, for Mr. Binkley was not smiling.

"I shall be getting back to work. Or rather to assisting Mr. Cavendish."

It was hard to tell in the dim light, but she thought she saw Mr. Binkley roll his eyes.

Turning back to the earl, she bowed her head. "I bid you good day, my lord."

"Will I dream you again?"

Mr. Binkley coughed.

"I promise you that I am real."

"Then also promise me that you will return. Tomorrow," the earl insisted.

She glanced at the admiral for permission. He hesitated, then nodded.

Why did that fill her with warmth instead of dread?

"Yes, my lord. I will come see you again tomorrow."

Simon Devere visibly relaxed. "I will stay awake until then."

Oh dear. She rushed to reassure him. "If you go to sleep, I will awaken you when I come back, and you will be right here in your own home."

"If you say so." He didn't sound convinced.

Nodding, she slipped quietly past the piercing stare of Mr. Binkley.

AFTER THEIR EVENING MEAL, Jenny lost no time in telling Maggie of all that had occurred. She wanted her sister to understand that the earl was not a monster as found in Perrault's fairytales, nor was he insane, merely tortured by his own dreams.

They were sitting on Jenny's bed in their cramped bedchamber, where no one could overhear them. Having returned to the library after her encounter with the earl, she'd placated Ned with a heavily-laden tea tray carried by the maid who followed behind. The shortbread, cream, and strawberries distracted Ned from wondering how it could have taken her so long to find the kitchens.

Leaning against the headboard, shoulder-to-shoulder with Maggie, Jenny shifted her skirts, raising them up to her knees to combat the summer warmth that had gathered in their room despite the open window.

"Lord Despair is a truly troubled man," Maggie said, fanning herself. "And you intend to go back?"

"I promised him."

Maggie considered her sister's profile. "Is he safe?"

Jenny shrugged. "I didn't feel afraid of him for a single moment. When he touched me, he was——"

"Touched you?" Maggie asked, a flash of concern crossing her pretty features.

Jenny felt the heat creep into her face.

"Briefly, he took hold of my arm but was ever so gentle."

Maggie smiled, saying nothing.

"What? Why are you looking like a cat in front of the cream?"

"Is his lordship handsome?"

Jenny clucked her tongue. "I could hardly see him. I told you it was dark."

"Well, did you get the sense that he looked like an ogre?"

They both laughed.

"Very well. I will tell you. The Earl of Lindsey is a pleasant-faced man from what I could make out in the darkened chamber. His hair was a little longer than fashionable, but someone has taken care to shave his daily growth. Most likely Mr. Binkley, although there must be a valet there somewhere, don't you think?"

Maggie nodded. "No doubt. What else?" She nudged her sister with her elbow.

Jenny considered. "He smelled clean and his voice had a rich timbre."

"When he wasn't shouting and moaning?"

"Yes, Mags. When he wasn't shouting and moaning. Poor man!" she uttered, thinking of how terribly he'd suffered. "We should all have compassion for him. I'm sure I was looking at sanity and intelligence."

"You *like* him!" her sister declared.

"What? How can you conclude such a thing from what I've told you?"

"Do you deny it?"

Jenny squirmed. "I feel sympathy for the man."

Her sister snorted with amusement. "When will you see your earl again?"

"Stop it. You know very well he is not *my* earl."

"Well?" Maggie persisted.

"Tomorrow." Jenny jumped off the bed when her sister started to laugh. "I'm going to Mummy's room and finishing the baker's books."

"I thought you finished those already," Maggie pointed out.

"Then I'll do the innkeeper's," Jenny said, fleeing from her sister's amused expression.

SIMON SCREAMED, WAKING HIMSELF up. He shook his left leg where he could still feel a rat's claws. His heart was racing and he had no idea of the time of day or night. That was normal. What wasn't normal was that he was looking for someone. For whom?

He tossed the blanket from him recalling how Binkley had placed it on his lap after supper.

After eating, Simon had taken twenty turns around his large chamber, surprised at how weak his legs felt even after such little exercise, and then he'd collapsed into his chair again. He hadn't appreciated Binkley trying to tuck him in like he was an aged grandmother.

Still, Simon couldn't shake the expectant feeling that someone should be, could be, in his room. Then he remembered her. The woman! He would focus on her, recalling her sweet voice and her kindness as she gave him water—and maybe she would reappear.

As long as he stayed awake.

Hadn't he asked her to return the next day? Was it tomorrow already?

Rising to his feet, he stretched. He was able to maneuver the room easily in the dark now after many weeks of doing so. Going to the window, hesitantly, Simon pulled one drape to the side. He cringed, expecting to see the bars and smell the thick pungent air of the Burmese teak forest. Instead panes of glass, fifteen of them, in fact, sheltered him from the cool English night air. By the look of the stars, it was early in the morning, perhaps a couple of hours until dawn. Such a long time to wait if she was in truth coming back to see him.

He desperately didn't want to go back into the last nightmare. The rats had been particularly voracious. Simon took a few more turns around his room. He would get his strength back eventually, but perhaps he should be trying harder. If only he could stay out of the cell long enough to exercise.

He almost laughed at his own convoluted thoughts.

For now, a book would do. Binkley had brought to him a stack of Simon's favorite adventure stories from his youth. *Robinson Crusoe*, *Gulliver's Travels*, even *Tom Jones*, although he hadn't been allowed to read the bawdy tale until he was fourteen. Now after having had an adventure of his own, and a rather terrible one, he wanted to read something more peaceful.

Against his usual practice, he lit a lamp and perused the offerings. Picking up *The Sorrows of Young Werther*, Simon glanced at it, considered the protagonist's solution of suicide, then hurled the book across the room. A moment later, he went and picked it up, setting it back on his bookshelf. The burst of spontaneous violence felt foreign to him, especially perpetrated on an innocent book.

What else? Ah, a collection of Robert Burns. A little poetry from a man who loved life and women and drinking. One could do worse. Unable to sit anymore, Simon opened it and proceeded to read while standing in the light of the lamp.

THE NEXT MORNING, JENNY decided not to bother keeping up the pretense with Mr. Binkley. It was insulting to the man. Much relieved, she told Ned he could remain at home. Of course, her cousin protested loudly.

"It's not safe for you to go there alone," he said.

"But I go there alone," Maggie pointed out, "and Jenny has before, too."

"You are with the children," Ned said, "while she will be without a chaperone."

Jenny stayed quiet. She wasn't going to argue.

"In any case, I'm going this afternoon," Maggie added, "and I'll check on you, shall I? When Peter and Alice are having their tea."

"If you wish," Jenny conceded.

Ned was unsatisfied. "Well, I don't like this arrangement at all. Lady Blackwood, what do you say?"

Jenny's mother was reading the *London Times*, a week late since it had to travel, and had clearly not been listening to a word. Upon hearing her name, she raised her head and looked at her daughters and her guests.

"Did I miss something?"

"No, Mummy," Jenny said. "Any news worth sharing?"

"Oh, yes," Eleanor added. "Anything about the queen?"

"Or the Countess of Dudley?" asked Maisie.

"I shall read further, but so far, all the news is bad. Of course, there are countless stories still of the famine. Those poor souls. Terrible, terrible," she said, and they all paused a moment to think of the people starving in Ireland.

Then she sipped her tea and scanned the next sheet. "The Duchess of Montrose has passed to her great reward.

And Frederick Douglass has returned to America after writing to the editor that he had a lovely stay here."

Maggie snickered, and Jenny joined in.

"What?" Anne Blackwood asked, looking at her elder two daughters.

"I'm sure he didn't say to the *Times* that he had a 'lovely stay,'" Maggie put forth. "He must have had something more profound to impart after being here for a year and a half," Maggie said.

Lady Blackwood shrugged. "I'm sure he enjoyed his time here. Anyway, let me look on the social pages."

While her mother regaled them with stories, Jenny excused herself and got ready to leave. In truth, a tiny sensation of eagerness sizzled through her at the prospect of seeing the earl again.

"Enjoy your morning," Maggie called after her as she climbed onto their two-seater. "Say hello to Lord Despair for me."

Glancing back, Jenny watched Ned questioning Maggie on her remark, and she sat back on the worn leather seat, happy to be escaping the confines of their country home and the oppressive Ned Darrow.

SOON, JENNY ALMOST WISHED for the ease of dealing with her cousin, or at least of handling merely the innkeeper's books. The Belton ledgers were in a terrible state. Money that should be there was simply not. How Mr. Binkley continued to run everything to their normal standards, she could not imagine. He must be a magician.

When the library door opened, Jenny hoped it was the butler for she had a few more questions for him. She had nearly decided to recommend to him that someone embark on a trip around the earl's vast holdings to get some understanding of how such a mess could have occurred.

Instead of Mr. Binkley, however, a woman she'd never seen before entered the room. By the style of her gown, Jenny could see she was not a servant. By the color of it, unwavering black, she could be only one person.

"Your ladyship," Jenny said, standing and bowing her head briefly.

"Do you know me?" The woman's voice betrayed the slightest of French accents. Obviously, she had as perfect a command of English as her native tongue.

"No, my lady. I assume you are Lady Tobias Devere."

Of medium height and slightly plump, the blonde-haired woman was dressed in an elegant black brocade gown and carried a crumpled handkerchief, which she seemed to be passing from hand to hand.

"I am. You've met my children, I understand."

"They are charming. My sister will be attending them shortly."

Lady Devere smiled, perhaps at the thought of her children.

"Miss Blackwood is excellent with them. Their French is much improved. My family's home is in Nice, and when Alice is another year older, I intend to take them both there for an extended stay."

Jenny nodded. She had nothing to contribute to the notion of such a wonderful journey, having never set foot off of the British Isles.

Then she glanced at the much-worn handkerchief and considered what it represented.

"I am very sorry for your loss."

Maude Devere looked down at the ground. "Thank you. I know people think I'm silly for my grief. After all, according to Lord Lindsey's account, my Tobias has been deceased for over two years, but for me, it is as if it has only just happened."

"I am sure it is very difficult. Also, to lose your home." Jenny would like to know why the widow was left penniless and to whom she'd sold Jonling Hall.

The woman eyed Jenny, who confessed, "We, too, had to leave our home in London because of my father's death. It has been an adjustment."

Without commenting on Jenny's family's fate, Lady Devere walked toward the library windows, overlooking the back of the estate.

"The children and I were lucky that the earl's staff took us in without his being in residence."

Jenny considered that. It was, in truth, quite remarkable that Lord Lindsey's staff should take it upon themselves to open his home without his permission. It testified to the closeness of the cousins, she supposed.

What would happen when Simon regained his faculties and took control of the earldom and the estate? Would he allow his cousin's widow to remain until she left for France? It would certainly raise eyebrows in certain circles.

Maude Devere spoke again. "My husband was content to stay here in Sheffield and handle whatever his uncle needed. I am not sure that his contribution was fully appreciated." She sniffed and dabbed at her eyes.

"It seems," Jenny said gently, "perhaps poor planning that both cousins should go away at the same time, leaving the aging earl alone."

"I doubt that my husband would have gone, but he felt it his duty to fight beside the heir." A note of bitterness had crept into her voice.

Was that why they both went? Perhaps the old earl, himself, had sent Tobias to guard his only son. Certainly, neither of the men could have foreseen the Earl of Lindsey dying while they were away.

"Yet, if something had befallen both men . . ."

Apparently, Jenny had overstepped her place, for Maude visibly bristled. "My son was here, in case both men did not return."

"Yes, my lady, but I didn't mean because of an heir. I meant the necessity of having someone run the Devere estate."

The woman made a noise that was incomprehensible and very Gallic before saying, "There was always my husband's father, the old earl's brother."

"Oh?" This was the first Jenny had heard of such a person.

Then Maude seemed to think better of her words. "I do not believe my father-in-law has any involvement in anything here at Belton, not since the current earl returned to his rightful place."

Jenny's ears perked up. "Do you mean your father-in-law was here during the time that your husband and the earl were away?"

"Yes, of course. When the former Lord Lindsey fell sick, his brother came at once. Why, it was my father-in-law's suggestion that I move with my children into this house. After all, he could see that Jonling Hall was simply a terrible drain on my resources."

"The earl's brother suggested you sell?"

Maude stiffened. "Yes."

"If your husband had returned, wouldn't he have been upset at the loss of his home?"

Jenny realized she might have overstepped her bounds. The lady confirmed it by lifting her chin and offering Jenny a withering glare.

"I'm keeping you from your *work*," Maude said, ignoring the question, and emphasizing the difference in their stations. "I intended only to meet you since you have already spent time with Peter and Alice. Normally, I interview personally each of their tutors."

Jenny refrained from asking if Maude found her acceptable to be around her children. She merely bowed her head once more and raised it to see the retreating form of Lady Tobias Devere.

She couldn't help but wonder if the woman's father-in-law had purchased Jonling Hall to keep it in the family. Yet, why wouldn't that have been in the records? And if he had, why wouldn't he have let his daughter-in-law and his grandchildren stay in their home?

No, Jenny decided she must be surmising incorrectly.

Another two hours passed, the teapot that had been brought to her stood empty, and Jenny decided to stretch her legs and perhaps visit her sister, who would be assisting the children in the blue parlor.

As she began to wander the hallways of Belton, though, Jenny couldn't pretend that she was going anywhere other than to the earl's chamber. Since the moment she'd arrived that morning, all she had wanted was to see him, to speak with him again, and to make sure he was well.

As she approached his chamber, this time, it was quiet. Was he sleeping peacefully or wide awake, staring alone into the darkness?

She nearly turned tail and fled, but at the last moment, tapped on the door.

SIMON HAD BEEN LISTENING for hours, waiting, beginning to think the female demon had been a dream after all, when he thought he heard footsteps. Indeed, he prayed he had.

The light knock on his door nearly had him jumping from his chair. But sudden movement sometimes caused him to awaken. He remembered that and froze, recalling vividly the time he dismounted from an enjoyable ride on Breton only to find his horse gone and his liberty once more curtailed by the confines of the dreaded cell.

"Enter," he said. Nothing happened. Was it the unknown woman? Had she heard him? Had he imagined her entirely? Most likely he had, for a stranger's existence in his home was entirely improbable.

Then the door opened. He held his breath, knowing by the cautious, slow movement that it was not Binkley.

A face appeared in the dimness of his room, and then the rest of her.

He felt like smiling. To think that his own private apparition had returned.

"Good day, my lord."

"Good day, phantom beauty."

Simon watched her falter. "No, don't hesitate. Come in," he told her. "Come closer so I can see you."

She did as he asked, but still, he couldn't see her well. All at once, the darkness of his room irked him instead of comforting him as it had done.

"Is it daytime?"

"Yes." Her voice was as soft and gentle as he recalled.

"Open the drapes," he said.

She didn't move.

"Why do you hesitate? When you open them, will I see the jungle?" He hoped his voice didn't betray the fear he felt at that prospect.

"No, my lord. You are in Sheffield and there is no jungle. But I am not a servant and am not used to being spoken to in such fashion."

"I see."

He considered that. Why was a strange woman wandering around his home if not a servant?

"*Please* open the drapes."

"Certainly." She brushed past him, and he smelled the same scent as before.

He'd forgotten about it, but there it was, crisp and fresh, like lemons and white flowers. He liked it even more than the Pears soap he was going through like fire through dry kindling ever since his return. To be clean, to smell good, two luxuries he'd thought never to experience again. Because of this, he bathed more often than he ever had before.

As the woman drew open the drapes on the window directly next to him, it was as if she'd lit a hundred candles.

The sunlight streamed into his room. Fear shot through him for a second, causing his heart to race.

Gripping the chair's arms, he held his breath, fighting not to scream, aware of the sudden clamminess of his own skin and the sweat that trickled down his back, dampening his shirt.

"My lord," she said, sounding concerned.

She was able to see his distress. He should feel humiliated but didn't. There were too many other emotions for him to contend with, including annoyance for he still couldn't make out her features. She was now entirely backlit by the bright light, which turned her hair into a shining halo.

"Are you well?" she asked, stepping toward him.

He couldn't speak to her. Couldn't reassure her. He just needed a moment. Shaking his head, hoping he was imparting his need to get his bearings, he closed his eyes. That only made things worse. What if he opened them and he was in his cell? What if she disappeared?

Tears sprung to his eyes. He was trapped. Too afraid to reopen his eyes.

What if? What if?

Simon heard himself scream before he realized he was doing so. It felt good. He yelled, and there were no reprisals although he thought he heard the woman gasp. He screamed over and over. No one ran him through with a saber however. He was alive.

Yes, he was alive and screaming, and too afraid to open his own goddamn eyes.

"What is going on here?"

CHAPTER SIX

B inkley! Simon knew he was home if Binkley was there. Immediately, he opened his eyes. There was his butler, whom he'd known most of his life. There was his room, lit by the warm sun that made a pattern of crosses on his carpet from the window's many panes and glazing. There was the woman, her hand over her mouth in distress, her eyes open wide and afraid.

"I'm sorry," he said to her immediately, and he was. He had never been the kind of man who would frighten a member of the fairer sex. He'd been extremely fond of one and bedded a few, but never had he scared a woman.

Still, she said nothing.

"Stand over . . . *please,* stand over there," he gestured to the other side of his chair, "in order that I may see you better."

Lowering her hand, she did as he asked. Her face was pale, making her lips appear quite red. And she had the most entrancing eyes he'd ever seen. Dark lashes, rich coffee-colored eyes that reminded him of his favorite horse when growing up, and they were beautifully large. Intelligent eyes in a pretty face. Currently those eyes were scrutinizing his own appearance, and briefly, with ridiculous vanity, he hoped she liked what she saw.

He nearly laughed, for how could she find him appealing when he'd just been screaming like a madman?

"I'm fine, Binkley," Simon told his butler. "I'm sorry to say that I ordered this lady to open my drapes, and the results were a tad abrupt."

"She should not be in here," Binkley asserted.

"I invited her." *Why shouldn't she?* he wondered. This was *his* house. He could entertain in it whomever he wished. And right then, he wanted to talk to her. Alone.

"I will call you if I need you," he told his butler.

"She has duties to which she must attend," Binkley argued.

He looked at the woman again. "You said you weren't a servant."

"I'm not, my lord."

"She is a bookkeeper, my lord."

"Is she?" He was correct. Those were intelligent eyes staring back at him.

"She will be along soon enough, Binkley."

His butler nodded to him, glanced at the woman, whom Simon realized, now that he could see her clearly, was younger than her voice, manner, and disposition indicated, perhaps barely out of her teens. Then Binkley left and they were alone.

"Have you come to Belton to look over the accounts?"

"Yes, my lord."

A flash of rage shot through him. Toby should be handling the ledgers. Toby, who had been murdered with utter disregard for his life or his family awaiting him. The quite awful truth was that his cousin's life had been wasted. The man never should have gone to battle. Better he had remained at home in his study, hunched over the numbers. Certainly, he never should have been in that infernal cell!

Simon pushed the impinging dark thoughts out of his mind. They would return later, he was certain. Meanwhile, he concentrated on tamping down his futile anger. The girl certainly hadn't earned it.

"What is your name?" he demanded, not caring if he sounded rude. He'd gone past caring about niceties. After all, she'd heard the uncivilized wounded animal that lurked inside of him.

"Jenny," she offered at once.

"Jenny! Sounds like a housemaid's name."

She seemed to take no offense. Rather, a puzzled expression crossed her pleasant face.

"How can a name sound like a servant's? That's ridiculous."

She had called him ridiculous.

"I don't think so," Simon said. "How many Betsys do you know in high society? None, I'd warrant. Elizabeths all. Perhaps if you'd said 'Guinevere.'"

"*Pish!* What if I were standing in the middle of the Strand and about to be hit by a carriage."

It was his turn to feel puzzled.

"Why on earth would you do that? Are you simpleminded?"

She shook her head. "Of course not."

If not simpleminded, then maybe merely illogical? "Then what are you asking me? If you are going to stand in the middle of a busy street, you deserve to be hit whether your name is Jenny or Guinevere."

"I wouldn't actually do it, of course. Besides, that's not my point."

Simon felt the urge to scream again. Normally, he gave in and did so. Instead, he kept his tone level and said, "There is no point."

"There is. If you were to yell out to me, 'Guinevere, take care,' why, I would be dead before you got to the third syllable of my name. But if you yelled 'Jenny,' I might have a chance."

Her meaning, despite her having taken a roundabout way to get there, came clear to him and lightened the moment. In fact, he had the strangest urge to smile.

"I see. In that instance, I might say 'Jen.'"

She paused and considered him. Then she smiled, and her face went from interestingly pretty to breathtakingly lovely. A surge of desire shot straight through him, completely taking him off guard. It had been a long time since his body had had a reason to come to life in such a manner. It felt damn good.

"In that instance," she continued, "I hope, my lord, that you would take liberties with my person and push me out of the way in order to save me."

They stared at one another for a long moment, her words in the air between them, and in his mind, at least, the idea of her *person*.

"Indeed," Simon said, unable to stop himself from taking the briefest of glances down the front of her blue gown to her feet that were hidden under her skirts. She was certainly shapely, lithe yet curvaceous, completely to his liking, and utterly off limits. At least for the moment.

As his gaze returned to her face, it skimmed over her décolletage noting the generous swell of her bosom and the mysterious valley between. Yes, his body was definitely awake.

"I might take liberties with your person," he agreed, "but what if *I* were to perish in your place under the horse's hooves."

They stared at one another for an even longer moment. Her cheeks were decidedly pink. What was she thinking? Was she still dwelling on his impolite assessment of her person?

She took a step back and broke the tension that had been created so swiftly.

Hands clasped before her, she said, "I would be extremely grateful and attend your funeral."

At her words, he not only smiled, Simon began to laugh. He laughed harder than he thought possible. He laughed until tears streamed down his cheeks, and then he sobbed and, quite surprisingly, he felt her put her arms around him.

For a moment, he froze at the entirely unexpected and strange sensation of being held and comforted.

Burying his face in the soft place of her neck, which held her appealing fragrance even more strongly, Simon cried in a way he hadn't done since he was a child. He didn't feel embarrassed. He didn't feel anything except intense sadness. Then, as the tears flowed and the minutes passed, he started to feel a little relief.

Yes, relief, as if he'd held something terrible deep inside, which he had now released.

He also felt bloody exhausted by the entire exchange. Lifting his head, he wiped the column of her neck with his shirt sleeve before she had a chance to straighten up. Then the urge to sleep hit him, precisely the way he thought it would feel being knocked in the street by those imaginary horses Jenny had mentioned.

He wanted to lie down and close his eyes. *How insane!* Wanting to do what he'd fought against all these weeks. He should accept his fate—sleep and let the nightmares come.

Watching as she rubbed a hand over the small of her back and then gently kneaded her own neck, Simon thought how kind of her to lean over him as she had for so long simply to comfort him.

"I'm going to lie down," he told her and, feeling rather like a child, he rose from his chair, crossed the room, and climbed onto his long-neglected bed.

Lying flat on his back, Simon glanced at the familiar canopy above him. He didn't ask her to leave. He wasn't sure whether he wanted her to go and let him save face for his humiliating behavior, for which strangely he didn't feel humiliated at all, or if he wanted her to stay and sit close by.

Yes, he did know! He realized he wanted her to watch over him while he slept, but he wouldn't ask that. Couldn't ask that.

To his amazement, this Jenny person, this bookkeeper, said nothing about his emotional demonstration. Instead, she reached for the large blanket folded on the chest at the end of his bed. Silently, she lay it across his prone form and unfolded it, pulling half of it down toward his bare feet, actually tucking the blanket around them, before pulling the other half up to his chest, smoothing it over him without making eye contact.

She was gracious in her caring, making sure to cause him no discomfort or embarrassment.

Simon could study her closely without her looking at him. It was an amazingly intimate moment, yet lacking any sensuality. He liked looking at her calm and lovely face, liked seeing her hair slightly mussed because she had let him grab onto her for support.

Yawning broadly, Simon closed his eyes, then felt her tuck the blanket up under his chin. He smiled again, and his face muscles felt strained with lack of use.

Jenny was caring *for* him as if she actually cared *about* him.

That was his last thought as he drifted off into a deep slumber.

UNSURE WHAT TO DO after his lordship went to sleep, Jenny spent a few moments simply staring at his face, now peaceful. Naturally, he looked younger without the frown lines and the tight, compressed lips. He looked more like the very young man from the Christmas parties of her youth.

His chest rose evenly and he seemed entirely calm. Lord Devere looked positively appealing in every way. Now Lord Lindsey, she reminded herself. *An earl.*

Recalling how his eyes had sparkled when he'd looked her up and down—rather insolently, although perhaps an earl could not be deemed insolent—and thinking how his lordship appeared a little surprised by his own reaction, she felt no insult. Only curiosity.

This strange man had found her attractive, she was certain of it, and that pleased her right down to her toes.

What's more, she could finally look her fill of him without embarrassment. He was fine-looking indeed, even more than she'd believed when telling Maggie of the shadowy figure she'd encountered. Tall, yet at present too slender for his height, his shoulders were broad and once he gained some weight, she was sure he'd cut a grand figure. His hair was not simply brown, it was richly umber, and she had felt its silky softness for herself when she'd held him against her. His eyes were a dark, blue-gray color that seemed endlessly deep, and it saddened her to think what painful memories were lurking in their depths.

After another minute of simply watching him breathing peacefully, Jenny backed slowly and silently away until she was standing by the door. She couldn't imagine he would appreciate having her looming over him or even sitting in attendance, a veritable stranger, when he awakened. With that in mind, she tiptoed from his room.

Despite what he'd professed about sleeping, he seemed like a man in desperate need of a long, uninterrupted slumber.

Finally, she was on the other side of the closed door, and she rested her back against it, closing her own eyes and considering the emotional encounter with his lordship. Lord Despair indeed! She would examine her own feelings about holding a crying stranger, a male one at that, later that evening. At that moment, she wanted to get back to the library in case Mr. Binkley came looking for her again.

"WHY WON'T YOU TELL me what happened yesterday?" Maggie asked, following Jenny into their mother's room after breakfast. Even though Ned now knew about her bookkeeping services, she had no wish to share the parlor with him. Better to remain at her makeshift work area. Henry had brought home another client's ledgers whilst she was away the day before.

Jenny supposed she should tell him to stop soliciting other clients until she finished with the earl's accounts.

"I told you. I don't wish to gossip about his lordship. I've confided in you about Lady Devere. Wasn't she strange and interesting enough?"

"I don't care about Lady Devere. I speak with her nearly every time I go to the manor. She is lonely and bored, and so she comes to speak French with me."

"Thank goodness she didn't do that with me," Jenny said. The very idea of speaking French with someone whose native tongue it was terrified her.

Maggie sat on the edge of the bed and crossed her arms. "Stop switching the topic."

"The topic is officially switched. Do you have any idea when Ned is leaving? I mean, what on earth is he doing here?"

Maggie stared at her. "Don't you know?"

Jenny feared she did but was afraid to think about it.

Her sister tossed herself back onto their mother's bed, her legs remaining hanging over and her feet nearly on the floor. "You could have quite an easy life."

"Whatever do you mean?" Jenny asked.

"As Mrs. Ned Darrow, mistress of the house in Dumfries."

Jenny groaned and heard Maggie's soft laughter.

"You could, you know. The Darrow family has a small house in London as well."

"Do not even think such thoughts," Jenny told her.

Maggie was silent for a few minutes while Jenny worked. "I feel terribly guilty," she said at last.

Jenny frowned. "Whatever for?"

Maggie didn't answer immediately. "When Father died, I was angry with him."

"I was, too, a little," Jenny confessed. "He should have had his affairs in order long before. He should have considered Mummy and the three of us. Don't feel guilty about your anger."

"It's not simply that. I thought of myself more than anything. I had started my first season, and then I realized I would have no more. However, Eleanor may never get to experience even one ball. And even one is glorious."

"I would say that one is the perfect number," Jenny considered. "After you get to forty balls in a season, especially on top of the drawing room teas and the early rides and the breakfasts with other eligibles, and the picnics and the boating parties, and the cricket matches at Lord's. Good God, it all seemed like more of a chore than anything."

"Be that as it may, you and I both experienced it. Eleanor may never do so. Yet, I didn't think of her or you. Only myself. And I should have thought mostly of you, who not only made it through your first season but secured a husband during your second one. And then lost him through no fault of your own. I never even considered that your heart might be bruised."

Jenny shrugged. "Dearest sister, do not for a moment worry over my heart. Not where Lord Alder was concerned. Nor do I regret not finishing my second season. I shudder at the notion of a third."

"But a husband—"

"There is always Ned," Jenny quipped, and they both laughed.

When Maggie left her to finish her work in peace, Jenny pondered her sister's morose words. Maggie might never get to finish an entire season. Eleanor might never have one at all. No, it was unthinkable! That her lovely sisters would languish in the country and not find suitable husbands.

Burying herself in the numbers, Jenny resolved as never before that she would earn enough for both her sisters to go to London. Come hell or high water!

A terrible outcry brought her out of the ledgers sometime later.

Even though she knew at once it was either Eleanor or Maisie, still, her thoughts flew to Simon Devere. How her heart grieved for the man. By all accounts before leaving for battle, he was well liked, dutiful, intelligent, and helpful to all those around him. No one had doubted he would take over his father's estate with a capable hand.

And now?

Rubbing the crick in the back of her neck, Jenny raced down the stairs and found the house empty. Hearing noise from the back, she ran to the terrace and saw that her family were gathered at the paddock.

Thunder!

Sure enough, the horse had nipped Maisie's arm, when the girl had not heeded warnings over Thunder's current unpredictable and surly temperament.

Maggie held a cloth over Maisie's forearm, while Anne instructed George, the stable boy, to fetch the local doctor. Ned strode back and forth talking about shooting Thunder between the eyes, causing Eleanor to sob uncontrollably, for she loved all creatures, except inexplicably hedgehogs.

Jenny rolled her eyes at the drama unfolding.

"Everyone, let's go inside and have Cook put the kettle on. Maisie, I think Cook said last night there would be a cream and strawberry sponge with our meal today."

Jenny particularly remembered that, for she thought of the expense of an extra dessert.

Mention of the sweet treat worked a miracle. Eleanor and Maisie brightened up and stopped their tears. Before long, everyone was sipping tea in the parlor and awaiting the doctor. At his arrival, he proclaimed the young lady would have no scar since Thunder had barely broken the skin.

While there had been a scrape of blood, it was merely a bruise that Maisie would have to bear for a week or more.

Ned, however, was not satisfied. Looking squarely at George, their cousin's face was red with anger. The rest of them waited in silence while Ned gave the lad a stern talking to, as if the boy were responsible for Thunder or could do anything about the horse's attitude. Although none of the ladies agreed, they couldn't gainsay him in front of the servants.

As soon as the doctor left, Cook put a thin layer of arnica infusion on Maisie's arm and said there would be only the slightest bruising of the skin at all.

"Certainly not for a week!" she muttered.

"I still think we should put that animal down," Ned proclaimed. From day one of his visit, as soon as the first warning had been issued about Thunder, their cousin had expressed this opinion.

"Absolutely not," Anne said, and Jenny was glad of it. She didn't want to usurp her mother's authority, but no one was shooting their horse.

"My brother is terrified of horses," Maisie blurted into the thick atmosphere of uneasiness that had clouded the room.

"Maisie," Ned snapped at his sister. "Of course I'm not! Anyone should be careful of such a brute, and you had better heed Lady Blackwood this time and stay clear. Terrified of horses," he repeated as if it were preposterous. Then he sat down and quietly drank his tea.

"Don't worry," Jenny told George who looked a little ill after Ned's dressing down. "Everything is fine. Why don't you go check on the horses? I'm sure they all need a bit of soothing."

Anne looked at Maisie. "You may ride Lucy, and you may pet and even feed the old Bay, but you must stay clear of Thunder."

"Yes, Auntie," Maisie agreed, despite everyone knowing it wasn't the first time she'd been told.

"I wonder if we can get someone to look at Thunder's leg," Jenny mused. "We should have asked the doctor while he was here."

Maggie chuckled. "He seemed rather full of himself for a country doctor. Somehow, I don't think he would have appreciated being turned into a veterinarian."

They all laughed.

Jenny glanced at the clock on the mantle. Were the hands deliberately moving more slowly today? Restlessly, she got up and went into the kitchen to see how long before they were served the midday meal. She wanted to get to the manor. She had a few more figures to look at in the ledgers. However, she was honest enough to acknowledge it was not only the Belton accounts that fascinated her. She fervently hoped there would be an opportunity for another encounter with the earl.

CHAPTER SEVEN

Jenny was sequestered as she had been the day before in the library on what was probably her last day, taking notes, recording irregularities, and writing a summary for the butler. Of all people to be receiving the master report of the estate's accounts!

When she heard footsteps go past the door that she'd purposefully left ajar, she knew it must be him and hurried to catch up.

Spying the hurrying form of the very man with whom she wished to speak, she called out to him.

"Mr. Binkley, a word if you have a moment."

He stopped and turned.

"Could I speak with you in the library?"

He hesitated, then nodded, walking back to her and gesturing for her to proceed him into the room.

"What may I help you with, Miss Blackwood? More tea?"

"No, nothing like that. I know I've been a pest about this, but I am only thinking of the good of the Belton estate and the many people who live here and work for the earl. I wish to know if there is someone who can act as overseer until . . . until Lord Lindsey is able."

The butler narrowed his eyes.

"Why do you ask?"

"It is unusual for no one to be at the helm," Jenny began.

"Do you have a great deal of experience in running large estates?"

"I understand your point, Mr. Binkley. Although my father was only a baron, I believe I possess the common knowledge that landed nobility do not usually do their own bookkeeping."

"You refer to Sir Tobias."

"Yes," Jenny confirmed. "Also, when you were telling me who was making notes in the ledgers, you failed to mention the other Lord Devere."

The butler appeared startled. "How did you learn of him?"

"Lady Devere paid me a visit and told me her father-in-law stayed here when her husband and the heir were away."

"I see."

When Mr. Binkley said nothing else, Jenny wanted to sigh with exasperation. What was going on here?

"The former earl's younger brother came to Belton upon his death to help run the estate? Have I got that correct?"

"No, that would be precisely not correct. Lord James Devere, the earl's brother, visited *before* his brother died. They sat together for many hours. However, the earl did not make any changes in his will or change allowances or even appoint his brother as a proxy. There is nothing disreputable for you to find if that is what you're alluding to."

His having said that made her think that there certainly was something for her to discover, perhaps not exactly dishonest but not standard practice either.

"If Simon Devere had been killed alongside his cousin," Jenny persisted, "would the old earl's brother have taken over?"

"I fail to see what that has to do with anything." Mr. Binkley's expression was sour. "Fortunately, the heir is alive."

"It is unconscionable that the housekeeper should be made to think of the estate's ledgers, is it not? Was the groom called in as well to make his mark upon the books?"

Mr. Binkley clearly did not appreciate her sarcasm. His face clouded over, and she wondered if he would simply throw her out. *Without* paying her.

"I apologize," Jenny said quickly. After all, it wasn't his fault. "I fear that due to my own situation, with my father dying and leaving my mother in a perilous financial situation, I have little tolerance for poor judgment, especially on the grand scale of an earldom, with countless others' livelihoods at stake. Including your own," she added.

He glanced around, as if thinking about his situation.

Taking a deep breath, she tried again. "There is another person's neat handwriting, beginning not long after Lady Devere moved in. Did she also make entries?"

"Of course not," Mr. Binkley answered.

"Then who?"

"Master Dolbert," the words were said through clenched teeth.

Jenny frowned. *Dolbert? Dolbert?* Where had she heard that name? Then she recalled the children. *Master Cheeseface!*

"The math tutor?"

Mr. Binkley nodded.

Well, she supposed, *at least that was better than the groom.*

By coincidence, she'd arrived at the same time as the tutor that morning, and they'd met at the side door. Unable to recall his real name, she'd nodded and smiled. The man was unremarkable except for a face pockmarked from some childhood illness. Moreover, he was utterly unsmiling in return.

It was that last trait, appearing to have a miserable outlook, that caused Jenny to immediately dismiss him as a suitor for Maggie. Pity. To have found a husband for her sister right there in Sheffield would have been handy and taken a weight off her shoulders. Regardless, Maggie would most likely not have looked kindly on a tutor as her mate in any case.

"You gave Master Dolbert the amounts to enter?"

"He was given the receipts directly to enter and then the deposits were sent to London."

Jenny didn't say a word. In fact, she bit her tongue. Yet how positively simple it would be for the man to record incorrect amounts and keep some of the income for himself. Especially a man good with numbers.

"Most of the income goes directly into the Devere bank account in London," she pointed out. "Why would some receipts come here?"

"Only the local agricultural revenues come here to pay for small daily household expenses."

She would ask the butler one last time about what alarmed her. "If both of the young Deveres had not returned, then who would be in charge?"

"The earl returned, Miss, so there is no reason to—"

"To worry. Yes, I know. You've said that." This was getting her nowhere. "Very well, Mr. Binkley. I suppose it would be helpful if the earl could actually leave his room and tour his estates as he used to."

"In time, yes," was his grudging answer.

"In time, and not too long from now either, the earl's coffers will be empty since the revenues are, in fact, dwindling."

Mr. Binkley nodded. "Yes, I am aware of that. Hence, my hiring you."

"There is little else I can do here," Jenny admitted. "I cannot make the money reappear, but I can tell you—I can show you if you care to look—precisely when things started to go awry. I can even pinpoint which holdings are not giving the earl his due. Are you the one to whom I should show these figures?"

Now the admiral looked out of his element, his face quite grim.

"If you can summarize your latest findings, that will do. For now, anyway. I have other duties to which I must attend at present."

He hurried out of the room as if afraid of looking at the numbers. That didn't surprise her. Many people felt that way when faced with detailed accounting.

Should she go see the earl? In his current state, could he handle information about his financial affairs? She recalled that Mr. Binkley said Lord Lindsey had no head for numbers. Unfortunately, at present, he didn't seem to have a head for much of anything. Could she help him? She was determined to try.

If his strength was interacting with the people in his employ and in the village and at other estate holdings, then that was what he should be doing. At the very least.

BLOTTING THE LAST PAGE of her notes, Jenny stood. There was no excuse to go roaming the manor, not to see Maggie, who had probably left already, nor to see the children, whom she'd met only once. She didn't need any refreshments as she'd already had enough tea to float the royal barge.

In fact, she really ought to be heading home. Instead, she was soon passing from one wing to the next and walking along the corridor toward Simon Devere's chamber, with no viable reason she could give anyone if she were caught. She would have to admit she was going to see Lord Lindsey even though this time, he had not invited her.

To her amazement, the earl's door was ajar. Still, she tapped on it. Instantly, she heard his voice.

"Enter."

Why did the timber of this man's voice cause something inside her to stir?

Pushing the door open, Jenny was surprised to see him standing and looking as if he were in mid-pace. One of the drapes was drawn partially open and enough light was streaming in that she could see him easily. Clean-shaven, hair brushed back, and wearing more formal attire than she'd previously seen. He had on a natty waistcoat over a starched white shirt. The collar was pinned in place, too.

"Good day, Guinevere," he said. "Have you been standing in the middle of any streets lately?"

Caught off guard by his humor, she laughed.

"No, my lord. Nor have any horses tried to run me over." That brought to mind Thunder. Hadn't Binkley told her that the earl was quite skilled with equines and their ways.

"My lord, I have a horse problem."

"Indeed? Tell me all about it."

His tone indicated that he was taking her quite seriously.

"If you were walking, my lord, may I suggest we continue to do so, since I have been sitting in your library for quite some time today."

"Certainly." Simon glanced out the window. "The weather is fine, it appears."

Would he go outside with her? Was he indicating such a thing?

"It is, my lord."

However, he only sighed deeply, causing her heart to ache on his behalf.

"If we open both those doors," he pointed to the doors on either side of his bed that led to the next chamber, "we can make a circuitous path of the two rooms."

"Let's do that," she agreed, wondering if and when he would leave his suite for the broader world outside. Or even for rooms beyond his chamber.

They walked from one room to the next in silence at first. She took in the space she had not seen before. A dressing room as well as a private office. It looked unused. Not a stitch of clothing showing from the wardrobe, nor a piece of paper on the expansive desk. Still, it was a beautiful area, with a thick rug under foot and lovely wallpaper.

"I prefer my bedchamber," he said, watching her.

"That seems odd, my lord, for a man who doesn't wish to sleep."

He nodded. "True enough. However, it is the scent."

Jenny couldn't help herself, she sniffed and sniffed again. The faint smell of wood polish was the only aroma she could detect. The earl stood to the side and let her pass through the doorway first, back into his bedroom. She sniffed again. In this room, there was no detectable scent at all.

She looked at him questioningly.

"I believe it is the beeswax. The aroma assaults me in the antechamber."

"Shall we not make the circuit, my lord?"

"It is fine, as long as I am walking through. I just don't like remaining in there."

She brushed aside any unkind thoughts about his strangeness and continued to walk with him.

"First, tell me about your horse troubles, and then, if you will, I would like to hear about the estate ledgers."

She had a momentary flash of guilt. Was she betraying Mr. Binkley? Then she realized the nonsense of such a feeling, for ultimately, every sum she added or subtracted was done on this man's behalf.

"When my family was moving up from London, one of our horses was injured. The leg seems to have healed, but Thunder is now skittish and ill-tempered as he never was before."

The earl frowned. "Have you had a vet look at the leg?"

"I'm afraid it seemed too costly an expense when it first happened."

"And now?"

"Now, I believe I have the funds, but, as I said, the leg seems to have mended nicely, according to our stable boy."

"Your stable boy?"

"Yes, George. His mother is our cook. We brought them both from London with us."

"And what are his qualifications to tend horses?"

Jenny considered. "He doesn't mind shoveling their excrement, my lord."

He barked out a quick laugh at her remark, a sound that seemed to surprise him as much as it did her.

Then with a slight smile, he told her, "Horses deserve a knowledgeable caregiver. They are complicated, intelligent beings."

"Like people, my lord?"

"I will not go as far as to say they are like people, but horses do develop damaged psyches, and then they need help. I've seen it happen before. What's more, they *can* be helped to return to their normal condition, be it ill-tempered or sweet."

"And thus, *exactly* like people."

He stared at her. "God, I hope so, Guinevere."

And just like that, Jenny knew they were speaking of him now, and his devastated mental state. She nearly touched his arm to express her sympathy but restrained herself from making such a forward gesture.

Instead, she focused on his twice-made error. "Why do you call me Guinevere?"

"Because it is your name."

She smiled, recalling their conversation from a previous day. "No, it is not."

"I understand you prefer 'Jenny.' What with your fear of being run over and all that."

She quite liked his sense of humor. "Whether I'm in the center of a street or not, my lord, still, Guinevere is not my name."

He stopped walking and frowned down at her. "You said it was."

"No, you said better it should be Guinevere than Jenny. Something about ballrooms, I think. As if no gentleman would write his name on my dance card if I were Jenny, or

89

was it Betsy? I'll have you know that no less than a viscount not only danced with me last season, he proposed."

The earl's eyebrows shot up.

"Why do you look surprised?" she asked.

Suddenly, she felt her cheeks grow warm. Perhaps the earl did not like her looks after all, which she'd been told were quite regular and symmetrical, and hence considered attractive. Certainly no one had ever called her a phantom beauty before, but still, she'd hoped—

"I am not surprised that you received a proposal, only that your viscount allows you to be alone with another bachelor, namely me. Not to mention the broadness of mind to let you practice the profession of bookkeeping."

A breeze of relief seemed to blow over her. Lord Lindsey didn't think it beyond the pale that she had received a proposal. He merely questioned her actions were she an engaged woman.

Still, she had to correct him. "I do not answer to anyone regarding my actions. And Lord Alder is no longer *my* viscount."

"You turned him down, then. Quite the correct thing for you to do. An intelligent, lovely girl like yourself should hold out for a duke, if not a prince."

Now it was her turn to laugh wholeheartedly, and she did.

"Oh, my lord. Perhaps we need to fully open the curtain. I do not believe I am a catch for a duke or a prince. Indeed, I was grateful for the interest of Lord Alder. Even a courtesy baron or a baronet would do."

"Nonsense!" he muttered. "A baronet indeed!"

And she found herself the object of his scrutiny once more.

"Thick shiny hair, the color of a dark chestnut mane. No balding patches?"

"No, my lord." She nearly choked at the idea as she lifted a hand to her head.

"Eyes that can hold a man in their sparkling depths. I assume they don't cross regularly?"

Jenny began to smile. "No, my lord."

"A sweet mouth with straight teeth and soft-looking lips of a healthy pinkish hue. Do you spit often, drool, or lisp?"

"No, my lord."

"A slim, fair-skinned neck. Prone to warts?"

"No, my lord, no warts." The very idea!

His gaze dropped lower, and her breath caught in her throat. As previously, he regarded her figure frankly, and she felt the heat creep into her cheeks.

"A pleasing physique with the right amount of curvature. Any unsightly bulges of fat hidden beneath your gown?"

She coughed, and when she answered, her voice was a whisper. "No, my lord."

"Thick ankles then?"

She shook her head, not speaking, but simply waiting for his inspection to end.

"Are your feet the size of tree branches? Go ahead, show me the ankles and the feet."

Without hesitation, she lifted her skirts a few inches.

Simon Devere examined her boots and her slender ankles. His brown hair fell forward as he did. The utter impropriety of her standing in the earl's chamber while holding her gown and undergarments up struck her all at once, and she released them.

His gaze caught hers for a moment, and then he started to walk again.

"Well then, as I said, you were too good for the viscount. With or without more light, I believe I see your assets quite well. You are lacking in none of them."

Goodness! Jenny hurried to catch up with him and continue their promenade.

How unbelievably awkward. What's more, she felt as if she should reciprocate and tell him what a fine figure of a man he was, but that was entirely out of the question. All she could do was thank him for his outrageous listing of her attributes since he had ended with a compliment.

"Thank you, my lord," she said into the silence.

"No need to thank me. Apparently, you don't own a mirror," he told her with mirth in his voice.

After another turn about the rooms, he asked, "Then what *is* your name?"

"Do you promise not to laugh?" She glanced at him, and he looked back at her with a gleam in his eyes.

"I do not promise. If I find something to laugh at, I assure you, I will do so."

"Very well." She paused. "My name is Genevieve."

"That does not make me laugh." He blinked at her. "Why would it?"

She sighed. "It is pretentious and long and foreign. What's more, no one can ever spell it."

"Hence 'Jenny.'" His gaze roamed over her face, and she wondered what it was he thought he saw. Turning from him, she continued their stroll.

The aroma of polish seemed to permeate the air now that she was aware of it. Beeswax, strong and fusty. They didn't speak again until they were back in his bedchamber.

"Jenny suits your no-nonsense, mathematical mind, I suppose." He stopped. "I'm done walking around in here like a nag on a mill wheel."

They stopped in the middle of his bedchamber, and Jenny considered again how shocking this situation truly was. The eyes of every member of the *bon ton* would be bulging, their eyebrows raised, their tongues waggling with the impropriety, certain of her ruin. She smiled, and Simon tilted his head.

"You are thinking something amusing, demon?"

"If I had not already lost the viscount over the downturn in my family's financial condition, my being here . . . with you . . . would certainly have caused its swift expiry."

Surprising her, the earl suddenly lifted his hand and stroked her cheek, then held her chin with his fingertips.

"Perhaps there's another side of you that Genevieve suits perfectly. I, for one, like the way it rolls off my tongue."

CHAPTER EIGHT

"Genevieve."

As he repeated her name, Jenny found herself staring at his mouth, which now fascinated her beyond anything else.

"Perhaps," she murmured, unsure of what she was saying as her breath had suddenly caught.

For a moment, they stood frozen, his fingers upon her upturned chin, her heart pounding painfully.

She licked her lips and thought perhaps interest flared behind his gray-blue eyes. If there *was* a demon in the room, it might be lurking within the earl.

Within her, however, she couldn't deny there was definitely an answering spirit.

Was he leaning closer?

At last, she shook her head, dislodging his hand at the same time as she took a step back.

"I've had my last Season," she insisted as if her real name belonged to the woman who graced the ballrooms of London. "I'm resigned to being Jenny."

Walking to the window, she turned her face toward the warm sun. She needed to calm her emotions and regain her senses. Not usually prone to flights of fancy, being alone with a man—this man, who had a wildness about him at times, who didn't seem to recall the boundaries of polite society—she was letting her imagination run amuck.

Certainly, he had *not* intended to kiss her.

"In fact, I'm proud of plain Jenny if it represents, as you say, my practical nature. I am slowly paying off my father's debt and keeping my family from losing any more than we have already lost."

"Admirable." The earl sounded as though he meant it. "If you are doing well, then what troubles you?"

Startled by his words, Jenny turned to stare at him. "How do you know anything is troubling me, my lord?"

"I could hear it in your voice. And now I can see it in your eyes. I'm sure it has to do with more than an irritable horse. Is it your broken engagement? Did you have a written contract? I could have the bounder brought to heel, made to honor his proposal."

"Oh." Her mouth went dry. How peculiar he made her feel. Off balance from moment to moment. What's more, inexplicably, she believed she could tell him anything and he would understand.

"No, my lord. It is not on account of Lord Alder. Besides, he broke only a verbal agreement, and I care not a jot about it. In truth, it is my sisters. I worry for their futures. We cannot have three spinster Blackwood sisters."

To her amazement, Simon Devere laughed, sparking a flame of outrage inside her.

"I see nothing funny. I hate to speak ill of the dead, but my father was quite irresponsible in how he left his affairs."

"Let me tell you then," the earl said, sobering. "Your worries are for naught. I've seen one of your sisters, all those complicated-looking curls and dressed in a fetching trim waistcoat. Why, she sways her bustle even for old Binkley, and I believe he notices, too."

Jenny couldn't help but smile slightly at his description.

"That would be Margaret. When did you see my sister?"

Simon shrugged. "From this window, I've watched her arrive many times, although I don't know why she comes here. I've seen you, too, for that matter."

She shivered, imagining his gaze upon her when she had no knowledge of him.

"What's more, I've seen your sister stroll down this hallway, with Binkley sending her on her way."

"I see." Jenny was about to tell him that her sister came to tutor French when suddenly she had a brazen idea and spoke before thinking.

"Would *you* wish to offer for Margaret? That would remove at least one of my concerns, finding her a suitable husband. She speaks French like a native, plays the harpsichord, and would make any man, even an earl, a wonderful wife."

As long as Simon didn't mind a sometimes critically sharp tongue and a tendency to selfishness.

Simon's face became expressionless, and she feared she had overstepped the boundaries of propriety with her half-serious jest. Moreover, she may have insulted him. After all, he was an earl, and Maggie, a mere baron's daughter.

"No," he said firmly, yet with no hint of annoyance. "I would not suit as your sister's husband. Or anyone's."

Jenny opened her mouth to protest, when he added, "I could, however, see my way clear to pay for your sister to have a Season."

She blinked, opened her mouth, closed it again, and then shook her head in wonder. "That is . . . why, I cannot . . ."

She wanted to say she could not possibly accept such unthinkable generosity, yet how could she not? For Maggie's sake. Maybe God was indeed answering her nightly prayers, working miracles through Simon Devere.

At her momentary speechlessness, the earl simply looked amused.

"Why would you do such a thing?" Jenny finally managed.

"Not quite the statement of gratitude I had imagined." He sat in his chair and crossed his legs, looking entirely relaxed, as if he hadn't just changed the course of her sister's life.

This could mean a husband for Maggie and a completely different existence than the one Jenny had accepted as her own lot, that of a country spinster.

"I would do it because I can," the earl said, "and because you seem quite nice. You've certainly been kind to me. It seems that your family has fallen on difficult times through no fault of your own. Moreover, you are trying to help yourself, not wallowing in your situation."

All of that was quite true. What's more, despite any appearance of impropriety in letting a stranger finance her sister's Season, Jenny would not be an ungrateful fool.

"I accept your offer on behalf of the Blackwood family." After all, it was not unheard of for a family patron to do such a thing. Was that what the earl now was?

"And you have a younger sister, do you not?" he asked.

"Yes, Eleanor."

"A beauty in her own right, I'm sure."

Jenny considered. "I hadn't thought of her yet in that way, my lord, as she is not yet fifteen. However, yes, I suppose she will be." She held her breath, hardly daring to believe his generosity was going to be doubled.

"As I recall, many girls are presented at court by age fifteen. In any case, whenever your family deems her ready, I shall provide for Eleanor in the same manner as Margaret, even if it is the same Season. Unless there is some rule about sisters and how many may be out at any given time. Of that, I am blissfully unaware."

Again, Jenny had no words. She knew she was gaping unattractively. Yet, how could she express her all-encompassing gratitude? How could he ever understand what this meant to her? Just like that, her worst fears had been alleviated. A terrible weight had suddenly lifted.

She wanted to laugh and cry at the same time. Moreover, she had the insane urge to hug him.

"And what about yourself, Miss Genevieve Blackwood? Would you like another Season in London's ballrooms? Perhaps to find a replacement for your fickle viscount?"

Like Perrault's Cinderella, she was being offered a wonderful chance by the most unlikely of godmothers. However, she had only the smallest scrap of interest. Recalling the rounds, the silly, posturing people, the stuffy rooms, the endless worry over gowns, who would dance with whom, and whether one's dance card was entirely filled, or if one might be left standing by the wall or the drapes. Not to mention the overarching dread of being left on the shelf.

Far better to put oneself upon it and stay there!

"God no," she said emphatically, then at his shocked expression, she added, "Thank you, my lord. I am quite past the age at which a Season is seemly, particularly with a younger sister ready for her turn."

"How old are you?" he asked bluntly. "Thirty-four?"

"Not quite," she admitted, before laughing at his little joke. "I suppose I am not *past* the age precisely. I know ladies who went for five Seasons, and to be honest, I felt nothing except sympathy for them. I certainly have no intention of putting myself in that position."

Then, to lighten the moment, Jenny made her own little jest, "If I become desperate, there are always the matrimonial advertisements."

However, Simon didn't laugh. He merely frowned with puzzlement. "I have never heard of these advertisements."

Realizing the matchmaking announcements had probably come to their height of popularity in London whilst Simon Devere was in Burma, she glanced at her feet. Not only that, they were rather vulgar for her to be reading, although the advice columns had not seemed quite so scandalous. One could read those for amusement and sometimes even glean a nugget of good sense, whereas the adverts were positively base.

"In such places as *The London Journal*, my lord, one can place an advertisement requesting a husband—or a wife, for that matter—though one must abandon all sense of modesty or humility and list one's attributes both of appearance and abilities."

Simon looked rather taken aback. "Rather the way we discuss good horseflesh before purchase, isn't it?"

"I suppose so, my lord."

"And would you do this?"

Oh, dear. What must he think of her?

"No, certainly not. I was joking, my lord. I believe the advertisements are full of untruths and exaggerations. Moreover, it makes forming an attachment rather . . . ordinary."

He thought for a moment. "Yet, as a practical woman named Jenny, shouldn't you find the enterprise of advertising for your mate comfortingly pragmatic, not to mention offering a far greater return on time invested than twirling about a ballroom hoping to be noticed? Think of the numbers and how many eyes in London might look at your advertisement versus the few hundred in a ballroom."

He sounded as if he were pushing her to place an advert, and the idea irked her.

"I was only jesting at the outset, my lord. I prefer helping my mother to run our home, and frankly, I like the challenge of being a bookkeeper. In every way, I prefer Sheffield to being in London."

"You are a strange lady," the earl said without a hint of rudeness. "Who will accompany your sisters for their Seasons if not you?"

"Why, my mother, of course." Lady Anne Blackwood enjoyed dressing her daughters and appearing with them in society.

"Leaving you alone in your house?"

Oh. That could be a problem.

"There is a housemaid and our cook."

"And the hapless stable boy," Simon reminded her.

She nodded. "And Henry."

"Henry? Is that the man I saw accompany you here one day?"

He had seen her arrive with Ned? Jenny preferred not to delve into her failed ruse.

"No, Henry is my late father's personal servant. My mother felt badly letting him go and, thus, did not. Having him puttering about seems as if my father is also present in some way. Henry earns his keep by being my ears and eyes regarding bookkeeping clients."

She closed her mouth at that. For goodness sake, she was chatting away like a magpie.

His gaze was suddenly piercingly sharp. "You know as well as I that none of the servants counts as a chaperone. Not really, nor as suitable companions or as safe escorts for you when you are at home alone in the country for an extended period. Certainly not for an entire Season. Especially a male servant."

The earl was quite serious and, unfortunately, correct. Moreover, he was looking at her as if she were a delectable morsel that any man might want to snap up if given half a chance. It confused and thrilled her at the same time.

"You are right, of course." Servants could be ordered to leave one alone with a member of the opposite sex, and thus no one in polite society considered them as reliable attendants. What if Ned dropped in for another visit while her family was away?

"Some might say that having the widow here without a proper chaperone is equally improper. More so even."

Obviously, Maude was in mourning, but what happened when she came out of it? Jenny couldn't imagine living in close quarters with Simon and seeing him every day without yearning to become closer. He was by far the most interesting, plain-spoken man she'd ever met.

However, the look of utter confusion on the earl's face made her wish she could recall her words.

"Maude?" he asked, his voice a little hesitant. "Tobias's widow lives here?"

Jenny realized her error. "I'm dreadfully sorry, my lord. I spoke out of turn."

"No, it's all right. Tell me. For apparently, if you don't, no one will."

"You have been indisposed until late," she reminded him in defense of Mr. Binkley and his staff.

Simon waved off that excuse.

"Tell me," he ordered again, sounding every bit an earl in command.

"Lady Tobias Devere resides here at Belton in private apartments. With her children."

Simon's eyes widened at the information. "That explains the loud noises, the shouting that I sometimes hear." He rubbed a hand over his face, nodding slightly. "I actually thought I was going insane."

"Yes, my lord. Peter and Alice can be quite loud. My sister tutors them in French."

"I see." He frowned. "No, actually, I don't see at all. Why aren't they all at Jonling Hall?"

Was it really going to fall to her to break the news?

"Perhaps I should get Mr. Binkley." She glanced around the room as if the butler might pop up from behind the bed.

"Jenny," Simon Devere said, his tone pleading.

She could not refuse.

"Lady Devere relinquished ownership of Jonling Hall while you were away."

Simon stood slowly. "Relinquished it? She *sold* the hall? Out of my family?"

Jenny shrugged. "Before you ask me, my lord, no one seems to know who bought it, and no one has, as yet, taken up residence."

With agitation, he crossed the room to the window, then strode back to the chair, repeating the short journey three times. It made the large chamber seem very small.

"I am utterly confounded," he said at last.

What if this triggered another incident?

"Should I fetch Mr. Binkley, or your valet?"

But he latched onto her arm as he had before. "Are there other nasty surprises?"

Only the very real possibility that his cousin had been stealing from the family. Or perhaps the math tutor had.

"I must be going, my lord. My family will begin to wonder at my lateness for dinner."

"We haven't discussed the ledgers."

Anyone would be foolish to think this man did not have all his mental faculties.

"You will return soon," he added, then remembered what she'd told him before. "Please."

"Yes." She gazed at his large hand still gripping her arm.

Swiftly letting her go, his tone was lighter when he spoke again. "And you will let your mother know that her daughters will not rot in the country next Season?"

Her heart soared once again and she nodded.

"And you will agree to go with them to London rather than stay alone in the country?"

It would be a humiliation for her, attending a third Season but only as a chaperone.

"My mother and I will cross that bridge when we come to it. However, I cannot let the threat of having to escort my sisters to London dampen my utter relief at what you have so generously given us." She felt how large the smile was upon her face. Undoubtedly like a beaming idiot.

"I honestly don't know what to say or how I can ever repay you."

Her words were met with silence.

It dragged on until it became uncomfortable, and all the while, he stared at her, his face neutral, his thoughts a mystery. The earl's glance eventually drifted from her eyes to her lips, causing an unexpected frisson of excitement to rush through her.

Then his gaze dropped lower, to her bosom.

Unexpectedly, her nipples began to tingle, causing her to be extremely aware of precisely where her shift brushed over them. At the same time, to Jenny's extreme embarrassment, she knew her cheeks must be bright red.

The very air around her crackled with tension. *Did Lord Lindsey feel it, too?*

When Simon's eyes caught her gaze once more, something flickered in their depths. Not a demon after all, but still, something quite uncivilized, just as she'd seen before. Swallowing past the dryness in her throat, Jenny prepared herself for his kiss.

Instead, he glanced away. "No repayment is necessary." The earl's voice sounded rough, and he cleared his throat. "It is time for you to go."

She took a step back, realizing she'd been leaning toward him. What a fool she had made of herself. He'd been waiting for her to simply thank him and leave. Instead, she'd stared silently at him like a ninny.

"I apologize for overstaying, my lord."

He nodded, looking for all the world like a dignified nobleman and not at all like a broken soul who'd once sobbed on her shoulder.

"Do not trouble yourself," he added. "I meant only that you had wasted enough of your day on me."

She was already backing toward the door, eager to escape from the scene of her mortification.

"Jenny."

She halted.

"I appreciated your company today."

The man was a puzzlement.

"Thank you again, my lord." She slipped out the door before she could ruin the moment. Before she did or said something else entirely inappropriate.

As soon as she stepped out of his chamber, however, she wanted to yell with pure joy. *A Season for both her sisters!* Dear God in Heaven. What a miracle!

Running carelessly as Eleanor might, Jenny was halfway along the corridor before she noticed the admiral. She nearly tripped as she abruptly slowed to a normal pace.

Mr. Binkley stood ramrod straight, at the top of the stairs and had clearly seen from whence she had come.

The impropriety of the situation dawned on her once more. Alone with the earl in his bedroom. Again. Only this time, she was wearing a delighted grin!

She remained silent, tamping down the urge to defend herself. Trying futilely to regain her dignity and look respectable, she merely nodded politely to the butler as she passed him and descended the stairs without haste.

She was nearly at the side door when she realized she had left her bonnet, coat, and gloves in the second-floor library. Jenny retraced her steps, even being brave enough to pass by his lordship's door, which was still ajar.

"Yes, my lord, as you say, far more than a nuisance." Mr. Binkley's words came clearly through the opening. "I don't think she belongs here."

"Of course she doesn't belong here! But whose fault is that?"

Silence greeted the earl's terse question until he asked another one.

"When will she be gone?" Simon's voice sounded irritated.

"My understanding, my lord, is that she'll be gone soon enough."

"No, not soon enough. Too much damage can be done in the meanwhile." His tone was sheer exasperation. "Her presence is highly irregular."

"Yes, my lord, and some may think that you should offer for her hand."

Jenny gasped, then clamped a hand over her mouth, hoping they hadn't heard her. What was the butler thinking? Why would Lord Lindsey have to offer for her hand?

Sweet mother! It was because she'd been alone in his room on more than one occasion. No doubt the staff was beginning to gossip. A female bookkeeper was abnormal, and who would believe she could really sort out the ledgers if she sauntered happily out of his lordship's bedroom?

As she tiptoed away, the earl's words pursued her down the corridor, "Marry her? Are you mad? Not if she were the last woman on earth!"

Jenny tried to ignore the pang of hurt. Of course, his sentiment was quite natural given the difference between their stations. Perhaps if she'd been a renowned beauty or had a fortune.

Yet, she was simply Jenny Blackwood, a baron's daughter. The last woman on earth he would marry.

CHAPTER NINE

"What do you mean you're not going back? Mummy, what can she mean?"

Maggie was persistent, but Jenny couldn't face it. Couldn't face the manor or Mr. Binkley, and definitely not the earl. Not today. Maybe the next day or the day after. Her emotions were in turmoil, and her feelings had been trifled with and tread upon, and a butler—*a butler!*—had disparaged her.

Moreover, a peer of the realm had looked as if he might kiss her one moment yet insulted her the next. Or had she misinterpreted the expression on his face?

"What if the earl withdraws his offer?" Maggie sounded worried.

No, Jenny did not want to go back. Not ever. In fact, there was probably no need. She had completed her work. Someone at the manor needed to go upon an estate-wide tour and sort out the mess.

Perhaps the earl should write to his uncle, James Devere, and ask him to carry out the charge if he was unable.

"After what that man is doing for us," her mother said, addressing her sternly, "I think you should finish your bookkeeping task for him in short order. And make the numbers look good so the earl doesn't change his mind about his generous gift."

Jenny sighed. As if math could be manipulated to show something other than what was true.

"Mummy, I have completed the task that Mr. Binkley set out for me." Snatching a piece of toast from the silver toast wrack in the center of the table, she buttered it with ferocity until it crumbled into a pile on her plate.

"Last night you said the earl invited you to return," Maggie pointed out. "If not to finish the bookkeeping, then why?"

All heads at the breakfast table turned to her. Ned was scowling fiercely, which made him look like an irritated ferret.

"He wishes me to explain my findings." Jenny kept her attention on the food before her and shoveled it into her mouth in an unladylike fashion.

"And so you shall," Anne Blackwood decreed.

Jenny looked up at her mother, knowing she would have to obey. Tearing off a corner of her toast, she popped it between her lips. As she crunched loudly, crumbs went flying across the lace tablecloth around her plate.

Seeing her mother raise a delicate and disapproving eyebrow, Jenny lowered her gaze again.

What was the matter with her? Behaving like the unsuitable woman that both the butler and the earl seemed to have already judged her to be.

"I left a summary in writing. There is nothing more *I* can do until *they*—" she gestured in the direction of Belton Park—"do something."

"How can Lord Despair *do* anything if he remains in his room?" Maggie asked.

Jenny fixed her middle sister with a particularly hard stare. After all, the man was now their benefactor.

"Sorry," Maggie muttered. "I mean, Lord Devere."

"Now Lord Lindsey," their mother corrected. "I am sure a strong man such as his lordship will improve with time.

Maybe he needs some of Cook's porridge to stick to his ribs."

Jenny thought of him sobbing and fearful of the light rather than the dark. "I believe he needs more than a full stomach."

"It's a good idea, though," Maggie said. "Not porridge, of course! However, I will take his lordship one of cook's strawberry tarts to thank him for his kindness."

"Apples," Jenny said, gazing at the bowl of fruit in the center of the table. "The earl is fond of apple Charlotte."

They all turned to look at her.

She felt her cheeks grow warm. "That's what I heard Mr. Binkley tell one of the maids."

"Cook can't possibly whip that up in time for you to take with you today, but she can for tomorrow."

Now why had she lied? Jenny had done nothing wrong by visiting the earl. Still, she didn't want her mother and Ned to discuss the unseemliness of her being alone with Simon Devere, and therefore, she wasn't about to tell them.

Glancing at Maggie to indicate she would greatly appreciate her sister's silence on that matter, she tucked into the rest of her breakfast and ignored her mother's words about taking anything to the manor that day.

"I cannot believe we shall be in London together after all," Maisie said, grabbing Eleanor's hand, causing her to drop her scone, which rolled toward the center of the table. Both girls giggled.

"If Lord Lindsey wasn't an earl and thereby above reproach," Ned said, "I would advise you to turn down his offer." The entire breakfast gathering went silent, even though he spoke directly to Lady Blackwood.

By his smirk, he enjoyed grabbing all their attention.

"After all, it seems entirely too forward a thing for the earl to do, with absolutely no ties to the family."

Anne set her teacup down.

"I would do exactly as you say, Cousin Ned," she agreed, causing Maggie and Eleanor to gasp in dismay. "That is, if some member of our family wants to step in and pay for each of my girls to attend a Season."

She stared pointedly at him until Ned looked down at his soft-boiled egg, a chagrinned expression on his face.

Crisis averted, Jenny dropped her fork onto her plate and excused herself from the table. All caught up with her other customers, she had no ledgers to look at. With the pressure off regarding Maggie's Season and with enough earnings set aside to carry them through a few weeks, she need not ask Henry to solicit any more clients as yet.

What would she do with a day off? For one thing, she would stay away from Eleanor and Maisie so as not to get dragged into another game of *Puss, Puss in the Corner.*

As the weather was fine, Jenny set out on a leisurely stroll, ending up in the vicinity of Jonling Hall, which she had never entered, not even as a child. The earl had been startled at its loss, Jenny wished she could at least tell him good news that a pleasant family had moved in. Perhaps she would see the trappings of domesticity or encounter a gardener as she passed by.

"I say, do stop for a breath." Turning at the sound of her cousin's voice, Jenny's heart fell. She preferred her own company. And if she had to have company, Ned's name was near the bottom of those on her list of whom she wished to spend time. It was awkward and uncomfortable as he continued to drop hints about his feelings, which were decidedly unwelcome. He didn't seem to notice.

Why didn't the man understand her utter disregard for him, as far as a romantic association was involved? Having to state it plainly, word for word, would humiliate him and cause hurt feelings. And she had no interest in hurting him. She had no interest in him at all. That was the problem.

"Is it safe for you to be roaming the countryside without an escort?"

"I assume it is," she answered. "No one has bothered me except you."

He laughed. "You are amusing."

Was she? "Then I must try harder to be disagreeable."

Now he frowned, apparently unsure whether she was joking.

His look of perplexity stung her. Feeling like a shrew, she added, "Thank you for worrying over my safety. You may walk with me." If only he would not speak.

However, he started to talk as soon as he fell into step with her. "I wanted to explain why I didn't take up the gauntlet that your mother threw down at breakfast."

Jenny tried to recall the gauntlet to which he referred.

Ned shrugged. "If I was in a position to pay for your sisters' Seasons, then I would most happily do so. If only to please you," he added, looking sideways at her.

She tried to offer him a smile but feared it looked more like a sickly grimace.

Oblivious, he continued. "However, I cannot put myself in any type of financial peril simply because your father chose not to prepare properly for his daughters' futures."

Jenny was tired of thinking that same thing, and thus, she said nothing. Still, Ned should not speak ill of the dead. It was not his place, especially not to the dead man's daughter. Perhaps if she didn't respond, he would fade to silence.

No such fortune befell her.

"I suppose your mother could appeal to my parents, whom I believe are in a way to help out your sisters, but since the earl has already offered, and since that doesn't drain any of my future inheritance of which you might have an interest, I believe it is for the best if things stay as they are—despite any hint of oddity that the earl would take it upon himself to bestow such upon your family. Without recompense. Without asking for anything in return."

He paused, then glanced over at her, even though she had not slowed her pace. "His lordship didn't ask for anything in return, did he?"

Only half-listening, Jenny let Ned's words echo in her brain, until his question suddenly made itself clear to her.

She stopped in her tracks, annoyed at the intimation of impropriety.

Her cousin continued walking a few steps, then realized she was no longer beside him and turned back to her.

"The scoundrel!" he blurted out. "What is the price of his aid?"

"Ned, what on earth are you talking about? The earl has asked for nothing." She would not let Simon's reputation be sullied any more than her own.

"And whatever do you mean by my having an interest in your inheritance?"

"*Ah,* that caught your attention, did it, Miss Jenny?"

The smug look on his face actually caused a physical reaction in the pit of her stomach. It was not pleasant. How she wished she could take back her question.

"I believe I have been overly discreet in my regard for you. Perhaps too discreet if you do not yet know how I feel. Let me tell you this instant that I—"

"Look there," Jenny said loudly, simply to stop him from making a declaration of love. For if he did, then she would have to tell him there could never be anything between them, and that as far as she was concerned, he could spend his inheritance on cards and women. That would not go over well.

For one thing, he would no longer be able to play the part of the fond cousin and remain in their home.

Most likely, with his pride intolerably pricked, he would return to their cottage, pack up his things, and leave, taking Maisie with him. That would cause Eleanor great distress.

Eleanor's distress would become everyone's.

"What is it, Jenny?" Ned looked around this way and that.

"The hall," she said lamely, pointing at the Deveres' minor residence. Or rather, their *former* minor residence. "Did you know it has been sold out of the earl's holding, and no one knows to whom?"

His exasperated expression was replaced by one of interest.

"Really? I wonder why the earl had to sell it?"

She didn't bother telling him it had been done while the current earl was out of the country. It gave Ned something to chew on, like a dog with a bone. With any luck, he would forget about his near declaration.

"For your sisters' sakes," Ned added, as Jenny started walking again, "let's hope this is not an indication that the Devere family has fallen on hard times. Perhaps you should get that promise of patronage in writing, or better yet, have the earl transfer funds immediately to your London bank."

How uncouth! As if she would do either.

"Come." Suddenly, Ned grabbed her arm and turned toward Jonling Hall. "Let us knock and see if there is anyone at home. Even a servant can tell us who the new owner is."

She dug her heels in, but he continued to tug her in the direction of the long drive.

"Really, Ned, that's not how things are done. If you're truly interested, I'm sure you've got connections in London who can tell you."

"Perhaps," he allowed, "but we're here. Why not simply present ourselves as neighbors? Even more than that, you are the earl's bookkeeper."

The man had no sense. "You must never speak of that to anyone. Are you listening?"

He didn't seem to be heeding her at all.

"Ned!" She yanked her arm free, and at last he turned to her.

"Listen to me. I have gone to great pains in this community to maintain the disguise of Mr. Cavendish. Only you, Mr. Binkley, and the earl know otherwise."

He rolled his eyes as if dismissing her concerns.

"Please!" Oh, how she hated beseeching her cousin. "Only think how it might damage my family, not to mention hurt my sisters' prospects. While they are grateful for what I provide, they would be humiliated if anyone should discover that I work at a profession. As well they should." Then she added, "By familial association, that could damage Maisie's chances as well."

His eyebrows rose slightly. "Very well. But if there are occupants and they look at us askance, we can at least say that the earl is your family's patron."

Jenny let him drag her the rest of the way to the front door, a pretty arched arrangement with large potted plants on either side. Unlike the manor, there wasn't a massive flight of stone steps to ascend, thus she assumed the working rooms were at the back of the house instead of in the cellar. Still, the house had an air of shabby aristocracy, conveying both comfort and gracefulness.

"To show up unannounced and uninvited," she whispered. "We shouldn't do this."

"I am curious as to who lives here. I'm sure the Deveres would appreciate any information we discover." Ned raised his hand and rapped upon the large door with his knuckles. "I wish I had my cane," he muttered.

After a few moments, Jenny said, "No one is here. Isn't that obvious?"

"We shall see." He rapped again with more force.

Jenny had taken a few steps away from the door, retreating as she most desperately wanted to do, when it opened at last.

"What ya' wan'?" came the voice from the shadowy interior. A woman's voice with a strong Cockney accent.

"I say," Ned spoke up, "is your master or mistress at home?"

"No," the answer came quickly.

Ned was not to be got rid of so easily. "Perhaps a cup of tea for thirsty neighbors?"

Jenny rolled her eyes at her cousin's bold request.

"'Ere now, if you're a neighba', ain't ya' go' no tea at 'ome?"

Jenny almost laughed at these blunt words from behind the door.

"Why, of course, we have tea," Ned said, spluttering with indignation. "That is not the point of neighborliness."

"The 'all ain't receivin' no one. Strict orders."

"I demand to know who your master is," Ned said, giving over all pretense of simply passing by.

"Who's askin'?" asked the servant.

Jenny tried to stop Ned from responding, running back toward him to grab his arm. She didn't want her name associated with such ill-mannered prying.

Too late.

"I am Edward Darrow, and this is Miss Blackwood. The Earl of Lindsey is her benefactor. Show yourself, woman!"

Jenny felt her cheeks grow decidedly warm.

"The earl!" It sounded like the servant was muttering to someone else.

"Close it," Jenny thought she heard, this time from a man.

"Strict orders," the woman repeated and closed the door firmly, not even five inches from Ned's nose. They both heard the latch slide into place and the bolt turn.

"Well! I never." Ned's face went quite ruddy with annoyance.

Jenny dropped her hold on her cousin's arm, turned heel, and walked away.

Why? Why had he given her name? If asked in the future, she could pretend it was Eleanor who might not know any better than to try to barge into someone's residence. How humiliating!

This was far worse than having her erstwhile viscount send word through a footman that he would not be officially announcing their engagement after all. Jenny remembered a momentary annoyance and even feeling sorry for the extra burden upon her mother, and then she had thought of Lord Alder no more.

Today's dreadful scene, however, played and replayed itself in her head as she marched home, aware of Ned striding behind her.

He called to her a few times, and she steadfastly ignored him. What a buffoon! Moreover, what if Lord Lindsey somehow heard that she was snooping about? *And why was that even a concern?* She did not know. She knew only that Ned had acted insufferably, and with all her heart, she wished to be away from him.

Not slowing her pace, Jenny slammed the garden gate after going through it. She would have done the same with the front door, right in Ned's face and let him experience the effrontery twice in one day, except her mother was in the front hallway.

"Mr. Binkley was here while you were gone," Anne told her without preamble.

"What did he want?" Jenny realized her tone was inappropriately sharp when her mother took a step back.

"You don't sound well," Anne said. "Did you get too much air?"

Sometimes her mother held the oddest ideas.

"No, I don't think that's possible, Mummy. One cannot get too much air. I think one can get too much sun, but that was hardly the case today, as I had on my bonnet and I kept moving. Except when I was forced to stand still on a doorstep." *Against my will,* she almost added.

"Really? Where did you go?"

Jenny turned to Ned. "Why don't you fill my mother in since it was your idea?"

He had the grace to look a tad sheepish. "I caught up with Miss Jenny near Jonling Hall and thought it a good idea to inquire as to the new owner."

A myriad of expressions crossed Anne's face. No doubt she considered their expedition to be forward, if not downright rude. Yet perhaps also interesting.

"Before you ask," Jenny explained, "we did not learn the new owner's identity. Only that he has poor taste in servants but exceptional taste in gatekeepers."

Removing her hat and gloves, Jenny linked her arm through her mother's and walked toward the dining room, hoping Ned would not follow.

"Pray tell, what did Mr. Binkley want? Before you tell me, though, did he leave payment?"

An excited gleam glinted in Anne's eyes. "He did leave an envelope addressed to you, which he said was your compensation. I left it on your bed."

Thank goodness! Her presence at Belton might have caused some consternation on the part of the butler and his master. However, she'd done them a good service. That, they couldn't deny.

"The other matter, though," her mother added, glancing behind at Ned, who followed them like a determined hound. "Mr. Binkley said the earl has requested your company this afternoon, and he also said he very much wished to speak with you himself."

"More ledgers?" Jenny asked.

Anne shook her head. "*Mm,* no, he didn't say as such. He wants you to let the staff know when you've arrived so he can have a word with you."

Ned made a disapproving noise, and Jenny rolled her eyes. If her cousin said one thing about impropriety, she might be forced to perpetrate violence upon him.

"Did Mr. Binkley specify a time?"

"Any time this afternoon," her mother said, "and mind you, he was quite pleasant about *asking.*"

Ned cleared his throat. "Shall I escort you?"

How dare Ned even ask such a question!

"I think not," she snapped, then saw the expression of disbelief upon her mother's face.

Looking at Ned who seemed quite crestfallen, Jenny's heart softened. She supposed he had not meant to cause a scene at the hall. Moreover, she could not fault the man for misplacing his affections.

"Thank you, Cousin, but that won't be necessary. The earl is a private man. I'm sure if he had wanted me to bring someone else, he would have said as much."

Ned nodded and moved past her to the parlor. Her family's parlor! Yet she would turn her thoughts from all things irksome.

She'd been summoned to the manor. Asking or not, it seemed like a royal command. It wasn't as if she could claim she was away.

Would she go? *Of course!* Her feelings had been hurt by eavesdropping, but she wasn't a child. Nevertheless, it struck her as strange that Lord Lindsey would want her to return after what she'd overheard.

Moreover, why did the butler wish to speak with her?

A terrible dread filled her. Perhaps after the men's discourse the night before, pondering whatever damage she could do to the earl by her presence—with the very distinct possibility of wagging tongues shredding her reputation—what if Lord Lindsey decided helping her sisters was too intimate a gesture, as Ned had suggested?

What if, as Maggie had feared at breakfast, *the earl had changed his mind or the admiral had changed it for him, and it had fallen to Mr. Binkley to tell her?*

Certainly, that made sense. If someone truly could think his lordship should offer for her hand simply because she'd spent time alone at the manor, what might people think if they found out the earl had paid for her sisters to go to London?

Why, that would practically brand her as Simon Devere's mistress!

CHAPTER TEN

As if she had been invited to sup with the earl, Jenny dressed in her best day gown. After all, she was not going there today to work in the library as a bookkeeper. She decided to look like a visitor and not a tradeswoman.

"Ooh," Eleanor cooed when she entered the dining room where her family always sat since Ned had taken up residence in their parlor.

Maisie looked up from her seat next to Eleanor and smiled. "You look as if you're going courting."

Courting? Should she change into something more demure? Perhaps she looked *too* fetching, as if she had designs on Lord Lindsey. Or as if she enjoyed his long appraisals of her person.

That was too outrageous to consider even for a moment!

At the sideboard, she lifted the lid on each platter to see what Cook had laid out for the midday meal.

Ned came in a moment later, and Jenny could feel the disapproval coming off of him in waves. Yet uncharacteristically, he said nothing, merely helping himself to coffee and sitting down.

"Brother, aren't you going to have some mutton pie?" Maisie asked, buttering a piece of bread.

Ned ignored her, keeping his eyes trained on Jenny, who felt more ill at ease the longer she stood there. Quickly, she placed a piece of pie on her plate before ladling it with gravy and sitting down. As she reached for bread, Ned did the same.

"After you," he said, pulling his hand back.

Jenny offered him a tight smile, which he did not return, and delicately grasped the last piece from the plate.

"Eleanor, go tell Cook that we'll need more bread."

"Don't trouble yourself on my account," Ned said.

How odd! As if asking Cook for more bread was troubling. Yes, it would be lovely if they had a bell system in the cottage, but her father had never seen the need to have one installed. With the home's rather compact size, calling for service was not a problem if you had a good set of lungs.

"Maggie and my mother will be in soon, and I'm sure they'll want some."

He nodded and sipped his coffee, and then he seemed to come to some decision. Jenny saw it the moment it happened as his expression was an open one.

"When are you leaving?" Ned asked her.

"Soon after I've finished eating. Why?"

"I should like a private word with you before you go."

She had put her cousin off since the day he'd arrived, yet it seemed he was determined to make his declaration. Jenny was equally determined not to let him. She needed a distraction. Eleanor and Maisie were discussing ribbons, the merits of satin versus silk skirts, and other such nonsense. They were no help at all.

Cook entered at that moment, giving Jenny time to think.

"More bread, please."

The woman nodded and turned to leave. Stalling, Jenny stopped her with a question, "How is George?"

Cook looked perplexed. "He's fine, miss. Thank you for asking."

"And Thunder. Has George made any progress in that regard? With the horse, I mean?"

Cook shrugged. "I don't know, miss. Do you want me to fetch him?"

Eleanor giggled, no doubt at the idea of their stable boy coming into the dining room during their meal.

Jenny shook her head. "No, that's fine. I'll check with him later." The woman must think her mad.

At that instant, her mother and Maggie entered, each getting a plate of food before seating themselves.

"My, don't you look lovely," Anne said. "As if you were at dinner during the Season."

Maggie fixed her with a knowing smirk, and Jenny wished she had stayed in her room until it was time to leave.

"I've ordered more bread," was her only comment, before she ate her pie in silence.

Seeing her mother raise a questioning eyebrow, Jenny lowered her gaze and kept it firmly on her plate. Even with her mother opening *The London Times* that the housemaid had set by her place setting, and Maggie opening the *Journal*, Jenny was quite aware that Ned's eyes were still upon her, waiting for a response.

Sipping her coffee to wash down the last of the crust, Jenny finally returned his gaze. She wanted to tell him how rude he was to stare. Instead, she gave him the second polite smile of the morning.

"Perhaps when I return, Cousin, for I have no desire to keep the earl waiting, not when he is, as you said, our benefactor."

Appearing resigned, Ned nodded. "As you wish. I'll be here upon your return."

When Jenny arrived at Belton, feeling strange in the absence of her abacus and satchel, she eschewed the servant's entrance and went to the imposing front door. Mr. Binkley answered the bell, ushering her in.

"Will you step into the drawing room for a moment, Miss Blackwood?"

Wordlessly, she followed him into a cavernous chamber, the great room she remembered from her childhood. A *drawing room*, he called it. More like a ballroom! Certainly, one could fit a hundred guests in there easily.

Glancing toward one end, she recalled precisely where the massive Christmas tree stood each year. In fact, she could picture Simon nearby, greeting people with boyish humor and a warm smile.

Except for two sofas by the colossal marble fireplace and two wingchairs beside her, the room was blatantly empty, looking nothing like her memories of candles and musicians, holiday decorations and treats. Clearly, it had not been used in a long time.

"I understand you discussed Lady Devere with his lordship."

Jenny blinked. She had not expected such a question, instead thinking she would hear immediately something about the withdrawal of the earl's offer to pay for Maggie's gowns and event tickets.

"Yes." *Should she apologize? To the butler?* "I didn't realize that he was unaware of his cousin's family living here. Until I told him."

"Yes, just so. There are a number of things that his lordship has not been told regarding changes that have occurred while he was away. The earl has been in an introspective state of near unresponsiveness since his return. There was no way you could know that, of course."

She stared hard at the admiral. It was not regular for a servant, indeed, an entire staff, to keep secrets from the master. Yet, she could understand how it might have been difficult to impart anything of great importance to a man sitting in the dark.

"I see."

Mr. Binkley nodded. "Good."

She waited. What did the man wish to impart to her?

"His lordship understood clearly when I told him about the sale of Jonling Hall," she added into the awkward pause. She wondered if the butler had thought the earl was unsound. "Do you know that he wants me to tell him about the ledgers and the accounts?"

"Yes, I'm aware. I think it extremely important that he knows everything, and I'm glad you will be explaining it to him."

What, then, was the hesitancy in the man's voice?

"Is there something amiss, Mr. Binkley?" Would he now mention her sisters' fate?

Very slowly and carefully, the butler spoke. "Lord Lindsey believes himself to be as yet Lord *Devere*."

Jenny frowned, mulling over the words for a moment. Then their import struck her.

"Dear God!" she muttered before sitting down heavily in the closest brocade-covered, wingback chair. "He doesn't know he is the current earl?"

Mr. Binkley, hands clasped behind his back, shook his head.

"You mean he doesn't know his father passed away."

"Correct."

"And you wish me to be discreet and not mention it to him?" After all, there was no need for it to come up. They'd already had numerous conversations without any mention of his father at all.

"In that, you would be precisely *not* correct."

She frowned, not liking his turn of phrase, and this was the second time the butler had corrected her in the same manner.

"His lordship reacts well to you. When Lord Lindsey returned from his captivity, he spoke little and gave very few orders. However, he was adamant that none of his friends or acquaintances be allowed into the manor. What's more, he instructed me and the entire staff to leave him alone. I have overstepped my bounds and disobeyed his orders as much as possible, but you, Miss Blackwood, you have made him speak more than I have been able to in all these weeks. What's more, he has actually requested your presence."

Jenny swallowed. "I believe he is not helping himself with the isolation nor especially with the darkness. Don't you agree?"

The butler seemed to move his weight from one foot to the other. "It is not for me to counteract the earl, but I do think a convalescence that included daily walks in the garden, weather permitting, and the company of others would do him good. Again, it is not for me to say."

"Then who? He has no family left here."

"You," Mr. Binkley said. "I believe you can get him to come out of his room. And you must also explain that his father has passed away and that he is now the Earl of Lindsey."

"I must?" She stood, feeling agitated. "There is no *must* about it. We should send for his uncle. Surely James Devere should be the one to explain the circumstances to his nephew."

Mr. Binkley's face twisted into a sour expression. "I sent word to Lord Devere directly upon my master's return. I sent word again when I understood the extent of Lord Lindsey's issues. Still, there has been no word from his uncle."

Jenny realized she was chewing on her lower lip. Her fingers were fiddling with the cloth of her skirts, and she sorely wished she had her abacus in her hands so she could slide the smooth beads back and forth.

Mr. Binkley said nothing more, but fixed her with a stare worthy of Maggie's nickname for him. Only an admiral who knew how to manipulate his troops could have such a half-pleading, half-demanding look. She'd never experienced anything quite like it!

"I will endeavor to bring him outside," she conceded.

The butler still didn't move.

"I will find the right way to tell him of his father's passing," she added, feeling resentful at being pressured to handle this duty that really had nothing to do with her. She was used to doing whatever was necessary for her own family, but how on God's green earth had she got herself mired in this mess?

Mr. Binkley's face remained passive, but his eyes crinkled in the corners and he nodded before bowing quite low, which she took to be an expression of his gratitude.

"The earl is waiting," he said, turning away as if she had been dawdling. Then he strode from the room, clearly expecting her to follow.

Remaining silent as he led her upstairs to the earl's chamber, she wished she had more time to gather her thoughts or even plan for how she would tell him.

Mr. Binkley knocked on the chamber door, then, at his master's response, he turned the brass knob, pushed the door open, and gestured for her to enter.

After she stepped across the threshold, instead of leaving the door open as propriety dictated, the butler pulled it shut behind her.

That small gesture caused her heart to pound. Simon Devere was waiting for her, standing by the window. When he turned at her entrance and saw the closed door, his eyebrows seemed to lift.

No doubt he believed she'd done it. She dropped her gaze to the beautiful rug. How should she start?

Coughing slightly as she realized her throat had closed up, Jenny wondered if she could ask for water and use the earl's glass. Was there another glass in the room? There ought to be. What kind of chamber held only one glass? Obviously, the earl had not been entertaining, but still . . .

Calm yourself, she ordered, wrenching her hands apart to stop from ringing them, then locked them behind her back in the style of the admiral.

"You wished to see me?" she asked at last.

"Yes." Simon hesitated, glancing back toward the window, his gaze fixed on the world beyond. "I want to walk with you."

"You wish to walk with me?" Jenny repeated. "You summoned me here to walk with you?"

Me, the last woman on earth whom you would marry? How she wished she was brave enough to add those words!

"Summoned you?" He sounded puzzled. "I didn't order you to come as if you had no choice to visit with me."

She smiled. "True enough, my lord. Still, it is not every day that one receives an invitation from the lord of the manor."

Nodding, he still looked uncertain. An air of trepidation surrounded him.

"Will you walk with me? Outside," he added.

Oh, so this was more than a stroll through his chambers. And he wished to go outside.

Fulfilling the first of the butler's requests was going to be easy if the earl was willing. Yet, it didn't sit right that he'd asked her back for this reason, not when she still felt the sting of his overheard words.

"Why?" she asked.

He tilted his head, considering.

"Because I fear that I am hampering my recovery by recreating the environment of my captivity. That is, no sun, stagnant air, no long walks."

"You mistake me, my lord. I understood what you meant about going outside—and I wholeheartedly agree you should. I meant, why me in particular? Why don't you walk with your valet? Or with Mr. Binkley?"

"I do not wish to walk with my valet or my butler." His expression softened. "I want to walk with a friend."

A friend. She hadn't expected that. All at once, her heart contracted, thinking how she had her sisters and her mother if she needed companionship or comfort, whilst his lordship had no one.

At her silence, the earl frowned. "I do have friends, Jenny. I was not always this way." He spread his hands indicating his situation in the room. "However, none of them live close by. They are in London or abroad. I've had letters," he admitted, "from those who wish to visit with me since my return. I have ignored them all."

"Perhaps it would do you good to write to them, even to share your experiences with those closest to you. And then, if you are up to it, let them visit."

She hoped she had not overstepped with her blunt advice. "I do not think isolation is good for you. In fact, I'm positive it is not."

Against all expectations, he smiled, ever so slightly. "That is why I wish to walk with you. Binkley would have remained silent on the topic of letters and friends, or said that I was doing the right thing, whatever it is that I am doing. Or not doing, for that matter, because he is a servant."

"You wish to walk with me because I don't instantly defer to you or agree with you. Is that right?"

"Exactly," he said. "For that is how friends behave."

Apparently, even though he could never have a friendship with his servant, he could disparage her in an intimate discussion with Mr. Binkley. However, to help the earl, indeed to help the entire estate, she would push that petty thought out of her mind.

"Very well." Jenny was glad she wore sturdy ankle boots and not her fancy kidskin slippers. "Are you ready?"

Simon looked startled. "What? Now?"

"No time like the present."

"Would you care for tea first? Or sherry?"

She didn't answer immediately. Was the earl going to need her to literally push him out of doors?

126

"My lord, I will wait for you in the front hall. I will wait five minutes by that splendid chiming clock I observed next to the main staircase." She walked to his door before glancing back at him.

Still, he hadn't moved.

"If you are not there after the minute hand has moved five times, then I shall depart."

He blinked, then nodded.

"Do you have a valet?" Jenny asked him belatedly, for she'd not seen one, although she supposed that was not unusual. Many such grand houses had hidden passages for the servants so they could serve almost invisibly.

Again, he nodded.

Jenny closed the door behind her and went directly to the front hall where her lightweight wrap and her reticule lay on the small tufted divan precisely as she'd left them. Slowly, while eyeing the pendulum of the grandfather clock, she donned her outerwear. Then she waited.

Should she have stayed with him and urged him onward? Simply because the earl wanted to go out, that didn't mean he could. Maybe . . .

His footsteps on the landing captured her attention. He still wore what he was wearing when she had arrived, but he had added a coat, and boots now covered his stocking-clad feet. She had never seen him in boots or shoes for that matter. In fact, seeing him on his staircase, fully dressed and staring at her warily, he seemed far more imposing. He looked every bit the earl of the manor that he truly was.

And for some reason, he wanted to walk with her.

She swallowed.

"I'm glad you made it on time."

"You have a sharp tongue."

"No, that is my sister, Maggie. I have a sharp brain."

"I think you have both," he said, taking her arm just as Mr. Binkley appeared as if by magic and opened the front door for them.

She noted the admiral's hopeful yet wary expression. It mirrored what she felt inside.

They got as far as the edge of the top step when the earl halted. Then he turned heel, taking her with him.

The door that had already closed behind them reopened. Mr. Binkley now wore a resigned, defeated look.

"My lord?" Jenny asked.

"This is all wrong," the earl muttered.

"I don't understand your meaning. You do see that this is your home and you're in Sheffield, England, don't you?"

He looked down at her, frowning at her question.

"Yes, of course. I am not in a delusional state at present, I assure you. I simply don't want to walk out the front. The last time I went down those stairs, I got into a carriage and didn't come back for three years."

He kept on walking, still holding her arm, striding directly through the foyer, taking a quick right down the first hallway until they reached her usual side door and kept going. They finally arrived at the very back of the house.

To her utter amazement, Mr. Binkley was there to open the door for his master. She noted he was breathing hard. He must have run like the hounds of hell were at his back, down a different route, in order to appear there exactly as they reached the door.

Bravo, she cheered him silently for his devotion to duty.

The earl appeared not to notice but only because he was focused on this difficult adventure. His grip on her arm had tightened and, glancing at his profile, she could see a muscle jumping in his jaw.

They took a few steps onto the spacious veranda. He halted and breathed deeply, then they took a few more steps.

"Shall we stop here?" he asked, sounding wary.

There was a table with a large umbrella set up.

"Let us keep walking," Jenny suggested. "Don't you think?"

He nodded. "That is the point, I suppose."

"Yes."

They lapsed into silence again as they descended a wide granite staircase to a large brick patio. This was surrounded by arbors, each one arched over a different path leading to a different garden enclosed by yew hedges.

"It's lovely," she told him, hoping to make him really see the place that he now inhabited.

"I know," he said. "I spent many, many hours out here as a boy, pretending it was a different world from Sheffield. That one on the right, I imagined led to Europe, and that one straight ahead led to the wilds of the African continent."

"And this one?" she asked, as they headed under a clematis-covered arbor and down a path on the left of the patio.

"This one went to an entirely magical world of sword fights and buccaneers, and nothing real at all. Sprites, fairies, witches."

"Fairies," she repeated.

He shrugged sheepishly. "I suppose I have always had a vivid imagination. It doesn't serve me well now, but as a boy, it kept me amused."

"I would have spent my childhood counting the number of bricks on these paths and hoping they were all equal, one to the other."

He laughed, yet not like the hysterical laughter that had turned into despair. This time, the sound was rich and full of actual joy. Merely a momentary laugh, quite normal, and her heart that had jumped with unease calmed.

"Practical Jenny, even as a child?" he asked.

"I suppose. Eleanor, my youngest sister, would absolutely adore this." Indeed, it was a fanciful garden with lush, large fragrant blush roses, clumps of sweet William, and towering foxglove.

"She sketches and finds much pleasure in sitting outdoors in nature, drawing what she sees."

"Invite her to come with you next time. The more exotic plants are in my pretend Africa. I'm sure she would see some there she has never before seen."

"I will. Thank you." That they were planning a *next time* seemed a tad premature when Jenny still had the unpleasant duty of telling him about his father's death.

They had reached a central area with a small fish pond, stone benches, and a bird bath. With comfortable like-mindedness, they headed to a bench and sat.

"I should have told Binkley where I was taking you. If I'd known myself, that is. Then, no doubt, he would already be here with refreshments."

Picturing him rushing between the tall plants and crawling under the hedges to beat them to the spot made her laugh.

"That's a lovely sound," the earl said, and her laughter died in her throat. At the same time, heat bloomed in her cheeks.

If they were courting, their current situation would be utterly beyond the pale, to have walked deep into the secluded garden and to be sitting alone together. She could only guess what the members of high society would have to say. What would her mother say, for that matter?

"One should install a very long pull cord in the center of each garden," Jenny suggested. "Then you could summon a servant whenever you wished. I'm surprised no one has thought of that."

Simon Devere's eyebrows rose. "That's a rather unusual and brilliant idea, Miss Blackwood. However, it does rather remove the feeling of remoteness and solitude that one often seeks deep in a country garden, not to mention the tranquility being disturbed by servants scurrying hither and yon with refreshments."

"Only think of the added work for the staff, too," she pointed out.

"They might like getting outside more," he considered. "I will look into your proposal. Perhaps long ropes could be laid out or strung from the trees."

She was sure her face expressed her shock.

"I was only speaking in jest, my lord."

The earl grinned. "As was I."

Her breath caught. Who could believe the man sitting in the dark a week ago could now be making jokes? "You fooled me."

He nodded slightly. "I very much like spending time with you."

Before she could say anything, he added, "I cannot quite believe I am sitting out here in this garden. And with you."

Picking up her gloved hand from where it rested on her lap, his fingers touched her lap briefly, brushing across her inner thigh. She felt a tremor of shock rush through her. The earl didn't seem to notice.

"This is precisely one of the places I used to imagine while I was captive. In precise detail, with my eyes shut." He closed his eyes while she looked up into his face, feeling off balance by his mercurial change of topic and interest.

Moreover, she was dealing with the strange sensation of a man holding her hand tightly in his. The viscount had certainly never done more than tuck her forearm under his and promenade around the veranda of whatever ballroom they were attending. Nothing before in her limited experience had ever felt as intimate as the earl's touch.

"I would reconstruct this place in my mind. Exactly. The feel of this cold stone bench seeping into my trousers no matter how hot the day. The scent of roses and how the garden's fragrance changes with the seasons. The appearance of the honeysuckle to our right and the pear tree arching overhead."

He was right in each instance.

"Go on, close your eyes and smell the various flora, and see if you can picture the plants in your mind."

She hesitated, but his eyes were still closed, so she did as he asked. As soon as her sight was shut off, she became overly aware of their joined hands. His thumb caressed her gloved palm, sending tingling sensations up her arm. Squirming a little, she stilled when he squeezed her hand encouragingly.

"Are your eyes closed?" he asked.

"Yes."

"Can you smell everything more strongly now?"

"Yes."

"When I was in the cell, I swear I could smell the flowers if I tried hard enough. And I did try. Every day. I hoped if I recalled each detail of my home, that eventually, I'd be able to stand up from the imaginary bench and not only walk around the garden but make it all the way into the house."

"That's an understandable hope," she said, her heart aching for the idea of him in confinement.

"If I'd known you, Genevieve, I would have envisioned sitting with you, exactly as we are now."

Hearing the earl say her name with her eyes closed, with her hand clasped in his, caused another tremor through her. When he said her name, it didn't sound silly, it sounded romantic, even sensual.

Snapping open her eyes, she leaned away from him. *What was she doing?* Even someone as occasionally eccentric as herself, who often flouted the conventional boundaries, knew this was going too far. She yanked her hand from his grasp, expecting him to open his eyes, but he didn't.

The earl gasped, squeezed his eyes shut more tightly, and then, with an anguished howl, he covered his face with his hands.

Dear God, what was wrong? Jumping up, Jenny stood before him, her knees nearly touching his.

"My lord?"

"No, no, no," he groaned. "You are not real. None of this is real."

"Please," she begged, crouching down. "Open your eyes. It is all real. I am here."

He moaned loudly. "I don't want to go back." He lifted his hands from his face, his eyes still closed.

"Demon, are you still here? Were you ever here?" His breathing was erratic and he was shaking his head.

Realizing he had slipped back into his former hysteria only after she'd broken their contact, Jenny quickly grabbed hold of his hands with both of her own.

He stilled and almost instantly his breathing became more regular.

"I am afraid," he whispered, and her heart melted.

"Simon," she said his Christian name for the first time out loud. "I *am* real." She squeezed his large hands. "You *are* home. I promise you. Please open your eyes."

The earl said nothing more, but became visibly calmer. His face relaxed, and finally, answering her silent prayer, he opened his eyes.

Such beautiful, yet troubled blue eyes, she thought.

Looking directly at her, sadness emanated from him like the rich fragrances from the flowers he had vividly recalled while in captivity.

All at once, the earl yanked her forward, turning her so she landed firmly on his lap. He released her hands only to bury his own in her hair, tangling his fingers on either side of her head and destroying the carefully styled ringlets.

"You are real!" He lowered his head and claimed her lips.

Jenny tried to protest, but her words were muffled against his mouth. Then, when he moved against her, slanting his mouth to fit more perfectly with her own, she decided there was nothing to complain about.

His kiss was divine. Its effect sizzled through her from her head to her toes that were now curling inside her boots while he continued his sensual assault. What's more, the heat from his thighs penetrated her day gown, warming the areas that had been chilled by the unyielding marble bench.

"You taste like sunshine," Simon murmured against her mouth before claiming it again.

It was her turn to keep her eyes firmly closed, for Jenny found she could not lift her lids while the earl practiced his skilled kissing upon her.

When he lowered his hands from cradling her head to encircle her waist and hold her firmly, she found it only natural to slip her arms up the front of his coat and clasp her hands behind his neck, feeling the silkiness of his dark hair. Their kiss continued, and she could not think of any reason why it should ever end.

And then she heard the sound of children's laughter, and it was coming closer.

CHAPTER ELEVEN

Jenny's bemused brain didn't seem to know what to tell her body. It was Simon who lifted her from his lap to her former place on the bench before he jumped up and moved away from her. In seconds, Alice and Peter appeared.

It was the first time Jenny had seen his lordship in the presence of the children. She hoped he didn't scare them. For her part, she resisted the impulse to lift a hand to her hair and draw attention to her disheveled appearance.

Maude Devere's offspring came to a crashing halt when they entered the circular center of the garden and saw it already occupied.

"Oh," squealed Alice.

Peter said nothing but stared from Jenny, whom he recognized, to the earl, who momentarily kept his back to all three of them.

"This flower is the one I meant, Miss Blackwood," Simon said loudly, plucking a pink hollyhock in full bloom before turning to her, appearing startled by the children's appearance.

Not a bad actor, she thought. Although he would have to be quite hard of hearing to be sincerely surprised at seeing them when he turned around.

His pretense gave way to genuine wonder. She could see it in his face. He looked, in fact, fascinated by them.

"How you've grown! Why, you were only up to here," he said to Peter, holding his hand at waist level. "And you," he said, looking at Alice, "still had leading strings."

"Did I?" she asked. "Who are you?"

"I am Simon Devere."

"I'm Peter Devere," the little boy said before giving a grown-up bow.

"That's not necessary. We're family," Simon insisted. "Your father . . ." He looked uncertainly at Jenny, and she nodded encouragingly. "Your father was my cousin and great friend."

"I don't remember you or him," Alice stated and went over to sit with Jenny.

Peter, however, stood staring at the earl. "Were you with our father when he died?"

"I was."

Jenny could see a play of emotions cross the earl's face. Doubtless, memories were assaulting him unwillingly. Would merely thinking of Tobias Devere cause the earl to have another episode? She sent up a silent prayer for his sake that he didn't.

Peter still stared at this unexpected man in the garden. Simon walked closer to the boy and stared down into his face.

"You are the very spit and image of your father."

At that, the boy fairly beamed.

"He spoke about you often and with great pride," Simon added.

"What about me?" Alice asked from where she leaned against Jenny's side.

The earl turned to her. "You were his little angel. I'm sorry you don't remember your father, but he thought of both of you all the time."

Jenny's heart ached for them. And then she remembered all at once that she had not yet told Lord Lindsey about his own father. Thankfully, the children had not said anything untoward regarding the old earl.

"Isn't my sister here today?" she asked the children, wishing to change the topic of fathers.

"Master Cheeseface just left," Alice said.

Jenny heard the earl softly repeat "Cheeseface?"

Peter spoke up. "Miss Margaret was here this morning."

"Oh, yes," Jenny should have remembered that, but she had lost all track of time being with Simon. Talking with him, touching him, being kissed by him! "Still, you shouldn't call the man such a thing, Miss Alice."

The little girl only giggled.

"What do you call my sister when she is not within hearing?"

Alice smiled, "Miss Pretty."

Jenny glanced at Simon, wondering what he thought of that. After all, he had mere minutes earlier been kissing her, and she was the plainest of the Blackwoods. How much more suited to such a handsome, powerful man was Maggie? Yet, the idea of her sister forming an association with Lord Lindsey caused her distinct uneasiness. More than that.

She stood, grasping Alice's hand as she did.

"I suppose we ought to head back to the house," Jenny said. "I should take my leave." She could hardly linger in the garden until the children went in and then pounce on him with news of his father's death. Perhaps she could visit again on the pretense of telling him about his accounts.

Unable to offer Jenny his arm whilst she held Alice's hand, Simon could only draw close on her other side and ask, "May I show you the rest of the gardens another day?"

"Yes. I would like that. To see Africa and Europe. And I will fill you in on everything I learned from the estate ledgers."

She offered him a smile. Truthfully, she would like him to kiss her again, but that was definitely asking for trouble. Besides, it had occurred not through a genuine passion between them but due to his mental state. The poor man had only needed reassurance that he was truly in this world and not another.

With Peter and the earl falling into step behind them, Jenny and Alice led the way back along the path. They had nearly reached the veranda when she saw Ned appear from around the corner of the house. He was half walking, half trotting toward them.

"Jenny," he called. "I've been looking for you."

She felt her cheeks grow warm at his use of her given name, a man that the children and the earl did not know. So forward of her cousin. So embarrassing! Yet, by his tone, something was amiss.

"What has happened?"

Ned paused to bow to the earl, then he looked directly at her. "It's Thunder. That wretched animal. He got spooked and practically killed George—"

Little Alice gasped, and Jenny dropped the girl's hand, stepping forward as the earl did the same.

"Who is this George?" Simon demanded

She glanced at him. "Our stable boy."

Realizing she had yet to introduce the earl to her cousin, she began, but before she could say anything more, Ned added, "Your mother wants you to come home at once. I've brought my carriage to collect you."

"Has the doctor been sent for?"

"Henry was dispatched there directly."

"Our manservant," she told Simon before he asked. Then to Ned, she said, "I need only collect my reticule from the front foyer on our way out."

"If there is anything I can do," Simon offered.

"That is kind of you, my lord. I'm sure we can handle it."

Ned reached for her arm, and she let him take it.

"Also, the damned horse has gone missing," he added.

Poor Thunder. If he had truly injured George and then run off, what would become of him? And Cook must be in a state of panic as any mother would over her son.

"Come, Ned, let us hurry." With a nod over her shoulder toward Simon and the children, Jenny rushed away, directing him toward the back entrance rather than going around the entire house.

As soon as her cousin's driver helped her into the brougham and secured the door behind Ned who climbed in after, he urged the horses into a fast trot. To Jenny's dismay, her cousin remained close by her side, too close with his boney thigh and shoulder touching her own.

Sighing inwardly, she didn't reprimand him, too grateful that between Ned and Henry, the situation that otherwise would have fallen squarely on her shoulders was already well in hand.

"When the butler said you were out in the gardens with the earl, I must confess, I was worried," Ned said, drawing her from her private thoughts. "I was greatly relieved to see that you were escorted by two children. Unsuitable as chaperones but effective, no doubt."

Effective, indeed! As if without the children, she and Simon could not be trusted. As if alone they might suddenly grab hold of each other simply because they were a man and a woman.

Jenny nearly snapped at Ned when she recalled precisely how easily she and the earl had gone from chatting like friends to kissing like lovers. Instantly, the flame of embarrassment leaped into her cheeks. Leaning away from Ned, she turned her face toward the carriage window.

"Honestly, Ned, I fail to see how my whereabouts or my companions are your concern."

"That is only because we have not yet had our conversation that I requested this morning. I believe the happy conclusion of which will very much make your activities my concern."

Jenny clucked her tongue. Thankfully, they were nearly home.

"This is hardly the time what with young George injured and my horse missing. Hardly the time," she repeated, hoping he would take the hint and realize there would never be a good time. "I do thank you for fetching me."

Ned plunged ahead. "I will help even more when our households are joined."

She could see her sweet house coming into view but jumping out of the moving carriage was certainly not the best course of action.

"Our households are already joined, in a way," she told him, still looking out the window. "After all, we're second cousins."

"Only by marriage," he reminded her. "If circumstances go as hoped, you can stop being your mother's helpmate, always at her beck and call."

"I like helping my mother," Jenny insisted. And her current state was far more desirable than being at Ned's beck and call.

Nearly there. She gripped her fingers on the small brass door handle.

"Your mother should remarry. It is the natural course of things. A woman marrying a man. Don't you agree?"

Jenny didn't agree. In fact, she thought him downright rude. "In my mother's case, I think it too soon after my father's passing."

"And in your case?" Ned persisted. "Guinevere, will you—"

She nearly laughed at finding out Ned didn't know her real name. Except this was no laughing matter.

The carriage had stopped but was still rocking when she turned the handle and thrust the door open before jumping down to the ground, shocking Ned's footman who was still climbing sedately off the dickey.

"I must check on George. Thank you again." With that, Jenny dashed inside, leaving Ned still in his carriage.

THANKFULLY, GEORGE HAD, AT most, a cracked rib where he'd been kicked by the horse's hind leg. Bruised and resting, George was effusively apologetic.

Jenny tried not to think of the physician's cost. It had been a necessary expense. She let the boy tell his story.

"One moment, Thunder was facing me, looking calm as you please, and the next, he must've heard a sound. He swiveled where he stood and kicked me."

"You're lucky it wasn't in the face," Cook said. She sat on the edge of the bed beside her son. "You could've lost an eye, my poor Georgie."

"I'm fine, Mum. I'll be right as rain soon. You heard the doctor."

"He'll be fine," Jenny said to no one in particular because the words sounded reassuring. "But we must find Thunder before he does himself any more injury."

Turning to her mother who stared back at her expectantly, Jenny realized that it would fall upon her to do exactly that, find the blasted horse. Henry didn't ride, and George was not fit to do anything but rest and heal. Then there was Ned who had not even offered to go, loudly complaining that it was a fool's errand and that the cursed horse had probably fallen into a ditch.

"And good riddance!" he'd added, making himself scarce.

She couldn't find it in her heart to be annoyed. As it turned out, he was terrified of horses, exactly as Maisie had proclaimed days earlier, due to having been thrown when he was a boy. After all, Jenny didn't like spiders yet she had no such excuse.

After donning a well-worn riding habit, Jenny saddled Lucy, putting a coiled rope and bridle in one saddlebag and a bunch of carrots in the other. Certain that her stable boy was in good hands, she set out alone to wander the surrounding countryside looking for Thunder

Maggie, Eleanor, and Maisie discussed accompanying her, but she told them to stay put. The former was too feminine, in Jenny's estimation, and unless she needed someone to flirt with Thunder or speak French to him, Maggie was useless. As for the latter, younger girls, they were too loud, always talking and laughing. They would scare Thunder before she could get within fifty yards.

Luckily, George had seen the direction in which their horse had run, and she and Lucy dutifully followed. It wasn't terribly difficult to pick up the animal's trail. What with his large size and cantankerous disposition, he'd broken shrubbery and crushed many plants in his path. Still, it took her long enough to find the beast that Jenny was prickling with sweat and annoyed when she finally spotted Thunder.

Relief at seeing her horse, and seeing him upright and apparently unharmed, quickly gave way to fear when she realized his predicament. Thunder had crossed a narrow stream, probably running blindly, and then come upon a rocky outcropping and a low hanging tree preventing farther passage forward. Unfortunately, the horse was clearly unwilling to re-cross the stream now that it had time to think about it.

There seemed no point in forcing docile Lucy to traverse the stream merely to join the irritable and unpredictable Thunder on a tiny patch of grass.

Dismounting, Jenny tethered Lucy to a low-hanging elm. Then she retrieved a carrot from the saddlebag and held it toward Thunder. The horse actually tilted its head, staring at her and at the offering as if she were asking a great deal of him for very little.

Whistling and calling to him for a few minutes, she finally declared defeat in keeping her feet dry. She would have to face down her own fear of traversing the stream and of staring down a horse that towered over her. Feeling inadequate to the task and beaten at the start, she knew that the one person whom she wanted to ask for help was in no position to provide it.

Thus, Jenny found herself at the edge of the stream, facing an agitated horse. Holding the carrot in front of her like a talisman of safety, Jenny lifted her skirts with her other hand and stepped into the stream. Water rushed into her riding boots.

"Thunder!" she exclaimed rather than unleash the unladylike oaths that she wished to utter. It was terribly uncomfortable, and she moved swiftly to the other side.

At her approach, the horse took a step back, coming up against a prickly branch that caused it to drum its hooves into the moist earth and toss its head.

Hesitating and feeling foolish standing there with a carrot in her hand, still she reached out to the animal. Obviously, she should have grabbed the bridle and rope instead but had thought only of soothing Thunder with a treat.

As she stepped closer, sure enough, the horse reared. From her place upon the sloping bank, Jenny discovered Thunder looked larger. Terrifyingly so. She had made a miscalculation, she feared. Perhaps a costly one.

Hastily backing into the water, she considered her position. Were they at an impasse?

"Jenny!" Impossibly, the unmistakable voice of Simon Devere sounded. In no way, however, could she imagine how the Earl of Lindsey was there.

"Get out of that stream," he commanded, "and away from that horse."

If Ned had ridden up and said such a thing, she would have felt a flash of temper at being ordered about like a child, and then, most likely, she would have done the opposite to whatever he'd said. However, with Simon, she obediently obeyed.

In a moment, she was back on his side of the stream, watching Lord Lindsey dismount from a lovely dappled gray gelding.

SIMON LOOKED THE YOUNG woman up and down. Jenny appeared unhurt, while obviously wet and in some peril. If she'd gotten closer to that terrified animal, she could have been struck. Right on her lovely head.

"I cannot believe you came out here alone to retrieve a possibly injured and assuredly distressed horse."

"If not I, then who?" she asked, gaping at him as if he were a spirit from the other side.

"Your friend," the earl said. "The one who grabbed your arm and dragged you off."

"Oh, Ned," she said dismissively. "My cousin."

Hearing the man who'd snatched Jenny from his midst was her cousin did nothing to eradicate Simon's feeling of annoyance. The man had been unforgivingly forward with Jenny back at Belton Manor, then had the gall to let her attempt a perilous rescue by herself.

Obviously, this Ned person lacked every single esteemed virtue, including chivalry.

"Cousin or beau," Simon said, "*he* should be here, not you."

She shrugged. "The question is, my lord, how can *you* possibly be here?"

"Honestly, I hardly know myself." He tied his horse near Lucy. "To be frank, which I feel I can be with you, when you headed away to deal with your injured stable boy and your horse, I was unprepared for the anger that overcame me."

"Anger?"

He nodded. "Yes, at myself. Everything in me wanted to help you, yet the idea of venturing out seemed an impossible task. How ridiculous!"

"No, my lord. Not ridiculous. Not after what you've been through."

"Nevertheless, the momentary depth of my own fear did, indeed, anger and then shock me. When you left me behind with the children, I realized how tired I am of being afraid, especially when I can't determine precisely of what I am fearful. I wasted precious time standing in my room willing myself to follow you."

"You are here now," she said softly. "And I am exceedingly grateful."

He brushed off her placating words. "I am not a cowardly poltroon, a nidget who lets others do what I can ably do. I am good with horses, or I used to be."

Simon always had an affinity for equines. Riding had come naturally to him and he had gentled his fair share of horses for inclusion in his father's stables. He hoped he still had the knack. No need to tell Jenny how he had sweat buckets and gritted his teeth until he nearly cracked them while waiting for his own horse to be saddled. He'd nearly fled to his room half a dozen times.

Once he was astride Luster, his favorite mount who seemed to know him at first sight even after three years, Simon had been relieved to find he felt perfectly at ease. He'd then ridden hell bent to her family's cottage, only to discover she'd set out alone.

"I am truly grateful, my lord. Thunder seems bigger somehow out here in the open." She waved her hands around, one sad limp carrot still in her grasp.

Ignoring her reasonable statement and her lovely, endearing smile, Simon went to the mare that Jenny had securely tethered and began to rummage in the closest saddlebag.

More blasted carrots! What on earth had she been thinking?

"I know you have a bridle and rope with you somewhere."

"The other bag, my lord. I still cannot believe you are here! How on earth did you find me?"

He shot her a glance. She looked particularly attractive in the late-day sun, with a little grime on her nose and her dress plastered around her ankles showing the outline of her legs. In fact, she looked infinitely kissable, and he was counting on another opportunity in the near future to taste her sweet lips.

"Please, call me Simon. It seems we've become good enough friends for that, don't you think?"

Her cheeks became infused with pink. He hadn't meant to embarrass her. If anyone should feel embarrassed, it should be him, especially after his last emotional display in the garden.

"How did you know I had a bridle and rope?" she asked.

"Because you are a practical girl."

"Yes, of course."

She almost sounded as if he'd insulted her.

"How did you find me?"

From her other saddlebag, Simon pulled out a rather old, short rope, which caused him to roll his eyes, and then a worn but usable bridle.

"I'm not a military tracking expert, but this was a rather simple expedition, and your mother pointed me in the right direction. Now stay put and let me take a look at this animal."

Making sure she nodded her agreement, for he did not want to find her suddenly at his elbow and again in harm's way, he entered the chilly water. In moments, he'd forded the stream and found himself face to face with the unfortunate Thunder.

"You don't look happy," Simon muttered in soft tones. "Look at the whites of your eyes. And those are some very flared nostrils. Come on, ol' boy. No one wants to hurt you.

I only want to get you back on the other side of the scary water."

The more he spoke, the calmer the horse became. Eventually, it lowered its head and grabbed at some green grass, ripping it from the earth and chewing.

Simon still hadn't touched Thunder, but very slowly, he lifted his hand before the horse's nose, making sure it saw him before he stroked it from forehead to muzzle. Then he leaned in to stroke its neck.

So far, so good.

Raising his other hand, letting the horse clearly see it, Simon brought the bridle in close and slipped it over the horse's head. Easy as eating custard. Yet, as soon as he moved to the horse's left side and attempted to close the buckle, it shied away. He tried again, and it jerked its head to the side, pawing at the ground.

An impasse.

CHAPTER TWELVE

"How is it going, my . . . *um,* Simon?" she asked. Jenny could perfectly well see how it was going. He didn't answer. Instead, he asked her a question.

"Tell me again what happened to this horse."

"Something spooked him, and he kicked our stable boy."

Simon shook his head with impatience.

"No, before that. What caused him to behave differently than he ever has?"

She tilted her head to the side. Her chestnut-colored hair, which had come undone during her ride, lay draped over one of her slender shoulders. With the last rays of the sun on her, Jenny was all warm and inviting, with those large brown eyes and gently parted lips. Lips that had been luscious and soft under his. He realized she was speaking.

"First there was the injury to his cannon, front right, as I recall."

Simon looked down. Thunder's leg below the knee looked healed and was properly bearing the horse's weight although he could see by its marred hair where the injury occurred.

"Then he got his head deep into a raspberry bush. After that, he has not been the same. George and I deduced, from the way Thunder behaves, that he might have scratched his left eye."

Simon looked at the horse. Certainly, the left eye was watering profusely, but he saw nothing that looked like infection. He brought his hand up toward it, and the animal didn't move. When Simon's palm got quite close, however, Thunder shied away as if entirely surprised.

"What would soothe you, beastie?"

"What did you say?" Jenny called out.

Simon considered. "I don't suppose you have a rag or lightweight cloth?"

"There is a blanket on Lucy, under my saddle. She has boney hips and—"

"Too heavy."

They stared at one another over the stream.

"There's nothing for it, then." With that, Simon shed his jacket, which he hung over a nearby branch, and then removed his collar and cuffs, which he wedged into his jacket pockets.

"My lord?" Jenny queried.

"You're supposed to call me Simon," he reminded her, unfastening the front of his shirt.

"You're not supposed to be undressing," she pointed out.

"My shirt is the perfect weight of cloth to cover Thunder's eyes. The only other garment that might work would be if you are wearing a cotton chemise. I don't suppose you wish to strip down to that garment."

"Absolutely not," she said, her tone strangled, as he finished removing his shirt and stood before her bare-chested.

Simon couldn't help glancing at her. There was the adorable bloom that suffused her cheeks whenever certain emotions flowed through her. In his mind's eye, he could picture her standing before him with only a cotton shift clinging to her curves.

How deeply would she blush if she knew what he was thinking?

"Anyway," he said, bringing his thoughts back to the task at hand, "what Thunder can't see won't scare him."

If only Simon could say the same about himself. Yet in truth, it was a similar issue. If his eyes were open, he needed to see clearly where he was and hang onto that reality with every fiber of his being. When he closed his eyes, if he kept them that way, he stayed safe, neither in the hellish prison in Burma, nor in the heavenly English countryside that might be unreal. With eyes shut, he existed in a place where nothing existed and nothing could be taken from him.

Clearly, Thunder needed that reprieve as well.

"Hang on, Thunder boy," he murmured. "You're going to like this, and that's a promise. Just like that lovely girl standing over there made promises to me and kept them. She said she would return, and she did. She said she was real, and she is."

Keeping up a soothing, one-sided, foolish conversation with the horse, Simon managed to tie his shirt around the horse's head, covering its eyes and securing it in place with the sleeves. Thunder didn't protest, nor did he try to shake off the garment.

And when Simon was finished, he fastened the bridle straps that were still dangling, attached the rope, and stepped into the stream.

"Your coat," Jenny called out.

Ah, yes. He was still unclothed from the waist up. Glancing at her, he realized she was staring hard at him. Did she like what she saw? He wished he had the physique he'd had three years earlier. He'd been far more muscular then, from riding, boxing with Toby, and rapier practice.

Now, he was too thin, although thanks to his cook's ministrations and his butler's insistence that he eat, at least Simon was not the gaunt man he'd been when he'd first returned to England. His ribs were no longer clearly outlined at least.

Still, he was no prize for Jenny to dote over. He could change that. He *would* change that.

Turning, Simon grabbed hold of his coat from the nearby branch with his free hand. Time to test his premise. Walking again into the stream, he tugged the rope for Thunder to follow. The horse did so, barely hesitating with the smallest of startles when its front hooves touched the water. In a few moments, they'd crossed the stream and were safely on the other side.

Jenny clapped her hands softly, as if afraid to startle Thunder but obviously too excited to remain still.

"How did you do that?" she asked, looking at him as if he were God.

Admittedly, her admiration, however fleeting, felt damn good. After losing a battle, getting captured, and failing dismally at protecting Toby, helping Jenny seemed like a step in the right direction, no matter the insignificance of his success. What's more, he had left the grounds of Belton. He was free!

"Horses are basically trusting pack animals," he told her as he walked Thunder to a tree a few yards away from the other horses. He tied him securely and patted the animal's smooth neck.

Turning, Simon found Jenny's appreciative gaze still fixed upon his person. Understandably, he wanted to pull her close and feel her bountiful curves against his naked chest instead of simply eyeing her magnificent breasts surreptitiously like a schoolboy. What's more, he wanted to claim her mouth again. This time, with his eyes open.

God, if she knew what he was thinking! That delightful blush would be a permanent stain upon her cheeks.

Shrugging into his jacket, as well as shrugging off the improper thoughts, Simon added, "Most horses will follow a leader just about anywhere. I think you are correct that Thunder's eye is injured. He's startling every time something that he isn't expecting comes close, and it's watering profusely, ruining his vision. Let's keep the blindfold on him until we get him home. Let him rest in the darkness."

Jenny looked at him curiously, and he knew what she was thinking: Comparing him to the wretched horse, and being quite correct.

Damnit!

"MY CARRIAGE IS STILL at Belton," Jenny pointed out, after Simon had successfully led Thunder behind his horse all the way back to her mother's cottage.

For her part, Jenny had ridden at the front of their procession on sweet Lucy. While very much aware of the shirtless man following behind her, she had tried to keep up a normal conversation.

Nevertheless, even while chatting, her thoughts kept drifting to the vivid memory of his bare torso, something she'd never seen before. Not any man's.

The earl was thinner than he ought to be, Jenny noted, yet he had a very fine form. Moreover, she'd been fascinated by his flat brownish-pink nipples and the dusting of tawny hair that curled in the center of his chest and headed downward toward the waistband of his trousers, leaving her to muse on what lay below!

When they'd arrived at her home, her family, particularly Eleanor, were overjoyed to see Thunder. All except for her cousin.

"He should be shot," Ned said upon exiting the house and seeing the horse. Then he took an exaggerated second look upon seeing Simon's shirt around the horse's eyes.

Swiveling his gaze to the earl and taking note that his lordship wore nothing beneath his coat, a frown settled across her cousin's brow.

"That's rather irregular, I do say," Ned avowed, his tone almost one of complaint.

"His lordship helped tremendously," Jenny said, addressing her mother and ignoring Ned entirely. *Shot, indeed!*

However, Eleanor was clearly worried. "Oh, please don't say Thunder has to be put down."

Before Jenny could do more than glare at Ned, Simon answered for her.

"Of course, not." The earl approached her mother. "If I may advise you, Lady Blackwood, this animal needs a veterinarian to look at its eye. There may be something embedded, although hopefully it is merely a scratch that will heal. In the meantime, unless you have a proper set of blinders, a lightweight feed sack should do to keep it calm. Far better than my shirt. It ought to have its head covered at all times."

"I fail to see how that will help," Ned said.

Jenny was in no mood to argue. Simon had been quite right. Ned should have helped her rather than pouting in his room. In *her* parlor!

Yet on second thought, she certainly wouldn't have wanted to receive an eyeful of her cousin without *his* shirt!

This time, Simon did respond directly to Ned. "The poor vision in Thunder's left eye is causing the animal to become increasingly skittish." Then the earl fixed her cousin with a hard stare. "Quite frankly, it was dangerous for Miss Blackwood to be out there recovering the animal. I'm surprised that she was allowed to, nay, forced to."

Jenny watched Ned swallow. Duly reprimanded, he had nothing more to add.

Simon spoke again to her mother. "Since you are now lacking a stable boy and, clearly, shorthanded when it comes to help," he shot Ned another disparaging glance, "I will tend to the animal and get him to his stall. After that, I can send assistance from Belton to help out until George—it is George, isn't it?—until he is up and around. Meanwhile, I will send for the veterinarian that my family has used for years. He is an excellent animal doctor."

Thus, it was that Lord Lindsey ended up acting as their stable boy. Once Thunder was back in his stall with a feedbag on his head, and Lucy had been stabled with fresh oats and water, then Jenny reminded Simon of her family's carriage, which still remained at his estate.

"I shall deliver your carriage to you first thing in the morning," he said.

"Oh, no, my lord," she protested. "I can walk to the manor and retrieve it myself."

The smile he offered her seemed like a warm bath. What's more, it silenced her as she took in his handsome face.

"Miss Blackwood, there is no need for you to worry. You've done enough as it is. Let me handle this one small task for you." He held her gaze for a long moment, until she nodded, thrilled to her toes at his offer.

Then turning to Jenny's mother, he said, "You have a remarkable daughter, and I am very pleased to have made her acquaintance. And all of your acquaintances, of course."

"Thank you, my lord. Will you stay for our evening meal?"

"That's very kind, but I will not impose unexpectedly." And with a bow to Jenny's mother and nods to the rest of her family, he took his leave. Only his glance to Jenny indicated his desire for her to follow him as he led his dappled gray to the road.

"I will send for the vet at once. I hate to think that your horse is in pain needlessly. If there's something under the lid or even, God forbid, in his eye, this man will flush it out. Even if there is some vision loss, Thunder's nature should return to normal after that."

With the only blight upon her happiness being the size of the veterinarian's cost, she felt blessed indeed.

"May I confess, my lord, although I don't wish ill on Thunder or George, for that matter, I see the benefit in what has happened today."

He cocked his head in an endearing fashion.

"Meaning?" he asked.

"Meaning you are here, where a few hours earlier I would have wagered my soul you could not possibly be. If I may say, my lord, I am quite proud of you."

To her delight, the Earl of Lindsey blushed profusely before bidding her a good evening and riding away.

IF HE COULD DO one impossible task, he could do another, he reasoned. He'd left the manor, left the grounds of Belton itself, and made Jenny proud. Now, he stood beside his bed, staring at it.

Glancing over at his favorite chair, which had, in a way, also become his most despised chair, he released a large sigh.

Genevieve Blackwood had done it! She had got him to go outside, and not merely into his own garden but out to rescue that bloody unfortunate horse. The thought of her needing him had compelled him to overcome the paralysis of his own fear and to bolt after her. He still could hardly credit that he'd ridden Luster.

Thank God he'd found her and the horse! Even now, though, anxiety trickled down his spine at what he'd done, but he *had* done it. What's more, he was determined he would not ever lock himself in his room again for being outdoors was far preferable to being indoors. He knew he wouldn't walk beneath an arbor and find himself imprisoned in his cell. He felt no fear that he might doze off while riding his horse and end up covered in rats. It was a miracle! All due to Jenny.

But the cursed bed! And sleep. Those were another matter altogether. They practically ensured a swift return to his cell, and he honestly wasn't sure he was strong enough to survive if he went back. Not after experiencing the joys of his home again and the pleasantries he'd felt with one particular woman.

Finally, feeling like a coward, he snatched up the same poetry book of Burns, lit three lamps, and sat in his chair to read through the night. Hours later, when he awakened on the dirt floor of his cell, he nearly wept. Going home had been a cruel dream. Riding his horse hadn't really happened.

Bitterly, he waited for the noise of the rats to assault his ears just as their claws and teeth would assault his skin if he wasn't vigilant. Yet he heard nothing. It was strangely quiet. Where was Toby? Lifting his head enough to glance around the dimly lit cell, he saw his cousin propped against the far wall, unmoving. Suspicion grew that something was wrong with Toby, something Simon already knew and didn't want to face.

"Speak," he tried to scream to his cousin, but he couldn't make a sound. Not wanting to face whatever was bubbling up to the surface from deep in his pool of memories, Simon lay his cheek back down on the floor.

Then he heard the guard coming and all his senses perked up. If he could kill the guard, he could prevent anything bad from happening. He could save Toby. Or was it too late?

JENNY WAS ON TENTERHOOKS all morning. When would their little yellow gig be returned? Would Simon come himself? Most likely not. He would send a footman to return the carriage and walk back to the manor.

After glancing out the upstairs window for the hundredth time, she sat back on her bed.

"Drats!" Extremely tired of her own impatience and her futile thoughts, she picked up the book she'd been unable to read for the past hour. If only she could take a walk. However, she was practically imprisoned in her room. If she ventured downstairs, Ned was sure to assail her with an invitation to speak privately. Even if she slipped from the house, she knew with certainty he would follow her.

Blessedly, Maggie had brought her a scone and a pot of tea before leaving on foot for her lessons at the manor. Jenny knew it was wrong but couldn't deny a surge of envy over her sister's position. She tried not to imagine the earl, whom she almost thought of as *her* earl, encountering Maggie in his home. With Simon's newfound strength and willpower, he might decide to check in on the children with whom he had seemed enchanted the day before.

How easy would it be for him to fall for the most beautiful Blackwood sister!

Jenny vowed it had been worth the wait when instead of a footman delivering her family's gig, Simon shocked her by arriving in his own carriage.

"I thought we could go reclaim yours together," he told her, standing, hat-in-hand on the cottage doorstep.

She grinned at him as she collected her bonnet and gloves, feeling almost breathless with delight. The Earl of Lindsey had come calling to collect her and had clearly gone out of his way to do so. After all, he could have sent a servant.

In no time, Simon had helped her onto the plush and polished leather seat of his sporty tilbury. They delayed only long enough for Cook to hurry out the door after them clutching a basket with a cloth over it. After having this thrust into her arms, Jenny found herself whisked away from home, her bonnet ribbons blowing in the breeze.

It was a far more enjoyable ride back to Belton with the earl than it had been coming from the manor with her cousin the day before. Although Jenny wouldn't have minded feeling Simon's thigh or shoulder against her own, like a gentleman, he stayed on his side of the carriage seat.

For her part, preoccupied by their close proximity, she kept imagining turning her face toward him. He would only need to lean down slightly to be able to kiss her again.

Sighing loudly, for if she were honest, another kiss was what she most desired at that moment, she nearly missed his concerned words.

"Do not despair," he said, mistaking her sigh. "I am sure your horse can be rehabilitated and restored to its former nature. It needs only a gentle hand and a kind, understanding soul to oversee its recovery."

At his words, Jenny did turn her face toward the man seated beside her. The earl's intense expression made her consider what he had said. There was no doubt in her mind he was speaking about himself as much as about Thunder.

"I'm sure he will be fine," she offered. "He has already made incredible progress."

Simon rested his forearms on his thighs, holding the reins loosely. A smile played about his mouth.

Clearly, he knew she meant him, and just as clearly, he was not bothered by it.

"As I said, an understanding soul."

Jenny accepted his compliment. Helping came easily to her, and there was something in this man that called to her womanly heart, drawing sympathy from her without pity.

No, he was too formidable a man to pity.

"I don't know how the scratch to your horse's eye will heal," Simon broke into her musing, "but even if he never properly regains his vision, if you accustom him to blinders, he will be far happier."

"I fear I would still be stuck in the stream had you not come to my rescue."

Dear God, now she was flirting shamelessly. Of course she would not still be standing in the water unless she were an absolute ninny.

"I have every faith that you would have found a solution, what with your tempting carrots and your frayed rope."

They both laughed, and any awkwardness of the morning dissipated.

"I took the liberty of sending for the vet today, and I will be honored if you'll allow me to pay for him."

Jenny shook her head. "You have done too much already. And I do truly thank you for everything you did yesterday. We shall pay for our own horse's care."

She heard Simon sigh. "You are stubborn. And you do not need to thank me. We are far from even in good deeds performed."

Lifting a hand, he softly brushed her cheek with his knuckles, then along her jawline.

"Oh, goodness," Jenny murmured as heat suffused her cheeks and her entire body seemed to warm.

His eyes widened. "What is amiss?"

"I'm certain my face is already red as a beetroot and most unbecoming."

Turning away, she broke the disturbing contact, staring toward the gully beside the rude country road.

"Jenny," he said softly.

She didn't look at him, and indeed, she did feel as stubborn as he'd accused her of being. Where Maggie could perpetrate a delightful dusting of color on her high cheekbones, Jenny feared she had two large red apples for cheeks.

"Genevieve," he implored, his voice low and husky to her ears.

She nearly smiled, realizing he was teasing her. However, when Simon gently grasped her chin and brought her head around to face him, she sobered entirely. His intense, scrutinizing expression stole her breath.

The horse had stopped at his command. There she sat, in an open-air carriage in the middle of the road, hardly able to breathe and utterly unable to move.

"No," he said, shaking his head slowly yet never breaking eye contact.

"No?" she repeated, feeling as if she had cotton wool between her ears rather than a brain. All she could do was look into his piercing gray-blue eyes, entirely captivated by his gaze.

"You are not at all unbecoming, nor does your face resemble a beet in any way. You have a perfectly delectable bloom on your cheeks to rival the sweet pink blush of England's fairest roses."

His thumb and fingers held her still.

She saw the flare in his blue depths, felt a responding surge of desire in herself. Undeniably, she was quite prepared, even eager, when he leaned toward her and kissed her.

CHAPTER THIRTEEN

Relishing the firmness of his mouth upon her own, Jenny nearly started to hum with pleasure. While not the desperate grappling kiss of their garden encounter, yet for all its gentleness, this kiss was entirely thrilling.

"Mm," she murmured against his mouth, before feeling the tip of his tongue trace the joining of her lips. Simon was like a sensual siege and she, the castle whose gatekeeper desperately wanted to open the gates.

Unhesitatingly, she parted her lips. He slid his tongue inside her mouth and tasted her.

Her hands fluttered up from her lap and the basket she still held. Clasping him behind the neck, she experienced everything he offered. *Such pleasure!*

Excruciating sensations of desire—for she'd read enough novels to know what this was—flowed through her, like golden honey across warm bread.

He released her chin, attempting to lay claim to her body, but the basket lay between them.

"What is in that infernal basket?" he demanded, picking it up and placing it at their feet. Yet, when he pressed his large, warm palm against her ribs, directly below the swell of her bosom, she couldn't form a thought or speak a word.

While sweeping his thumb upward toward her left breast, his fingers dug gently into her many layers of cotton and silk.

For her part, Jenny wished the earl had nothing on beneath his coat as the day before. How easily she could draw her gloved hand from behind his neck, down past his collarbone, and slip it across the naked chest she'd glimpsed yesterday. In her fantasy, however, she wore no gloves and stroked him with her bare hands. If only she could feel whether the curls she'd viewed sprinkled across his chest were soft or coarse. If only . . .

When their kiss ended, Simon rested his forehead against hers for a mere moment, and she could feel him breathing as hard as she was. When he sat back, releasing her, he broke all contact except for the intimate gaze they still shared.

"Are you terribly offended?" he asked.

At first, she couldn't reason past the roaring of her blood, certain he could hear the loud thumping of her heart. Still, he waited for an answer.

"I don't think I am." It was true. Jenny knew she ought to slap his handsome face for taking liberties. Moreover, propriety dictated that she jump from the carriage and race for the nearest home to demand sanctuary.

Instead, she smiled slightly. "Should I be?"

He threw back his head and laughed. Then he picked up the reins where they rested across his strong, lean thighs, and with a swift movement, got the horse moving once again.

"No, you should not. I meant no disrespect at all. Precisely the opposite. I hold you in the highest esteem and meant only to pay tribute. It is only because of you, and Thunder, that I was able to sally forth this morning. Think of that."

Her small smile became a large grin, and she faced forward again.

"It was quite an agreeable tribute," Jenny allowed.

They remained in companionable silence after that.

Back at the manor, her carriage was precisely where she'd left it, although currently without a horse attached.

As Simon gave her his hand and helped her down, stable boys came at once to unharness the chestnut mare. Another two led away the lightweight tilbury toward the carriage house. Yesterday, the same boys had gawked at their lord in his strange state of undress, yet they were too well-trained to say anything.

Drawing aside one of the lads, Simon instructed him, "After you get my horse rubbed down, go to Miss Blackwood's home. You are to assist with their horses until they dismiss you. You may ride Luster."

She could see by the stable boy's shining eyes that riding Luster was a treat for him.

"It is the small stone house just past Norman's Corner," Jenny told him.

"Yes, Miss. I know the place. George is your stable boy."

She nodded. "Yes. He has sustained an injury but should be well soon."

"Yes, Miss," he said again and hurried off to finish his duties so he could leave.

"That was very kind of you."

"Will you take a refreshment with me on the terrace?" When he chuckled at his own words, she tilted her head.

"What is funny, my lord?"

"Merely, the extreme civility and properness of such an invitation after you've spent hours in my room, it strikes me as nearly absurd."

She shrugged and laced her arm through his. "We are friends, as you said."

Instead of entering the house, they took the long way around, through the side garden opposite the stables.

"Your cousin is a useless toad," Simon said unexpectedly and with enough ire to surprise her, although she couldn't argue with him.

Having been taught not to speak ill of people, particularly family, she remained silent.

"I cannot stomach such a man," the earl continued. "You could have been hurt."

"Ned is only visiting, and most likely didn't think it his place to interfere." She forbore mentioning her cousin's fear of horses. Why humiliate him further?

Still, the earl's mouth nearly dropped to his chest. "*Interfere?* Are you saying that is what I did?"

Jenny rushed to respond. "Oh, no, my lord. Your assistance was invaluable. And I am beyond grateful."

Was that a gleam appearing in his blue eyes?

"How grateful? And stop calling me 'my lord.' I've given you leave to use my name, so use it."

"*Exceedingly* grateful. Thank you, Simon." That one word, his name, struck her as intensely intimate.

He smiled broadly at her. "Your cheeks are quite pink again. What *are* you thinking?"

Curse her fair complexion and tendency to blush! Yet, she did not have to tell him anything about her thoughts. Luckily, he didn't press her for a response. Instead, on the terrace, he drew out a wrought-iron chair with a soft cushion upon it and gestured for her to sit. After he'd taken a seat, Binkley appeared.

"Lemonade," Simon requested. "And if you have any biscuits."

"Of course, my lord." However, the butler didn't hurry off to do his master's bidding. Instead, he hovered a moment until Jenny looked up at him, shading her eyes in the sun to see the man's face.

Was he widening his eyes? And then scrunching up his face? What on earth?

Simon noticed the man dawdling. "That will be all, Binkley."

"Yes, my lord."

This time, there was no mistaking the intense, pleading look the butler gave Jenny, even gesturing with his head toward Simon before he withdrew.

She was not going to be let off the hook, not by the staff. Yet, was this really the time and place.

Coward! she admonished herself. Was any time a good time?

"I think he likes you," Simon interrupted her inner war.

"A very devoted servant, isn't he?" Jenny offered. How to begin?

"He has been with us for as long as I can recall. My father hired Binkley after he got out of the king's service." Pausing, musing, he looked out at the gardens. "My father has always been very good at choosing staff."

And there was the beginning she needed.

"Your father . . . is . . . was . . . That is, are you close to him?"

He shot her a puzzled expression. After a moment, he looked away. "Yes. Like many fathers and sons, I suppose. Were you close with yours?"

No, she didn't want to talk about her father but his.

"Well, I loved him. And he seemed like a good father, right up to the end. As I mentioned, it turned out he was in a bit of financial trouble." This was not helping. They were straying farther from the topic.

Simon nodded. "Still the worth of a man's bank accounts is not all there is to a man." He reached out and patted her hand as if consoling her. "Baron Blackwood had three daughters who seem to be smart and lovely, and that is his legacy."

Jenny was perfectly at peace with her rather careless father. That was not the issue.

"Yes, but, Simon, about *your* father. The earl. The old earl. That is, Lord Lindsey. Or rather formerly—"

"You are trying to tell me that my father is dead." His tone was flat, unemotional, unexpected. Resigned.

She quickly covered his hand with hers, making a layering of their hands. He looked at them all pressed together on the table, then lifted his gaze to her eyes.

"You knew?" she asked, her voice low and soft.

He nodded. "He would have come to me the moment I set foot on the property, no matter my state. I suspected it. I didn't want to ask, though. I could almost believe he was simply away. I went to his rooms one evening, very late, and found everything shrouded in sheets."

"I'm sorry."

Just then, Mr. Binkley arrived with a maid who carried a silver tray of refreshments. Worry was etched upon the older man's face, but in his hands was her basket.

"Another reason to stay isolated," Simon added. "I didn't want to hear anyone from the outside call me Lord Lindsey."

The butler flinched but didn't speak until Simon spoke to him directly. "Binkley, old man, I thank you for your careful attention to my feelings along with everything else."

"Yes, my lord," the butler said as if Simon had commented on the weather. However, Jenny noticed the man's jaw tense and knew he was not unaffected. "Will there be anything else, my lord?"

And the only outward demonstration of sentiment was that Mr. Binkley set down his small burden and hurried off even before Simon could answer.

"Did he ask you to tell me?"

"Yes."

"Kind of him," he murmured. Then he noticed the basket. "Not that again. What in God's name is in there?"

Laughing, Jenny slipped her hands free from his and pushed the offering toward him. One of the stable boys must have found it on the floor of the carriage.

"It's for you."

He frowned at her a little suspiciously. Then lifting the cloth cover, he peeked inside. Reaching in, he withdrew a porcelain covered dish and placed it on the table before him. He took another look and noticed a single silver spoon. Looking suddenly like a little boy at Christmas, Jenny nearly blurted out the surprise.

He lifted the lid and his expression became one of absolute wonder. Slowly, without taking his eyes off the contents of the dish, he set the lid aside.

"Is that . . . ?"

"It is."

Without another word, he picked up the spoon. Then with lightning speed, he thrust it into the very center of the apple Charlotte and shoveled in a massive mouthful. And then another. Simon closed his eyes, causing Jenny a momentary fear that he would lapse into a state of terror. He chewed, savored, and swallowed. Then he snapped his lids open and looked at her.

"It's positively wondrous. Would you like some?"

She shook her head, unable to conceive of depriving him of a single morsel.

But he insisted, spooning some more up, he held it out to her.

"Taste," he commanded.

Because she could see that it would please him to share with her, she leaned toward him and let him feed her. It was one of Cook's most heavenly desserts. Swallowing, she sighed.

"Thank you, but I insist you eat the rest."

Staring at her, his gaze fell to her mouth. Raising his hand, he wiped the corner of her lips, coming away with a drop of thick custard on his thumb. This, he lifted to his own mouth and licked away.

Jenny's mouth went dry. *Good God but he was an attractive man.* She wanted to be that drop of custard encountering his tongue. At the same time, she was fascinated by the idea of licking his thumb herself.

Clearly, he knew his effect on her, for he offered her a wicked grin before focusing on finishing the rest of the dessert.

God bless his stomach, she thought, after he finished about four portions' worth. Hopefully someone in the manor knew enough to give him some mint tea later if he felt an ache. When he was done, he sat back in his chair.

"You listened and remembered. Thank you."

His words warmed her from her toes to her heart. It was rather easy to make him happy, and it pleased her to do so.

"You're most welcome. I'll tell Cook that you approved."

For a few moments they were silent, looking out at the gardens in full bloom.

"I reclined on the bed last night," Simon's voice drifted toward her softly. "To sleep."

The import was not lost on her. Could she ask him a personal question? Would he mind? She thought not.

"How did you fare? Did you sleep well?"

Simon didn't hesitate to answer. "No, not well at all. In truth, I ended up in a heap on the floor."

Gasping, she raised a hand to her mouth. "Were you injured?"

"Only my pride. I was grateful for the floor's assistance in awakening me."

She had to stifle a laugh, only because he was clearly comfortable telling her, even making a jest of the whole thing.

"Are you going to try again?" she asked, taking a sip of the forgotten lemonade.

He shot her a glance from under his lashes.

"Are you envisioning me in bed, Genevieve?"

She coughed, choking on the chilled tart beverage.

"No, my lord," she said when at last she could speak.

"Pity."

TWO HOURS LATER, AFTER they had talked of everything and nothing, she stood. "I must get home before the next crisis befalls my family. Also, I'll give Maggie a ride, as she hates the long walk."

"Long walk? From here to your cottage? Why, I could sprint it in five minutes. Or I could have. Before."

Before! No doubt, a part of him would always divide life betwixt the years before he'd been held captive and after. He was, as she'd noted, a little thin. Yet, if the way he wolfed down Cook's dessert was any indication, Jenny had no doubt he would fill out his clothing again in no time.

Not that his filling out was any of her business.

What were they talking about? Maggie . . .

"Nonetheless, it's different when one is wearing impractical footwear, as our Maggie. She has a fondness for soft slippers, more suited to a parquet ballroom than a country road."

"Let's go find her then. I'm sure she'll be glad of your gig to take her home."

In fact, Jenny's middle sister was thrilled to be rescued from the last half hour of tutoring, not even minding that Lord Despair, himself, stood there in the doorway.

After curtsying deeply to the earl, Maggie looked him directly in the eye. "I understand you saved our horse and did so bare-chested, my lord. Bravo!"

Jenny wanted to slap her own forehead, and then slap Maggie's. One didn't say "bravo" to a peer of the realm.

However, Simon only laughed. "That was an unintentional consequence, I assure you."

Jenny sought to catch her sister's eye and get her moving toward the carriage before she said anything else embarrassing. However, Maggie surprised her by an expression of gravity.

"I wish to offer you my sincere gratitude, my lord, for your generous sponsorship of my sister, Eleanor, and myself. This means a great deal to us and also to our mother."

He gave a wonderfully deep bow that removed the hint of charity from his gift and turned it into a token of respect.

Jenny watched as the earl and her sister smiled at one another.

Oh, dear. The green-eyed monster was swishing around Jenny's skirts again. Maggie looked perfection itself, even in an ordinary day dress of pale blue with her thick, caramel-colored hair braided effortlessly over one shoulder. And, of course, Simon was her equal in his gray pants and waistcoat, his crisp white shirt and perfectly tied cravat.

Suddenly, Jenny felt every bit the plain sister who had been easily tossed aside by a viscount. Her feelings, nay, her strong reactions to Simon's touch should warn her she was delving into deep waters in which she had no business swimming. After all, he was the Earl of Lindsey.

"Your sister is my new and very good friend," Simon told Maggie.

His words permeated Jenny's thoughts, which had been spiraling with doubt. When Simon's gaze caught hers, they shared a smile, and she let go of her misgivings. His friendship was a great gift she'd never expected when being forced to move to the country.

Not caring how she blushed in front of her sister, Jenny felt instantly lighthearted. Even more so when he said to her, "I hope you will come again soon. We still need to go over the ledgers."

"Yes, my lord," she agreed. "Of course."

As soon as the three of them appeared in the courtyard, with a gesture from Simon, one of the stable boys brought out the Blackwoods' old Cleveland Bay and harnessed him swiftly and efficiently to their carriage. It was difficult not to notice how the horse's coat shone. Someone had even waxed its hooves.

"The Bay's had a night of pampering," Maggie remarked. "His mane is nearly as glossy as mine."

Jenny rolled her eyes at her irrepressible sister.

As the old horse waited docilely, Simon helped first Maggie and then Jenny into the gig. She noticed he managed to also touch her arm and then her waist in his efforts. She was greatly aware of each place where the earl's hands branded her. In fact, her body seemed to sizzle under her clothing.

What was wrong with her?

"Jenny." *Her* name on *his* lips sounded equally as intimate.

"Yes?"

"You are incredibly helpful in a crisis. I would be happy to have you by my side if and whenever disaster strikes."

Goodness! What could he mean by saying that? In London, during the Season, that would practically be a proposal.

"Thank you," she managed and flicked the reins to get moving as her sister elbowed her excitedly in the ribs.

Halfway down the long drive, Jenny, like the biblical Lot's wife, could not resist looking back. Simon Devere still watched her, his arms at his sides, his head cocked slightly. She couldn't tell for sure, but she had a feeling he was wearing one of his charmingly boyish smiles.

WATCHING HER LEAVE, A sinking sensation rolled through him. Nervous energy assaulted his body as she completely disappeared from his sight. This young woman had become important to him. He couldn't deny it.

The smart, capable Jenny made him feel safe. How outrageous! A slip of a thing. However, it was blatantly true. Her lovely eyes held him captive in this world more strongly than any bamboo bars could. His anxiety fled at the sound of her voice and the touch of her hand. Yes, he very much enjoyed the touch of her hand.

"My lord!"

Simon turned to see his butler hurrying toward him.

"Thank goodness I've found you."

"I was not lost, Binkley. I assure you."

The butler stopped in his tracks, then realized he was making a jest. "Of course, my lord, it's only that . . ."

"That I'm normally right under foot, precisely where you can find me."

Binkley stayed silent.

Simon supposed he should be grateful his servant cared about him to such a degree. Binkley had been holding everything together above and beyond his post.

"You wanted to speak with me about something important, didn't you? And I put you off the other day."

"Yes, my lord."

"Then let us do that now."

"Yes, my lord. I will meet you in your chamber."

Simon was loath to go indoors, yet he could hardly set up camp outside. No doubt his butler would feel the need to commit him to an asylum if he did that. Still, he could avoid his room until bedtime.

"No. The library, where Miss Blackwood usually works."

Binkley merely raised an eyebrow. "In that case, my lord, everything I want to show you is already there."

A half hour later, Simon almost wished he'd told Binkley that he would wait to hear about the accounts when Jenny came back. Of course, he grasped the larger problem—a distinct siphoning of their capital—but it would take more time to understand the details Jenny had uncovered. And even though he now knew the gist of it, he looked forward to her explaining what she thought it all meant.

Meanwhile, the pit of his stomach felt like a raven was clawing at his innards.

All factual signs pointed to Toby embezzling money and sending it . . . where? Obviously, he couldn't ask his dead cousin, the man he called a great friend. Yet, he could ask his widow.

Maude Devere was in residence in his home. Uninvited. Perhaps she would pay for her keep by explaining a few things to him. Besides, it was time he spoke with her about the unauthorized sale of Jonling Hall.

172

CHAPTER FOURTEEN

"There you are, Cousin," Ned's voice was too close. "I was starting to think you were hiding from me?"

"Don't be ridiculous," Jenny said from her hiding place in the branches of their crabapple tree. "I often come up here to . . . to read."

Unfortunately, she had no book with her, and even Ned was sure to notice that.

"And sometimes just to keep an eye on Thunder. I can see if he's going to bother Lucy or the old Bay."

"May I help you down?" he asked as if her being in a tree was perfectly reasonable.

Realizing after breakfast that Ned was looking for her, and fearing he would follow her if she walked anywhere, Jenny had climbed instead. She'd desperately needed a break from the accounts that Henry had brought her, which would keep her busy for at least a day. However, half an hour had gone by, and her backside was beginning to ache.

"Yes, please do," she said.

He raised his hands up to hers, and she failed to see how that would help her. Was he going to catch her?

Half sliding, half jumping, Jenny ended up plastered against Ned whose arms closed around her instantly like a vice. Pushing against his narrow chest with both hands, she dared not look into his face lest he take the opportunity to kiss her. That prospect sent a rush of revulsion coursing through her.

"Thank you," she mumbled, staring down to where their bodies touched and hoping her gratitude was all he wanted. In truth, she felt none at all. She simply wanted him to leave her alone.

Instead, he held on.

"Jenny, I should very much like to speak privately with you about a matter of grave importance to us both."

Christ! He was a determined soul, for certain. She struggled another moment. He was also stronger than he looked!

"I will discuss nothing," she assured him, still not raising her face, "not while you have me imprisoned and detained."

She was about to stamp on his booted foot when he released her. She tried to step back but came up against the tree trunk. If it were Simon keeping her between his body and a tree, she would have had no problem with it. In fact, she would not have demanded to be released in the first place.

That unexpected wayward thought brought the familiar heat to her cheeks.

"Dear Cousin, I consider your blush a pretty marker of your female mind, but you have nothing to be embarrassed about. True, I may have seen your ankle while you were in that tree, but I hope to see far more of you in the future."

Not if she had anything to say about it. Luckily, she had a lot to say about it!

"The way you held me was *not* very gentlemanly," she admonished him. Perhaps if she became more disagreeable, he would turn his attentions elsewhere. Maybe toward Maggie, although she could hardly wish him on her sister. "I do not wish to have a discussion or think on matters of grave importance. I have work to do. Henry brought the apothecary's ledgers yesterday evening."

She tried to push past him, but Ned held his ground, forcing her to stand still and stay put.

"That's partly why I am sure you will rejoice at what I have to say. As soon as we agree, you won't need to ever look at numbers again, unless they're *our* household accounts."

She swallowed. "What do you mean 'our' accounts?"

Of course she knew what he meant, and she also knew that disagreeability was not the way to navigate these murky waters. Neither by her nature, nor by her common sense. If humiliated, Ned could certainly make life uncomfortable for her sisters when they got to London. The *ton* would be sniffing the air like dogs at a hunt as soon as any of the tarnished Blackwoods returned for a Season.

Perhaps Ned might be made to depart while remaining on cordial terms.

"Our *marital* accounts," Ned said, a small smile crossing his lips. "In our home in Falkirk. Guinevere, I am asking for your hand." He took that opportunity to grasp hold of her right one in both of his.

Instantly, she tried to pull it free, but he held firm, his hold as strong as any trapper's snare.

"Since you have no father," he continued, "I cannot ask him. I can speak with your mother, if you insist, but I am not sure her permission is needed, nor is her opinion on the matter relevant."

What an ass! Sighing, Jenny closed her eyes and looked to the sky. Too late for prayer, she feared. Sure enough, when she opened her eyes, he was still standing there and still holding her hand captive. What could she do?

"You know I have no dowry."

"None at all?" Ned questioned, his ardor slightly cooled. At least she hoped it was.

"Absolutely none. Not a cent." She nearly smiled.

He hesitated, then to her amazement, he said, "I didn't think you did, but I had hoped for some small pittance. That is quite all right."

Her mouth opened slightly. Perhaps Ned wasn't quite as mercenary and boorish as she had thought. After all, if he wanted her despite her penniless state, then he must truly have affection for her. More's the pity that she could not return his regard.

Then he added, "I imagine you've made a pretty penny with your bookkeeping, not to mention what the earl paid you. As your new benefactor, Lord Lindsey will probably give you something more for a dowry, too. Whatever you have, it will be enough to bring to our marriage and turn over to me when I am your husband, *Lord* Darrow."

A shock of anger raced up Jenny's spine resulting in a torrent of words that she couldn't have stopped even if she'd wanted to.

"I have made that money, every *pretty penny* as you say, for my family. What's more, we live on that money. The food you've been eating has been paid for with that money. Our servants are paid with that money. The physician has been paid, as will the veterinarian, with that money. I am not saving it in a hope chest like a moon-eyed girl."

Finally, while he stood there surprised by her vehemence, she was able to yank her hand free.

"And if I were, I certainly wouldn't *hope* for a man like you to be my husband. You shall have to find another way to become a baron. You won't be stealing my father's title through me! By the way, my name is Genevieve!"

With that, she pushed past him and ran into the house, not stopping until she was upstairs safe in her room.

Almost immediately all sorts of commotion occurred, followed predictably by Ned's loud voice and then the shrieking of Maisie and Eleanor. After banging noises in the room next door, no doubt as Ned's sister—or more likely, the Blackwood maid—packed Maisie's things, there was then more thumping as someone dragged the trunk down the stairs. Although Jenny didn't hear the front door open, she couldn't miss it being slammed shut.

A few moments later, Maggie and Eleanor raced into the room.

"What did you say to dear Cousin Neddy?" Maggie's saucy tone was laced with delight as she crossed her arms and leaned against the oak wardrobe.

Eleanor was crying openly, dramatically, as only a fourteen-year-old could do and sunk onto the end of the bed as if melting.

Jenny didn't lift her head off the pillow. Lighter footsteps heralded her mother who sat on the bed beside her in the crowded room.

"The Darrows have left," Anne said without a hint of sarcasm, although she had to know everyone in the house, including Cook and even the stable boy had heard their departure. "Ned seemed rather infuriated by you, from what I could tell."

Jenny wanted to apologize to all of them for the uncomfortable scene that had occurred because of her. Yet she could not. She had always done her best for each member of her family, and she was sorry for Eleanor losing her friend. She was sorry for any distress the abrupt and ugly departure had caused her mother, but she would not say she was sorry that Ned had departed.

"He asked me to marry him," she began. She paused as Maggie barked out a laugh, Eleanor gasped, and her mother merely nodded.

"I feared he might," Jenny admitted, "and I was trying to stay away from him so he could not speak the words. However, he cornered me like an animal. He was rude and insufferable."

Anne patted her hand, and Eleanor dried her tears on her skirt.

"It didn't sound as if you tried very hard to let him down gently," Maggie said, her eyes sparkling with mirth.

"No," Jenny told them all. "In the end, I lost my temper. It was far easier than I imagined to tell him no. He only wanted to trade up from his plain Scottish 'mister' to Father's baronetcy anyway and thought to style himself 'Lord Darrow.'"

"That makes our dinner engagement much easier to attend, then," Anne said. "We can all fit in one carriage."

Jenny sat up at last. "What engagement, Mummy?"

"While you were in the garden giving Ned the glove, as my mother would say, I received this from Belton Manor." She pulled a piece of crisp cream-colored paper from her waistband.

"Tomorrow night, we are to dine with the earl."

Eleanor perked up tremendously. "How exciting! I am going to pick out my dress now in case it needs mending." With that, and apparently quite over the loss of Maisie, she dashed from the room.

Maggie raised a beautifully sculpted eyebrow. "The four of us are dining with Lord Despair?"

Her mother didn't correct her middle daughter. "The invitation was for the six of us, and thus there would have been two bachelors to two maidens," she nodded at Jenny and Maggie in turn. "Then the two younger girls and me, as dowager. It would have been quite a gay party."

"Dowager?" Jenny muttered, wrinkling her nose at her mother's use of the word.

"Well, I am one," Anne said, looking completely unaffected by her status.

"You're a *young* widow," Maggie said. "A dowager must be sixty at least, with hair on her chin."

Anne laughed. "In any case, now there are two maidens to one bachelor. That will be a strange dinner party indeed."

"Should we tell him?" Maggie wondered.

Jenny considered. "I don't think Lord Lindsey will be able to produce another bachelor out of thin air. He said his friends do not live close by." She frowned. "Do you think we should cancel?"

"Absolutely not," her mother said. "Eleanor will thoroughly enjoy this distraction, and I'm sure you two can share the attentions of his lordship." Again, she nodded at each of her daughters before rising to her feet.

"I should let him know of the change in order for his staff to alter the seating arrangements. I'll write a return missive at once. Maggie can take it with her when she goes."

Maggie sat down in the space her mother had vacated.

"I don't see the earl usually," she said quietly, perhaps anxiously.

Anne patted her daughter's hand. "You will give my note to that Mr. Binkley fellow, not to the earl."

After she left, the two oldest Blackwood sisters stared at one another. It was one thing tutoring Lady Devere's children or even poring over ledgers in the library. It was another thing to have their entire family seated in the dining room as guests of the earl.

"You're practically courting," her sister said, looking bemused.

"Don't be ridiculous!" But Jenny's heart was thumping. Talking with Simon Devere was easy, and she held him in such high-esteem for the way he was pulling himself out of the darkness of his own mental predicament.

"Why am I being ridiculous? The earl is quite handsome, if you like tall, dark-haired men." Maggie grinned. "Certainly, more than your fickle viscount with his thin lips and even thinner hair."

Jenny couldn't help chuckling. "It's true I never thought much about Lord Alder's looks beyond the fact that he didn't repulse me. However, I'm certain he had perfectly suitable lips and thick brown hair. In fact, I am sure many consider him handsome."

Then she shrugged. "I simply didn't know how differently I would feel when I truly admire a man's appearance and, of course, his character."

"And you do? With Lord Des . . . Devere, I mean?"

"He *is* rather lovely," Jenny admitted, then felt the dreaded heat on her cheeks. She put a cooling palm up to each one.

All at once, Maggie squealed. "Has he kissed you?"

"Ssh," Jenny admonished her. "Goodness, why on earth would you ask me that?"

Maggie laughed with delight. "Why would you stall and ask me why I'm asking you unless I have guessed correctly? Tell me everything." She wriggled on the bed, practically clapping her hands.

"What was it like? Has he kissed you more than once? Has he touched you anywhere else on your person?"

"Enough!" Jenny tried to sound formidable yet failed. Instead, she couldn't help smiling. Recalling when Simon's lips touched hers, she did feel like the moon-eyed girl she'd mentioned to Ned.

"I have had the honor of his kiss, yes. Merely gratitude for my helping him to feel more at ease."

"Gratitude?" Maggie said, sounding horrified, then she gave an unladylike snort of laughter. "You ninny! Men don't kiss out of gratitude. They kiss because they admire you. They kiss because they want to bed you."

"What!" She shot Maggie a concerned look. "How would you know? Exactly how many times have you been kissed?"

Maggie gave a small smile, causing her heart-shaped face to take on a catlike expression.

"I may have enjoyed *une petite bise* during my brief time in London."

Jenny's mouth hung open. "I had no idea. Are you saying, from your vast experience then, that some man, a member of the *bon ton*, I'm assuming, wanted to bed you?"

Maggie blushed in a way that Jenny had never before seen on the cheeks of her usually self-possessed sister. How interesting!

Maggie picked unseen lint off her sleeve. "Ultimately, it was unimportant since my Season was not long enough for anything serious to develop."

"I see." Jenny frowned, hoping that her sister had not had a perfect union yanked out of her grasp.

Maggie stood. "Well, you successfully managed to turn the focus from your own kissing to mine, so let's get on with the day, shall we? You've got ledgers, no doubt, and I have to prepare for tutoring."

She paused in the doorway. "If I see Lord Despair, shall I give him a message from you regarding how he honored you with his gratitude?"

Maggie disappeared just in time to avoid the pillow that Jenny threw at her sister's head.

THE BLACKWOOD FAMILY HAD been in high excitement for the past twenty-four hours until it was time to depart for Belton Manor. Luckily, Jenny had more than one good gown from her Season and a half, and no one in the country would know if her dress was outdated or had been worn more than once.

Maggie, too, had gowns from her Season, including a couple as yet unworn. They'd been packed away, a sad reminder of what had befallen their family. Now, however, they were brought out for a joyous dinner with the earl.

At last, all the Blackwood women were suitably attired to attend the Earl of Lindsey and not disgrace themselves. Even Eleanor, who had not grown much in a year, still could fit into her favorite satin party gown.

Henry drove them in order for them not to appear as country bumpkins without servants, but they'd had to get their traveling carriage out of storage and harness both Lucy and the Cleveland Bay, a very mismatched team.

"We should have walked, or I should have driven," Jenny complained when the carriage lurched as the old Bay pulled faster than Lucy, causing Maggie to slip forward off her seat and stand on her sister's foot for the umpteenth time in the very short journey. Henry was not the most skilled driver. However, when one of Lord Lindsey's footmen greeted them as soon as they stopped in front of the manor, Jenny was glad not to be perched atop the dickey with windblown hair.

Moreover, quite unexpectedly, Simon appeared at the top of the stone steps as if he'd been waiting for them, perhaps looking out the window. That thought brought a smile to her lips, which grew even broader when he threw decorum to the wind and briskly descended the stairs.

Beginning with a respectful bow to their mother, he greeted each of the sisters in turn, offering a wink to Jenny that she hoped the others did not see. When he grasped hold of Maggie's hand, bringing it to his lips, he became the dapper earl again, formal and polite, as if he hadn't once told Jenny about her sister waggling her bustle.

Then he reached Eleanor.

"How is your horse, Miss Eleanor?"

"Fine, my lord. Thanks to you. It is good to see you in a shirt."

The older three ladies gasped until, after a stunned pause, Simon laughed outright.

"I shall endeavor to keep it on through the entire evening."

Then he took Lady Lucien Blackwood's arm through his and led the small group up the steps.

Before long, they were seated at dinner. Since they were such a small party, there was no lingering for drinks and trifling conversation in the anteroom. They took their assigned chairs at one end of the long table with Simon at the head, the baroness to his right, and Eleanor to her right. Jenny and Maggie sat opposite, on Simon's left.

Jenny's third time in the dining room was definitely the most pleasant, she decided. Finally, it was alive with flickering, long tapered candles, delicious aromas, and happy people.

"Most unfortunate about the hasty departure of your visitors." Simon broached the subject of Ned and Maisie's leaving as their wine was being poured. "They must have had pressing business."

Although it was impossible Simon could know what had occurred between her and Ned, still Jenny sensed an undertone of satisfaction that her cousins had left Sheffield.

Her mother spoke first. "Had they known of your invitation, my lord, I'm sure they would have delayed their departure."

"Then how fortunate for us that they did not know," he said.

For a moment, they were all silent, digesting his words, then Eleanor giggled.

Simon looked innocently nonplussed. "I meant only that I wouldn't have wanted to inconvenience them or have them change their plans on my account."

Jenny hid a smile by looking down at her lap and arranging her napkin. She knew precisely how Simon felt about Ned and was quite certain that he was unconcerned over inconveniencing him.

"As long as you were not insulted," Anne added, "then we are untroubled by their departure."

"Then rest assured, you should be entirely untroubled."

Maggie spoke up. "My lord, I should very much like to take this opportunity to once more offer my most sincere gratitude regarding a Season for myself and for Eleanor."

He nodded and shrugged at the same time.

"Please, think nothing of it, Miss Margaret. You have already said as much. I am happy to do it. I would extend the offer to Miss Blackwood," he said, looking at Jenny. "However, she has already expressed her disinterest in such an undertaking."

She was even more disinterested since beginning her blossoming friendship with him! If Simon truly wanted her to go away in January and find a husband, she would be most downhearted.

Raising an eyebrow at her oldest daughter, perhaps wondering why Jenny and the earl had discussed such a topic, Anne said, "Nevertheless, Lord Lindsey, we are, as a family, immensely grateful. Aren't we Eleanor?"

Caught sipping wine and staring up at one of the enormous chandeliers, Eleanor choked, coughing profusely while her family looked on with chagrin.

"Some water for our youngest guest," Simon ordered one of the servants standing by the sideboard. Immediately, the woman stepped forward and filled Eleanor's spare glass with water.

While she regained her composure, Jenny filled the silence.

"If Margaret is to attend the upcoming Season, we will need to begin preparations shortly. We need to find a skilled local dressmaker or go to Manchester or Nottingham."

Simon regarded her with thoughtful eyes. "Practical planning, Miss Blackwood. Unfortunately, I cannot help you with ascertaining where local ladies obtain gowns. I must confess that I have never even considered the matter."

"Perhaps Lady Devere could assist us. I've only met her once, but she was dressed beautifully."

"I've met her a number of times," Maggie added, "and she is always fashionably clothed."

Simon frowned slightly. "I invited her to our dinner tonight, but she refused. Something about a headache. Perhaps Miss Margaret can speak with her directly next time they meet over a tutoring session."

Their mother spoke up. "Please tell Lady Devere we hope she is feeling better. Such a shame to miss this delightful evening."

Simon nodded. "To be frank, she and I have never dined together when not in the company of her late husband. I have not seen her since my return."

All the ladies murmured a platitude of condolence over his cousin's death. Yet, not one of them thought it odd Maude Devere chose not to dine alone with Lord Lindsey. Indeed, Jenny knew the same thought ran through each of her family member's heads—how scandalous had it been otherwise.

She also realized that Maude must be desperately lonely. No wonder the woman wanted to return to her family in France.

"Did Sir Tobias and his wife not have a home in London?" Jenny asked. "I only wonder since I am sure she would be more at ease surrounded by the social engagements open to a widow in the city, as opposed to the intense isolation she must feel here in the country."

She glanced at her mother. "Not meaning any disrespect for my dear mother, of course."

Lady Lucien Blackwood drew herself up tall. "No disrespect taken at all, dear. If I didn't have you three girls with me, I cannot imagine how I would have endured this past year."

The Blackwood women all shared a moment of mutual admiration until Simon coughed and spoke.

"I'm certain it was difficult nonetheless, to leave behind your home in London for good."

Anne nodded. "Yes, my lord, it was. I have many happy memories there, but I am also extremely grateful that we had a place to come to here. And I am even more grateful that we shall be returning to London by your munificence. I hope you will not mind if I accompany my daughters."

"Of course not. My home in London has ample room for all of you, including Miss Eleanor and Miss Blackwood should they choose to accompany you."

Jenny remembered her conversation with him on this very subject. Was he trying to get rid of her for the many months of a season? How would she earn any income for her family if she were in London? Moreover, if she didn't take part in the Season, what would she do with her days? No, the idea of going to London was not palatable at all. She would definitely be seen as securely on the shelf and, furthermore, entirely irrelevant to all society.

She shuddered.

"Do you feel a draft, Miss Blackwood?"

His question indicated that Simon had been scrutinizing her carefully.

"No, my lord."

Before they could make any further conversation, the first course was served.

Hours later, they were full of fish and fowl and sweet warm treacle pudding. There was no man to retire with Simon to his smoking room for port and cigars, and the ladies would feel foolish sitting drinking tea while waiting for him to return alone. Instead, the evening was declared a great success, and the Blackwoods donned their capes in the front hall.

After expressing his delight at their company, Simon turned to Jenny.

"Miss Blackwood, regarding the bookkeeping issues that you have recently uncovered, will you come tomorrow so we may discuss them in depth?"

Jenny was caught off guard by his request for her rapid return.

When she hesitated, he added, "Binkley informed me in a general fashion of some discrepancies you discovered, and I spent a goodly amount of time going over your summation. I appreciated it immensely. However, I need your skilled mathematical proficiency to explain in person what I am looking at in the ledgers."

Taking a deep breath, she tried to stave off any blush creeping into her cheeks. The sooner she and her family departed, the better. Elsewise, she feared that her mother would somehow guess that the last time Lord Lindsey summoned her to his manor, it had ended in a rather compromising situation in his garden.

"Certainly, my lord. I will be here at whatever time suits you."

Simon waved his hand nonchalantly. "Anytime you wish, Miss Blackwood. I will be here awaiting your arrival with anticipation."

With no greater anticipation than she would feel, of that Jenny was certain.

CHAPTER FIFTEEN

Simon knew he'd been rather wicked asking Jenny to return in front of her family, when she could hardly put up a fuss or start protesting over possible impropriety without insulting him. Practical Miss Blackwood couldn't, or wouldn't, insult him after he'd had them all there to dine.

On the one hand, he knew he should have invited one of her sisters to accompany her. However, if Jenny wanted to succeed in the professional world, she would have to swallow any squeamishness about meeting with gentlemen in their homes. After all, most of them would be too busy worrying over their finances rather than thinking inappropriate thoughts.

On the other hand, Simon knew it was a preposterous and highly dangerous idea. The only gentleman's home in which he could countenance the beguiling Jenny being unaccompanied was his own. And he certainly had some vastly improper thoughts running through his head— leading to some even more shocking feelings running through his body.

Sighing, he poured himself a healthy portion of port and retired to the parlor. He was starting to feel quite at home . . . being at home. Having the Blackwood family, delightful in every respect, dining with him had been easy. At no time had he felt the urge to yell or close his eyes or run.

Perhaps he was nearly back to his old self entirely.

Thanks to Genevieve Blackwood!

"THERE YOU ARE. AT last." He got to his feet and bowed slightly in greeting.

Jenny frowned at his words. Simon had distinctly told her that he didn't mind when she showed up. Thus, she'd been determined not to appear so eager as to arrive on his doorstep before taking her midday meal.

"Yes," she said, "here I am. I didn't expect you to be waiting in the library."

"No matter," he said. "I like it in here. I was always an avid reader. I'd nearly forgotten how much I missed the luxury of opening a book and flipping through its pages."

Staring down at the book in his hand, he seemed to drift off into his past.

"I spent a great deal of time going over stories while I was imprisoned, trying to recall details. Sometimes, I would have to go over a book many times before I could remember a character's name. In the end, it gave me something to do and kept me from going entirely insane."

"You're not the least bit insane," she assured him. She was going to ask him if he'd had a better night's sleep. However, by the ruffled appearance of his hair and the dark circles under his eyes, she knew he had not. Instead, she nodded at the book. "What are you reading now?"

Looking slightly sheepish, Simon shrugged. "No great literary work to improve my mind, I'm afraid." He held up the book and showed her the frontispiece with the title of *Captain Singleton*. "Just an adventure story."

"A good one," she said.

"You've read Defoe?" He appeared surprised. "I thought Archimedes would be more to your liking."

Jenny made a sour face. "Do you think me so dull, my lord, that I wouldn't like an adventure story?"

He didn't respond but merely raised a disapproving eyebrow.

"Do you think me so dull, *Simon*?" she repeated. "And you know it is entirely improper for me to call you that. Why, I've known husbands and wives who never use their spouse's first names."

He laughed. "I've known them, too, but I can't say I liked them."

She smiled. "True enough." How good to hear him engaging in light banter.

For her part, she wanted the type of relationship in which she felt comfortable proclaiming her husband's first name not only in private, but also in front of others. It was a wife's right to intimacy.

However, she and Lord Lindsey did not have that relationship, nor any such rights.

Looking around, Jenny saw the ledgers already opened and spread upon the large oval table. "I suppose we should get started."

He balanced the open book on the chair's thickly upholstered arm beside him.

"I suppose."

An hour later, she felt he had a sound grasp of the issues. On her part, she'd had to work hard to keep her focus on the numbers, something she'd never had a problem with before. Simon's nearness, the way he brushed her arm with his as he reached across her to turn a page. The way he leaned close to pore over an account. The way he smelled deliciously of the distinct Pears soap scent. Perfectly fresh, not sweet, not musky, simply clean.

"Jenny." He repeated her name, and she realized that she'd been leaning close sniffing him. *Oh dear.*

"Yes, my lord . . . Simon."

He grinned. "My lady Jenny," he teased. "I asked if you thought any of these were simply unfortunate errors, perhaps due to unqualified people making entries."

She hated to say this, particularly when a dead man could not defend himself.

"No. I do not. From what I understand, your cousin was adept at accounting, as you know. Or at least, your father believed him to be, and the lessening of recorded income started then."

Glancing into his blue eyes, Jenny wanted to be utterly clear.

"Since your cousin left for battle, certainly there have been careless, even sloppy, entries, but the sustained, diminishing of funds began while he was overseeing the ledgers. I'm sorry."

He shook his head. "There is nothing for which you should be sorry. I appreciate your trying to sort this mess out, regardless of how it got this way. I tried to speak with Maude the other day. I fear she has been avoiding me. Strange though."

"What is?"

Simon sat back and crossed his arms. "She hasn't gained from anything Tobias did, if indeed, he was siphoning off family income. Where is the missing revenue? Why did she have to sell her home, indeed a Devere holding that she should not have let go without permission from my father or me."

"You were not here," Jenny pointed out. "After your father's death, to whom should she have sought permission if she was in dire straits?"

"My uncle, I suppose, her father-in-law."

"Perhaps he did give her permission to sell Jonling Hall."

"I have sent him a letter asking as much. What's more, I still don't know who my neighbor is going to be."

Jenny felt heat creep into her face at the disgraceful scene that had unfolded on the hall's doorstep.

"What is it?" Simon narrowed his eyes. "Do you know something about the new owner that I do not?"

"No." She stopped. What could she say? "I did find myself passing by there, with my cousin."

Simon's own expression darkened.

"We learned nothing," she rushed on. "However, I must say, the servants were quite rude and protective of the residence."

"They were, were they?" He stood and stretched his arms overhead.

She gaped at the casual display of his physique, again reminding her of how she expected spouses to behave in front of one another. He continued to twist his torso this way and that, unnoticing of her observation.

Until he turned suddenly and caught her gaze.

"I think I should pay a visit to the hall," he said. "Would you like to accompany me?"

Recalling her last visit there and thinking of what the servant might say, she balked.

"I should be getting home."

"Nonsense. A quick carriage ride?" He waggled his eyebrows, taking her thoughts to their last time in his tilbury.

"Perhaps a stroll," Jenny suggested.

Beside her once more, Simon offered her his hand. Taking it, she let him draw her to her feet. He continued to hold on to her, staring down into her upturned face.

"In answer to the question I left hanging earlier, no, I do not consider you dull at all. Quite the opposite. I believe you to be adventurous and brave and even unconventional. All the while, remaining pragmatic. How do you do it?"

Rendered speechless, Jenny shook her head. *What could she say?*

Simon looked as if he might add something more. However, in the next instant, she thought he might simply lean down and kiss her.

Instead, after a long moment, the earl released her hand, stepped back, and gestured for her to precede him out of the room.

The very honest and utterly feminine Jenny admitted disappointment to herself. The practical Jenny knew it to be a narrow escape, indeed. Where would all these intimate encounters end?

SIMON THOUGHT HE'D MANEUVERED the situation well to end up taking a long unaccompanied walk with Genevieve Blackwood, although a covered carriage would have afforded the privacy they might both have enjoyed.

He was determined to find an opportunity for another one of their astonishingly sizzling kisses. He'd nearly done so in the library but thought it might scare her away from walking with him, and he was not ready to part company. Yet now, as he donned his coat and she picked up her reticule, kissing her was utmost in his mind once again. Each previous time, he had felt a punch of shock at how exciting it was to kiss her.

Truthfully, that surprised him. After all, he'd made love to women before, and it had not always progressed slowly from kissing to petting to carnal copulation. Depending on the woman, of course, each knew what they wanted out of the encounter and how far they were prepared to let him go. Despite the reputation of country girls, he'd found that the London set were far more likely to lift their skirts in a vacant room a mere closed door away from a ballroom full of dancers.

During more than one social season in Town, he'd had his share of furtive encounters with doe-eyed misses, sick of dancing, tired of teasing and being teased. They wanted to be kissed and touched. A couple expressed their desire to feel a man inside them, and Simon had been more than willing to fulfill their wishes.

Looking back, his actions were dangerous as hell. He could've been caught by any one of them if they'd wanted to trap him into marriage.

He took Jenny's arm in his. This woman had snared his attention and affection in a much more sublime way, by earning both.

The only sound for a few minutes was that of their footsteps crunching on the gravel which then fell nearly silent upon the dirt road beyond his estate. She had let him take her arm and tuck it against his side. It felt utterly correct to do so. He could imagine walking with her this way anywhere, perhaps strolling in Bath from his townhouse to the mineral spa, or enjoying the sights of Paris and Prague together, or entering Blessington's gorgeous home in London to show off his new wife.

His wife? Yes, that felt right, too.

"How is it that you cannot tell by a purchase agreement who has bought the hall?"

Simon nearly laughed. While his mind was floating ever more romantically toward wedded bliss, hers was focused on the practical matter at hand.

"I am sure if someone were to investigate properly, the name would be evident. However, Binkley was in no position to question Lady Devere."

The short silence indicated Jenny's disapproval of such lackadaisical handling of important affairs.

"I confess that I haven't had too much interest in what was happening beyond my chamber's four walls, as you know. Until quite recently."

Glancing down at her, he was rewarded with her upturned face and a sweet smile. She understood. What's more, Jenny seemed to hold him in no less regard for his failings. Her kindness and her trust in him bolstered his resolve to recover wholeheartedly and to improve. Every day. If only he could sleep without the cursed dreams.

By St. Nicholas's Day, they held the first large party. After that, people were in his house, it seemed, every weekend through Twelfth Night and its culminating ball of hundreds.

"There were many guests," he apologized.

"I usually held an abacus."

He barked out a laugh. "You didn't, did you?"

"No." Jenny smiled broadly at him, and her face was beyond beautiful. "I am joking. I can see no reason you would recall a plain, brown-haired girl in a—"

"A blue and green tartan!"

Her eyes widened. "Good God! You do remember."

"I do! It's just come to me. That could only have been you. You wore it more than one year. That's why you stood out."

She blushed. "I did. It was too big at first, then I grew into it and then out of it. I loved that dress. Perfectly warm at the coldest time of year."

"The second year I saw you in it, I thought to myself, I remember that little girl in a striking tartan last year. And the following year, I looked for you. Sure enough, in you came with your plaid dress and a little sister in tow."

She covered her face with both hands. "It never occurred to me anyone would notice."

"Why should it matter? You, Miss Practicality, were warm and happy." He took hold of her wrists and pulled her arms down. "Weren't you?"

"I was. My childhood was a very happy one. Was yours?"

His thoughts jumped to his mother, and he could see the instant Jenny realized that. His mother was not in even his earliest memories, as she'd passed before his third birthday.

"I'm sorry. I should not have asked you such. I know you lost Lady Devere when you were very young. I never saw her when I visited your home."

"I was three. And you can ask me anything. I am not nursing any deep sadness over my mother. Except to futilely wish I could have known her. Sadder for my father who loved her beyond anything."

This discussion was not going in the direction he wanted. Pressing Jenny against the tree suddenly, he imprisoned her with a hand on either side of her.

"And, no, before you ask, I am not overly traumatized by my father's death either. Yes, I wish to God I'd been here, but I know it wasn't my fault that I was not by his side. Besides, I spoke with Binkley about it after you and I talked. He said my father went so quickly as not to suffer. We can ask for no more than that, any of us."

"True enough," she murmured, looking delightfully distracted by the position he had her in.

"You and I are here now. That is all we can control at the moment."

"I can't say that I feel I can control anything since you have caged me at the four-hundred tree. Why?"

"Can you guess?"

CHAPTER SIXTEEN

J enny felt her cheeks rouge over instantly, and then saw his answering devilish grin.

Simon lowered his head, keeping eye contact until the last moment when her lids drifted closed precisely as his lips claimed hers.

"Mm," she murmured against his lips. How she loved kissing this man! The delectable feelings that pulsed through her entire body when his mouth contacted hers were a marvelous sensation. Why, she could be happy for hours simply standing in his embrace and kissing him. As long as no spiders or other creepy crawlies descended the tree to investigate.

She shuddered, causing him to lift his head.

"Are you cold?"

"No." She licked her lips, watching his glance dart to her mouth, following her movements. "I was thinking of bugs."

His lovely blue eyes rounded. "Pardon me?"

She giggled at his deflated look. "Oh no, my lord, the kiss was beyond delightful. It's only that I can easily envision what lives in this tree."

He swore under his breath. "Then this is the wrong place. For I would like to have your whole attention."

Before she could protest, he had taken her hand and was moving along at a quick pace back toward Belton's gate.

"Simon, are you cross with me?"

He glanced down at her but didn't slow his pace. "No, far from it. I merely want you to be comfortable. Let's go back to the garden where we were interrupted before. Lightning, as they say, rarely strikes twice, and I'm sure we will have it to ourselves."

Almost as soon as they passed through one of the arbors and ended up under overhanging boughs of a willow, he swept her into an embrace, lowered his mouth to hers, and soundly kissed her once again.

At his warm lips and firm thrusting tongue, not to mention his deft hands that seemed to be wandering her body, halting only to grasp her waist or—goodness!—grab her derriere, she shivered as before.

"Cold or insects?" he teased.

"Neither."

"Comfortable?" he asked.

"Extremely." Except that every nerve in her body seemed to be sizzling. She had to calm her mind and slow her heartbeat. What better way than with facts. "And they're not insects. I don't mind insects. You know, grasshoppers and butterflies, and the like. I just don't like spiders and other arachnids."

Simon was staring at her mouth but she didn't think he was listening to her. "May I kiss you again?"

"I think that's the first time you've asked my permission."

"Then I have been a rogue of the first order." His tone indicated he didn't care if he had been rather roguish.

"You may."

After another long kiss in which Jenny thought the world had entirely fallen away and left them on an intimate island of sensation, he raised his head again. She swayed toward him before she caught herself, opened her eyes, and regarded his face.

An expression she could not interpret crossed Simon's features.

"Jenny?"

His tone sounded serious and she matched it. "Yes?"

"I would like you to accompany me to my various holdings and get to the bottom of the income depletion."

She couldn't help taking a step back and out of his embrace. In fact, his unexpected words caused her feet to start walking again as if to escape such lunacy. He fell into step beside her as they wandered the garden path.

"First, that is impossible," she told him when she could find her words. "Second, why would you ask me of all people?"

He sighed, then ignoring her first point, he asked, "Who better than you?"

"Obviously a trained bookkeeper, a male one, or perhaps someone from London's detective force."

He chuckled. "I hardly think a detective is needed, and why would I need another bookkeeper? I have you, and you are entirely capable of sussing out whatever is amiss. We would be on the road a week. At the most, ten days."

Jenny stopped in her tracks. The earl had gone too far! Had he no care whatsoever for her reputation? Or did he believe her so loose for having let him kiss her, he thought she would let him do even more when they were away from the civility of their genteel country life?

"I could not possibly do such a thing, and you have leaped the boundaries of decency to ask it of me. You must go with Mr. Binkley."

Simon gave a short bark of a laugh. "So he can fetch my tea and port? Taking Binkley is pointless. He can't do what you can do. No one can. Not even me. I wouldn't have noticed or understood those errors if you hadn't explained them to me."

Aghast, Jenny persisted in dissuading him. "Since I did explain them to you, you can go to your estates and decide for yourself."

"I agree that I should go, accompanied by my overseer."

She breathed again. He was seeing sense. "Yes, precisely."

"That's settled, then." Simon sounded agreeable. "*You* shall be my overseer."

"What? No! I shall be looked upon as a freak—as a masculine female. An abhorrent creature at best."

The earl gave her a quick glance up and down that lingered upon her bosom and eventually settled upon her lips. "I can attest that you're a very feminine female."

She could see he was teasing her. Perhaps this whole notion of his was merely a jest.

"You know it is not possible. Not without a companion." She shouldn't have said that. It was still an outrageous idea. "Even then . . ."

"Would Binkley do as your companion?" Simon asked.

Jenny felt like screaming. "Of course not. That's even worse, my setting out on a trip with two men! Even with a female companion, it is absurd to go traipsing about the countryside as your overseer. And you know it."

"Why?" he asked, yet the smile playing about his attractive mouth showed her he knew exactly why. Clearly, he wanted her to blush. And blush she did.

"Improper beyond belief," she muttered and continued walking again until they came to the center of the fairy garden. There were tall larkspur in every shade of blue and purple with richly scented geraniums in large clusters, and everywhere grew beds of brilliantly colored pink phlox like rich floral carpets. The aroma of wisteria, which clung to trellises, perfumed the air. The entire effect was, indeed, as magical as a fairy.

Simon stood close. For a moment, they were both silent. She could see he was thinking, considering, hopefully coming to his senses.

"I do not wish to bring any shame upon you or embarrassment to your family," he said at last.

"Agreed." Jenny relaxed. Perhaps this had merely been a prank on his part.

Against all expectations, however, the Earl of Lindsey, suddenly dropped to his knees in front of her.

All the air instantly seemed to dissipate from Jenny's lungs, leaving her with no ability to take in more. If Simon didn't at that very instant start hunting for some lost article, perhaps his pocket watch, then she would know what he was about.

She could not be correct!

He took both her hands in his. Jenny gasped.

"I am quick to decide and quick to act. I know what is important in life, now more than ever. I have learned the hardest lesson on earth—that there is very little I can control. I lost my freedom and, more importantly, I lost people I loved."

Sounding thick with emotion, he paused before continuing, "I could do nothing. Neither for Tobias, nor for my father. I now know people are all that matter in one's life. Truly." He squeezed her hands gently. "We should live with people who make us happy and bring them happiness in return. You make me exceedingly happy."

"Simon," she whispered, not able to say more, feeling a lump of emotion like a plum pit in her throat.

"Genevieve," he continued, "I am asking you for your hand."

Dear God! The most unexpected phrase out of the earl's mouth, and it was the very mimic of Cousin Ned's. Except her name was correct on the earl's lips.

"Two proposals in one week!" she exclaimed before instantly regretting her thoughtless words yet unable to retrieve them. In the next moment, her legs felt wobbly. "I need to sit."

She half-stumbled to a wrought iron bench with fanciful scrollwork, sitting down with the weight of astonishment and uncertainty weighing heavily upon her.

Simon rose from his position with an oath of annoyance.

Instead of sitting beside her like a civilized gentleman, he circled the bench like a tiger about to pounce.

"Two proposals! What on earth are you talking about?"

"Sorry," she offered at once. "I am in no way equating the previous proposal to yours. I am simply astounded. The minute a girl puts her own person firmly upon the shelf, men become more insistent upon pulling her off it again. I should wonder that it doesn't become yet another coy tactic for the *ton*. Create a room at each ball designated 'the shelf' and see if the suitors don't flock there to conquer the as-yet unconquered."

"Most women are on the shelf due to some perception that they are undesirable," he protested, "whether fair or unjust. However, that is blatantly not the case with you. Yours was a shelving due to financial circumstances beyond your control."

He swore loudly yet again before coming to a standstill in front of her.

"Why are we discussing the bloody *ton* and wallflowers. I demand an explanation."

Hm. Simon Devere demanded, did he?

Her mind was still going in every possible direction, refusing to settle on the one important issue. He had asked her to marry him. Jenny slowed down the thought to see if it made any more sense. He. Had. Asked. Her! To. Marry. Him!

"Well?"

"The reason my cousin left abruptly was because I turned down *his* proposal. I knew he had feelings for me and had been trying to put him off for days. Once he declared himself and I refused, I knew he would leave in high dudgeon. And he did."

"Ha!" Simon exclaimed. "I knew it." Then he laughed, a genuine full laugh. "What a dunderhead! How could that puffy-faced, weak-willed maggot hope to win your affection if he wouldn't even help you rescue Thunder?"

Jenny shrugged slightly. "It would have made no difference even if he'd brought me an entire team of prize stallions."

The earl quieted and finally sat upon the bench beside her.

"I had no feelings for him," she explained.

He didn't speak for a moment. Then in a low voice, she heard him add, "That is understandable."

She couldn't help a quick giggle that slipped from her. Beyond nervous, Jenny desperately wanted to examine the feelings swirling inside her. She was flattered, appalled, somewhat insulted, and intrigued—all at once.

And curious.

"You would marry me in order to have a bookkeeper by your side?" It sounded as absurd as she thought it would

Simon smiled. "Well, I wouldn't marry merely any bookkeeper."

"This is not the time to be joking with me, my lord."

"No, perhaps not. However, I will confess that I think we will be, if I may say so, well matched. We converse easily, laugh often, and . . . ," he trailed off.

"And?" she prompted.

"And we have already discovered that we enjoy a certain passionate response to each other. Wouldn't you agree?"

She would definitely agree but not out loud. Besides, there was the delicate matter of his mean-spirited and quite definite words to his butler.

"I must tell you that I am entirely confounded by your proposal."

Simon frowned. "Really? Have I not made love to you nearly every time we are alone?"

Her face heated. In truth, he had. And she had let him. Moreover, her feelings for him had grown quickly from the concern one would feel for any suffering being to a genuine desire to help him heal.

Even more than that, his wellbeing now mattered to her. She enjoyed every moment with him except for when he suffered, and then she suffered, too.

However, there was the matter of his proclamation.

"Quite plainly, you said that you would not marry me even if I were the last woman on earth. What has changed in two weeks?"

It was the earl's turn to look confounded. "I never said such a thing. Where did you get the idea that I had?"

"I heard you with my own ears. You were speaking with Mr. Binkley, the same day that you offered to pay for a Season for my sisters."

Frowning a moment, Simon looked up at the sky, down at his lap, and then back into her eyes. At that point, recollection dawned on his face, smoothing the lines.

"I remember now. However, we were not discussing you. We were speaking of Maude Devere. It was after you first told me she'd moved in. I had questions for Binkley about the how's and the why's of it. My butler is of the opinion that Tobias's widow should not be at Belton."

Simon paused as he always did when discussing his cousin, his gaze becoming distant and distracted. Jenny understood that his keen mind took him back to the moment of Tobias's death. Sure enough, the earl shuddered slightly before refocusing on her.

"Binkley thinks, in his bourgeois way, that with Maude and the children living here, what with them all being practically my family, people will start to suggest I marry her."

He sighed. "There is a slight unseemliness to the arrangement, I suppose. At least one could conclude that, seeing as we are of an age and both without partners."

Jenny nodded. That made sense. A weight lifted off her shoulders and off of her heart. His words had been hurtful,

compliant in his arms, she was everything he'd ever hoped for. Yes, he'd done well. And now that he'd kissed her again and seen her off in her carriage with the promise of calling on her mother that evening, he had the far less pleasant task of hunting down Maude Devere.

When he could find her in none of the common rooms, he told Binkley to announce him at her private chambers. Feeling like David bearding the lion in his den, Simon entered behind Binkley while Maude was still deciding whether to see the earl or not, or more likely, she was thinking up another prevarication to keep him away. No one could have that many headaches!

He had a right to see her. After all, now that he had returned, she was living in his home by his inclination. Granting him an audience, or rather not granting one, was not a choice Simon felt like giving her. He wanted some answers.

She sat on a small salmon-colored settee with a newspaper on her lap. Her children, he noted, thinking of what Jenny had said, were nowhere to be seen. It seemed as good a time as any to talk.

"Thank you, Binkley. That will be all." Simon sent the butler on his way. If Maude was squeamish about being alone with him, then she could ring for her maid.

"What is the meaning of this?" Maude asked. She didn't stand but gave an indication of towering indignation nevertheless. Her French accent thickened with her unease.

"I didn't intend to alarm you, Lady Devere. I simply wish to speak with you regarding some affairs of my estate, and of course, the sale of Jonling Hall."

She paled, and Simon knew it was not going to be an easy discussion.

"I didn't know I shouldn't sell it, I swear to you. I thought it was entirely mine to do with as I pleased."

"Yet it was not."

She reared back as if he'd slapped her. "There is nothing that can be done now. Tobias should have told me that we held the hall only by your father's pleasure, and now yours."

"Yes, I suppose he should have. I have only your word that he didn't."

Now, he had brought forth her ire as her skin flushed. It was far preferable to pale skin and cowering eyes for he didn't like to think he was harrying a woman.

"Why would my father-in-law suggest I sell it if I didn't have the right?"

Simon was taken aback. Had his uncle truly counseled her to do such a thing? He had heard nothing yet from his missive to his father's younger brother, but he was starting to think he would have to take a trip to South Wingfield and speak directly to him. Meanwhile, he still needed answers.

"Where is the profit from the sale?"

"Profit?" She blinked at him, and he sensed her stalling.

"Yes, the earnings, the proceeds, the takings. You sold a dwelling that you had not paid for, nor had ever made payments on, therefore whatever Jonling Hall sold for would be pure profit. Where is that money?"

She glanced down at her lap. "Gone," she said, her voice low. "Mostly."

"Gone?"

"Yes, my lord. There were debts to pay."

"Debts? Whose? Yours, or are you going to attribute them conveniently to your husband whilst he is no longer here to deny or verify your words?"

"That is not my fault. I wish he were here more than anything else on earth. I certainly wish he had come back instead of . . ." She clasped a hand over her mouth.

Thankfully, Maude didn't complete the heinous statement. Simon had thought more than once how much better it would have been for everyone if Toby had, in fact, been the one to return. He had a family, an heir, a living father. The transition of the earldom from one side of the family to the other would have been quite simple.

Instead, Simon had returned to find he had no father to whom he could ask advice, and only someone else's widow and children. And he'd been mentally unstable for months. He couldn't hold Maude's words against her. If their situations were reversed, he would feel the same way.

But they weren't reversed. What's more, he was taking himself in hand and doing what he could to get back to the person he had been, and now, there was Genevieve Blackwood who made him want to live again. Because of her, life was once more extremely precious.

He nearly smiled thinking of his Jenny, except that would have been unkind to Maude.

"You know I am aggrieved over my cousin's death, and extremely sorry for your current circumstances." He took a few steps farther into the room. Then, although she didn't invite him to do so, he sat upon a very feminine wing chair opposite her. It might have come from the hall, or it might have been his mother's. He didn't recall.

"You have no money, no income. Tobias left you without any savings either?"

She nodded.

"Why would he do something so out of character? He always seemed responsible, even earnest in taking care of his family. He looked after my father's ledgers." Saying this, Simon kept a keen eye on her, and sure enough, she tightened her lips and looked away from him yet again.

Had Toby truly been stealing from the estate's coffers? If he had, where was the money?

"I cannot get any information out of you that you do not know. However, here is an easy question?"

She raised her gaze to his once more.

"Who purchased Jonling Hall?"

"I do not know, my lord. It was handled by my solicitor."

"Yet you told the new master's servants at the hall not to speak of their new master to anyone, not even to me. Why would you do that if you didn't know who he was?"

She opened and closed her mouth like a carp. He had her, thanks to Jenny.

"I don't know why you'd say such a thing," Maude finally said.

"Because it is the truth. I know it."

Silence. Long and unbroken. Until the lady began to cry.

Simon rolled his eyes. Clearly, she was expert at this—deny, deceive, and distract.

How long could she keep it up? He waited. She cried, then sobbed, then sniffled. He supposed all that performance would give her quite a headache.

When finally, she quieted, he said simply, "Give me the name of your solicitor."

Her wide eyes and her face now blotchy indicated they were back where they started.

"Lady Devere, I will not toss you out of my home because of Peter and Alice, as well as a sense of duty to my cousin. However, my patience will only go so far. I will not be made a fool of. You will tell me now your solicitor's name and how to reach him, or I will march you over to the hall and we will speak to the staff together."

After a moment's hesitation, she thrust the newspaper from her lap and stood. "Very well."

Oddly, she no longer seemed tearful. Stomping to a writing desk against the far wall, she yanked open the top drawer and withdrew a piece of paper. A quill sat in an inkwell upon the desk. Snatching this up, Maude dripped ink all over the paper as she scratched out a name before sanding the words and folding the note.

Returning to Simon, she held it out to him with little grace. "My lord."

He took the paper, fighting off the temptation to read it while in her presence. That show of mistrust would be too insulting for both of them.

"And you avow you do not know the owner of Jonling Hall and you know nothing of Tobias doing anything untoward regarding keeping the Devere accounts."

"I know nothing," she declared, lying through her teeth.

"Very well. I bid you good day." With that, Simon offered her a small bow of his head and left. Refraining from unfolding the page until he was in his own study, he did so as soon as he entered the room.

"Ballocks!"

Almost illegibly, she'd written, *Sir Agravain*.

"HE'S HERE!" ELEANOR YELLED from upstairs where she'd installed herself as lookout on Jenny's bed.

For some reason everyone around her seemed in an agitated state, while Jenny felt exceedingly calm. Everything had fallen into place and seemed precisely as it should. Her future and those of her sisters were secured, and all because she hadn't run in the opposite direction out of fear of the unknown. *Lord Despair* had turned out to be neither a madman nor one of Perrault's ogres, but a perfectly wonderful man.

Greeting him at the door, she experienced an overwhelming surge of affection. Whereas previously, she'd tempered her emotions when it came to Simon Devere, now Jenny gave them free rein and found they were strong and deep.

Hoping he felt the same, she smiled and gestured for him to enter.

"It's good to see you again," she offered and was answered with a broad grin.

"Yes," he agreed. "I know it has only been a few hours, but I found myself urging my horse to a faster gallop."

"Everyone is waiting for you on the back terrace. I hope you don't mind sitting outside. Also, we have only wine or sherry. Nothing stronger."

By the time she finished her short welcoming speech, they had walked the depth of the house and were stepping outside together. Her mother and Maggie were exactly as Jenny had left them when she'd scampered inside at hearing Eleanor's yell.

As the ladies started to rise, Simon hurried forth to take Lady Blackwood's hand. "Please, don't get up on my account."

Bowing briefly over Anne's knuckles, he then moved to Maggie, who immediately outstretched her hand and wiggled her fingers at him.

"Such a pleasure to see you again, Lord Lindsey."

Jenny had to hold back a chuckle at her sister playing the lady, as if men arriving and kissing her hand was a regular occurrence.

Still, she thought it dear of Simon to do it.

"And where is the third Blackwood sister?" he asked. "For I cannot begin until the whole family is present."

"Here I am," Eleanor said, rushing onto the terrace and practically skidding to a halt before dropping into a low curtsey in front of the earl.

"How is Thunder today, Miss Eleanor?" the earl asked her.

"We are keeping his eyes covered, my lord, as you instructed. And he seems calmer, I think. Your stable boy is very nice, too."

Jenny startled. This was the first she'd heard that Eleanor had noticed their temporary help. Exchanging a glance with her mother, Jenny wondered if she should send him back for a more surly one.

However, her youngest sister added, "And your horse, my lord, is most magnificent. I've never seen such a beautiful animal." And with Eleanor's tone being much more enthusiastic over Luster than over the boy, Jenny instantly relaxed.

Simon laughed softly. "I'm glad you approve. Will you sit with us?"

Once the ladies were all seated, Simon took up a position, standing between Lady Blackwood and Jenny.

"You may already know why I have come."

Indeed, Eleanor's giggles gave away what they all knew.

Simon continued, "I have asked Miss Blackwood for her hand in marriage, and she has graciously agreed to be my wife. The only blight on our happiness is that I didn't have the privilege of making the request to Baron Blackwood, nor get to meet the man who created such a lovely family."

Jenny's heart swelled with affection for the earl. How extraordinarily kind of him to bring her father into this proposal and to elevate Lucien Blackwood back to his status as cherished patriarch, rather than disgraced debtor.

A hush had fallen over her sisters, and her mother dabbed at her eyes with a handkerchief daintily pulled from its concealment in the sleeve of her gown.

The earl addressed Anne. "In the absence of your husband, Lady Blackwood, I hope you will see your way clear to allow me the honor of marrying your daughter. I vow to take care of her for the rest of my life."

Jenny felt tears prick her eyes. Although never having considered she needed to be taken care of, she appreciated Simon's sentiment. Moreover, it was the perfect declaration to make to her mother, who'd feared for her daughters' futures. Anne could be at ease, at least regarding her eldest.

"Where and when?" Maggie asked, breaking the serious tone and reverting to her less ladylike, more direct self.

Without hesitation, Simon answered, "At Belton Chapel and as soon as the banns have been read."

"Why such haste?" Again, Maggie being Maggie! Jenny tried to catch her eye to fix her with an admonishing look, but her sister managed to avoid her.

Simon stood from his bent position next to Lady Blackwood. Turning, he took hold of Jenny's hand and drew her to stand by his side.

"Firstly, because everyone important is right here." He gestured around the table. "Unless you wish to invite extended family from Baron Blackwood's northern relations. Cousin Ned, perhaps?"

Jenny laughed. "I think not."

Nodding, Simon continued, "We have no need of a large occasion, invaded by hordes of nosey inquisitors, all masquerading as well-wishers whose only motive is to poke through my house and gape at Lord Despair."

They were all silent at his use of the cruel moniker.

"It is no matter, ladies. Yes, I am aware of what I have been called. Yet I am not the same man I was when Miss Blackwood heard me moaning in my room. Am I?" He smiled at her, and she smiled back, mouthing the word *no*.

"Where was I? Yes, to the point of haste. I have only an uncle, whom I am certain will not be insulted by missing a few moments in the chapel and a wedding luncheon, especially as I've determined we will call on him during our wedding trip. Which leads me to the second reason for marrying sooner rather than later, because this delightful woman has an exceedingly good brain. In lieu of a frivolous honeymoon trek that accomplishes nothing, Miss Blackwood—by then, Lady Lindsey—and I shall tour the Devere holdings. Jenny is going to take a look at all the accounts."

"How romantic," Maggie muttered, and Eleanor giggled again while Anne tried to hush them both.

Taken aback, Simon looked doubtful for the first time. "Unless that displeases you," he said to Jenny, "in which case, we shall take a wedding trip to Paris first."

"No," she protested. "We don't want to go traipsing off to the continent while your estate is in disorder, do we?"

Glaring at Maggie for bringing romance into the perfectly acceptable marriage proposal and wedding plans, she squeezed Simon's hand encouragingly. After all, there would be room enough for romance and, she hoped, love later on. There was certainly already passion. Why not assume love would follow?

Embracing her practical nature, she saw no reason why they couldn't put the Devere house in order. "We will take the ledgers with us and see if we can't straighten out a few things."

Meanwhile, she was enjoying the feeling of Simon's fingers interlaced with her own ungloved hand. His warm skin against her only reminded her of what delights were to come. If she were to confess her innermost feelings, which she would not, she'd have to say she was already in love with Simon Devere.

However, as inexperienced as she was in the ways of desire, she wondered if she loved him because of the sensations he created in her body. Or, rather, if he made her feel so tingly because she already loved him.

As long as she was marrying him and getting to explore all these new tantalizing feelings, she could not care a whit.

"A toast," Lady Blackwood said.

They all reached for a glass of wine, including Eleanor.

Standing, Anne raised her glass. "To the newest member of our family." She nodded to the earl, then smiled at her daughter. "And to a long and happy marriage for the Earl and soon-to-be Countess of Belton."

Jenny's heart skipped a beat. How strange to hear herself called Countess. What a day it had been! Looking at her beloved family, she could only hope for similar happiness for her sisters.

SPENDING NOT EVEN A single night in her new home, Jenny looked longingly at Belton Manor as it disappeared from sight through the rear window of their coach. She had married Simon that morning, two weeks to the day after the banns, with only her family, Maude Devere's children, and both their households' servants filling the pews.

Now, changed from her new gown of peach silk, purchased and altered in Nottingham specially for her wedding, into a rich, blue wool travelling gown, Jenny glanced at her new husband. *Her husband!*

Simon was as dashing in his travelling clothes as he had been in the chapel, in slate gray with a white ascot.

An early celebratory feast, replete with one of Cook's enormous almond and fruit cakes infused with brandy, had left Jenny feeling full and lethargic. Ensconced in the earl's luxurious clarence, they would not stop until they reached the market town of Wirksworth. Their first night as husband and wife would be spent in a small country manor that had been in the Devere family for generations.

Simon promised the start of their journey, at least, would be like a traditional wedding trip. Moreover, each night would be like a honeymoon, he'd added in a low tone for her ears only as they left their well-wishers behind.

"What has you smiling so delightfully?" he asked her as the horses picked up the pace.

Jenny blinked at him. She could hardly confess it was the idea of going to bed with him that night. However, the more she'd read from *Aristotle's Masterpiece* during the days between their engagement and the marriage ceremony, the more curious and excited she'd become. If done correctly, she read, the act of copulation could be very enjoyable. Moreover, she had a feeling, simply from how wonderfully Simon kissed her, her husband would make love quite skillfully enough for both of them to enjoy it.

"When are we stopping?"

His eyes widened, and she knew in an instant he was aware of where her thoughts had taken her. In the next moment, his handsome mouth stretched slowly into a slightly lopsided grin. He crossed to her side of the carriage and sat close, draping his arm behind her.

Simon encased her in warmth and affection, and as his free hand touched her cheek, turning her face toward him, her entire body began to tingle.

"Mayhap we don't have to wait until we stop for the night to begin our honeymoon."

Her face heated. "Here?" she asked, glancing nervously around the interior.

True, the carriage was plush and spacious. However, the book had indicated they needed a few items for successful lovemaking. Hen eggs, almonds, and parsnips would cause Simon's "yard" to rise to the occasion. And surely, she needed space to recline in the correct position to receive him.

On the other hand, the manual indicated simply by engaging in the act that occupied her thoughts, she and Simon would feel better in every way, in mind and body. It sounded like a cure-all.

But here, in his carriage?

CHAPTER EIGHTEEN

"I think I would prefer our first time to be rather more comfortable," Simon admitted before Jenny could express her own doubts. "Especially for your sake. However, there is nothing to stop us enjoying ourselves for the next few hours."

With that, he leaned down and kissed her. Immediately, his hand dropped from her cheek to the underswell of her breasts, palming one in his large hand.

She nearly squeaked against his mouth at his bold touch.

At his tongue's insistence, she opened her lips and let him inside. Long moments passed—how much time, she had no idea—during which he kissed her and fondled her gently while she tried to touch him anywhere she could through his traveling clothes. Heat pooled unbearably in her lower regions.

Realizing she was squirming with frustration, Jenny broke their kiss, breathed deeply, and asked, "How long do you think it will be before we arrive at Wirksworth?"

Simon chuckled. "I am rethinking the idea of comfort, too, my lady. Perhaps if you lifted your skirts and sat upon my lap."

Her face heated even more furiously.

"You still blush, sweet Genevieve, even as my wife. I like that."

"The daylight," she murmured.

He sighed, and reaching past her, deftly attached the shade, then did the same on his side as well as the front. They were plunged into near utter darkness.

"What think you?"

She thought this was the strangest situation. Yes, she wanted him and wanted to experience everything she'd read about. However, she was still somewhat frightened. Not to mention shy. And his coachman was a mere foot away in the front and a footman in the back. No doubt they could hear every word and everything else, too, such as a moan or a scream. And what if a horse threw its shoe at precisely the wrong moment, causing the carriage to reel wildly and one of them got hurt?

Yanking her shade back down, she let the lovely brocade fabric hang, flapping nearly to the floor.

"I think I am too practical for my own good."

He tilted his head in query.

"I'm sorry, my lord. My mind is attending to the situation at hand, to the men nearby, even to the potential for you or I to be injured."

At his expression, she added, "Do not laugh at me."

"Never," he said, yet he appeared to be holding back from doing exactly that. "Dearest Jenny, I dare say there is nothing unusual about your reticence. I also believe after some experience, you shall come to enjoy engaging in our marital rights even here in our carriage, as much as elsewhere. For now, let's simply anticipate the evening before us."

With that, he pulled her to his side and leaned his chin upon the top of her head.

"I for one will do precisely that until the moment I can be alone with you."

Grateful for his understanding, Jenny relaxed against him. After a moment, she asked a question about his childhood, and they spent pleasurable hours talking before she drifted off to sleep.

The carriage coming to a halt awakened her. She found her head upon his shoulder and her hands clasping his lapels, with his arms around her.

Feeling wool-headed, she sat up. "I must have drifted off."

"You did. As did I, until a gentle beaver began gnawing wood close by."

She looked up at him, then realization dawned on her. Gasping, she covered her mouth with her hand. "I snore?"

"You do. Charmingly in fact."

How could he find such an unladylike habit to be charming?

"In any case," he added, "we have arrived."

At that moment, the footman opened the door and helped her down the leather-clad folding steps into the dim light of a warm evening.

Oh, but it was lovely to stand and stretch, even if she was on display upon the gravel drive of Hopton House. Updated from a once-simple fieldstone dwelling to an elegant three-bay residence, at the moment, Jenny cared not what the house was like, as long as she was on solid ground and standing straight.

Watching Simon exit the carriage and raise his long arms overhead, she hoped he would be willing to take a refreshing walk after they greeted his staff.

THAT NIGHT, THEY DINED on a meal of minced beef with egg garnish, glazed carrots, and pureed cauliflower. The eggs, Jenny knew, were the cook's way of stimulating her fertility.

Glancing at her new husband as she swallowed a delicious morsel, her gaze caught his, revealing all the tamped down desire shining fiercely in his eyes.

"You take my breath away," Simon told her.

"As do you," she confessed.

In moments, they were mounting the main stairs to their bedroom. As soon as he closed the door behind them, he took her in his arms.

"You were quite right in the carriage. This is how I want us to enjoy each other, where I can strip you completely and lay you across that decadently thick mattress."

Her heartbeat drummed at his words, and she looked toward the bed, which was already turned down and did seem about six times the normal thickness. A small fire crackled in the hearth to warm the room even though it was late summer. No doubt the staff had taken into account they would be quickly unclothed. There was a decanter of claret on the bedside table and two glasses. Everything was perfect.

"May I help you undress?" Simon asked, his hands already roaming over her back and up her sides.

"Yes, please." Was her voice so husky? She coughed slightly to clear it. "If I may do the same for you."

As if unwrapping presents at Christmas, they took turns. Her spencer jacket, his cravat, her travelling gown, his waistcoat and suspenders. They paused, each to remove their footwear, her satin pumps, his boots.

Standing in her undergarments, Jenny felt on the verge of great change. In a moment, a man would see her bare for the first time, and she, in turn, would see her first naked man.

She would never be the same after, could she?

Simon unbuttoned the fall of his trousers and dropped them. Instead of being bare underneath as she'd expected, he faced her in a pair of short drawers. Bending down, he slipped his knee-high stockings down his calves.

Jenny noted with satisfaction he had put on enough weight in the passing weeks to no longer look the part of an underfed captive.

"Your turn," he prompted, when she remained frozen. "Maybe this will help," he added, blowing out half of the many candles that were dotted around their bedroom. "I think the staff got carried away with romance."

A nervous laugh escaped her as she undid her corset with practiced hands and let the garment drop, followed by her waist-to-ankle petticoat. Then, she reached up under her shift and untied the ribbons of her stockings before undoing her garter.

"May I?" he asked.

Nodding, she pointed the toes of her right foot toward him, allowing him access under her shift. As he slid the stocking down her leg, he softly, sensually caressed her from thigh to ankle. Her knees wobbled, and she grabbed for one of the bedposts before holding out her left foot and inviting him to do the same again.

"Nearly done," Jenny muttered, taking the hem of her shift in her hands.

"Let me," he said, approaching her and pulling her into his strong arms. However, instead of removing the last barrier on her body, Simon kissed her thoroughly until she felt her toes curl into the thickly woven carpet.

The pulsing heat returned, causing areas of her body to throb, chasing away any fears until she was more than ready for him to claim her as his own. When he started to tug at the hem of her chemise, she raised her arms to assist him.

In an instant, Simon had whisked the white cotton over her head and tossed it with the rest of their clothes upon the low divan.

Taking her hands, he held her away from him and looked down, appearing to feast with his eyes.

"You are magnificent, a diamond of the first water."

His words warded off the blush that had threatened her cheeks, and for once in her life, Jenny merely accepted the attention without embarrassment. After all, under his worshiping gaze, how could she be embarrassed? She felt like a queen.

Clearly, he liked what he saw. And exactly as *Aristotle's Masterpiece* had predicted, Simon's yard rose to its duty, tenting the front of his drawers.

Boldly, she stepped forward and tugged at the small satin drawstring bow, releasing his last undergarment, which slid down his muscular legs.

"Oh," was all she said. "You are the one who is magnificent. Truly."

And those were the last words she spoke as he smiled, drew her to the bed, and proceeded to make love to her.

Even without parsnips, he seemed quite up to the task. More than once, in fact.

After the second culmination, lying entwined with her husband, still breathing heavily and feeling a sated heaviness to her limbs, Jenny knew she could stay awake hardly a moment longer. She had to tell him what she'd discovered between his taking her virginity and both of them spending—first her, with an astonished cry, followed by his guttural groan as he pumped into her tight sheath.

"Simon."

He ran a fingertip between her breasts. "Yes, Genevieve."

She giggled at her own name, giddy with happiness, still marveling at the unimagined pleasure.

"I love you."

She heard his breath catch.

For a moment, he said nothing.

And then she heard the sweetest response, his voice choked with emotion.

"I love you, too, wife."

IN HER DREAM, JENNY walked in a field of wildflowers, the sun was shining brightly, and she was warm and happy. Simon was on the other side of the pasture beckoning her. Crossing beneath a copse of drooping willows, to Jenny's horror, the snaky branches seemed to tangle around her slender neck and tighten. The more she struggled to escape, the tighter they became.

"Simon," she screamed to him for help. "Simon!"

Hearing his answering yell, she awakened at once. However, the pain at her throat did not diminish. Fighting for air, she reached up to feel her husband's hands at her throat. Too strong for her to break his hold, his grip was not loosening, and she hadn't the breath to scream again.

Clawing at the backs of his hands as blackness seeped into the edges of her vision, she then pummeled him with her fists, and finally, as her last strength left her, she managed to slap his cheeks.

All at once, the tension in his hands ceased, although for a moment, Simon still didn't release her.

"Jenny," he said, his voice groggy and confused. "What is happening?"

She could only groan in response. Realizing their situation, he pulled his hands away from her as if scalded.

"What in the hell?" he swore, sitting up and grabbing a flint to light a bedside candle.

She didn't move but simply remained lying on her back, her own hands pressed against her aching neck. Stunned terror still trembled through her.

As Simon realized what he'd done, a moan of anguish escaped him. When he reached for her, she flinched without meaning to, and he swore again. As he slowly moved toward her again, however, she let him take her in his arms, smoothing her hair behind her shoulders before propping the pillows up for her to lean on.

"Dear God, I don't understand," he ground out.

Swallowing painfully, she coughed to clear her throat. Snatching up a glass, he poured her some wine. Gratefully, she sipped at it, keeping one hand on her tender neck.

"You didn't mean to do it," she whispered at last. "I could tell. You were completely asleep."

Gingerly, he lay his hand on the counterpane where it covered her lap.

"Are you hurt?"

Yes. "No," she assured him. "You stopped nearly as soon as I awakened."

Silence. Then he rose from the bed, unmindful of his nakedness. "This is not good."

"I'm sure you were having a nightmare. It isn't your fault."

"Fault, be damned. What matter fault if you are hurt?"

"I will be fine. I *am* fine." She hoped the painful ache would go away soon.

Pacing in front of the bed, Simon was not growing calmer.

"I was having the same dream of Burma. I've awakened before with all the bedclothes not only in disarray but on the floor as if I had been violent. I've even found *myself* on the floor, as I told you once, yet with no memory of falling out of bed. Yet I never thought I could do something so brutal as try to strangle you. It's madness. It goes against the natural order of how I should protect you."

Setting her wine glass on the bedside table, she crawled to the end of the bed.

"Simon, please. Do not berate yourself. You are neither mad, nor unnatural. Simply troubled. I'm sure it won't happen again."

Reaching her arms toward him, ignoring her own unclothed state, she hoped he would settle down and return to the bed. Moving into her embrace, he held her, her check pressed against his warm body.

"Everything is fine," she soothed. "Come back to bed."

He stiffened. "No. Not tonight, Jenny. I can't."

"Please."

"I will sit in the chair by the fire. I can sleep there as easily, and I can also be assured I won't harm you."

"Tsk, you won't—"

"I already did!" He released her. "Let me do what I must. I will watch over you until you fall asleep. Come now," he circled the bed and patted her pillow. "Try to go back to sleep."

Feeling miserable at the unthinkable turn of events, she settled her head on the pillow, wishing her husband's side of the bed were not empty and already growing cold.

"Take a blanket off the bed," she insisted as Simon tucked her in.

"Yes, wife." He smoothed her hair off the side of her face and leaned down to kiss her. "I'm so very sorry," he whispered.

"I know."

In the next moment, he blew out the candle and plunged the room back into the pre-dawn darkness.

CHAPTER NINETEEN

When Jenny awakened the next morning, it took her a moment to remember. Sure enough, Simon was not in the bed, but he also was not in the chair. She was alone. Hurrying with her toilette, merely washing her face, using her tooth powders, and brushing her hair before twisting it into an easy chignon, she then dressed in traveling clothes, the easiest to fasten by herself.

After a quick stop at the water closet, she descended to the main floor and went to the dining room in search of her husband. It was empty. As was the parlor, the drawing room, and the conservatory, and every other room she searched. Where was that man?

Not knowing enough about her surroundings to risk venturing outdoors alone, she instead found the kitchen by following her nose toward the smell of coffee and sausages.

Simon was not there, but a round woman with a ruddy face was seated on a stool drinking coffee.

She jumped up as Jenny entered.

"Oh dear, it's the countess," the cook uttered before bending into a low curtsey from which Jenny feared the woman might not easily straighten. "You should have rung the bell, my lady."

"Sorry to bother you," Jenny said, causing the cook's eyes to bulge at her apology. "I smelled the coffee, and also, I'm looking for Lord Lindsey."

"Let me pour you a cup, dear." The woman was staring at her now with unfeigned interest. "I did see his lordship a couple hours ago. He took his coffee in the parlor, and I believe he went out riding, my lady."

The cook set the cup and saucer on a tray, her gaze still fixed upon her new mistress. "We don't keep a big staff here, my lady, unless someone from the family is staying for an extended period, if you see what I mean. I do apologize for not sending a maid to your room."

Jenny wondered if she could take the coffee cup off the tray, but had a feeling that would not make the woman happy.

"No matter. I appreciated the chance to sleep in." How was she going to get the hot beverage before it was stone cold?

They stared at each other. Finally, the cook said, "Will you take your coffee in the dining room or the parlor, my lady?"

Jenny sighed. "I suppose the dining room, if you please." Then, realizing she was hungry after her night of being turned from maiden to wife, not to mention the startling event afterward, she asked, "And I would like eggs and sausage."

At the door, she glanced back. "Perhaps a couple pieces of toast, too. With preserves if you have any, or honey will do."

At that moment, the maid entered and froze stock-still upon seeing Jenny in the kitchen.

"Oh, dear," she said, curtseying even lower and more agilely than the rotund cook. "My lady." She also stared at Jenny as if she had a squirrel on her head.

"Tilda, take her ladyship's coffee to the dining room and come back for her breakfast."

Thus, Jenny found herself being trailed by a maidservant carrying a large silver tray with only her saucer and cup of coffee. Once in the dining room, she took a seat on one side of a long redwood table with gold inlay, waiting while the girl set down her beverage before her.

"Sugar, my lady?"

"Yes, please," Jenny said, and the maid grabbed a glass bowl from the sideboard and set it down before her with a spoon. "I'll go grab your breakfast, my lady." The girl backed out of the room, keeping her eyes fixed on Jenny the entire time until she turned and ran down the hallway.

Instead of the girl's light tread, however, it was Hessians she heard upon the floor, and suddenly, there was her new husband in the doorway.

Unable to keep from smiling, Jenny stood and held her hands out to him.

To her dismay, his expression went from pleasant to thunderous in an instant, and he strode over to her.

"Bloody hell!" he exclaimed, peering closely at her neck. "I should send for a doctor."

With her hands fluttering up to her neck, Jenny shook her head. "Whatever for?"

"Don't you know? Can you not feel your own injuries?"

"My *injuries*?" Glancing around the room, she spied a looking glass artfully placed behind crystal decanters in one corner, causing the light to sparkle wildly and brighten the space.

Hurrying toward it, she hardly dared to look at herself. When she did, she gasped.

Craning her head to the right and left, she was amazed at how bruised her neck was, with red patches and some already deep purple. Anyone could see she'd been nearly strangled to death. Why, there were even fingerprints. Oh dear! What must the staff think? No wonder they had stared.

"Honestly, it is a little tender," she admitted, turning to Simon, whose stricken visage tugged at her heart, "but I certainly don't need a physician. What could he do? Perhaps your cook has some arnica infusion."

Just then, the maid returned, stopping short at the sight of the earl. An expression of fright crossed her face, and Jenny wished she had the words to protect him. What could she say? She'd become tangled in the bed clothing?

Better to simply ignore the bruising and ignore the staring.

"My breakfast?" she prompted the girl, who gave Simon a wide berth and set down the tray overflowing with food.

"Will you eat with me, my lord?"

"I have no appetite," he said tightly.

Jenny decided she'd ignore him as well. Simply let everything return to normal.

"That will be all then," she said to the maid. What was her name? "Tilda, isn't it?"

"Yes, my lady." The girl curtsied again and left, her glance going from her new mistress's colorful neck to her lord's fearsome expression, until she rounded the corner.

Jenny sat down and finally sipped her coffee. Lukewarm but still delightful. She picked up her silverware and tucked into the hearty breakfast. However, as she chewed and swallowed the first bite of juicy sausage, she halted. Chewing was easy but the swallowing was a painful process, made worse by her attempting to hide how difficult it was.

Of course, Simon's scrutiny saw everything. "I knew it. You are injured. You cannot even eat."

"Of course I can," Jenny said, proving she could by taking another bite. Chewing as long as she could, at last, she had to swallow. Coughing, she took another sip of coffee. That went down fairly easily, at least.

Simon yanked so hard on the bell pull, Jenny feared it would come away in his hand. In mere moments, Tilda had returned.

236

"Ask your cook if she has any arnica. And we will need only soup for the rest of the day." He looked at Jenny again as she pushed the eggs around her plate. "Most probably for tomorrow's breakfast, too," he muttered after the maid had disappeared.

"Breakfast?" she exclaimed. "I thought we were going to the first of your holdings today."

Simon sat in the chair beside her. "We should wait until you heal."

"Nonsense," she uttered. "Let us forget this matter and continue our journey. I have no intention of hiding out here."

He sighed and grabbed a piece of toast from her plate.

"Very well. However, you must wear something high-necked or wrap a shawl around the mess I made of your lovely skin."

"If only I could wear a cravat." She laughed.

He didn't even smile. "There is nothing humorous about this."

"Perhaps not. Yet it is not the end of the world either."

Deciding she'd better buck up before her new husband decided to put her on bedrest, Jenny forced the fluffy eggs down her aching throat, swallowed the last of the coffee, and rose to her feet.

"I will check on the arnica and then dress in such a way no one else will even notice, I promise."

With her husband's distraught expression haunting her, Jenny left to prepare for her first trial as an overseer.

SIMON WANTED TO BREAK something. Something valuable, as if breaking something expensive he could pay for would absolve his sins. Glancing around at the modest furnishings, he noted there wasn't a vase that looked expensive enough to bother hurling across the room.

However, the blasted mirror in which Jenny had seen her injured neck, he could cheerfully toss onto the floor and crush beneath his boots.

He didn't do anything of the kind, of course. He'd never been a violent man. Thus, waking up with his hands choking the life out of his wife—the kindest, most helpful person he'd ever known—had shaken him to his core.

And mere hours after having made love to her, the most intense, fulfilling sexual encounter he'd ever experienced. His practical Jenny was also fiercely passionate. He'd deflowered her, and then he'd nearly snuffed out her vitality.

Nauseated by his thoughts, his stomach churning, Simon knew he was going to be sick. A delayed reaction, he considered, as he ran out the back door into the garden and lost the toast he'd only just ingested.

That's what came of tamping down the terror of what he'd nearly done. Moreover, he'd been holding that fear in check ever since his new bride had gone back to sleep trustingly while, filled with horror, he'd sat in the chair staring into the darkness.

It had been too easy to think himself healed.

Wiping a handkerchief across his mouth, Simon stared up at their bedroom window. With Jenny by his side, he'd known a smug satisfaction that everything would be well. Indeed, he'd thought he had conquered the demons inside him. At last! He would be utterly *normal* again. And, of course, he had looked forward to their wedding night with particular glee after a long period of abstinence.

Bah! What a fool! Perhaps he was cursed.

Unexpectedly, Jenny appeared at the window, looking out over the garden and his breath caught in his throat. He saw the moment when she spied him. A smile lit her lovely face and she held up a hand with a slight wave.

He waved back. He would do anything to protect her, even from himself.

OH DEAR, WAS SIMON brooding again? That was definitely not good for him. Jenny had seen him in the garden looking pensive before they left. Now, he leaned his head back in the carriage but didn't look peaceful.

Being ever practical, she knew there was no solution her husband could come up with in his own mind. Therefore, spending long minutes going over the events of the previous night would do nothing but upset him.

She tapped his knee to get his attention. "Tell me more about this mill."

And she drew him out of his thoughts with question upon question about the mill manager, George Marley, how well Simon knew him, how long the Deveres had owned it, and more. Until they arrived in Derbytown.

It was an impressive operation, grinding all manner of grain for the surrounding townships, as well as a large baking company that sold in Wirksworth.

The mill manager seemed neither nervous nor guilty when Jenny and Simon were shown into his office.

"Lord Devere," Mr. Marley said rising from his desk and bowing. "I had no idea you were visiting."

In truth, they had told no one, in case they needed to take advantage of the element of surprise.

"It's Lindsey now. May I introduce to you my wife, Lady Lindsey."

"You don't say? Wonderful! I'm honored, my lady." Marley bowed again in her direction, then he became all business. "I doubt you came all this way to show off your lovely countess to me, my lord. Is there a problem?"

"Mayhap," Simon said. "However, my wife is more suited to the task of explaining the issue."

"You don't say!" Marley repeated, taking another appraising look at Jenny, glancing over the shawl wrapped around her neck like a man's cravat.

Simon gestured with a wave of his hand to his footman who waited by the door with the appropriate ledger. Bringing it forward, he deposited it on Marley's desk.

"I am good with numbers," Jenny blurted, grateful Simon nodded in agreement.

"My wife has found some discrepancies and some oddities. I am sure you will be able to explain these. Meanwhile, I'll take a look around, if you don't mind. I'm sure one of your men can show me."

They'd agreed ahead of time that the footman would stay with her and Simon would look around as he used to do, taking the measure of the operation. Marley's raised eyebrows did not deter them from the plan, and in a moment, Jenny was seated opposite the mill manager.

She got right to it, flipping open a ledger to a marked page and pointing out the time a few years back when the payments no longer were entered in the household accounts.

Marley frowned. "That's been years! Why hasn't anyone asked before?"

"You know his lordship was away," she said delicately. "As was his cousin, Sir Tobias."

At the mention of Tobias, Marley's expression turned grave. "Shame about that one. Terrible thing to leave a widow and children."

"Yes," she agreed.

"Well, my lady, I can show you precisely what the profits are on a monthly basis and how much we've sent to the estate quarterly, if you understand my meaning."

"Yes, I assure you, I quite understand." Amazing, Jenny thought, that the man had accepted the situation as easily as he had.

Marley had a shelf full of ledgers behind him. Pushing his spectacles up his nose, he reached the shelf without standing and pulled the closest leather-bound book in his direction.

"The very last one is this figure." He tapped a somewhat dirty fingernail upon a handsome sum of money.

Jenny nodded. "That's what I was expecting, given the amount from about six years back."

"Depending on the time of year, that's about what his lordship always receives for the months when we're grinding." He flipped to the front of the ledger and ran his finger down a handwritten note tucked inside.

"Payment goes to an H. Keeble in London, as directed."

"Pardon?"

"Is there something wrong, my lady?"

"I have never heard of this person."

Marley frowned, then he shrugged. "He's been receiving the payments these last six years.

"I suppose that was upon Sir Tobias Devere's edict?"

"Yes, my lady. Exactly."

Poor Simon. How distraught the news of his cousin's deceit would make him. It was not simply the loss of the funds, but the betrayal by one whom Simon had loved and trusted.

NOT TEN MINUTES LATER, after Mr. Marley had escorted her to where Simon was discussing the fineness of the ground wheat with a worker, they were on their way.

"You've discovered something," he said at once.

"Unfortunately, yes, confirmation of perfidy."

Telling him where his income was going, she watched Simon's face cloud over. "Did you get this Keeble's address?"

She nodded.

"Perhaps he is the mysterious Sir Agravain."

Jenny frowned. "I beg your pardon? Why would King Arthur's villainous knight have anything to do with whoever was helping himself to the Devere fortune?

"Maude was less than forthcoming with the name of her solicitor. Yet I suppose it will be easy enough to determine if this man is one and the same."

"We are traveling away from London," she pointed out.

"For now."

IT WAS LESS THAN an hour's ride to the next stop, a bleach mill. The fumes were overwhelming, but Jenny found out the same information in short order. H. Keeble was collecting the income. After directing the mill manager that payments should no longer be sent to London but directly to Belton Park, they hurried on.

"Another hour to my uncle's," Simon told her after they'd stopped to stretch their legs at an inn and eat a late luncheon.

"Will you ask him if he knows anything about his son's . . . *um* . . . diversion of funds?"

He shrugged. "I don't know yet. Toby was fond of his father, and I imagine the man is still quite stricken with grief. How will he feel if I start interrogating him about my cousin's bookkeeping skills?"

"Will we spend the night there?"

Simon eyed her thoughtfully, his glance predictably going to her well-covered neck.

"I was planning on it. We could take a room at an inn instead."

She considered. Either way, Jenny had the feeling they were going to have a strife-filled night unless she was extremely careful.

"Staying at your family's home in South Wingfield is perfectly acceptable to me. I'm sure your uncle will want to spend time with you," she said, hoping she was correct.

Alas, she wasn't. In the front hall, instead of Simon's uncle, the man's second wife, Lettie, awaited them, draped in a gown of black bombazine, signifying her mourning for her husband's son.

The woman's job, it seemed, was to admonish them for not giving enough notice in advance of their arrival. For although Simon had sent word two weeks earlier, apparently, it was considered bad form by Lettie's husband.

"My lord is most unhappy that you find us in such a state."

Truthfully, Jenny thought it would have taken far longer than a week or two to put the place in order. The tapestries looked dingy, the foyer floorboards were unwaxed, and the place held a general air of both neglect and paucity.

Even the butler's uniform was missing a button, and she could see his stocking through the worn toe of his shoe. If Jenny looked carefully, she had no doubt she'd be able to see his toe through his torn stocking, as well.

"We are family," Simon insisted, as if nothing they encountered could matter.

However, they spent the better part of an hour trying to enjoy a cup of watered-down sherry with the peevish mistress of the house while seated in a sadly furnished room with peeling wallpaper and one boarded up window pane. Moreover, there was a chip out of Jenny's drinking glass and something very uncomfortable poking up into her thigh from a hole in the sofa.

"We didn't want you to go to any trouble," Jenny added again when Lettie brought up for the umpteenth time how inconvenienced they were by the unexpected visit. Simon's uncle had still not appeared.

"With more warning," Lady Devere declared, "we might be eating a slightly better cut of meat tonight, and there'd be a grand pudding to top it off. We eat rather simply when we're on our own."

By the thinness of the woman, not to mention her hollowed cheeks, it appeared they were alone for many meals. And if two weeks were not enough to see they had a fitting evening meal, then Jenny doubted this woman had any business running a household.

"In any case, the maids have got your room ready," Lettie continued.

"Thank you for your welcome," Jenny insisted, despite feeling anything but.

Simon was oddly quiet, perhaps distracted by the black crepe draped everywhere, over mirrors and windows and doorways.

Jenny tried to see past the mourning decorations. With a little spit and polish, although less than a fifth the size of Belton, the house could be made quite hospitable.

"You have a lovely home," she lied, hoping to set the woman at ease over the joyless, rundown residence.

"Compared to Belton, it is a hovel," came gruff words from the doorway, as James Devere, styled as a lord by courtesy only, finally deigned to grace them with his presence. "Which is why I can't understand why you've come all the way here."

Simon stood at once and strode across the distance between them, arm outstretched in greeting.

Jenny's heart skipped a beat when for a moment it appeared as if her husband's uncle would not take the proffered hand. After a moment's hesitation, he did. She imagined a warm embrace would have been more fitting given the circumstances, but could tell instantly that would never happen. This man seemed as rigid and cold as her husband was yielding and warm.

He must be deeply grief-stricken over his son, she concluded.

"I came to introduce you to my countess, Lady Genevieve," Simon said, and the use of the title and her formal name gave her pause. Her husband was offended, or hurt, by the cold reception and clearly wanted to remind his uncle who they were, not some petty relations to be treated badly.

James Devere glanced toward her, raking her with his disinterested glance as she stood and curtsied. Jenny swallowed her intense feeling of dislike. *He is suffering from melancholia,* she reminded herself.

"You are the new bride." He said the last word between gritted teeth. "The woman who has captivated my nephew so quickly following his return."

Frowning, Jenny couldn't say why, but his words seemed insulting. What's more, his tone implied he couldn't for the life of him see why Simon had chosen her. Be that as it may, she decided to react with the respect the man deserved as the patriarch of her husband's family.

"I am pleased to meet you, my lord."

His response was a thinning of his lips and a low-murmured, *"Hmm."*

Oh, dear. This was not going as she'd hoped at all.

"I offer my condolences on the loss of your son," she added.

His head whipped up, his expression tightening as his gaze locked onto hers.

Lettie gasped audibly, and Jenny had to steel herself. Surely the man was about to let loose with a tirade.

Perhaps sensing the same, Simon came to her side and took her arm under his.

"I am truly sorry, Uncle, to be the one to bring back sad tidings. Toby was not only my cousin but also my beloved friend, as you know."

Bless him for taking the focus onto himself, when apparently, she'd committed a *faux pas* for bringing up the dead man.

James's mouth worked as if he was trying hard to get words out. In the end, he merely nodded to his nephew before turning to his wife.

"Is our meal ready?"

Lettie moved forward to her husband's side. "I'm certain it is."

And with that, they left the parlor for the dining room and an unfashionably early, utterly cheerless dinner, the long stretches of silence broken only by the scraping of the silverware upon the plates and an occasional remark from Lettie.

For his part, Simon tried to begin a conversation by describing the holdings they'd recently visited. This elicited nothing but a sour expression from his uncle whose stare remained fixated on his wine glass except when he was drinking from it.

Jenny remained silent, unable to think of what she could add to this unhappy occasion.

When, after a copious amount of wine, James Devere did at last speak, she couldn't help wishing he had remained silent.

"Since you had the good fortune to return from that cursed, useless war when my son did not, I thought you might have had the good sense to marry his widow."

CHAPTER TWENTY

Even as he said the words, Simon's uncle's gaze never lifted from the table.

"Seems as if it would've been damn convenient, what with a readymade family and all."

Lettie closed her eyes a moment, exactly in the instant Jenny felt hers go wide with the rudeness of the man's statement.

Across from her, Simon bristled, appearing to grow larger as he took in a deep breath.

"As it turned out, Uncle, I was lucky enough to find precisely the right woman for me." He offered her a smile that took the sting out of James Devere's words and warmed her to her toes.

"Well," was all their surly host said.

Clearly, Simon had had enough. "I think it high time the countess and I took to our chamber."

God, yes! She couldn't wait to get away from the taciturn, unwelcoming James Devere. Grief was an excuse only up to a point.

Poor Simon, she thought, *having merely this man as his last living relation!*

At her husband's nod, Jenny stood, waiting for his uncle to stand as well. He did not. Perhaps he was too far in his cups to recall his manners.

"Good night, Lady Devere," Jenny said to Lettie before turning to James Devere. "Good night, my lord."

"Hmm," he said.

In response, Simon bowed to Lettie, bid her good night, and ignored his uncle altogether.

As they reached the top of the stairs, her husband murmured in her ear, "That went well."

Jenny couldn't help the first giggle that escaped her. Her nervousness had built up to a bursting point. Now, it came in full-throated laughter that brought tears to her eyes.

At first, Simon seemed surprised, yet by the time they reached their room, he was laughing with her.

"After all," she said as they sat upon the bed holding onto each other, "if we can handle Ned in my family, we can handle James in yours."

He stroked her cheek.

"I did not like that my uncle insulted you."

"I didn't feel insulted. He doesn't even know me. He merely wanted to keep a connection to his son and expressed it badly."

Simon's thumb brushed over her lips, causing a delightful tingle to begin.

"How did you get to be so understanding, Lady Lindsey?"

He moved his hand and cupped the back of her head.

Locking gazes with him, she answered before all her thoughts were scattered by the kiss she knew was coming.

"Born this way, I suppose."

And then his mouth descended upon hers.

A little while later, she admitted, "I'm rather glad your uncle drove us from the dining room. I much prefer being alone with you."

"Agreed, wife." Pushing her back upon their bed, Simon's kiss deepened. She curled her fingers in his hair and opened her mouth to his.

However, when he would have trailed kisses from her jaw down her neck, he growled.

"Will you remove the shawl, please?"

Knowing this would ruin their romantic encounter, she sighed. "It's keeping me warm. Have you noticed our room is like ice? I think there is one tiny piece of coal in the fireplace."

"I will keep you warm."

Slowly doing as he asked, Jenny didn't need a mirror when she had her husband's wincing face to tell her how she looked.

"Christ! I should be whipped."

"Stop it," she ordered. "I'm sure the arnica helped. Undoubtedly, my neck will appear bruised for a few days."

"Your flesh is colored like a juggler's cap, purple, black, even green."

"Then let us go to bed and put the light out, then you don't have to look at it."

Still, Simon hesitated.

"I am asking you to come to bed with me and hold me in your arms."

His mouth twisted. "Unfair, wife. You know I cannot deny such a request when I've wanted to touch you all day."

More slowly than the night before, they made love. His hands upon her skin, stroking and teasing her, brought Jenny quickly to throbbing desire. His mouth left off kissing hers to perform wickedly delightful acts on her heated body. By the time he settled his hips between her thighs, she was nearly begging him to fill her.

It was perfect, and Jenny couldn't imagine how she'd gone without such sensations for the first two decades of her life. Nor how she could ever do without her strong, passionate husband ever again.

SIMON'S HEARTBEAT STARTED TO slow as he lay beside his luscious, soft wife. However, the satiated feeling dissipated as the minutes passed. Their lovemaking had been intense and sweet at the same time. Rather like Jenny. Moreover, each time he touched her naked body, each time he sunk into her, he loved her more.

For certainly, this was love causing his abject terror at the idea of falling asleep and possibly hurting her again.

Having decided the best course of action was to wait for her to drop off to sleep, then creep from the bed to the chair, he would spend this and every night away from her. For he knew precisely what would happen if a certain dream started. And it would start, as it had almost every night since his return.

Knowing he might hurt her the next time he touched her gnawed away at him, keeping him awake. When her breathing became deep and even and her body's movements stilled, then he left her safely to her slumbers.

JENNY AWAKENED TO SUNLIGHT and birds chirping and smiled, feeling like a princess. No, she corrected herself, she felt like a countess.

Glancing over to where her husband slept beside her, she frowned. *Gone!* He moved very quietly for a large man. She'd not heard or felt him rise from the bed.

Recalling the night before, she had planned to lie awake, keeping alert. If Simon began to move and thrash about, perhaps due to a disturbing dream, then she was going to go to the large, threadbare chair by the window.

However, after all the travelling and the meal—as well as the glorious lovemaking—she'd dropped off to sleep very quickly. And nothing bad had happened. So, she'd been correct. The events of the previous night had been an aberration. They had slept peacefully together.

Smiling to herself, she dressed quickly, making sure to apply more arnica from the pot Tilda had given her before wrapping a pretty, lightweight shawl around her neck.

Jenny found her husband in the dining room, breaking his fast with Lady Devere. His uncle was absent, perhaps simply sleeping in.

"I hope you slept well," Lettie said, as Simon pulled Jenny's chair out for her. "I'm sure if you'd given us more notice, we could have had the sheets aired longer and the carpets cleaned. Maybe the windows needed repointing," she trailed off and bit a piece of dry toast.

Jenny nearly rolled her eyes. Glancing at her husband, his enigmatic expression gave no clue as to his thoughts. Perhaps he was thinking of their lovemaking. For certainly, that was the only memory she would hold onto when recalling her stay in James Devere's home.

"Perfectly well," Jenny said pointedly, hoping Simon realized they had passed a night without incident. "The bed was quite comfortable. Wasn't it, my lord?"

"Quite," he agreed. "Tea?"

WHEN THEY LEFT MID-MORNING for the Devere coal mine, Simon's uncle had not appeared. Given the man's disposition, Simon would not have asked him anything about his son's potential thievery in any case. Jenny could see broaching the topic of Tobias and the ledgers would have gained nothing but potentially James Devere having an apoplectic fit.

"Still, if he'd come to say goodbye, you could have asked him if he'd given Maude leave to sell the hall," Jenny pointed out. "I suppose now we know why he advised her to move into Belton Manor. If you had died, Tobias would be next in line and his family would already be installed at the seat of the earldom."

Simon stared out the window. "But Toby died, and his father seemed to think I should have picked up the pieces of his family."

"I'm sorry if this visit was a disappointment to you."

Simon shrugged. "I merely wanted to see my uncle after all this time. It had been years, as you know. He's bitter, but it looks like his house has been long-neglected. If Toby were skimming funds, why would he let his father live in squalor? I guess I should simply be relieved my uncle didn't ask me for any details of Toby's death."

Jenny patted his knee, and he imprisoned her hand under his.

"I wish *I* could forget the bloody details."

"I know." Reaching up, she stroked his cheek with her other hand. "In time."

The next stop, at a lead mine, went as the previous two, and they procured a room at an inn in the late afternoon, with only a brewery to attend the following day.

When the innkeeper led them to a spacious suite, Simon told him they would take dinner alone in their room.

"I always stayed here when I went around to visit the accounts. I never dreamed I'd be in this room with my lovely wife."

Considering his words, Jenny didn't particularly care for the flash of jealousy that sizzled through her.

"Were you ever in this room with another woman?"

An expression of surprise crossed his face, and Jenny felt her cheeks warm. In truth, the forward question surprised even her. It was none of her business, and no good could come from knowing the answer if he had.

Instead of looking uncomfortable or guilty, however, Simon's face stretched into a smile.

"You cannot know how very pleased I am to be able to say unequivocally that, no, I never had a woman with me.

You are the first and only I shall ever bring to this inn or on my estate travels. For you are a rare gem, Lady Genevieve Lindsey. And I still cannot believe I plucked you from a garden so close to my own home. Proof the *bon ton* with their tedious rounds of the Season haven't a clue how to find a proper mate."

Was she glowing? If not, it would be a crime against nature, for Jenny felt happiness in every fiber of her being.

Crossing the room on eager steps, she tossed her arms around her husband.

"I am grateful I was blessed with a gift for mathematics."

He laughed at her statement and held her close.

"However," she added, leaning back and looking him in the eyes, "my sisters cannot rely on our good fortune. I cannot believe that luck, like lightning, will strike again in our little village. Thus, a Season each, they must have."

"I have not forgotten my promise, wife."

And then they spoke no more for a long time. In fact, Simon had to get up and don his banyan hurriedly, allowing his countess to hide absolutely naked under the bed covers, when a knock on the door heralded their evening meal.

Sitting on the bed, unclothed, they ate cold chicken, bread, and pickled onions. Talking and laughing together, Jenny couldn't imagine a better repast had she been at court dining with Queen Victoria herself.

However, all too soon, the earl grew hesitant as bedtime approached.

"I shall ask you every night to come lie down with me and hold me in your arms."

He smiled tentatively. "And every night, I shall not refuse you."

SIMON SAW THE FILTHY jailer approaching. *What did he want?* Surprised to find himself back in his cell after such a long dream of happiness, a dream in which he'd not only been back at Belton, he'd even fallen in love, Simon knew if he could get his hands on the bastard's throat, he could choke the life out of him and possibly escape.

He had someone at home to whom he desperately wished to return.

No. Shaking his head, he knew that was an idiotic fantasy. He had no ladylove. Yet he knew he must kill the guard. Only then could he save Toby, who sat against the cell wall staring at him.

Yet something troubled him. Some reason why he felt a new sense of dread. Not the rats. Not the cold. Not the hunger. If he could remember what was bothering him . . .

No matter. Strangely, as if not understanding the peril he was in, the jailer walked close by the enclosure and even stood where Simon could reach him. Fool. Dead man!

Reaching for him, Simon felt his hand touch warm flesh, but then the jailer dodged just out of reach. Once, twice, and then too far to touch.

Disappointed, Simon lay back down on the cell floor. It felt far more comfortable than it had before, and he realized he could most likely sleep easily. Even the rats had disappeared for the time being.

JENNY'S HEART WAS IN her mouth. That was what it felt like anyway, ever since Simon had reached for her, his fingers grasping for her neck. Quickly, she had scooted to the edge of the bed. He'd tried twice more until, as quietly as possible, she'd slipped from the covers to huddle beside the bed, trying to see him in the dark.

His visage was tense, thunderous, not peaceful as it should be.

Thank goodness she'd stayed awake, or had reawakened, she wasn't sure which. For certainly, if Simon hurt her again, he would be devastated.

Snatching up the robe her husband had discarded, she snuggled into it and sat down in the chair by the dying embers of the fire, tucking her feet up underneath her. She would stay until morning, and then get back into bed when he started to stir, with Simon none the wiser.

"WHAT IS THE MEANING of this?"

Jenny jerked awake, her neck cricked uncomfortably and, oh dear, was she drooling slightly while sleeping sitting up?

Wiping her cheek upon her own shoulder, she tried to clear the web of sleep from her brain.

Simon stood before her, stark naked. And apparently livid.

Recalling what had driven her from their bed, she cursed herself for not waking up in time to return to it.

Even worse, she'd neglected to come up with a credible reason for sleeping in the chair.

"Don't bother," he said, as if reading her thoughts. "Any tale you tell, I already know is a fib. I know exactly what happened because I had the cursed dream."

Hanging her head, Jenny hoped he would let her stay silent on the events of the night before.

Alas, he was not going to let it rest, even in the nippy morning air and him without a stitch of clothing.

In fact, as she tried to come up with something less damning than what had actually happened, her brain became distracted by the sight of him in daylight, his muscular frame, his long limbs, his impressive . . .

"Tell me," Simon ground out, turning to pace to the other side of the room giving her a superb view of his magnificent rear.

He spun around, giving her the other view again. Her mouth went dry, for it seemed with the slight agitation, he was becoming aroused in other ways.

"I . . . ," she trailed off and stared.

"Yes?" he prompted. Then he glanced down. "*Christ!* Where is my banyan?"

Realizing Jenny was wearing it, he grabbed his discarded drawers and yanked them on.

Feeling slightly disappointed when everything interesting disappeared from sight, she sighed. Then in order to ease his mind, she gave lying a try.

"I thought you seemed a tad restless, so I decided to let you have the bed to yourself."

"Restless?" Simon demanded.

Her gaze slid from his to a point over his shoulder.

He waited.

When she said nothing more, he crossed his arms.

"Did I touch you?"

"Not really."

"*Damnit!* You were afraid of me, weren't you?"

"Don't be silly," she said quickly. "But I know better than to stand in front of a runaway carriage, even if the horse means me no harm."

"Not the bloody metaphorical horse and carriage again!"

Jumping up, she ran to his warm body and slipped her arms around his waist.

"I'm not afraid of you, and I never will be. This will work itself out. Maybe if we talk about—"

Instead of enclosing her in an embrace, he turned away.

"There is nothing to talk about. I cannot control what happens in my sleep."

"But maybe if you discussed your dreams. Is it one in particular, did you say?"

"No."

"No, it's more than one?"

"No, I don't want to discuss it." Simon's mouth tightened. "I suggest we dress, break our fast, and go to the last account."

"Very well." What could she say? Every night, it seemed, and perhaps every morning, too, would be a new battle. Looking at her troubled husband, Jenny vowed to fight— with him and for him—in order to keep him.

"I AM GLAD WE'LL be home by tomorrow night," Jenny said as Simon assisted her into the carriage after their last stop. "Though clearly it has been well worth these days of traveling."

"It has been an enlightening trip, and at least we have a name and address."

Her husband should have been content knowing they could easily hunt down Mr. H. Keeble in London, but his brow held the hint of a frown as it had all day.

It didn't take an intellectual bluestocking to know what was troubling him.

"I'm sure you look forward to seeing your mother and your sisters again," Simon added.

"Truthfully, I'm most looking forward to starting in my role as countess and helping you run Belton. I want to build a life with you, and, if you'll let me, make our house feel like my home as well."

At last, she elicited a smile from her earl.

"Of course. You may redecorate or renovate as you see fit. I trust since you know what is in our coffers, better than anyone, you won't bankrupt the house of Devere."

She grinned. "No, my lord. That would hardly be in our best interest."

"Just so."

After, he'd seemed in better spirits. They returned full circle to spend another night at the Devere home in Wirksworth, with the watchful Tilda and the round-faced cook.

As she expected, Jenny awakened alone with clear signs Simon had slept in the chair. What would happen when they returned to Belton?

In the comfortable clarence, they at least could celebrate the triumph of having successfully redirected Simon's rightful income back into his own coffers. Yet, when the familiar stone wall and black gates of Belton Manor came into view, her husband's eyes took on a look of uncertainty.

Picking up her gloves from her lap, Jenny tugged them on, flashed him an encouraging smile, and vowed to herself to help Simon become quite certain of his decision to marry her.

IT WOULD BE JENNY'S first night in her new home, her first evening as Countess Lindsey, and the servants had gone over the top to make her feel welcome. She nearly pointed out to Simon the absolute opposite reception they were receiving from that of his uncle's home. Then she thought better of it. No need to pick at a wound.

The admiral was front and center to greet them with other staff lined up according to rank. Fresh flowers decorated the front hall, a scrumptious dinner had been planned, and, if Jenny wasn't mistaken, every window had been cleaned. She'd warrant they were completely out of vinegar, there were so many sparkling panes winking in the last rays of the late afternoon sun.

Feeling an immediate bonding with these people with whom she would spend the rest of her life, she sent up a silent prayer of gratitude. Things could be terribly different. As the staff bustled about to bring in their bags, get the lord and lady seated in the parlor, and bring them refreshments, it seemed as if blind Fortuna had spun her wheel and bestowed upon Jenny the greatest of good luck.

Suddenly, instead of someone else's efficient and happy staff, they were hers. She added the burden quite happily to her load as mistress of Belton.

Even Peter and Alice appeared, showing up as the sugared orange slices and ladyfingers also arrived. Watching as her new husband spoke animatedly to his young cousins, it wasn't difficult to imagine him with their own children.

"What are you thinking, Lady Lindsey?"

She felt her cheeks grow warm.

"Ah," he said.

"I don't understand," Alice said.

"What *are* you thinking?" Peter asked the same question.

Smiling at them, Jenny said, "Only what lovely children you are and how pleased I am you are living here. Where is your mother?"

Peter shrugged and grabbed for a second ladyfinger.

Alice, sucking on an orange segment, spoke around the juicy morsel, "In our parlor."

Lord Lindsey raised an eyebrow. The woman had been hiding out, it was his contention, in order that no one could ask her any more questions. Sir Agravain indeed!

Thinking of her husband and their staff, who all depended upon the solvency of the estate, Jenny was determined to get to the bottom of any disreputable dealings, even if it meant storming the widow's private rooms.

At bedtime, Simon saw her to the door of her own chamber, which now contained all her personal things from the Blackwood cottage along with a very large bed.

When he paused at the threshold, Jenny clenched her fists at her sides. Would she have to convince her husband each and every night? For while she knew it was the fashion to have their own rooms, she had no desire to spend her married life sleeping alone in a four-poster bed with only occasional visits from her husband.

Not giving him the option to abandon her, she asked, "Which room shall we take tonight, yours or mine?"

"Well played, wife."

"What do you mean?" She blinked her eyes.

"Both options ultimately are the same."

She wanted to stamp her foot. Didn't he want to hold her, caress her, make love to her? They'd been married merely a week.

"Don't you want to sleep with me?" she demanded.

"Frankly, no."

CHAPTER TWENTY-ONE

Jenny took a step back into her room, feeling as if he'd struck her.

Simon followed her, grabbing both her hands.

"Don't misunderstand me, Jenny. I want to lie with you. I certainly want to give you pleasure and watch you spend in my arms. And I wish to hold you, every night and every morning *if* it were possible. However, the part in between, the sleeping? No, I tell you without lying, I don't want to sleep with you. In fact, the idea terrifies me."

"Nothing more has happened," she said, hoping she didn't sound as desperate as she felt at this turn of events, a lifetime of separate beds.

"It has actually. The nights you slept safely, I got out of bed and sat in a damned chair."

"The same way I found you when I first entered your room." As it turned out, she had not really helped him at all.

He let her hands drop. "I stayed in a chair for a far different reason then. To keep from sleeping."

"And when you did drift off in the chair, did you have the same violent dreams?"

"I don't want to talk about it," he insisted to her dismay. "We shall compromise. Get ready for bed here, and I shall do the same in there," he pointed toward the door that separated their bedrooms. "Then I shall come back and . . ."

"Yes?"

"Spend time with you until you fall asleep," he finished, the glint in his eye bespeaking of how they would spend their first night together at Belton.

She supposed that was the only arrangement with which he would feel comfortable, and she had no choice but to agree. For now.

THE NEXT DAY, WHEN Lady Tobias Devere had still not put in an appearance, Jenny decided to take matters into her own hands. She wandered through her new home to the apartment on the second floor in the east wing that somehow the widow had commandeered for herself and her children when she'd moved in uninvited.

Tapping on the door, Jenny waited patiently for a response. Simon had told her of his inability to extract information from the widow. Upon her only encounter with Maude in the library, Jenny had seen how easily the woman went from speaking freely to closing up like a miser's purse.

However, it only made sense that some answers must lie with the widow. She tapped again. Nothing.

Turning away, Jenny took two steps down the hallway before stopping. Squaring her shoulders, she turned and approached the door again. *Her* door in *her* home. She would enter unbidden, since she had been assured this was not the woman's bedroom but a sitting room.

With a swift turn of the brass knob, she swung the door open. It was apparent that the room was empty. Moreover, Jenny could see this parlor was merely the first of a string of rooms, all joined like Simon's chambers by two sets of doors, allowing one to stroll in a loop if one wished.

Somewhere, in one of the rooms, the children must be playing, for their voices echoed on the parquet and high ceilings, reaching Jenny's ears.

The talking and occasional laughter was quite comforting, and she guessed the apartment would seem extremely lonely if it were silent. Walking farther in, she came to the next room that was set up as a charming dining room where no doubt Tobias's family ate. How sad to think of their lives going on without the young man.

"Non, j'ai dit non!" Maude's voice came from behind the closed door to the next room, speaking in French perhaps because something—or someone—had upset her. Then she said in English, "You must go tell him it is finished. At an end. *Finis!"*

A man's voice, one she didn't recognize, argued with her, "He won't like it, my lady."

"If the new earl sees you, he may recognize you, and then there will be questions."

The entire puzzling exchange had taken only moments, and suddenly, Jenny realized their footsteps were drawing closer to the door between the rooms. Running, in her slippered feet, she made it back into the center of the parlor when she heard them enter the dining room. All she could do was turn and face them, standing in the middle of the room as if she'd only then walked in.

Lady Devere and Master Cheeseface were already in the parlor when they looked up and saw her. Maude gasped, and they both halted.

Jenny held her ground. She could not curtsey first without losing face, but she could speak first. Indeed, protocol demanded it.

"It is good to see you well, Lady Devere, after your many headaches."

The widow flushed and then remembered whom she now addressed. She curtsied, low enough to seem respectful but without showing any true deference.

"Thank you, my lady. I wasn't aware you had returned from your wedding trip," Maude said, despite Jenny knowing this could not be true. "This is my children's arithmetic's tutor, Master Dolbert."

The man bowed low, and Jenny was doubtful he even remembered their brief encounter at the side entrance. Did it matter? Should she mention she'd met him before? He had the same disinterested expression now as he had then, a man who preferred to look anywhere but directly into one's eyes.

"Congratulations on your nuptials," Maude added, clearly wishing to keep Jenny's attention from the man at her side.

Jenny thanked her, wondering not for the first time why the widow hadn't come to the chapel for the wedding or attended the breakfast feast, although both Peter and Alice had been there. It would be impolite to ask, of course.

"I was not even aware the earl was courting you," Maude said a little offhandedly.

"I can certainly understand how some might say they were surprised," Jenny allowed. If more was said, however, by Maude or anyone else, it would be inappropriate. Any implication of undue haste was beyond rude, except when her own dear Maggie said it.

Maude shrugged in her Gallic fashion, and an awkward silence descended. Politeness demanded the woman invite Jenny to sit and have tea. She didn't. Instead, she turned to the tutor.

"You may go. Thank you for the update on the children's progress."

Master Dolbert nodded, bowed deeply again to Jenny, a shallower bow to Maude, and then he departed through the open door to the hallway as quickly as a rabbit with a fox on his tail.

The two ladies stared at one another.

"We visited my husband's uncle while we were away. Your father-in-law."

Ah, that got a reaction, Jenny noted with curiosity.

Maude paled and sat down, then jumped up once more as if she'd sat on something hot.

"My apologies. Will you sit?" she invited at last with little enthusiasm.

"Thank you." Jenny would keep this civil, but she was not leaving without learning more. Seeing a book on the chair, she asked, "What are you reading?"

"Voltaire." The woman said nothing more.

"I have read him only in translation."

"It is not the same," Maude pointed out, looking disappointed.

Feeling a sliver of insecurity, especially in light of the woman's superb command of both English and French, Jenny explained, "Unfortunately, I do not have the command of your native tongue like my sister has, which is why she and not I tutor Peter and Alice."

It would've been boorishly defensive of her to mention she had other talents. In any case, discussion of tutoring reminded Jenny of a question that had been nettling her like a pebble in her slipper. Was she not the Countess of Lindsey? She supposed she could get away with asking Maude whatever she wanted.

"Speaking of which, who pays my sister to come tutor your children?

Maude stared as if the question, or the asker, made no sense.

Jenny waited. If she put words into the woman's mouth, she would never learn the truth.

Finally, the widow's gaze slid to the floor.

"Why do you ask? Why would you assume I am not the one who pays?"

Hmm, two questions for her one. Not really an answer. Certainly not a forthright one.

"Forgive me, Lady Devere, however, I am under the impression, perhaps wrongly, that you have no income of your own. Yet you pay my sister and Master Dolbert?"

A long hesitation, as well as the widow's pursed lips, met Jenny's questioning words. When Maude at last realized Jenny was not going to fill the silence with idle chatter or retract the question, the lady sighed.

"You are quite correct. However, I have a little money from the sale of my home." She lifted her chin, looking rather mutinously proud. "When that is gone, then . . ."

Jenny understood the fear of financial ruin and wished to comfort this rather prickly woman. "I am sorry for your situation. I am certain my husband will keep you and your children under his protection for as long as you need. In your place, I can see why you sold the hall, but why won't you tell us to whom you sold it?"

Maude shook her head. "I do not know."

Jenny persisted. "The servant at the hall said you did."

"She lied. How does she even know me?"

"The maid said it was Lady Devere who told her not to tell my husband who her master was."

Frowning, Maude kept her gaze on her own hands resting in her lap. All at once, she looked up at Jenny, and her puzzled expression cleared.

"There is more than one Lady Devere at present."

It was Jenny's turn to frown. Then she realized she had met the other one, Letitia, James Devere's irritating wife.

Why would *she* have any say at Jonling Hall? Simon's uncle's home bespoke of miserliness or an extreme lack of funds. Certainly, he didn't seem like someone who could afford to purchase the hall, although Jenny could quite believe he would turn out his own daughter-in-law. Especially when James had hoped to push her into the arms of the new earl.

"Is there anything else you can tell me?"

Maude merely pursed her lips before muttering, "I don't know anything."

She knew something, as evidenced by the conversation Jenny had overheard.

"The mathematics tutor, I met him once before."

Blanching, Maude whispered, "Dolbert."

A strange reaction to a seemingly banal man.

"Is something wrong?"

The widow shook her blonde head.

"I . . . I have a megrim coming on."

Ah, the ever-at-the-ready headache that kept the widow from dinners or wedding nuptials and now threatened to send Jenny from the room.

"My mother always uses oil of peppermint on the back of her neck and temples. Shall we ring for some? Or perhaps simply a strong cup of tea?"

Maude's eyes widened, then she got up and strode to the bell pull. "I shall ring for tea," she said.

"Very good."

They sat in strained silence, first while they waited for the response from below stairs, and then while they waited for the ordered tea.

"Sublime weather," Jenny said, at last. "Why, there were flowers in bloom everywhere we went."

Maude nodded.

Sighing, Jenny decided to wait out the other woman. She would busy herself reciting the multiplication tables, which she often used to help her fall asleep. Having reached the table of five, she was pleased the tea had arrived as she was already beginning to feel a tad drowsy.

Jenny was even more pleased to see there were shortbread biscuits.

"Nothing like a biscuit to perk one up in the afternoon." She took a bite of one as the maid poured their tea.

Maude nodded noncommittally.

Goodness, Jenny thought. *I'm starting to sound like my mother.*

"Anyway, where were we? Discussing Master Dolbert, I believe."

Maude's eyes opened wide, but Jenny would not be put off. This was too important to the Deveres, and now she was one of them. Taking a sip of the bracing hot beverage, she waited.

Maude drank her tea, nibbled at the shortbread, and even put her fingers to her temple, but Jenny simply sat and said nothing more.

"My father-in-law suggested I hire him."

Jenny almost missed the woman's words, spoken softly.

"I beg your pardon. Do you mean to say James Devere suggested you hire a mathematics tutor, or Master Dolbert in particular?"

"Dolbert."

Jenny tried to reconcile such interest in the education of his grandchildren with the curt, stingy man who seemed to neglect his home and was perhaps starving his own wife.

"I am . . ." *astonished* ". . . pleased your father-in-law has such loving concern for Peter and Alice."

Mayhap the man's abhorrent behavior during their visit was entirely brought on by grief after all.

She had one last question. Dredging up the information given to her by the owners of the Deveres' investments.

"Do you know Mr. H. Keeble?"

Her face growing even paler if possible, Maude opened her mouth once, twice, thrice, clearly caught off guard. At last, stiffly and with bulging eyes, she shook her head.

"No? You've never heard of him?" Jenny almost laughed at the woman's obvious perfidy.

Maude shook her head once more.

"Who is he?" Her voice was little more than a whisper.

"No matter," Jenny said, dismissing the topic. She wouldn't be made a fool of, explaining what little she knew to this woman who clearly knew more.

Standing, Jenny took her leave. It had been an interesting visit, but in her heart, she felt it would be best if the widow left Belton sooner rather than later. It was beyond disconcerting to have a liar, and potentially a thief, in their midst.

Determined to keep a close eye on Maude for the sake of her husband's estate, Jenny turned at the door.

The woman had remained seated but stared at her from across the spacious room.

"My husband requests that you and your children attend the evening meal with us in the future. After all, we are one family."

Without waiting for a reply, Jenny left. If Maude dared to disobey such a request, she'd be forced to send in the admiral!

"IF YOUR COUSIN WAS acting on behalf of your uncle, then why wouldn't James have a palatial residence instead of letting his home become so rundown?"

They'd been going around the topic for the better part of an hour and getting nowhere. Simon was quite ready to drop it for the time being.

He took a sip of brandy and leaned back against the sofa. His intelligent wife was like a Bow Street runner, simply not going to let the matter of embezzled monies go until she'd sussed out the culprit.

"On the other hand, you firmly believe Tobias would not do such a thing to betray your father and you without being encouraged, or even forced. Correct?"

Nodding, Simon set his glass down on the table beside him and yawned before reaching for Jenny and dragging her closer to him.

"There," he said, when she was snuggled against his side. "That's better."

Encouraged by her soft laughter, when she looked up at him, he stole a kiss.

"My lord, we must focus on the issue at hand."

"My lady, we can know nothing more until we either go to London or send someone on our behalf to check into this Mr. Keeble. In the meantime, at least we have solved the mystery of the diminishing income."

Jenny worried her lower lip with her teeth. He loved seeing new things he hadn't noticed before.

"What is it?" she asked.

"What is what?"

"You're staring. Do I have the remains of something on my face?"

"No, wife. You look perfect as always."

This time her laughter was more of an unladylike snort that caused him to chuckle as well.

"I am far from perfect," she protested.

"Closer to it than I am," he pointed out.

Sighing, she gave him that patient look he wasn't sure he liked. She dismissed his nighttime violence as if it were inconsequential. All he could think of was how it felt to wake up and realize his hands were around her slender neck. And she was still wearing high-necked gowns to hide the last of the bruises, now a yellowish brown.

"When shall we go to London?" Jenny asked.

How could he take her without getting separate rooms at every inn as well as maintaining that status in his townhouse? She would fight him as she'd been doing most nights here at Belton. And when traveling, things could be even more unpredictable.

"Actually, I am thinking to go on my own." Simon ignored her puzzled look. "I will ride rather than take the carriage. I can get there more quickly, meet with Keeble, spend only one night in London, and return the following day."

"Why can't I go with you? I thought I was your estate manager?"

"You are. But there could be danger. We don't know what manner of man with whom we are dealing. Thug or gentleman."

"Which is why you shouldn't go alone."

He nearly laughed but sensed that would offend her.

"Dear wife, I can handle myself, and while I am sure any villain would be terrified by your stature." He paused when she punched him in the shoulder. "I would feel better knowing you are safely at home."

She was muttering under her breath about safety, and he wished he could make her realize how her wellbeing was now of the utmost importance to him. To protect her was his duty. And he would not fail her as he had Toby.

"Nevertheless, I should very much like to see the townhouse, especially as my sisters and mother will be residing there in a matter of months. Let me accompany you on the journey, and I will stay well away from Mr. Keeble. Or am I your estate manager in name only? Is it true or a lie?"

It was his turn to sigh. For she had certainly made mincemeat of his argument. How could he keep her home? If she were carrying his child, she would stay home, but he was rather premature with that hope.

"Simon, what are you thinking?"

"That we should have children immediately!"

"I beg your pardon?" She leaned away from him, perhaps to ascertain his seriousness.

"We should get you started on producing babes so you have appropriate concerns and interests. Not musty ledgers. You shouldn't be concerned with boring things, such as . . ."

"Going to London?" she finished for him when he trailed off lamely. "The most exciting city in the world?"

"Also filthy, crowded, and smelly."

In truth, he would love to go to Vauxhall with her and to the opera. Maybe even to Astley's. Jenny would simply have to agree to his rules for sleeping, both on the journey and in Town.

Thus, Simon found himself in his carriage with his wife a few days later, headed to London.

"Are you terribly annoyed I'm with you?"

Simon could tell by her expression she knew he wasn't, and also that she didn't care. She was simply thrilled, if her eyes told the truth, to be going with him.

"Yes," he lied, a slight smile upon his lips. "I'm dreadfully furious, can't you tell?"

He reached over and took her beloved face in his hands.

"Oh," she murmured, obviously waiting to be kissed.

Claiming her soft lips beneath his, he relished the way she clasped her fingers behind his neck. Slanting his mouth, he gently but determinedly slipped his tongue into her sweet warmth.

"Mm," she moaned.

When they parted, she had the slightly disheveled, distracted appearance that always stirred him to want to do it again, as well as a great deal more.

"That is my favorite part of traveling," Jenny confessed, as she lifted her heavy lids and smiled at him.

"Mine, too."

As he'd feared, she put up a fight when he said he would procure two rooms on the first of four nights at an inn.

"I will not have people thinking we are that type of couple."

"What type of couple?" Simon couldn't keep the exasperation out of his voice. He simply wanted her to be able to sleep safely.

"The type who don't have enough affection for one another to sleep together. As if we can't bear the other's company."

He sent his eyes rolling skyward as they stood outside the inn, arguing like fishwives.

"I believe no one thinks anything of the sort. It is perfectly normal to get two chambers. In fact, quite the contrary, they will think we are like rutting goats if we need only one room when travelling."

At her shocked and hurt expression, he wished he could call back his words.

"Never mind. We shall stay in one room, the better for me to keep an eye on you."

He should be flattered that Jenny wanted to be with him. In truth, he was moved by her deep affection and grateful beyond words. Moreover, at her apparent relief and happiness that he would share her room, he did, in fact, feel like a randy goat.

He was not looking forward to a night on the floor or a chair, but for Jenny, he would do either.

CHAPTER TWENTY-TWO

J enny awakened to the familiar sight of an empty bed. How chivalrous. At least they had enjoyed each other before he'd let her drift off to sleep and then abandoned her.

Her mouth twisted. That was unfair, he hadn't really abandoned her. She looked to the overstuffed chair and frowned. No Simon. Maybe he had left the room after all. Getting out of bed, she rounded the end of it and nearly tripped over her husband's prone form.

As it was, she kicked him in the head.

"Ouch," he exclaimed and sat up from his makeshift nest—a pillow upon the carpet and two blankets over the top of him.

"This is ridiculous, husband. You are not a dog to lie on the floor at the foot of the bed."

He grinned. "I've slept in far worse conditions, as you know."

Tossing her hands up, she tried to step past him to reach her clothing hanging in the wardrobe, but he grabbed for her hand and, with a quick tug, pulled her down on top of him.

Before she knew it, her shift was up around her waist and they were engaging in the best of *Aristotle's Masterpiece*, as she'd come to think of their lovemaking. Afterward, lying with her head cradled against Simon's shoulder and his arm around her, she couldn't help the giggle that escaped her.

"What is it?" he asked, still drawing tender strokes across her flat stomach.

"I am certain this is the first time an earl and his countess have made love on this floor, right next to such a comfortable down mattress. Like Bedlamites!"

He brushed a kiss across her forehead. "Truly, I am quite mad for you," he admitted, "but you are probably right. Let's break our fast and get on the road, the sooner you will see our townhouse."

Liking the sound of "our townhouse," she dressed quickly and ate even more quickly.

Three days later, as she supervised the unpacking of their trunks, Jenny was not disappointed. When Simon gave her a tour of the house, she tried to glean more about the man she'd married.

"My lord, I am surprised your family ever left Town for Belton."

For instead of the usual London house with barely any land, the Deveres' had a corner mansion with front and back gardens on Portman Square.

"We've had offers," he admitted, "from more than one duke and a member of the royal family. However, not needing the coin, we kept our place in Town. I don't know if my father came here when I was . . . away."

According to the downstairs maid, Lady Maude, Lord James, and Lady Letitia had all used the Devere townhouse in the past few years.

At that news, Jenny lifted an eyebrow to her husband. "The plot thickens."

"Such a mind for discovering deviousness," he said, admiringly.

"Tell Mr. Keeble, Simon Devere, Earl of Lindsey, is here to see him."

Simon was no fool. He'd hired a man to follow Keeble for two days to determine what kind of man he was and for whom he worked. The news was not good. A legal steward for the underworld, as best he could tell.

Because of that, he'd called upon one of his closest friends, John Angsley, the Earl of Cambrey, who luckily was in residence in London. After a great deal of "dear God in Heaven" and backslapping and "damned good to see you" and more backslapping followed by a few fingers of brandy, they'd set out together.

"No, I'd never heard of him either," Cam said as they rode to Keeble's office. "That tells us nothing, though. I don't run in his circle any more than you do. I doubt we'd ever come across the likes of Keeble at White's."

"White's?" Simon repeated, still staring out the carriage window. "I can't think of going back there, as if nothing ever happened."

"You will be welcome wherever you go. Moreover, none of us can imagine what you went through. But listen, every bloody one of us thinks you're a hero."

Simon flinched.

"If I was, Toby would be here, too."

"That's nonsense." Cambrey crossed his arms and sat back. He'd known Simon's cousin, but they hadn't been in the same class at Eton. "Utter rubbish. I suppose you should have saved Admiral Nelson, too."

Simon shrugged, not ready to absolve himself of any blame. Still, he'd had other triumphs lately.

"I took a wife recently." He turned his face to his friend and couldn't help smiling at the thought of Jenny. *His* Jenny, who now waited at their townhouse for his return.

"You are married? Why didn't I read of it in the papers?"

"Bad of me, I suppose. I wanted to get it done, and the lady didn't mind having a quiet country wedding."

"Lucky you. Her name?"

"She was Lady Genevieve Blackwood."

Cambrey nodded. "*Ah,* Baron Blackwood's eldest daughter."

"You know her?" Simon realized, for all he knew, his friend might have danced with Jenny during the Seasons when he was stuck in Burma.

"Not really. I've seen her, of course, at a number of events. Sweet face, as I recall." He winked at Simon. "I do know what happened with her father. And her viscount," Cambrey added pointedly. "It was common knowledge Alder dropped her like a hot tater and began courting a viscount's daughter from Wembley."

"Thank God," Simon muttered. "Alder's loss, my gain."

"You are in love!" Cambrey deduced by the look on his friend's face, the tone of his voice.

"Yes. Honestly, I don't see how I would even be here if not for her. I was in terrible shape when she found me."

"I'm glad you got a happy ending. You deserve that."

Simon brushed his words away with a wave of his hand. "What? Not happy?"

Hesitating, Simon wasn't sure what to tell Cam.

"A story for later. But as for my wife, she makes me exceedingly happy." The carriage had shuddered to a stop. "Will you come back to my home after we conclude this business, to meet her?"

"I'd be honored. Now let's give this fellow the what for, shall we?"

Thus, they entered Keeble's office, which was neither shabby nor sumptuous, simply two rooms above a successful stockbroker and below a commercial merchant in Bayswater, just north of Hyde Park. In the outer room, a thin middle-aged clerk sat at a desk and against Simon's expectations, there were no ruffians present to intimidate or attempt to scare him off.

The clerk's eyes widened at their entrance and grew larger at hearing the identity of the two earls.

"Well, is he in?" Simon asked.

"He must be," Cambrey pointed out, "or his office door would be open, no?"

"Why, yes," the clerk said, jumping up and stumbling backward. Keeping his eyes on the two men, he knocked on his master's door.

"Come," came a voice from within.

"Perfect," Cambrey said, "we'll take it from here." He gestured for Simon to proceed him.

Approaching the clerk until he could do nothing except step aside, Simon pushed the door open and entered. An ordinary office belonging to what appeared to be an ordinary man. Yet, this was the man who for years had been receiving the Devere family's income, from five different enterprises.

"You are Keeble?"

The man stood, obviously recognizing by their clothes he had two fine gentlemen in his office.

"I am."

Simon looked him up and down. He didn't look like a thug who funneled money to the top gambling clubs in London, but that was his job, to get money from debtors and pay creditors.

"I am Simon Devere, seventh Earl of Lindsey."

"My lord." The man bowed respectfully.

Studying him, Simon felt puzzled. The man looked vaguely surprised but not alarmed. Certainly not as Simon expected an embezzler would.

"This is the Earl of Cambrey." He gestured beside him to John without turning.

"My lord" Keeble bowed to Simon's friend in turn. Then silence.

"Do you know why I'm here?"

to the circus at Astley's Royal Amphitheatre and attending the rather garish and loud Bartholomew Fair, where they'd watched wire-walkers, acrobats, and fire-eaters. It had been most thrilling.

Tonight, she'd had the pleasure of entertaining as a new bride in the parlor until supper. Then over a meal of roast grouse and peas with a delicious minted vinegar sauce, Lord Cambrey had them all laughing with tales of his and Simon's time at school.

Now the men were heading out again, leaving her stuck with a library book. She had no one to go anywhere with besides her husband.

Poor planning! She should have brought Maggie for company, at least.

"Very well. I'll be waiting."

CHAPTER TWENTY-THREE

True to his word, Simon was back within a few hours. Jenny had already decided to make use of the townhouse's luxurious facilities and had enjoyed a deep, soaking bath in his absence. Warm and relaxed, she was drinking port—feeling very grown up—when her husband swept into the house in better spirits than when he'd left.

Pouring himself a drink, he joined her on the sofa.

"I like this robe," he told her.

She smiled. "I know." A deep purple velvet, finely woven, it clung sinfully to all her curves.

Touching his fingers to the opening, he started to tug on it.

"I like it best when it's on the floor or draped across a chair, not covering your body." He leaned toward her to nuzzle her neck.

She giggled. "You're tickling me."

"I will happily tickle you everywhere. Shall we go upstairs?"

"In a minute," Jenny insisted. "Tell me what happened. Did you find the man you were looking for?"

"I did." He paused and swirled the liquor in his glass.

"Are you going to make me drag each tidbit of information from you?"

"No, but I'm not sure how you'll take what I have to tell you, thus I think I'd rather wait until morning."

Alarm raced through her, making her sit up straight and offer him a hard stare. "Now you must tell me. For I could never sleep with wondering."

Sighing, he set his port down and then took her glass and put it beside his own. Holding both her hands in his, he looked her in the eyes.

"It's no secret I think you're marvelous and brilliant."

"Simon—"

"Don't be alarmed, I just wanted to tell you that first and foremost."

"Very well. Carry on."

"Cam and I found the man who gambles in my uncle's stead easily enough, right at a high-stakes table. He was playing deep, as they say."

She frowned.

"Betting heavily," he clarified. "With Devere money."

"Outrageous!"

"Yes. But how to put an end to this? He was surprised to see me but insisted he had done nothing wrong. He enjoys playing, and he's got a plum position doing it."

"What manner of man is he?"

"Harmless enough. About my age, I suppose. Looked oddly familiar yet I swear I've never set eyes upon him in my life. Cam thinks he may have been at school with us. Whoever he is, he fell into the right puddle."

"And how will you mop up this puddle and dry up his endless supply of gambling funds?"

"I told him it was going to stop, and he laughed. He said it wasn't up to me or to him."

"Then to whom?"

"The man to whom my uncle first got terribly indebted."

"And who is that?"

"*The Fishmonger* himself."

"Fishmonger?"

"Will Crockford was born to a fishmonger and destined to become one, except he didn't. Instead, he's one of the most powerful men in London. Unfortunately, he's also commonly called 'the Shark,' for good reason. Apparently, we Deveres helped build his gambling establishment, or at least our money did. And quite a nice place it is, too."

Simon released her hands and picked up his drink once more.

"Crockford's is every gaming man's fantasy. Luxurious, respectable, right on St. James Square, a liveried servant at hand every time you turn around. And a roomful of bored, wealthy young men who don't mind being pigeons."

"Pigeons?"

"*Mm,* easy marks for Crocky and his staff."

"Well, I don't care how nice it is. What are you going to do? Meet with this Shark person?"

"Oh, I'll be right there," he said fixing her with an intense stare, "beside you."

She nodded, and then Simon's words filtered through her brain. "Beside *me*?"

"Yes, dear one, beside the finest brain I know for handling numbers. That's really all it takes to win at cards. That and some luck."

Jenny opened her mouth, then shut it again. Then she picked up her glass and sipped her port before trying again. *No*, she still had no words to describe how petrified she felt or explain to him how she could not possibly do such a thing. Not even to save his family's fortune. For one thing, she couldn't go into a gaming establishment, for another, she was terrified of anyone called Shark, and lastly, most importantly, what if she lost and let Simon down.

"I know your head is probably swirling with thoughts," he said. "I also know you can do this. And right here, in our own home. I have invited Crocky here and he has accepted."

Suddenly, she couldn't take a deep breath. That usually only happened when her corset was laced too tightly. She also found herself unable to speak, not wanting to disappoint her husband who'd put his faith in her. Why, she had demanded to go with him to London to face whatever foe was draining the Devere coffers. Apparently, face him she would.

"Please say something, Jenny. I'm starting to fear I've sent you into a state of severe stupor."

She shook her head slightly to clear it.

"I know nothing about gambling except my father was terrible at it. If I have inherited his skills, we shall be lost."

"You have your own unique skills. You and Crocky will play a hand of piquet, all or nothing."

"That sounds ominous. In any case, if I am counting cards, there won't be much to count if we only play one hand. Secondly, what is 'the all' and what is 'the nothing'?"

Simon laughed. "You must score at least 100 points to win, and you have six hands in which to do it. And 'the all' is if you win, Crocky will accept it as debt paid and done on my uncle's behalf. If you lose, I will pay him the rest of the debt, including the interest, by selling off whatever I need to. In any case, there will be no more gambling on my uncle's behalf."

"You've cut him off and Mr. Crockford accepts it?"

"I have." Crossing his arms, Simon looked quite forbidding for a moment, every muscled pound of him the commanding earl who would take care of his estate and his tenants.

She considered it. "Either way, the drain will stop against your accounts?"

"Either way, this farce ends."

That made her feel better. However, the stakes were still extremely high. The Devere coffers would feel the blow of such a huge sum being paid out to the Shark all at once. Servants could lose their jobs, as Simon had said, and holdings might have to be sold. She swallowed.

"When is he coming?"

"Tomorrow afternoon."

Alarm skittered through her. "I must learn to play cards by then?"

"Only one *partie*. I'll teach you." He leaned forward and took the glass from her hand, setting it down. "But not tonight. There are other things I would much rather teach you tonight."

She started to shake her head, thinking it impossible to focus on anything besides her anxiousness, when his warm hand rested upon her cheek, turning her face to his. Blinking, Jenny waited as his mouth claimed hers. As they kissed, her insides melted along with her worries. This man had gone through hell and returned. Amazingly, he was still generous and warm and loving. He was gifting her sisters with a Season each. She would repay him by trying her best to beat the Shark. However, she wouldn't think about any of that now.

As she opened her mouth to let his devilish tongue slip between her lips, she vowed that tonight, she would concentrate only on being his willing pupil.

Awakening in the strange bedroom of their townhouse, as usual, she found her husband gone. Simon had slipped from their bed to sleep elsewhere, just as he did at home. Feeling helpless to alter their predicament, Jenny decided instead to focus on learning the card game.

WHEN THE VALET SHOWED Will Crockford into the drawing room, Jenny wished they'd brought the admiral with them instead of leaving him to look after Belton. The Shark was dressed to impress and could easily pass as a respectable business man. What alarmed her was he brought a large, rough-looking individual with him, a man who dwarfed their spindly young valet, sporting a nose that looked as if he'd been at the wrong end of a pugilist's fist more than once.

Instead of announcing their guests, their valet was trailing along behind, belatedly stammering their arrival.

With good forethought, Simon had invited his friend Lord Cambrey to attend. With her husband and his friend, Jenny felt perfectly safe despite the unsavory company who now stood in her drawing room.

The Earl of Lindsey made introductions of his wife and his friend, to which the Shark said, "A pleasure, a pleasure."

Glancing at his own man, he said only, "This is Busby."

At that point, Simon made it known it was Jenny who would play against Crocky.

The thin veneer of civility cracked for a moment, as Will Crockford's eyes bulged. He took a second look at the young wife of the earl, tilting his head and considering her.

"Is this a jest?" he asked.

"No," Simon responded at once. "My wife will play against you. First to reach one hundred and over."

Jenny remained silent as her husband had advised, holding her tongue to be a woman of mystery who may or may not be adept at cards. Let the Shark wonder what he was in for.

The man sighed. "I warn you, Lindsey. I can spot a cheat a mile away, and Lady Lindsey's pretty face won't distract me much."

Jenny felt her cheeks color at the backhanded compliment, but still said nothing, merely letting Simon pull out her chair as she and Crocky took seats at the table. The others remained standing. Neither the coarse Busby nor her husband or Lord Cambrey were going to relax for fear of missing a single movement of the hand and card.

If only she could calm the butterflies that fluttered against her rib cage. She glanced at Simon, who gave her an encouraging smile, then a wry tilt of his eyebrow. *Look at the situation we are in.* Smiling back, she felt calmer.

Will Crockford produced a deck he declared to be a piquet deck, already sorted to have only thirty-two cards. It took another few minutes for Simon and Cambrey to examine the deck to their satisfaction. It appeared unmarked.

Acting the gentleman, Crocky offered to deal the first hand to show her how to do it properly.

Before she could accept, Simon coughed, and she remembered what he'd told her.

"Mr. Crockford, as you are aware, the dealer on the sixth hand is at a disadvantage, therefore, I would like to deal first. Shall we cut to decide? High card chooses."

To her delight, Jenny drew the high card and dealt them each twelve cards. When she held the cards for the first time, a shot of disbelief nearly caused her to drop them upon the polished wooden table in front of her.

What on earth was she doing?

However, when the Shark made a clucking confident sound, she stiffened. There was luck involved, but there was also skill, and these were simply numbers, which had always been her faithful friends.

When after examining their hands, neither of them declared *carte blanche*, they settled in to play. As dealer, Jenny had the younger hand, and Crocky got to exchange first. He lay only three cards face down, withdrew an equal number from the talon of eight cards, and then, as his right, got to look at two more. Flustered, Jenny exchanged for all five left in the talon, even knowing the Shark had seen two of them.

For the first round, she could scarcely blink for fear of missing something, but then her brain took over as she counted what she saw and guessed what was to come and calculated the odds, and then . . . Crocky won, declaring his points, sequence, and set, each with a triumphant grin.

Jenny had to say "good" for each, meaning she could not best him in any of the three categories.

How quickly her luck had turned from winning the deal to losing the round. Glancing at Simon, fearing she'd see disappointment on his face, she saw instead an encouraging smile.

She would do better. She had to. For at this rate, Crocky would reach thirty points before she scored. If he received the repique of sixty points, the Deveres would assuredly lose.

The Shark dealt the next hand, and Jenny spent more time considering what she would exchange. Paying more attention, she realized she knew nearly every card Crocky had by what she had and what she'd seen in the talon. She had a better set and sequence, played her tricks, and won the cards in the next round for an extra ten points.

Crocky looked impressed but unbothered.

"Have you played before?" he asked her, as she shuffled the pile of cards.

"No," she said honestly.

"I see." He turned to Simon. "Will there be refreshments? I can't say much for your hospitality."

Instead of being offended, her husband only laughed. "I don't think you'll be here that long. Besides, you've had plenty to eat and drink on Devere money, haven't you?"

Crocky's mouth turned up on one side in a slight grin. "I suppose I have. Still, some brandy or even ale would be appreciated."

"I can provide you something one last time," Simon agreed and rang the bell.

In a few minutes, they all had a glass either set before them or in hand. Jenny didn't touch her drink. She found the pause in their play to be disconcerting enough, never mind tainting her clear thoughts with brandy.

Taking a long draught from his glass, Crocky smiled at her and nodded to continue. If he hoped to make her forget anything she'd seen and counted, he had failed. The next hand she took easily, out playing him in two of the three categories again, and won all twelve tricks for forty more points. Her score was mounting quickly toward one hundred.

They were at two to one, and she was feeling hopeful. And then he set down his hand, all twelve cards, face down, shooting her a smile that didn't reach his eyes.

"Are you declaring?" she asked.

"Perhaps."

"What are you playing at?" Simon asked, taking a step toward the table, which caused the silent Busby to do the same.

"Ease up, gentlemen," the Shark said. "I merely thought to make this more interesting. Odds are my hand wins and we're practically tied for points."

"Or it doesn't," Simon proposed, "and you've lost."

"Do you think I've won?" Crocky asked Jenny directly.

A glimmer of doubt snaked through her brain. It was possible he had received the six and eight of hearts. It was also possible he was bluffing.

"I believe if you had the best hand, you would play it. You have nothing to gain by changing the terms if you think you have the winning cards."

Will Crockford blinked, and she assumed she was correct. But then his expression changed.

"To the contrary, Lady Lindsey. I don't want to be tied and have to go through another two hands now that I see you have some skill. I'd rather end this with the stakes riding on a single card. We can ignore what's here in my hand," he offered, tapping the top of his stack, "and we can each draw one card, highest wins."

"You agreed to the terms," Simon pointed out.

What's more, Jenny could only exert what little skill she had if she could count cards and play cleverly. She could do nothing if they were relying on fickle fortune.

"I do not agree to a change in terms," she said. "Make your declarations, win or lose, and we play on to the end."

"Very well, I tried to give you a sporting chance."

He showed his hand, declaring his *carte blanche* first for an extra ten points and then his tricks. To Jenny's dismay, Crocky had indeed won the round, although not all the tricks. Still, she heard a groan from Lord Cambrey, which didn't help her mood.

Was she going to fail at helping her new husband save his estate?

A spark of anger burned deep within her. Gambling had destroyed her father and, by association, had greatly injured her mother and sisters. The consequences of whatever happened here could affect many people who depended upon the Devere estate.

Staring at the fickle cards, all of a sudden, Jenny realized Crocky had cheated. There was a card on the table that shouldn't be there for it was already in the talon. She was certain of it.

Looking askance at Busby, a big man with a wedge of a scar under his right eye, she had no doubt he had a weapon concealed upon his person. Accusing the Shark of cheating was most likely a dangerous proposition, and someone could get hurt.

She considered her options. Crocky knew he'd lost the hand and had thus tried to get out of revealing his cards in case she spotted the duplicate. They were, for all intents and purposes, tied. She could win the next hand fairly, which he could also do, or he could cheat and win. At which point, she would have to call him out, as they said.

Then Lord Cambrey said, "You know, Crocky, you should have declared the *carte blanche* sooner. Bad form really. Some might say it nullified the round."

The Shark bristled. "Now see here," he began, "I've been playing piquet a damn long time, and I've never had anyone say I don't know when to declare before."

Jenny didn't want the men to get into a fight over that technicality.

"Since I am the one playing him," she said, "while I thank you, Lord Cambrey, I am deciding Mr. Crockford may keep his extra ten."

Blowing a loose tendril off her forehead, she carefully dealt the next hand. Barely glancing at her own cards, instead, she stared hard at the Shark's hands, making sure they remained in plain sight, not going to his lap or fiddling with his sleeves, for certainly, he had cards concealed somewhere.

He went first, then it was her turn. The hand was surprisingly uneventful, six tricks each and barely a few points between separating them. It could still go either way with only one hand to go.

To Jenny, the room was deathly silent except for the pounding of her own heartbeat in her ears. Another play, then another, and she found herself staring down at what she hoped was a winning trick. Pausing, she stared at it, and then looked at Will Crockford over the top of the cards. Their gazes locked, and his eyes widened as he realized what was happening.

Coughing loudly, he covered his mouth with one hand, continuing to cough until his man stepped forward and thumped him on the back. Then Crocky made a great show of withdrawing a handkerchief and holding it up to his face.

"My apologies," he said at last, taking another long drink and finishing off his ale.

"Quite all right," Simon said, but before anything else happened, the Shark laid down his hand.

"I believe I have won again, not only the last hand but the most points."

Jenny pursed her lips. Nestled between a queen and a ten was a jack she was sure had been in the man's pocket before the interruption of supposed phlegm.

She glanced at her husband, who stared grim-faced at the cards fanned out upon his table. Lord Cambrey took a step forward and also stared down at the high-scoring trick.

Crocky's face broke out in a genuine smile, and he began to push his chair away from the table.

"A good *partie*," he said.

"Indeed," Jenny said. "And we shall abide by its outcome without any gainsaying, shan't we?"

"Yes, of course," Crocky said, beaming now.

"Then I must inform you, you have lost." She spread her run of cards upon the table, aces high.

"The Devere family has concluded its debt to you, Mr. Crockford."

With that, Jenny pushed her chair out and stood while the Shark stared, eyes bulging at her cards.

Simon gave an uncharacteristic whoop of joy and grabbed her to him in a tight embrace.

"Well, damn me," Lord Cambrey murmured. "Good show."

"Thank you," she told him from the circle of her husband's arms.

At last, Crocky stood slowly. His face was ashen, and his man appeared to be waiting for an order.

As the moments of bristling tension stretched from one to the next, Simon released her and somehow, before she knew it, he had placed his body between her and Crocky. Lord Cambrey was by his side. She held her breath.

Will Crockford faced them. He didn't smile, his body stayed taut, but he slipped his hands into his pockets.

"Very well," he said at last. "It was an interesting game. I would like to say enjoyable, but I've never found losing to be pleasant. That's why it almost never happens."

"I have this for you to sign before you leave." Simon pulled a single page from the pocket inside his coat. "There's a pen here." He picked it up from the sideboard and lay them both before the gaming house owner.

If anything, Crocky looked even more put out. Hardly glancing at the words, knowing they cleared the debt, he signed his name.

In another moment, after the briefest nod to Lord Lindsey and Lord Cambrey, he pierced Jenny with his gaze. To her, he offered another deeper nod, nearly a bow. And then he turned and walked out, followed by the still-silent, scarred man.

When the front door closed, the three of them let out a collective sigh.

"I think this calls for champagne," Lord Cambrey said, ringing the bell with an exuberant yank of the tapestry pull. "I hope you have some on hand."

Instead of answering, Simon took both of Jenny's hands in his. "You were wonderful. I thought he had us."

"He was cheating," Jenny explained. "Even if I hadn't won the last hand, I would have exposed him."

Simon's face flushed red. "The wretch. I should go to his club at once and call him out."

"No," Jenny pleaded. "It's over. We won. Let's leave it at that."

Simon looked at his friend, who shrugged.

"I agree with your lady. To confront the Shark in his own sea is asking for trouble. And I see no gain from it except to anger a man whom we already know has no scruples whatsoever."

Simon hesitated. "You are both right. At least the three of us will always know the mighty Shark lost to Lady Genevieve Lindsey." The summoned servant came in and was sent to the kitchen in search of champagne.

"I DON'T WANT TO go in a coach again for a very long time," Jenny said when they returned to Belton Park days later.

"It seems we've spent more time away from home than in it."

"I'm glad it feels like home to you." Simon took her in his arms. "I am eternally grateful. Without you, some drastic changes would have had to be made."

After visiting with her mother and sisters briefly before their evening meal, she acknowledged her exhaustion.

"Then let's turn in early," Simon suggested as the servants removed their dinner plates. "I'll rub your shoulders and your feet and your . . ." He raised an eyebrow, causing warmth to spread through her.

"Suddenly, I feel a modicum of energy returning." She let him lead her up to her room.

Her room. Not *their* room. The one blight on their happiness remained. Jenny had been so successful in London, though, she felt hopeful she could make a difference in that matter, too.

Simon eschewed the maid in favor of undressing his wife himself. She loved it when he did this, when his strong, capable fingers stroked her skin as he gazed lovingly into her eyes. When his lips replaced his fingers, whisper-soft against her skin, he placed kisses everywhere, and she found herself trembling. Then his wicked tongue tasted her skin, scorching her as he did.

Drawing her upon the bed, Simon kept his promise and kneaded her shoulders before rubbing the soles of her feet. However, she found it more frustrating than soothing. There were other parts of her that awaited his touch with extreme anticipation.

"Simon, please. Come up here," she demanded.

Feeling his smile where his mouth rested upon the delicate skin of her inner thigh, she added, "At once."

In another moment, he covered her body with his own. Their lovemaking was slow and sweet, and utterly fulfilling.

"Simon," she keened as the sensations peaked and her muscles involuntarily tightened. Her husband was deep inside her when she felt him reach his own release.

In a few moments, while held in his embrace, she was unable to fight the heavy-lidded tiredness that overtook her.

As soon as her body began to calm from the intense climax, she drifted asleep.

"SIMON." HER OWN VOICE awakened her from a nasty dream in which she was alone with Crocky. Realizing she was indeed alone, she felt overcome with sadness reaching her hand out to touch the cold sheets beside her.

Poor man! What demons tormented her husband each night, and how could she help him to overcome them? If one silly dream of the Shark had her lighting her lamp and wishing for company, what must Simon experience, especially when he awakened alone?

What if she tried again to be a comfort to him? To be an anchor for his ship of nighttime travels?

Hopping out of bed, Jenny slipped on her nightdress and carefully, quietly, opened the door that separated their rooms.

Letting her eyes adjust to the darkness of his chamber, she listened to his breathing, steady and deep. He seemed peaceful at the moment. Perhaps she should retreat. On the other hand, if he awakened to find her beside him, realizing they'd had a perfectly successful night together, then perhaps he would be willing to try it again the next night. And the next.

Tiptoeing across the thick carpet, she reached his bed to find little room. He was neither on one side, nor the other, but sprawled in the middle, the blanket around his waist.

Judging which side had more room, she circled the bed, sliding under the bed clothes, and settling beside him. It took her many minutes as she vowed not to wake him.

The familiar scent of her husband, the warmth of his bed, his rhythmic breathing, all soothed her into falling asleep nearly as quickly as after their romp.

CHAPTER TWENTY-FOUR

Simon opened his eyes and saw the bars of his cell. The anguish this caused was greater than usual. *Why?* He thought about it as he started to sit up. He remembered feeling blissful only moments earlier. Then he remembered Jenny.

Jenny! His wife. He had a lovely, sweet wife. How could he have married her and left her behind?

Confusion clouded his mind, but he knew he had to escape to get back to her. Perhaps he could break down the door. Scrutinizing it, the wood didn't seem too solid after all. Then he thought of Toby. He must release his cousin before the unthinkable happened. *Yes*, he had to protect Toby.

Turning his head, to search for his cousin, the sight that greeted him caused him to tremble. Toby was leaning against the wall, alive and yet not. Stiff, his eyes clearly plucked from his head, his body in various states of decay, yet he raised a hand in greeting.

Simon closed his eyes and shook his head. When he opened them, Toby lived again and was even smiling at him. Breathing a sigh of relief, Simon knew the only way to keep his cousin alive was to kill the guard and get the keys that always jangled from a large iron ring clipped to the man's trousers.

Turning away as the guard approached, a murderous rage shook him. If only Simon could move his limbs more easily, but they felt leaden. Still, for Toby's sake, for Jenny's, he would beat his captor to a pulp.

JENNY KNEW SHE'D MADE a terrible mistake, and now she was trapped. The blanket and sheet snared her as she tried desperately to scoot away. Her husband's sightless eyes were blazing and ruthless as his lethal hands reached for her.

Whimpering with fear, she flailed at his arms, trying to keep him from making firm contact with her.

Swiftly, however, his fingers found their target around her neck.

Before she lost the ability, she screamed as loudly as she could. First a shriek of terror, but then she yelled his name.

He hesitated, and she thought perhaps he would awaken.

However, with renewed force, Simon gripped her.

Hating to hurt him but seeing no other recourse, Jenny brought her knee up under the bedding, aimed at his midsection.

"Oof," he said, releasing his hold on her.

She turned and nearly succeeded in escaping from the bed, but his hand grabbed at her shoulder, and he yanked her back toward him. As his hands found her neck again, this time from behind, she pummeled his legs with her heels.

"Simon," she screamed again.

Suddenly, she heard knocking at their bedroom door.

"My lord! My lady!"

It was the admiral. Thank goodness they weren't still in London where she was certain no one would have come to her aid.

302

"Help," she screamed, only to find herself heaved onto her back on the bed.

In the next instant, the door burst open although she couldn't see Binkley from her vantage point. All she could see was Simon who held her by the front of her nightdress with one hand and had pulled his right hand back, making a fist.

"Oh God," she moaned, hearing Binkley's feet upon the floor.

Too late. Ducking to avoid the punch—or at least to protect her face—Jenny still caught a glancing blow against her ear and skull that caused her head to explode with pain while a loud ringing clamored within her brain.

And then mercifully, his attack stopped.

For as Jenny cowered with her arms up, her ear ringing, the butler went against all rules of servitude and attacked his master.

With Binkley hauling Simon away from her, right off the edge of the bed and onto the floor, she heard her husband awaken at last.

"What in blue blazes?" His voice was thick with sleep, groggy with confusion.

Binkley stood over him but was staring at the injured countess, his keen eyes boring into hers.

"He didn't mean to," she said, her voice hoarse. "Truly. He was asleep."

Almost imperceptibly, the admiral nodded before beginning to help the Earl of Lindsey to his feet.

If she could have, she would have snuck back to her room to avoid the unpleasant scene she knew would follow.

DAYS LATER, EVEN WITH the swelling in his wife's ear partly subsided, their relationship was reduced to the thinnest of strained discourse. Each encounter usually began with him cursing himself when he saw the state of her, and with her absolving him of any blame like a goddamned saint.

Simon had reached the breaking point.

"I can no longer stand to look at you."

Jenny cringed at his words, and her lovely pink cheeks paled.

"That is a terrible thing to say," she retorted. "You can't mean it."

"I do. I have told you to go stay with your family. Yet here you remain, like a battered reminder of my sick mind."

"I do not hold you responsible for what you do when asleep."

"Then you are as foolish as you are currently ugly."

She flinched, and he hoped it would take only a few more unkind words to get her to leave. For soon, he would need to take her in his arms and kiss her sweet lips and confess how he could not stand the notion of living without her.

"Be that as it may," she said, her voice trembling, "I will not abandon you, our home, or our marriage."

"This is not the marriage either of us intended."

She stood and, against all sense, moved toward him instead of away from him. "It may not be this way forever."

Involuntarily, he took a step back.

"It certainly will not," Simon agreed. "You are leaving. Today."

She shook her head. "You cannot force me. I made a mistake. I admit it. It is entirely my fault. I should never have entered—"

"You're right," he snapped. "You shouldn't have. If we hadn't retired early, if Binkley had already been asleep in the servants' quarters rather than doing his final walk through the house, then you might be dead."

He crossed his arms, looking formidable and absolutely unyielding.

"I understand you do not wish to return to your home here in Sheffield. People will talk. Your family will be disappointed."

He looked out the window considering what to do. When an idea came to him, he turned to face her.

"You will accompany your family to London. You can all go early for the Season and order Margaret's gowns."

She worried her lower lip, looking most unhappy. "For how long? When will you join us? Surely by Christmas."

His heart clenched when her voice broke on the word *Christmas*. How could he send her away? Every particle of him needed her close, wanted her there beside him. She was everything now, the only reason he wasn't locked away in his room. But he needed to heal somehow, to stop this madness. Desperately, he wanted to be the man he was before his captivity. *Was it even possible?*

All he knew for certain was hurting her was too painful. If he ever fell asleep by mistake in her bed after they made love . . . *no!*

"I don't know how long." He tried to say it calmly and kindly. After all, none of this was her fault.

"Please, Simon, I don't want to leave you." Grabbing hold of the front of his coat, she raised her gaze to his. "We love each other. I will not go."

Swallowing, he braced himself. One of them had to be strong enough.

"You will stay at our townhouse, or I will not pay for Margaret's season."

Gasping, Jenny released him. "You wouldn't stoop to such blackmail."

He narrowed his eyes at her. *Couldn't she see he meant what he said?*

"I would. Fight me on this, and there will be more at stake than merely your enduring a Season with the *bon ton*."

"What are you implying, Simon?"

"A divorced countess is infinitely better than a dead one."

Jenny reeled, her face as white as paste. Now he had her attention.

"You would let me go?"

He hated how small her voice sounded. Where was his strong, practical lady?

He balled his hands into fists at his sides. Any weakness at this point could endanger her life.

"I would save you from me. Either by living apart or, if you will not go willingly, then by divorcing you."

She put her hands over her ears, apparently unable to listen to his terrible words.

"We should call a doctor," she said, no longer looking at him, her gaze fixed on a spot past his shoulder and out the window. "You should discuss your dreams. We could make certain neither of us falls asleep when we are in the same bed—"

"We cannot take that risk! At least, I will not."

Finally, she raised her tear-filled gaze to his.

This is what I've turned her into, Simon thought. This sad-eyed creature.

"You are sending me away rather than fighting to keep me," she accused. "Then you cannot care for me as I do you."

She whirled away from his suddenly outstretched hand. When she ran from the room, Simon dropped his arm back to his side. He had persevered and won, the most terrible victory he could envision.

"YES," SAID LADY BLACKWOOD, fingering another fabric in the pale palette suitable for an eligible maiden, even if it was Margaret's second season. "That fabric is perfect. We've found four that suit you," she said to her middle daughter, "and nothing yet for your sister."

"We've found plenty that would suit her," Maggie argued. "If only she'd choose something."

Jenny raised her head when she realized they were talking about her. Sitting on a divan in the dressmaker's lounge, she had been staring into her cup of tea, her thoughts taking her many miles away.

"I do not need gowns, Mummy. I'm a married lady."

At least in name. Simon had let her remain his countess when he'd banished her to London.

"Of course, you do, dear. You are an earl's wife, after all. When the *little* Season starts, you will be in high demand, and you must represent your husband in the best light until he arrives."

"Yes, Mummy." She didn't have the spirit to argue. She feared the next question.

"When is the earl joining us?"

"This is about Maggie," Jenny pointed out. "Simon may not come at all, until Parliament opens."

"*Mm,*" her mother murmured but kept her thoughts to herself. "Still, you will need gowns. He gave you an allowance, didn't he?"

"He did." Jenny more than anyone knew exactly what she could spend. "Fine. I like the deep blue Maggie considered too dark for her. And the red silk and the cream and gold brocade. Done."

Setting down her cup, she stood. "If you will take my measurements, Madame Curry," she addressed the seamstress who was finishing up with Margaret, "then I will leave the choices of trim and buttons to your expert taste."

Eleanor was getting only a few day gowns to replace what she had grown out of. For the most part, she would remain inside the Devere townhouse when Maggie and Jenny began the endless engagements. Knowing her youngest sister would be bored and resentful, Jenny wondered if she could use her newfound status as a countess to introduce Eleanor to other girls her age, those similarly marooned in London.

In another half hour, they had left the modiste's shop and were heading along the high end of Knightsbridge Street, when they ran into Lord Cambrey.

"A pleasure to see you once more, Lady Lindsey. And so soon."

Jenny bowed and smiled, remembering her recent triumph and their champagne celebration.

"May I introduce you to my mother, Lady Blackwood, and my sisters, Miss Margaret and Eleanor."

It was not lost on her how Lord Cambrey managed to pay respectful attendance to their mother while keeping his lingering gaze on Maggie, and he seemed not to notice Eleanor at all.

Maggie, for her part, turned on her infamous charm and projected a dazzling smile. When Lord Cambrey could escape the pull of her sister, he turned to Jenny again.

"I thought you had returned to the countryside."

"Yes, we had. Lord Lindsey is there still." What could she say? "I am helping prepare my sister for the Season."

He glanced again at Maggie, and Jenny was certain of at least one name on her lovely sister's dance card.

"When is Simon returning?"

"I'm afraid I couldn't say." Did he hear the tension in her voice? She hoped not.

When an invitation for his lordship to come to dinner at the week's end had been offered and accepted, they moved on.

"He is adorable," Maggie said as soon as he was safely out of earshot.

Jenny rolled her eyes. "He's not a kitten or a young pup, for goodness sake."

Maggie giggled as if she were already half in love. "No, but he *is* adorable just the same. I wish I had a new gown for Friday."

"There are *pret-a-porter* at Mrs. Landsdowne's," their mother suggested. "Shall we at least go take a look?"

"We should, indeed," Maggie said.

SIMON HAD BEEN WITHOUT his wife a mere four days and thought he was losing what little was left of his mind. Oh, he was busy enough as there was always some task that needed handling on his estate or at one of his manufacturing holdings.

Yet, he couldn't focus on any one thing for very long. Since Jenny had left, his nightmares had only grown worse, evident by his bedclothes tangled upon the floor and sometimes himself as well, awakening only when crashing to the carpet.

In the mornings, he was increasingly exhausted and at night, he was considering sitting in the chair again.

"You coward!" he muttered to himself as he realized he was staring blankly at the shelves of books in the library instead of actually attending to the letter to his ale distributor.

"My lord?" Mr. Binkley asked as he happened into the room at that precise moment.

"Nothing," he said glumly. "What is for dinner?"

The butler blinked. "I'm not sure, my lord. You've never asked me before."

"I didn't care before, I suppose. The countess told me every afternoon what she'd asked Cook to prepare. It does get one anticipating a good meal."

Mr. Binkley nodded. "I see, my lord. Shall I go ask Cook?"

Simon hesitated. Everything tasted like the shavings from the saw mill since Jenny had moved out. What did he care whether dinner be lamb or beef?

"No, never mind." He had to focus on more important matters than what he would eat, especially since he didn't give a damn if he ever ate again. Not seeing his wife's beautiful face across from him at the table made every meal a torturous affair.

"Who is Dolbert? Have you heard of such a person?"

"Yes, my lord. He was the tutor Lady Devere employed for her children."

"I see. Where is he now?"

"Gone, my lord. He has not been to the house in weeks."

"If he ever does return, please bring him to me at once."

"Yes, my lord. Will that be all?"

As soon as Simon had dismissed Binkley, his thoughts returned to the same thing, his cowardice at not wishing to discuss his dreams with Jenny or with anyone. Wasn't it enough having terrible visions flit through his head when he was awake? Did he have to dredge up the ones that haunted him at night and examine those as well? And to what end? He was not like a carriage wheel with broken spokes, easily mended.

He did, however, begin to consider what could help, if anything. Crossing the room to the shelves of books, Simon ran his gaze along their spines. *What could help him?*

Jenny's words repeated in his mind, that he couldn't possibly feel for her what she felt for him. *Bah!* The only time since he'd known her that she had been absolutely wrong. He loved her deeply. Hadn't he told her? Apparently, not enough, and his words could never make up for his heinous actions.

That she cared for him at all astounded him, for he was fairly sure if she beat on him each night, his ardor would cool.

He wanted to scream his frustration. Instead, he grabbed at the first book his fingers touched. Shakespeare's *A Midsummer Night's Dream.*

With a sour expression, he shoved it back upon the shelf. Then, however, he espied the lowest shelf of works in foreign languages. His father had always had a collection of texts in French, German, and Italian. There, next to Perrault's volume of fairytales were two books by Wolff, *Psychologia empirica* and *Psychologia rationalis.*

"A man does not cure himself," Simon muttered aloud, then turned quickly, thinking somehow Binkley would be there once again, overhearing his master's strange ramblings. But he was alone.

In any case, these books were in Latin, and Simon had no way of knowing if an answer was in there. He doubted it. But what if there was someone somewhere who knew what was happening to him. He didn't even care why. He only wanted a cure.

One thing was certain, the best place to find the answers was not in the Sheffield countryside of England. Nor could he traipse around London looking for assistance. Not only was Jenny there, but so were many people who knew him, and they would begin to ask questions.

No, he had to seek the answer somewhere on the Continent.

JENNY WELCOMED JOHN ANGSLEY, Lord Cambrey into her London townhouse, all the while thinking herself a fraud. She was no more Simon's true countess than she was the lady of Belton Manor from which she'd been unceremoniously tossed out and banned.

Still, she could play the part of Lady Lindsey until . . . until Simon did actually decide to divorce her. In any case, Lord Cambrey was a gracious guest with stories of London that were of the appropriate nature for all parties at the table.

Moreover, to her delight, he brought his young cousin, Beryl, who was staying with his parents in Town. And immediately, it was decided she and Eleanor would be fast companions when they had to sit out the Season's many events.

"Thank you," Jenny said to Lord Cambrey as they were leaving the dining room for the drawing room. "It was thoughtful of you to notice Eleanor and bring her company. That has eased my mind. A young girl experiencing loneliness, especially in London, can get up to no end of mischief."

Out of earshot of her family, he asked, "And how about a new wife?"

Jenny looked at him sharply. There was no possible way he could have gleaned anything from a single meeting on the street and a dinner party.

"I had a letter from Simon," he continued.

Why did that make her heart start to pound? *Good God, had he told his friend before his wife he intended to break their vows?*

"You look alarmed. I apologize. He said only that he was not planning on coming to London at present, but rather, he has set off for the Continent."

She felt ill. If she were not the hostess, she would excuse herself at once so she could go sob in her room.

Lord Cambrey touched her arm. "I've made it even worse. Again, my apologies. Of course, I assumed you knew. Simon asked me to check in on you and your family in his stead. And it is a pleasure, I assure you, not a task."

She could hardly listen to him. Why was Simon going across the channel? And for how long?

"I appreciate your attentiveness, Lord Cambrey, but I'm sure my mother and I can shepherd my sister through a Season."

"I know perfectly well how capable you are, and if the rest of the Blackwood women are anything like you, then Miss Margaret's Season will be a rousing success. Yet, I would be honored to escort all of you to any functions you wish. Most likely, I would be attending them anyway."

"What are you two discussing over here with your heads together?" Maggie asked. It was boldly asked and implied something almost untoward. Except Jenny knew her sister was simply trying to enter into the conversation. She also knew she ought to back away and let them converse.

"We were discussing the best way to navigate the offerings of the *bon ton*. Why don't you tell Lord Cambrey which events we are planning to attend while I go see if we have any more of that delicious Spanish wine in the pantry."

Jenny walked away from the couple. In truth, a glass of madeira would certainly ease the sting of learning secondhand that her husband had left for parts unknown. Still, more and more families were returning to London from their country homes, and before long, the Christmas season would be upon them. Why, she would hardly notice her loneliness when the celebrations began, from Christmas Eve to the Epiphany.

Yes, that's what Jenny was counting on, a thoroughly busy end of the year and beginning of the next, and then the rounds of the Season as soon as Parliament resumed. *Oh joy!* And she wouldn't think about when or if she would ever see her husband again.

CHAPTER TWENTY-FIVE

Simon lifted the heavy knocker, letting it fall with a resounding clank. When no one answered, he pushed the door open and climbed the flight of stairs as he'd been directed. The man he'd come to see, this good doctor of philosophy, had supposedly studied all there was to know about his particular affliction. Indeed, when he found the right office, there upon the learned man's door under his nameplate were the words *"Praktiker der Psychologie."*

Simon rolled his eyes, barely countenancing his own weeks of futilely chasing a cure. And now, he was hoping to be seen, diagnosed, and treated by one Carl von Holtzenhelm.

"Enter."

Taking a fortifying breath, Simon pushed open the door and entered the small office on the upper floor of a dingy grey building in Heidelberg.

At a plain, wooden desk sat a man with a short salt-and-pepper beard. He looked up as Simon entered. For a long moment, the doctor took measure of him. Then he rose and leaned over the desk.

"Come closer, Herr Devere. Open your eyes to their widest."

Simon did so.

"Stick out your tongue," came the next order.

Again, Simon complied.

"You look healthy and sane," Holtzenhelm said at last.

"I hope I am both, *Herr Doktor.*"

"Have a seat, and we shall begin."

The man of science waited while Simon took the only other chair. It was slightly undersized and extremely hard, with a seat that was too short for his thighs and a plain wooden back that dug into his spine. Nevertheless, Simon tried to remain still and not wriggle like a child.

"It's uncomfortable on purpose," Holtzenhelm said after staring at Simon.

"Why ever for?"

"Keeps you from being able to dissemble or to create layers of invented happenings and excuses that would muddy the waters between us and the truth."

Really! A damned painful chair did all that? Or perhaps the man was nothing more than a quack.

"I have your letter here somewhere. I know you went to see Reichenbach. A smart man. We both have these on our shelves." With those words, he gestured to the books on the nearby shelf with titles Simon either couldn't translate or, if in English, didn't recognize. Nonetheless, it gave him a sense of confidence to see such works of philosophy and psychology in the man's office.

The small practitioner steepled his fingers and considered. "Why did you come to me?"

"Reichenbach suggested it. He's studied my issue, which he called somnambulism, but other than labeling me a 'sensitive,' he couldn't help me."

Simon fidgeted and crossed his legs. "He thought perhaps you could."

"Hmm." Holtzenhelm grunted. "Maybe. Tell me everything. Leave nothing out. I need to hear it more

thoroughly than in your letter. The descriptions of your actions were too vague."

Simon swallowed. He had specifically not gone into detail with what had occurred.

"I fail to see how the particulars matter. I am utterly asleep when I become violent. I have a wife, and I cannot trust myself to share a bed with her."

"You have injured her?" Holtzenhelm asked.

Simon nodded.

"You are dreaming, of course, at the time, and acting out your dream," the small man added. "Is it always the same dream?"

Simon considered. "The details vary slightly, but the dream is quite consistent."

"Tell me." With those words, Holtzenhelm leaned back in a chair clearly more comfortable than the one upon which Simon sat stiffly upright, for slouching brought only more discomfort to his back.

"I am in a very recognizable cell, in Burma. I was there for two years. In the dream, I am convinced I can overcome one of the guards and save my cousin."

"Is it always the same guard?"

Simon frowned down at his lap. "I believe so. No, maybe not. But I always want to kill him with my bare hands."

"Because then you can escape?"

Shaking his head, Simon nearly answered no. "Because then I can save Toby."

"Toby is your cousin?"

"He was. He died in the cell."

"Do you feel responsible for his death?"

"I *am* responsible," Simon intoned.

Holtzenhelm's forehead crinkled. "Why do you say that? You were both prisoners, no?"

"I was bigger, stronger. I should have protected him. It's the only reason I went along. He only wanted water."

"I see."

"No, you don't," Simon insisted. "He had a wife and children."

"I'm sorry," Holtzenhelm offered.

"And our guard was so . . . puny. On any given day, either Toby or myself could have beaten him with one hand. But that worthless scum ran him through for asking for water!"

The man across from Simon nodded.

"In your dream, you are not intent on escaping, only on saving your cousin?"

"I don't understand your question. If I kill the guard, both will happen."

"Is Toby alive in the cell in your dream?"

Simon pondered a long time, going over any of the dreams he could recall. He realized the answer.

"Yes, he is alive."

"In your dream, you save him by killing the guard. In reality, you can only save yourself."

"I shouldn't live while Toby died."

"That's ridiculous. I hope you see that. Of course, your cousin should not have died, but neither should you. Nor should you punish yourself or feel the tremendous guilt I can hear you are carrying with you still."

Simon jumped to his feet. "I am not carrying anything." Then he marched to the far end of the room in two strides, realizing he was beginning to sweat.

Turning, he shuffled back to stand behind the hard chair.

"Good God, man, this room is not much larger than the cell I was in. How do you stand it?"

Holtzenhelm shrugged. "I work with the boundless reaches of the human mind, the psyche if you will, and no room can confine it. I need only a place for you and for me to talk. Right now, confined in this room, can you recall the dream any better?"

Simon felt the sweat between his shoulder blades. "I can."

"When you are in the dream, do you know it is a dream?"

"I assure you if I did, then I would not be trying to strangle my wife."

The practitioner's eyes widened slightly, then he nodded.

"That is what we must work on then. We must make your brain understand you are in a dream. As soon as you are able to do that, then you will be in control."

Simon took in the man's words, and finally, he sat down again. The chair didn't seem quite as uncomfortable.

"How do I do that?"

"I will help you. We will find the cues that indicate a dream because they do not match up to what you know is reality. There will be some, I assure you, and when you see them, you must recognize them. Even if you cannot wake yourself immediately, you must not try to kill the guard."

"I must not kill the guard," Simon repeated doubtfully.

Holtzenhelm nodded. "I will help you."

JENNY THREW HERSELF INTO the spirit of the winter festivals and the jubilant parties that were being thrown all around her. Although it was inappropriate to host anything herself with her new husband away, her mother wouldn't let her brood indoors.

"Tonight is the Yule party at Lady Atwood's," Lady Blackwood reminded her.

Jenny grimaced. "And then some clever clogs will insist on a reading of Dickens's work. Because how very unusual and unexpected!"

Maggie laughed as she did a lot lately, obviously happy to be in London once more. "Gracious, I can't take that story one more time this month!"

"Even I am growing weary of Mr. Dickens's Christmas tale," Eleanor chimed in, "and I truly think it is very fanciful and well told. Anyway, I'm pleased I am permitted to attend."

"And Lord Cambrey's cousin will be there," Maggie added, making Jenny smile. Both the earl and his young cousin, Beryl, were keeping her two sisters occupied and happy, albeit for quite different reasons.

Jenny wished she could ask Simon more about Lord Cambrey his nature, and his possible intentions toward Maggie. Did the man treat women's hearts frivolously or with care? Had he many attachments in the past? How about currently? And what were the state of his finances and holdings?

Sighing, she looked around the sumptuous drawing room that was now hers, filled with her own family. Look how far they'd come from having to sell their own home and head for the country, facing permanent banishment. Yet here they were, preparing for a Season, enjoying an event-filled Christmas, reconnecting with old acquaintances. Still, she felt the yawning gap of loneliness.

THE MUSIC ENDED WITH a perfectly delightful rendition of de Pearsall's "Lay a Garland," and then their hostess, still clapping for the pianist and the singer, stood before the crowd.

"I have a special treat," she announced. "Lady Elizabeth Benchley, a friend to Mr. Dickens himself, will read stave one and stave five of *A Christmas Carol.* Isn't that splendid?"

This was greeted with rousing applause, although Jenny suspected it was made warmer by the appearance of nearly a dozen servants carrying trays with goblets of fizzy drinks and sweetmeats.

She stood. "I'm going to take a stroll and see the paintings in the gallery. Would anyone care to join me?"

Her mother shook her head. "I've promised Lady Delia that I shall go over the midweek carnival entertainment for Argyll House. Do you mind, dear?"

"Not at all," Jenny said. Eleanor had her head together with her new friend, Beryl, and for an instant, she wondered if Ned and Maisie would be attending the Season. That could be awkward, indeed.

Maggie stood beside her. *Ah,* here was company at last, but her sister looked right past her with that beatific smile that could only mean one thing—Lord Cambrey was close by.

Without even answering Jenny's invitation for a stroll, Maggie sighed.

"Isn't he handsome?" And with that utterance, she pushed past Jenny, who turned to see . . . well! Not Lord Cambrey but another young eligible bent over Maggie's hand and brought it to his lips.

Despite the momentary shock that Maggie already had another suitor, Jenny realized it was sensible for her sister not to get too attached to any man yet. This young man, not too tall but well dressed, invited Maggie to accompany him to the refreshment table for a lemonade.

So romantic. And so public! Jenny had almost forgotten how every single moment one spent with the opposite sex was on display for all to witness. How unlike her own hasty and private courting. Why, no one except Cambrey had even seen her and Simon together, except for Crocky and the strangers at Vauxhall.

For all anyone knew, she wasn't the Countess of Lindsey at all but a squatter who'd taken up residence in the Devere townhouse.

Turning away from the scene of her sister's starry-eyed encounter, she followed a flow of people between one room and the next. Behind her, she heard Lady Benchley begin the story in an exaggerated manner that grated upon Jenny's nerves.

"Marley was dead to begin with."

In a few minutes, she found herself in a long hallway enjoying a collection of massive landscapes, beautifully set in matching gilded frames. One looked as if it could have been painted near Belton Park. Backing up a few steps, she stared longingly at the countryside, recalling the many times Simon had caught her alone and made love to her, either with passionate kissing or something even bolder. Did he miss her presence as she did his?

"Miss Blackwood, is it you?"

Turning, she encountered Viscount Alder, her once-fiancé. For the briefest moment, a frisson of nerves danced through her. How she wished Simon were by her side to show this man someone else had found her worthy of giving her his name.

Many women would give him the cut direct and walk away. Rightly so, too. Yet, she had never been the type for such rudeness.

"My lord," she greeted, not curtsying. She would be damned if she'd lower herself an inch in presence. "However, I am Lady Lindsey now."

He nodded. "I heard rumor you had married."

"More than a rumor," Jenny said, feeling the heat bloom on her cheeks.

"Congratulations," he said. "And apparently, marriage suits you well. You look stunning."

Did she? She wondered at his gentle manner and his sweet compliment. True, he had been that way during their brief association. Yet, given the way in which he'd ruthlessly cast her off, she had thought to encounter a different Michael Alder if ever they met again.

"I had not heard you'd returned to London," he added.

Perhaps suddenly considering the matter, Viscount Alder glanced around them as if expecting Simon to pop out from behind the long draperies.

"Will I have the honor of greeting Lord Lindsey this evening?"

"He has not come to London," Jenny admitted, keeping her tone neutral. "He had business to attend elsewhere."

The viscount's eyebrows raised almost into his hairline. "A strange time to do business," he said. "What with a new wife and it being nearly Christmas."

She shrugged, offering him no more information, letting her eyes wander back to the painting.

"Will he join you soon?" Lord Alder asked.

"Mm," Jenny murmured noncommittally. Why on earth did it matter to the infernal man?

Alder drew a step closer. "I am glad we have run into each other if for no other reason than so I can offer you my sincerest apology."

That caught her attention. She stared at him. Her former beau looked a little older in only a year. No doubt, after all that had happened, she did, too. Yet there was a sadness to his eyes that had not been there before, a strained look causing slight creases in his forehead.

"Are you well?" she heard herself asking, although she didn't know why she should have any sympathy toward him.

At her words, his face relaxed, and he actually gave her the slightest of smiles. Maggie had been wrong. His lips looked fine to her. Not nearly as handsome as Simon's but passingly pleasing, all the same.

"Thank you for asking," Alder replied. "I don't deserve your kindness, I know that. In any case, there have been complications in my life with which I won't bore you. Perhaps some time, we may take a stroll around the park as old friends and talk. Married ladies have more freedom, nearly like men. Have you discovered that?"

Jenny perceived nothing nefarious in his words.

"What a peculiar thing to say, but yes, I know what you mean."

"I always admired you," he blurted.

Oh, dear. Did he harbor some hope of a reconciliation? Leaning away, she said, "It is inappropriate for you to say such."

He gave a nonchalant shrug that instantly, almost painfully reminded her of Simon.

"Circumstances occurred beyond my control and I regret how quickly you disappeared from my life."

As he spoke, she raised a gloved hand to her lips in dismay. For without a doubt now, she saw pain lingering in his gaze. Could it be he had genuinely cared for her?

At her continued silence, he added, "That was, no doubt, also inappropriate to say, particularly to a recently wedded wife."

Offering him a small smile in return, Jenny said, "I shall overlook it, my lord."

"You have moved on and look well. For your sake, I am very pleased."

She patted his arm because something about him drew her to do so. At the same moment, his hand covered her gloved one upon his forearm, she heard a familiar voice.

"There you are, Lady Lindsey."

Pulling her hand back as if burned, Jenny turned to see Lord Cambrey almost upon them. Hoping she didn't look guilty—knowing her cheeks were now scarlet—she feared she did.

However, instead of censure from her husband's friend, she saw only wariness in his gaze directed at Alder.

For his part, Lord Alder dropped his arm to his side and offered a bow to the earl.

Cambrey kept his eyes upon the viscount even while he addressed Jenny.

"Your sister noticed you'd been gone for a long while, and you never know what disreputable types lurk in these hallways."

"Do you know Lord Alder?" she asked, trying to initiate a more general conversation.

"Vaguely." Cambrey continued to stare hard at Alder, who began to bristle.

Apparently, Simon had left her in good hands, for his friend was championing her where there was absolutely no need.

Since the men were not about to discuss fox hunting and the best make of tobacco, Jenny decided she had better separate them.

"Shall we go back to the reading? I don't want to miss the ending, nor to further worry my family."

Cambrey only nodded and reached for her arm.

Lord Alder spoke again.

"Lady Lindsey, it was a distinct pleasure running into you this evening."

She knew better than to own to the same pleasure since it might sap the last of Cambrey's patience. She gave Michael Alder a slight nod.

"Good evening, my lord." With that, she let Cambrey lead her away.

However, after a step or two, he halted and looked over his shoulder.

"Just so we're clear, Alder, the countess is under my protection while her husband is absent from London. I consider it my honor to do any small service for such a war hero as our Lindsey. I will be certain to advise him as to your close attention to his wife when next I see him."

Jenny rolled her eyes at this absurd display of male posturing. Yet she would not gainsay Cambrey for risk of humiliating him. To do so would be a direct insult to her own husband. She hoped, however, that the viscount didn't give a moment's worry to the Earl of Lindsey with his dander raised for that was unlikely. She had done nothing wrong.

When they turned the corner, she felt Cambrey's stiffness relax.

"Thank you for coming to get me. The viscount surprised me out of nowhere, but he was quite harmless, I assure you."

"Rather like a maiden aunt at a family gathering, you think?"

She laughed. "Precisely."

"My lady, Alder is a tad more dangerous than a spinster with chin hair. I would advise you to steer well clear of him."

With that, they were back in the bustling, brightly lit main hall, and there was her family, along with Cambrey's cousin Beryl, laughing and talking, the reading of Dickens apparently over.

"May I escort you ladies to your carriage?" Cambrey asked.

"Oh, please let us stay another few minutes," Beryl asked. "I want to find Maryliss and introduce Eleanor to her."

"Very well," Cambrey said, and the youngest two scurried away clutching each other's arms excitedly while trying to maintain some demeanor of ladylike decorum.

"We are happy your cousin has taken to our Eleanor," Lady Blackwood intoned. "I imagine in a year or two, it will be their turn to come out."

Cambrey looked taken aback. He glanced the way the girls had gone.

"I don't believe my aunt and uncle have considered next year's Season for Beryl. She seems so young."

Anne Blackwood chuckled slightly. "They all seem young, my lord, until suddenly, they do not. And girls grow up in the blink of an eye into women."

Cambrey's glance took in Maggie, lingering for longer than perhaps polite, before dropping to the floor.

Jenny smiled. *Yes, this might be Maggie's second incomplete Season if Lord Cambrey's thoughts were going in the direction of one particular grown up female.*

Suddenly, more than anything, Jenny wanted Simon by her side, to look at her in the same way as if she were the jammiest bit of jam.

Simon's lovemaking had caused her to believe he truly wanted and needed her by his side. Could she possibly have been mistaken? Had he married her for business matters, to sort out the mess his accounts had been in? Was he even now with another woman in France or Italy?

Later that night, when she sat on her bed—what should be *their* bed—Jenny considered the possibility that given Simon's vexing nighttime condition, he might consider a mistress to be more desirable than a wife. One didn't expect to spend the night with a lightskirt, did one? He could toss her out or leave her side at any time.

Perhaps all she had to do was vow to never sleep with him or even attempt it again. After all, for the pleasure of his company and for being his wife in all other ways, she could make that vow. If he would only give her the chance.

The next morning was the first time she felt the nausea that plagued her for the next few weeks until her condition was confirmed. She was with child.

CHAPTER TWENTY-SIX

"Mummy, please, let things be."

"You must notify your husband, I say." Her mother started in on the same argument for the third day in a row since she had found out about her eldest daughter's condition.

Jenny had told Maggie, who instead of keeping it to herself had exclaimed with joy at becoming an aunt. In fact, Maggie was exuberant and joyful at nearly everything these days, wearing a constant glow that Jenny thought should have been hers.

In any case, her mother and younger sister knew almost before Jenny's cup of weak, milky tea had grown cold.

"Simply write to him. He's been absent from you too long. He is a caring man and would want to be with you. Besides, whatever business he has abroad cannot be as important as his heir."

Her mother had no idea how difficult her request was. Jenny would have to ask Cambrey precisely where her husband was and whether he could get word to him. *How humiliating!* Perhaps she could offhandedly inquire as to whether Cambrey had heard from Simon, and not let him know she had not. Still, Jenny would need an address if he were abroad, and how could she obtain it without telling John Angsley her plight.

The abandoned wife, and now abandoned mother-to-be.

How she wished she and Simon had been given the time to settle things between them before a child came along. On the other hand, it comforted her there would be no more talk of ending their union, not now that a son or daughter of the house of Devere was on its way.

Meanwhile, she could do nothing else but wait and continue to play hostess to her family, smile at everyone who congratulated her on her marriage, and prevaricate to those who asked after her absent husband. She would continue to pretend everything was as it should be until it became the truth.

SIMON AWAKENED IN HIS cell. Pressing down on the strangely soft dirt underneath him, he raised himself to a seated position and took stock of his surroundings. Despite the dim light, oddly there were no rats. He had a feeling that fact was important because there were always rats at dawn and dusk.

Still, gazing miserably at the bars, it was a cell like it always was. He'd been dreaming of Belton Manor and . . . a bearded man who had been speaking with an accent. *A doctor*, he thought.

Moreover, he'd been dreaming of a lovely woman with wide, knowing eyes and a lush, kissable mouth. He could almost remember her name.

Glancing sideways, there was Toby. His cousin sat on the ground simply gazing at him quietly. Toby needed him to kill the jailer, or he would die.

With quiet resolution, Simon knew he had to strangle the man who held the keys.

ANOTHER PARTY, ANOTHER NEARLY unendurable evening standing with the ineligibles, both the widowed, the matrons, and the wallflowers. She could stave off the boredom by imagining who was interested in whom. Then there were the brief conversations with those who had been her friends prior to her disastrous last Season and flight to Sheffield.

Obviously, most everyone probed for details regarding her missing husband, some out of malice, which she ignored, some out of pity, which she could not bear.

Indeed, Jenny was becoming increasingly aware of consolatory glances. Except for a few days in London when Simon had been dealing with Crocky, no one had seen her husband in over three years. However, they had certainly *heard* of him.

Immediately upon his return to English soil, the rumors that had originally blown on a cruel breeze from Sheffield to London had earned him the label of Lord Despair. Now that she was in residence in the Devere townhouse, boldly taking part in the little Season's activities with no earl by her side, the breeze was becoming a tempest.

"He is mad as a march hare," twittered a young woman, hardly concealing her mouth behind her fan, as she stared at Jenny.

"I heard they have restrained his arms and legs," said another.

"And he has to be fed like a baby," loudly exclaimed a third.

With most of the remarks that drifted to her ears, Jenny pointedly stared down the speaker. Occasionally, she rolled her eyes to show her utter disregard for their ridiculous speculation. However, lately, with her desire to sit down or to stay home altogether, standing tall and proud was becoming a far more difficult chore. She was tired. She was generally queasy from morning until nearly suppertime.

At some point, perhaps in two months, maybe three, she would have to enter confinement. Then how shredded would both their reputations become?

The missing earl and his disappearing countess!

And would her babe be born with his or her father still missing?

The tempest would reach biblical proportions.

"Jenny, stop frowning," her mother said, appearing by her side after doing the rounds of the room with her friend Lady Delia.

Maggie appeared at her other side. "I wish you would dance."

The idea of spinning and twirling held positively no appeal.

"Where is Lord Cambrey?" For certainly to see Maggie without him was an oddity.

"We cannot dance more than two dances in a night without someone crying out the banns," Maggie said, rolling her eyes, yet to Jenny it appeared the idea wasn't displeasing to her sister. "We have a dance coming up soon enough."

"Who is next on your card?" their mother asked.

Maggie angled the square paper dangling from her wrist, then she made a face.

"Oh," she exclaimed in dismay, glancing at Jenny. "I nearly forgot. Your former fiancé sketched in his name before I even realized who he was, but I am certainly not doing him the honor."

Jenny felt ill for more than one reason but stayed silent. Hopefully, it was a coincidence.

"Why would Lord Alder seek to dance with you?" Lady Blackwood asked her middle daughter. "He can be certain I would never allow an association between him and you, not after his shoddy treatment of our Jenny. I'm sure other parents feel the same way. Why, I can't even imagine why he is here!" she finished with some vehemence, scanning the crowd as if she might scorch him from the room with her gaze alone.

Jenny nearly smiled. Nearly. Her mother's dander was well and truly up. Yet she couldn't help wondering if Michael were using Maggie to gain information about her and, more importantly, her husband. The *ton* moved in such sneaky ways it wouldn't be surprising. Except regarding the viscount, it did surprise her for he had never seemed the type to deal in gossip.

"Mummy, I am more than pleased to miss this next quadrille," Maggie stated. "I'm sure Lord Alder was simply being polite." She looked sorry to have mentioned him at all. "Why, I doubt he will even show up to claim his dance."

Just then, another young buck, Lord Westing, the same who'd kissed Maggie's hand at Lady Atwood's, appeared in their midst. The only son of the Duke of Westing with dashing good looks to boot, the marquess had every girl's gaze upon him.

After bowing to each of the ladies beginning with the senior, he turned his attention to Maggie.

"You are not dancing, Miss Blackwood, which robs the room of much enjoyment. It is too late to begin this dance, yet perhaps I may have the next?"

Maggie eyed him up and down. Jenny, too, gave this new prospect the once over. After all, although Lord Cambrey was impressive, neither his attention was certain, nor were his intentions clear. Besides, Maggie had an entire Season and many young gentlemen to consider.

What would her persnickety sister think of this one? Westing certainly cut a good figure in his jacket and breeches. His ascot was perfectly tied. What's more, he had a chiseled jaw and very blue eyes under a thick head of dark brown hair. Both Jenny and her mother waited, breath bated.

Maggie's dazzling smile appeared as if she'd pulled it out of her glove and pasted it on, and she batted those glorious eyelashes.

Biting her lower lip to keep from laughing, Jenny had to give her sister her due. Men found Maggie's flirting to be beyond charming.

"Why, I believe my next dance is free," Maggie offered, without looking at her card.

Jenny sighed. Woe betide the man whose name was in the next space as, knowing Maggie, there most assuredly was one. Whoever he was, he would be left like a ship without its sail, uselessly stranded.

Westing took in the bustling room. "Perhaps we can go together to the refreshment table before our dance begins. It is less crowded there at present."

"A splendid idea." With that complimentary phrase, Maggie let her new admirer take her arm in his.

After bowing once more to Jenny and her mother, Lord Westing led her away.

The remaining Blackwood women looked at each other, eyes wide, until Lady Blackwood spoke. "I've heard good things of that young man. Not only fine looking, if I may say from my advanced years, but well-behaved. And in line to inherit a great deal. Every eligible miss here is envying our Margaret at this moment." She gazed in the direction they'd gone. "What do you think of such a match?"

"Mummy, every dance with a man cannot result in a match. Yet I agree, he is a handsome man. As long as he is kind and loyal," she added, thinking of Simon's finer qualities, "and loves Maggie so much he never wants to be without her."

Dear God, tears were pricking her eyes.

Her mother grabbed her hand and held it, clasped safely.

"Are you all right, dear one? Shall I get you something to drink? That helped me when," she lowered her voice, "when carrying each of you three."

"Something cold would be welcome," Jenny allowed, and her mother nodded and hurried off.

No doubt Lady Blackwood considered it a good excuse to spy on her middle daughter and see how she was faring with Westing.

Tapping her toe quietly along with the music, Jenny remained alone until the dance ended. Lord Cambrey appeared, obviously searching for Maggie. Oh dear, was his name next on her sister's card?

"Both your mother and sister have vanished," he observed.

As the music started up for a lively polka, Jenny realized Maggie must even then be dancing with Lord Westing. Would Simon's friend be annoyed?

Deciding to hold her tongue on the matter, she only nodded, smiling and observing passers-by. Let Maggie make her own decisions. Jenny had other concerns, including a matter not to be overheard by anyone.

With her mother still not returned, she decided to grab the broom by its handle.

"My lord, will you take a stroll along the gallery?"

Cambrey looked momentarily surprised, then quickly recovered.

"Certainly, my lady." And he offered her his arm.

She hoped no one took notice of their exit through the double doors behind them. Others were doing the same, and she had a certain autonomy now as a married woman that she hadn't had before. However, Lord Cambrey clearly wasn't her husband, and if someone wanted to begin a nasty rumor, they no doubt could. She would ask her question as quickly as possible and return to the ballroom.

"I will be brief," she said to him as soon as they were alone at one end of the long promenade. It must be nice in the dead of winter to have such a stretch of a hall in which to walk vigorously back and forth, especially if one had a worrisome issue, like the absence of a husband, to contend with.

"I simply wish to know if you've heard from Simon?"

As SIMON REACHED OUT for the filthy jailor, he received a slap on the face. From whence it came, he couldn't tell. He tried harder to get to the man's neck, then he received another sting to his cheek. After another, he awakened in a strange bed in a strange room.

Sighing, the earl knew precisely what had happened.

Holtzenhelm had come to Simon's apartment late in the evening and told him to sleep. And obviously, he'd awakened him in a manner that worked.

"Thank you," Simon muttered to the bespectacled man who sat on the chair beside him.

"You're welcome, but I take no pleasure in slapping you. Shall we begin?" Holtzenhelm asked.

Simon nodded, feeling weary.

"At the beginning. Every detail."

When Simon had explained the same dream in excruciating minutiae, he felt drained. After the doctor left, he took a walk in the frigidly cold city of Heidelberg.

Many of the shops were decorated with Christmas cheer, different than the English but recalling the spirit of the season all the same. *Nikolastaug* had come and gone, with all the children awaiting St. Nicholas, and even Herr Holtzenhelm had seemed to brighten days before when describing his two young sons' excitement for what treats had been in their boots the following morning.

Yet when the good doctor spoke animatedly about decorating the Tannenbaum and invited Simon to the end-of-the-year festivities, he felt an ache in his chest. As Holtzenhelm went on about the Christmas Eve dinner, describing the suckling pig, white sausage, and sweet cinnamon *reisbrei*, and then closed his eyes to describe to Simon the upcoming Christmas Day feast of plump roast goose, nutty, fruity *stollen*, and spicy *Lebkuchen*, Simon felt only sadness. He had spent the past three Christmas tidings away from England, recalling the celebrations and the familiar foods.

Now, he felt a lump in his throat at missing his first Christmas with his wife. What would it be like to see the candles reflecting in Jenny's eyes as they opened their door to carolers and toasted St. Nicholas?

He simply wanted to go home.

"I'M SORRY." LORD CAMBREY'S eyes, indeed, shone with apology. "I have heard nothing from him. It is as if Simon has disappeared into the heart of the savage nations of Europe."

As surely as he had disappeared inside her heart. Permanently, irrevocably. Hopefully, he would come out far more easily from the Continent.

She only sighed while wanting to weep. Her love for her husband was absolutely embedded in her being now, and she could hardly face each day without him. If she only knew where he was and when she might see him again, it would ease her mind.

"I would ask you to trust him and not to worry. Why, he was practically singing *Lady Greensleeves* in your honor the first time he told me about you. In any case, he must return soon," Lord Cambrey added.

His words sparked hope in Jenny's breast. "Why do you say that, my lord?"

"Parliament officially opens in a few weeks, and he had best be there."

"I see." The ramifications of an absentee representative in the House of Lords were not good, including a possible loss of Simon's privilege.

However, she doubted now she would see him for Christmas. Sure enough, when it came and went, she spent the holiday with her mother and sisters and with Lord

Cambrey's family who extended to the Blackwoods and the Countess of Lindsey more than one festive invitation.

"WHAT STANDS OUT IN your mind when you first find yourself in the cell?"

Simon bit back a curt retort and answered the doctor as simply as he could.

"That I am there again, or that I have never really left."

"It is that real to you?" Holtzenhelm asked. "You do not get the sense you are in a dream?"

Simon hesitated.

"What are you thinking?" Holtzenhelm asked.

"Each time I awaken in the cell . . . that is, when I *dream* I am back in the cell, the dirt is soft under me. It must be the bed I'm feeling. I believe I always have a moment of wondering why the dirt is comfortable after so many nights lying on the hard-packed earth."

Holtzenhelm nodded. "That is very good. If we can convince your mind the soft dirt indicates a dream, you may be able to control your actions."

Simon nodded.

"Is there anything else?" Holtzenhelm wondered. "The more signs we can reinforce to your sleeping self, the better."

Considering for a moment, Simon took himself through the dream that was more familiar to him than the environment in which he now found himself in the doctor's office.

"There is no stench. The absence of rats is also quite glaring. There were always vermin, and even more at night. They make noises, terrible noises." Feeling sweat prickle his skin, Simon closed his eyes only to have the vision of a rat appear in his mind, large and terrifying. Instantly, he snapped his eyes open.

"You seem to feel very strongly about the rats," the doctor said. "Good."

Simon stared at him. Holtzenhelm's ability to look dispassionately at Simon's trouble irked him, yet perhaps it was for the best and gave the man more clarity. But *good* was the last word he could use in conjunction with rats.

At seeing the earl's expression, *Herr Doktor* shrugged.

"I am sure you can use the absence of any strong odor and of rats in your favor."

At this, Simon barked out a laugh. "That would be a change, considering they were my nightly nemesis, and sometimes during the day, too."

"I understand," the doctor said, although Simon knew the man couldn't possibly truly understand the conditions. Nor could he know the emotions the cell invoked. The fear and anger and sadness. And guilt.

"Is there anything else? We must go through the dream again," Holtzenhelm said.

Simon retold the dream again. Awakening in the cell, no rats, the guard, his anger. Over and over. There was something else. Something on the edge of his brain, but he didn't want to think about it.

Instead of whatever it was dancing at the edge of his mind, he decided to think about Jenny, her sweet smile and shining eyes, her soft, pleasing voice. *His Jenny.*

"I will see you tomorrow," the doctor said. As he reached the door, the man added, "I bid you sweet dreams."

Did this short German have a sense of humor or was he mocking him?

Simon merely nodded.

That night, unfortunately, was no different. The dreams that had begun to happen less frequently during his brief months with Jenny now came nightly once again.

And each time he awakened, whether entangled in his bedclothes or landing on the rug, Simon thanked God Jenny was not beside him to be harmed. Would he ever find his way back to her?

CHAPTER TWENTY-SEVEN

Then the unthinkable happened. Another dinner party was underway in which Jenny was seated between two aged men with whom the hostess deemed acceptable for a married woman to converse all evening without causing a scandal.

Jenny hid her yawns behind her serviette and turned from the tediously boring man on her left who wished only to boast about his acreage and his grown children in excruciatingly minute detail to the leering, hoary nobleman on her right who kept his eyes fixed on the swell of her breasts as he inappropriately complained about his wife. That unfortunate spouse was seated as far away from her husband as the table allowed, no doubt having entreated their hostess, Lady Chantel-Weiss, to make it so.

To the old lord's only defense, Jenny's bosom had blossomed in recent weeks, and she had not yet had any of her gowns adjusted to hide the fuller figure of her condition. She doubted he had noticed her face once since they were seated together.

And then a late guest appeared, and Jenny felt a stirring of discomfort, Cousin Ned!

As soon as he caught sight of her, she knew he would cause her trouble for slighting him. His eyes narrowed and his mouth thinned while turning up as if in a smile. With a nod by way of greeting, he took his seat next to a lady halfway down the other side of the table. Jenny breathed a sigh of relief.

Normally, she and Ned might not even have cause to speak since it was simply not done across the middle of the table between the candles, the many crystal glasses, and the flowered centerpieces. However, since he'd arrived late, their hostess was determined to make him earn his dinner.

From her seat at the head of the table a few chairs down to Jenny's left, Lady Chantel-Weiss tapped on her fluted champagne glass with the long tines of her silver dinner fork.

"Everyone, hush now." Very quickly those at the table quietened and turned to their hostess.

"Since Mr. Darrow has seen fit to amble in nearly an entire half hour after we have all been seated, I demand from him reparation."

Knowing what was coming, many started to laugh, some slapped hands on the tablecloth in encouragement.

"Yes, my lady," Ned said at once, practically preening at being the center of attention where another might look abashed by his own rude behavior. "Whatever reparation you wish, I shall endeavor to satisfy and do so as befits this gentle gathering."

Jenny wanted to roll her eyes, only thankful she was not in fact Mrs. Darrow, nor even generally known as Ned's second cousin. His affected speech made her want to bring back up the shrimp paste on toast points that had greeted guests on tiny plates as they sat down to dine.

"You must tell us an entertaining story," Lady Chantel-Weiss said. "Isn't that right, my lord?"

However, Lord Chantel-Weiss either didn't hear her or didn't care, for at the other end of the table, on Jenny's right, the good man continued slurping his potato soup.

"But hear me, Mr. Darrow," their hostess continued. "Your story must be novel and interesting, or you shall be shown the door."

Many laughed again, but when Ned's eyes turned upon her, Jenny felt a frisson of dread. There was something in his gaze, a malicious glint.

"Very well," he said. "A story?" He steepled his fingers a moment in front of him as if considering.

All the while, Jenny's sense of dread increased, bringing on a racing heart. In turn, her skin felt clammy as she broke out into a light sheen of perspiration.

"A few months back, I took a trip to the country to visit family members who'd fallen upon particularly dire straits." Ned paused dramatically. "Financially, if you take my meaning."

With her soup spoon still clenched in one hand, Jenny stared down at the tablecloth in front of her plate and bit her lower lip against the physical discomfort she was experiencing.

"While I was there, I witnessed the strangest courtship imaginable."

"Do tell," said a voice from farther down the table.

"Speak up," said another.

"I will," Ned said. "What do you make of a young woman with no title and no dowry visiting a wealthy nobleman's house?"

Jenny nearly gasped her dismay aloud.

"Is this a riddle?" asked another.

"What if I told you she went day after day unchaperoned to sit in his bedchamber?"

A few other people around her did, indeed, gasp. Jenny took the opportunity to draw in a few breaths, as deeply as she could, given her tight corset. However, there was nothing she could do to tamp down either Ned's tale or the steadily rising nausea.

Warming to the attention he was receiving, Ned stood and actually paced down the length of the table.

"Moreover," he said, "despite this young woman being fair of face and form, the nobleman barely knew of her existence. At first."

"How can that be, if she was in his bedroom?" their hostess asked.

"This earl—oh, forgive me," Ned said, as if his slipping of any hint of the man's identity had been a mistake. "This nobleman was plainly *touched in the upper works*." He tapped the side of his own head.

"Gracious," exclaimed a woman.

Jenny could not raise her eyes. Were people already looking at her? Did they know?

"Still, this woman went to him to provide aid and comfort."

"I wouldn't mind that type of aid and comfort," said the lecherous fool to her right. A few men chuckled.

"In fact," continued Ned, "her services were in high demand around the entire township."

Another few gasps ensued, and the elderly Lord Chantel-Weiss, who until then had remained silent and let his wife run her party, exclaimed, "Here, now, I say, Darrow. Is this appropriate dinner talk?"

"Forgive me, my lord," Ned said, his tone placating as he walked around the end of the table behind the hostess, who was grinning and obviously enjoying the tale immensely.

"Perhaps some here have misunderstood my meaning, but this young woman was in service to the nobleman . . . as a bookkeeper, of all things."

"Stranger and stranger," someone intoned.

Jenny grabbed for her water with her free hand and nearly knocked over her wine glass.

"This lady," Ned continued, now looking directly at her, "nearly penniless, ironically had a mind for numbers and began to balance the ledgers for the whole village. She became the most dreaded of the sex, a masculine one."

"Oh, dear, dear," said Lady Chantel-Weiss.

"Yes! It is true. However, she ended up being of special assistance to the *despairing* earl."

Another gasp, and this time, Jenny was certain she felt their gazes upon her. Flexing her fingers, she dropped her forgotten spoon, which clattered onto the bowl and spattered creamy bisque across the white tablecloth.

Ned walked farther around the table as he talked, coming eventually to stand almost directly behind Jenny's chair.

"In fact, as if in this topsy-turvy tale, the woman were the famed fairytale prince and the earl were the sleeping beauty, somehow this ordinary girl awakened him from his deep stupor and, miracle of miracles, dear friends, he married her. Or thus she claims."

Jenny pushed her chair back, nearly knocking Ned off his feet as she did. The bile had reached her throat, but she would not add to her humiliation by retching here in the Chantel-Weiss's formal dining room while select members of the *ton* gaped at her.

And she certainly wouldn't give credence nor respond to Ned's awful tale, not while Simon was unable to defend himself from the pathetic portrait her cousin had painted of the earl as a drooling imbecile and her as a gold-digging Cyprian.

Why she had ever agreed to go to this gathering when Maggie was at another infernal ball and her mother was home with Eleanor, Jenny did not know.

Practically stumbling on the doorsill as the floor wavered beneath her feet, she fled the room without offering her apologies to her hosts. The murmurs of incredulity and horrified whispers mixed with the tittering of delight followed her into the hallway.

Ned was an utter scoundrel, and he would be sorry when or *if* Simon returned!

Reaching the water closet, Jenny retched into the bowl. A few minutes later, with the contents of her stomach completely vacated by violent heaving, Jenny stared

As soon as she saw her sister, she would ask her the cause of Lord Cambrey's strange behavior.

For the moment, though, she would read and reread Simon's letter, probably a hundred times. And as she sat again upon the sofa, Jenny finally brought it to her nose, inhaling deeply. Was there a lingering scent of Simon's shaving tonic or was that merely the smell of the inside of Cambrey's pocket?

CHAPTER TWENTY-EIGHT

Arriving on English soil after days of travel from Germany to the French coast, Simon admitted to a mixture of relief and trepidation. He'd been delayed in Calais by a storm that made passage impossible for a day. Then the choppy waters had caused their usually brief voyage to take nearly twice as long.

After a late-afternoon landing in Dover, he eschewed the offering of accommodations at the King's Head Inn and left at once by coach and six to London. He was exceedingly grateful his wife was not in Sheffield but, rather within a day-and-a-half reach in London.

Now that he was so close, the months of separation had shrunk down to an unbearable few hours and miles.

With his late start, the coach service reached only the port city of Rochester before halting for the night. Exhausted from the previous days of journeying followed by hours in the swaying coach, Simon fell asleep before his head hit the pillow.

As had happened for the last two weeks, when the dream came, he faced it with confidence, his mind trained to determine the falsity of it. In fact, the dream did not come steer me toward Lady Delia. When I learned the truth, I saw no reason to continue the farce of having any interest in that lady, certainly not to please my parents."

"I am very sorry," Jenny said and meant it. She could even admit to contrition over briefly thinking ill of him. "What point is there, however, in going over all this now? You know I am married."

"Yes, *Lady Lindsey*, I know." Alder gave her a long look. "I suppose I wanted you to know I had not cared a fig about your financial situation, and that the dishonorable action was not mine. After what my parents did, I also needed to know if you are happy. I've watched you from a distance. You are here for the Season and are quite obviously alone. A new bride alone in London does not bode well. Married, yes, but happy?"

A myriad of feelings coursed through her. Whatever she said could be construed as disrespectful to Simon and a betrayal of the intimacy between husband and wife. Yet, Lord Alder had been forthcoming, and his aura of sadness touched her heart.

Certainly, she could tell him something. That she had got over him quickly was probably not the right thing, nor was disclosing her present predicament.

"Let us walk again," Jenny offered, for there were, indeed, others who might be eavesdropping.

Back in the brisk air, strolling beside him instead of looking directly at him, she could more easily confess she wished her husband were in London.

"What prevents him?"

"I'm not sure." Realizing how vague that sounded, Jenny added, "I believe he will be here any day."

To her surprise, he stopped and, as he had hold of her arm, she halted beside him. There, on the Serpentine path, Alder turned toward her and looked down into her eyes with an expression she could not quite fathom.

In the back of her mind, she was aware this was not a good situation to be seen in if recognized. Furthermore, she could see from the corner of her eyes there were other people on the path.

Yet the viscount still held her gaze. In fact, his dropped briefly to her mouth, causing her to gasp slightly.

Recalling their surroundings, Alder stiffened, his glance securely upon her eyes once again.

"I accept you are no longer free, but I confess I wish it were otherwise." He gave a small grunt of pained laughter, and she reached up, putting her hand on his shoulder.

The poor man. She had no wish to be the cause of his pain.

"You are the woman I intended to spend my life with. And despite your marital status, I cannot help but care for you."

Jenny shook her head, yet he covered her hand with his, the warmth of him seeping through her gloves.

"Oh, Michael," she began, her voice sounding husky with emotion, "I am sorry." She wished he felt nothing for her.

"I would never dishonor you by doing or saying anything more. I simply wish you to know I am here for you, in whatever capacity you may need. If you are ever lonely and wish to walk, as we did today, I am at your service."

"She doesn't need your service," came an achingly familiar voice cutting through the cold air like an icy blade.

Jenny gasped again as she turned to face her husband. Shocked at seeing him there, she could only stare in disbelief.

She found her voice at last, but it came out in an incredulous whisper. "Simon."

Standing with arms crossed, his legs slightly apart, apparently, he had witnessed a few moments of her discourse with Alder. His expression was grim, and she realized all at once, he was angry with her for being with the viscount.

As if he had the right!

A slight pressure on her fingers had her glancing back to Michael. He frowned down at her, perhaps with worry for her safety. Certainly, Simon looked formidable, but she didn't fear him in the least.

Tugging her hands free, and realizing she should have done that immediately, Jenny turned to face her husband. She fervently wished the viscount wasn't standing quite so close, his shoulder pressing against her own. No doubt they looked guilty without even a hairsbreadth between them.

Uncrossing his arms, Simon held out his hand to her.

She hesitated, causing his eyes to flash in fury. In fact, her husband had never looked more daunting. His dark, windswept hair, as if he'd rushed through the park, brushed the upturned collar of his black travelling coat that swirled around his feet at the slightest breeze. Or was that because he was trembling with rage?

However, it took her only a moment to gain the courage necessary to answer his silent invitation and to disregard the uninviting scowl on his handsome face.

Reaching out, she let him take her hand. As soon as he gently yet strongly drew her close, she felt safe. He was back, he had come to claim her, and her heart would be whole once more.

"Here now, Lindsey, the lady and I were merely—"

"The lady is my wife, and I will thank you to remember that." Simon spoke without lifting his gaze from hers.

Without bidding Alder good day, Simon turned and started toward his waiting carriage, practically dragging Jenny along due to the length of his stride. She dared not glance back at the viscount, lest it further madden her husband.

Yes, Simon was positively rigid, and yes, she felt intimidated by his manner. However, he had returned and everything would be set to rights. Of that, she felt as certain as she knew one and one made two.

Once seated in the carriage for the short ride back to their townhouse, he remained stoically silent, watching her. She supposed a declaration of love after coming across her practically in the arms of another man was too much to hope for. Yet, her joy felt boundless.

Simon's very presence seemed a miracle! And in all of London, he should discover her at the Serpentine was even more of a miraculous event.

"How did you find me?"

"To my good fortune, you had told your mother where you were heading, although not with whom."

She wished his words didn't cause an immediate blush to creep onto her face, yet she could feel it. No doubt, she looked as guilty as the mythological Pandora peeking in the cursed box.

"I thought you had no feelings for Alder," he ground out the name. "The man who callously broke faith with you last year!"

"I don't," Jenny began, hardly believing they were having such a ridiculous conversation. His harsh tone was bordering on argumentative.

"That's not what it looked like while I stood there. You were gazing up at him with a mooning expression and, dammit, he was holding both your hands. In public!"

"A mooning expression. Are you mad?"

"I am most certainly not." His tone was like ice.

Exasperated, she raised her own voice a notch. "I haven't seen you in months. You could have been off doing anything with anybody, and you are going to argue with me over standing with Lord Alder in plain sight?"

He folded his arms again, looking thunderous. "You are not using his first name now, I hear."

The carriage rocked to a stop and without waiting for his assistance or the footman's, Jenny wrenched the carriage handle up and jerked the door open. Without the folding step, she had to jump down onto the pavement.

"You are being insufferable!" she said over her shoulder, stomping up the steps to their townhouse. Binkley had the door open for her before she even lifted her hand.

Not hesitating, she walked directly past the butler and up the stairs to the room she had had to herself for such a long time. She needed a moment to calm her temper for this was not the homecoming she'd envisioned. That they were starting like this was absurd.

However, without a pause, Simon was right behind her. As she entered her chamber, he was at her back propelling her into the room in order to shut the door behind them. And lock it.

"If you thought to keep me out while you contemplated your next meeting with *Michael*, you may think again."

Involuntarily, she glanced to her writing desk where she had penned a response to Alder's invitation that had led her to the Serpentine stroll.

"Dammit!" Simon exclaimed, before slamming his fist into his open palm, making her jump.

If he hoped to frighten her, however, he had failed.

"Stop it!" Jenny was half ready to weep and half infuriated.

Stripping off her gloves, she tossed them onto the bed before tugging at her hat pin and throwing her hat toward the dresser. Lastly, she unbuttoned her wool coat that normally Binkley or her maid would have handled.

Simon did the same, removing his great black overcoat. Then as if they were chivalrous knights preparing for battle, they both draped their garments over chairs and faced each other once again.

"What were you doing away so long and with whom?" Jenny asked, wishing she could keep the high thread of jealousy and uncertainty from her voice.

"I spent my time with Doctor Holtzenhelm, a squat, balding German with nose hair, whom I never once fancied tupping."

The image deflated her suspicions at once and even brought a sideways smile to her lips. After all, if it were a sexual encounter he'd been after, he could have stayed in England and had her.

"Can you say the same?" Simon asked.

Caught off guard by the question, she didn't respond for a moment, then hands on hips, she answered him.

"I assure you I spent absolutely no time with a short German doctor, balding or otherwise."

"I mean, were *you* with someone you fancied?"

Rolling her eyes, she crossed her arms. Oddly, she had not taken Simon Devere for the jealous type since he'd forced her to go to London, buy gowns, and attend a Season by herself, all after taking her for his wife and then abandoning her.

"I have been to countless dinner parties, and I've had men blatantly peer down my décolletage. I've stood around the edges of too many balls to count and watched couples dance, and I have turned down a lifetime's worth of dance requests. And during all that, I never once wanted to experience a good tupping with any one of the many men I've encountered."

He took a step forward. "Who looked down your décolletage? I'll kill him."

Was he even listening to her? She remembered the night Ned had humiliated her. Simon would have more to deal with once the *ton* knew he had returned. Rumors of his mental capacity were still dancing across the tongues of many.

"Honestly, that is not important. Shall we start over? Let me but change into a lighter weight gown and we'll have tea. I'll come down to the drawing room."

Needing to get out of the damnably heavy wool dress, Jenny was also desperate to get off her feet.

"I don't want to drink blasted tea with you, and I won't be dismissed from this chamber like a servant.

CHAPTER TWENTY-NINE

Jenny was sure her mouth formed a perfect O of surprise. "I didn't mean—"

Simon's actions interrupted her words as he reached her in two swift steps. "Just tell me, Jenny. Am I too late?"

Shocked by the question and even more so by the haunted look in his eyes, she shook her head in response.

"Of course not. Whatever can you mean by asking me that?"

He lifted his hands to her shoulders. "I had to go away to get help, but I fear I was gone too long. You are positively glowing with happiness after your outing with Alder. Have you given your affections to him?"

Sweet Mother Mary!

"Silly man. Alder means nothing to me. I am glowing with happiness at your return and for other reasons. There is much to tell you."

Looking mollified by her response, he took hold of her chin between his fingertips.

"And I want to hear everything." Lowering his mouth to hers, he spoke against her lips. "Later."

Claiming her mouth, Simon took it tenderly at first, but their passion caught hold like a flame to a dry wick. Thrusting his tongue between her parted lips, he encircled her with his arms, resting his hands low on her hips to pull her body against his.

Relishing the feel of him, Jenny couldn't resist pressing her full breasts against his chest and tilting her hips toward him. Grabbing his hair with both her hands, she held his head in place and let him ravish her mouth.

Quickly, it became insufficient for either of them. Drawing her to the bed, he made her sit before he bent down to remove her walking boots. Reaching up under her skirts, Simon unhooked and peeled down her stockings.

Lifting each foot for him, she let him slide the silken hose off her ankles, her skin raising in goosebumps where his fingers trailed down the skin of her thighs. When her stockings were lying on the floor, she watched as Simon removed his Hessians. In another minute, he had stripped off everything except his trousers.

Standing before her now, he undid the buttons of his fall and stepped out of his pants. He was wearing nothing underneath, and she was treated to the mouthwatering sight of her virile husband in full glory. It left her giddy with arousal. It had been so very long.

She no longer needed the tips of *Aristotle's Masterpiece* to know what would happen next and how best to please him. However, there was one small piece of information he did not yet have.

"Turn over, please," he said, his voice thick with desire.

She complied, kneeling upon the bed and giving him access to her buttons, the long line of them that had him swearing before he'd finished undoing half.

"I'm sorely tempted to destroy this gown," Simon muttered.

"No," she pleaded. "I like it, and it was quite costly."

"Because of the former and not the latter, I shall persist," he grumbled. "And also, because I do not intend to begin our reunion by simply tossing your skirts over your head, although I promise you, we would both thoroughly enjoy that, as well."

Blushing, she thought she might ask him to do precisely that. Next time. It sounded wicked, even for a married couple, and she wanted to experience everything with him.

As soon as Simon could open her gown wide enough, he slid it off her shoulders and down her torso to pool at her hips. Without turning her, he reached around her, using his large palms to cup her breasts through the layers that remained, kissing her neck as he did.

"*Zounds!* I can see why someone was looking at your breasts, sweetheart. I don't remember them being so bountiful. I have indeed been away too long."

Jenny remained silent. He would discover her secret soon enough. And she couldn't wait to be stretched out bare skinned before him, for her excitement seemed even swifter and stronger than usual, causing a pleasant but insistent throbbing between her legs. One only her husband could satiate.

Unlacing her corset, Simon removed it and peeled the shift from her shoulders. Turning, she lay on her back and lifted her bottom, giving him access to ease the many garments over her hips and down her legs.

Tossing these behind them onto the floor, he feasted his gaze upon her naked body, his scrutiny taking in her thighs and her stomach and her breasts. He frowned at her slightly thickened figure and luscious curves.

She saw the moment he realized her condition, for his eyes widened before his gaze flew to hers.

"You carry our child?" His voice was an incredulous and hopeful whisper.

Feeling the tears prick her eyes, Jenny could only nod, amazed to see her husband's eyes also fill with emotion.

"Over three months along," he said with wonder, stretching out beside her and lightly tracing a circle around the small roundness of her belly.

"How do you feel?"

Jenny was tempted to tell him the woes of her nausea, but instead, spilled out what was truly surging through her.

"I *feel* if you don't touch my breasts immediately and kiss me, then slide inside me and ease the ache, I shall scream."

The grin that spread across his face served to increase her anticipation.

"Say please, Genevieve," he demanded, lowering his head so his lips were hovering over one rosy nipple. At the same time, his hand stroked down toward the soft hair at the apex of her thighs where the curls were already dampened with her desire.

"Please," she murmured.

He suckled her breast and then the other one, all the while letting his fingers strum a heavenly chord where her ache was most intense. Her body raised to meet his hand, needing more.

"We'll go easy," he said, then nipped at her breast before licking over the tingling area, making her moan.

"Don't you dare go easy." Her voice was thick with desire.

"Dear wife," he replied in a teasing tone.

"Dear husband." She pulled him close.

As he slid inside her, she sighed in bliss.

UNFORTUNATELY, NOT MANY MOMENTS later, they lay entangled in each other's arms, already spent but only temporarily satisfied. Simon knew it wouldn't be long before they were engaging in the act again, more slowly, more tenderly. She'd been right, they'd mated like wild rutting animals, and it had been glorious.

"That was precisely what I needed," Jenny said, her eyes closed, appearing entirely worn out.

Simon chuckled. "Thank goodness I arrived in time." Then he sobered.

"I did arrive in time, didn't I? I could have lost you." He stroked her soft shoulder, almost unable to believe she was there beside him. Had she any idea how frightened he'd been seeing her with another man, gazing at Alder, touching him?

Without opening her eyes, Jenny shook her head.

"No, it was I who thought I had lost you."

"I went away to save us," he promised. "To try to give us a normal marriage."

Her eyes slid open, and she rolled onto her side to face him. "Did you succeed?"

Brushing a strand of her hair behind his wife's ear, Simon considered her question.

"I believe I did. Nothing is assured, of course, but I have been successful for many nights through many dreams."

Her plump breasts caught his eye, and he dropped his hand to caress them with the back of his knuckles, watching as her nipples puckered. Then he lowered his palm to her stomach.

"Now there is the baby to consider."

Her eyes sparkled. "Yes. Are you pleased?"

That was putting it far too mildly.

"I am over the moon, yes." *Except for the added worry*. He would hide nothing from her. "However, knowing there will be two lives beside me in bed does not ease my mind."

He watched her eyes darken, and then she sat up.

Gazing down at him, her earnestness was etched in her sweet face.

"I ask you not to leave me again. Not to leave us!" Protectively, she covered her bare stomach with both hands.

Simon reached for her and pulled her to his chest.

"I have no intention of it." His hand smoothed up and down her back, relishing the texture of her satiny skin.

"The *ton* has not been kind," she confessed.

He had figured as much. "I don't care what they say about me."

Her silence alerted him that there was something more.

"Tell me." Then it dawned on him. "Were they speaking of you?

He felt her nod. That they would attack her in his absence caused needles of anger to prickle his skin.

"Is there anything I can do?"

She shook her head. "I don't believe so. Before you returned, I had determined to enter my confinement early. My last social event ended with my fleeing the Chantel-Weiss's dining room and being ill in their water closet."

He would have chuckled if she hadn't sounded close to tears. He was only sorry he hadn't been there to support her.

"I'm truly sorry."

"It wasn't only that. Cousin Ned was there, and he humiliated me in front of everyone at the table."

The prickling he'd felt became blades of fury. How dare the man? Ned was her family!

"He told everyone how good I am with . . . with mathematics." Her voice broke.

"How good you are with . . ." As his anger ebbed, Simon struggled not to laugh. He must be missing the insult.

"Aren't your abilities something of which you should be exceedingly proud? I know I am."

"It was the way he said it and how he portrayed me as such an oddity. And worse, he mentioned how I was 'servicing' you and others in the village, leaving it unclear at first what services I was providing."

Now he took insult. "I'll flay him alive." At that moment, holding his soft, voluptuous wife in his arms, he could do it, too. He would gladly punish anyone who hurt her.

"I must confess, dearest husband, I, too, am concerned about the nighttime, now that I'm *enceinte*."

The air left his lungs. Her mercurial changes of topic were entirely new. That was unbalancing him enough. Yet, her concern on behalf of their baby because of him came so unexpectedly and mirrored his own fears, he didn't know what to say. Would she banish him from her room? Before he could even prove he was healed?

Maybe it was for the best. What if he lost control despite what Holtzenhelm had taught him?

JENNY FELT HIM HOLD his breath for a moment, and then he relaxed. Almost, she wished she hadn't voiced her fears. Yet, she'd had to. She could no longer blithely put herself in danger for fear he might hurt the life she carried. What would happen later that night, she could only wonder?

As it turned out, Jenny would never have guessed her husband's outlandish solution, for it was beyond the pale in many respects. Simon decided the admiral would remain in their room on a cot for the entire night

"Wouldn't a dog at the end of your bed be preferable, my lord?" Binkley intoned, his face deadpan at his important yet embarrassing position.

Jenny would rather have had a dog, too. Or her lady's maid, but Simon reminded her of the last time he'd attacked her, and a woman might not be strong enough to stop him.

Thus, it was after they retired for the evening and had concluded another long and delicious bout of lovemaking conducted far more languidly than their earlier encounter, Simon admitted Binkley to their chamber.

Jenny was under the covers in her night gown with a robe draped over her shoulders, sitting up to watch the proceedings. Simon padded to the door in his drawers and a dressing gown and admitted the butler, whom she assumed had been waiting in the hallway. *How mortifying!*

Earlier, while they'd dined, a cot had been brought in and put under the window where normally two chairs and a small table rested.

Jenny nearly laughed at the admiral's sour expression. Simon had insisted the man be comfortable and dress for sleep, thus Binkley paraded in with a nightcap on his balding head, a full-length night dress, and slippers that poked out from under.

"Nice cap," Simon said as the butler got settled.

"Thank you, my lord."

Simon climbed back into bed as Binkley turned down the oil lamps and then crawled into his cot by the light of the moon.

After a few minutes of silence during which everyone seemed to be trying to stay as quiet as possible, Jenny said, "This is the strangest night of my life."

Simon chuckled, rolling onto his side and punching his pillow into shape.

"For me as well, my lady." Binkley wriggled and his cot squeaked. "Good night to both of you."

"Let us hope," Simon muttered. "And then this peculiar arrangement can end as soon as possible."

WHEN JENNY AWAKENED THE next morning, both men were still sound asleep. The realization that nothing untoward had occurred filled her with pure happiness.

Simon was on his back, snoring slightly but appearing utterly peaceful.

Glancing at their butler, she tamped down an insistent snicker that threatened to erupt at the sight. Binkley was hanging off the side of the cot, one arm and one leg draped to the floor, and his head lolled to the side. One bony shoulder was exposed where his nightgown had slipped down, and his nightcap had popped off completely.

Could she get out of bed to use the water closet and the bathroom? She would have to tiptoe across the room past the admiral. No doubt Binkley, who had been instructed not to leave until one of them arose for the day, would welcome them getting up so he could attend to his morning duties.

Slipping out of bed, Jenny made it out of the room with both men still sleeping. Perhaps a dog would be more useful.

CHAPTER THIRTY

Simon found his lovely wife in the dining room sipping tea and munching on a slice of toast. He had never felt more grateful in his life.

Grinning at her as she looked up from the newspaper, he came to a halt and opened his arms to her. Her face broke into a broad smile, and she rose and ran to him.

After holding her close, he leaned back to look down into her lovely face.

"You seemed to sleep quite peacefully," she said.

He nodded, his throat closed with emotion. Coughing slightly, he said, "I did."

"Did you have a bad dream?" Her eyes were wide with concern.

"I did." Regardless, he couldn't stop his smile from reappearing.

She frowned. "Then why are you grinning like the village idiot?"

"Because I knew it for what it was, and I didn't let it provoke me to violence."

Shaking her head with wonder, Jenny reached up and touched his cheek.

"The time apart was worth it for this, for the rest of our lives."

"I think so." Should he explain about the guilt that had been gnawing at him, causing the violent beast that came out in his dreams? He thought not.

"Sit down, wife. Let me wait on you. Would you like more tea?"

The sound of her laughter was like the biblical milk and honey, nourishing his soul. She sat and patted the chair next to her.

"Are you waiting on me because poor Binkley is sleeping still?"

Helping himself to a plate of hot breakfast from the sideboard, Simon took the proffered seat beside her.

"I roused him with a swift kick to his side. He is rather like a hound, after all."

She giggled softly. "No, he is a dear to put up with us. But your idea was quite brilliant. I did feel more at ease having him there."

"And there he shall remain, at least for a little while."

Her nodding acquiescence heartened him. They would make this work.

"Is that all you're eating? Don't you need to start eating for two?"

"Gracious, no," she said. "If I did, I would be as large as a horse by the time our child came along."

"So, an autumn boy." He imagined a son with Jenny's chestnut-colored hair and soft brown eyes.

"Or girl," she reminded him.

Yes, a daughter with his wife's intelligence and beauty. Good lord, he'd have to battle the young bucks off with a stick. At the moment, however, it was simply the two of them, and he could ask for nothing more.

"Shall we start fighting over the name now?" he teased her.

Jenny laughed again, and Simon was delighted with how her eyes sparkled at him.

"Why don't we simply pretend we've had the fight and I've already won?"

"That sounds like a good idea." She was level-headed and practical, and he could trust Jenny wouldn't name their baby anything outrageous, like Napoleon or Gertha.

Before Simon had finished his eggs and bacon, Binkley entered, looking as if he'd slathered on an extra layer of reserve after the indignities of the night.

"Lord Cambrey to see you, my lord," he said stiffly, eyes straight ahead. "Shall I request he wait in the library?"

"No, show him in."

Wiping his mouth with his serviette, he glanced at Jenny.

"There are no secrets between us, and nothing I discuss with Cam that can't be shared with you."

She seemed to flush with happiness.

Suddenly he wondered, "Have you shared our news with him?"

She shook her head, eyes wide. "Of course I wouldn't, not before telling you."

"Telling him what?" Cambrey asked, entering swiftly and with great familiarity, tapped his thigh in greeting before pulling out a chair and lounging at their table.

"Do sit," Simon said.

With equal sarcasm, Cambrey held his hands up. "No matter how many times you offer, no, I say no. I don't need any nourishment. Don't push that delicious smelling food on me."

Jenny chuckled. "It's good to see you, Lord Cambrey. Please, help yourself to anything at our sideboard. It's a serve-yourself morning. But I will pour you some tea."

"I will say yes to tea, and no to the rest. I ate before I arrived. I'm here to discuss politics."

"Maybe I should leave you gentlemen alone," Jenny said.

Simon shook his head. "I welcome your company, wife. In fact, I don't think I can stand for you to leave the room."

Cambrey laughed at this open declaration. "Indeed, Lady Lindsey, don't leave on my account. I won't be long and the topic affects women and children as much as anyone."

Simon felt Jenny startle beside him. Should he tell his friend about his heir now, or would that embarrass her? He decided to remain silent until she was ready to speak. But he was well-aware to what Cam was referring.

"*Ah,* yes" Simon said. "Lord Ashley's bill."

"Indeed. Ashley is still pushing hard for his Factory Act, and I, for one, support it. I hope you will, too." Cam leaned forward in his chair.

"Of course," Simon agreed. "It's about bloody time."

Jenny set her teacup down. "It will pass this time, I hope. It is only right and just and humane. How can anyone be expected to work longer than ten hours a day? That should include the men, though. After a hard day's work, these women need their husbands at home, and the children need their fathers."

Cam smiled. "We should ask your countess to come speak before the ministers."

The two men laughed, but Jenny was adamant. "No, thank you. I think I've stepped outside my role quite enough."

"Have you given up bookkeeping then?"

Simon's ears perked up at his friend's question, awaiting her response. Obviously, as Lady Lindsey, she now had no need of working for the Belton townsfolk.

Glancing at him with her unassuming way, she sent him a questioning look.

He reached over and took her hand. "I had rather hoped you would continue to oversee our family ledgers."

She smiled. "I would love to do that, my lord."

"Well, then, now that's settled, I will be off." Cam rose to his feet. "I only wanted to make sure you were going to put in an appearance tomorrow, and I thought I might have to browbeat you into voting yea."

Having attended Parliament many times but only in the visitor's gallery, Simon had often watched his father conduct the business of the nation. This would be his first time taking the Lindsey seat.

"When our queen opens the proceedings, I assure you, I'll be there," he promised. "However, I doubt they'll push for a vote immediately. I'm sure a majority aren't in Town yet."

"True enough, but Ashley will try to use it to his advantage. He's spent the better part of Christmas and the past month visiting every member of the House he can. He would as soon have a vote tomorrow when he's nearly certain of a win.'"

Cam was at the door when it suddenly opened and Maggie stepped into the room.

"Oh," she stopped in her tracks at seeing Lord Cambrey in her path. Her cheeks blushed a pretty rose color.

"Miss Margaret," Cam said at once with a shallow bow.

"Lord Cambrey," she returned with a deeper curtsy. "Have you just arrived? Are you joining us for breakfast?"

"No, my lady, I was on my way out."

"Very well," Maggie said, and strode past him to the sideboard to help herself, keeping her back firmly to him.

"I'll see you out," Simon offered. He was glad for a moment alone to ask his friend if there was anything else he should know about either Alder or Darrow's actions.

"Good day, Lady Lindsey," Cambrey said, bowing to Jenny and offering her most of his usual cheery smile, which she returned. Glancing toward Maggie, he added, "And to you, Miss Margaret."

Simon noted his wife's sister received only a cursory nod from Cam, which she might have returned had she seen it, but she was staring at the choices of cold meat.

She did, however, answer. "Good day to you, Lord Cambrey."

JENNY WATCHED HER HUSBAND leave the room, oblivious to any possible undercurrents of emotions since he hadn't been in Town when she believed she was witnessing a burgeoning romance.

Knowing her flirtatious sister, the whole interaction surprised her.

"I would have expected you to invite Lord Cambrey to eat with us and not take no for an answer."

However, she recalled Cambrey's neutral voice when speaking to Maggie, lacking all the warmth it had held in the previous few minutes of discussion.

Perhaps she had got it wrong, Jenny surmised. It had been weeks since she'd been to a Season's event, and had not heard her sister mention dancing with Cambrey in all that time.

Maggie took a seat across from her with her plate piled high and a slight air of relief. Jenny wouldn't have been surprised if her sister had said, "Thank goodness he's gone."

That message was in every fiber of her being as she visibly relaxed.

"What has happened?" Jenny asked, resuming her seat and pouring more tea.

"About what?" Maggie asked innocently.

"With you and Lord Cambrey, of course."

"I have no idea to what you're referring. What about *me* and Lord Cambrey?" Now her sister was staring at her blankly, leaving Jenny feeling like a gossiping fool.

Jenny frowned. Had she created an association between them entirely in her own head?

"I thought . . . that is, don't you enjoy his company?"

Maggie shrugged and put jam on her toast. "He is nice enough, I suppose. Yet he is certainly no Lord Westing."

"I see." Cambrey had been pushed aside for the more dashing marquess.

"There is nothing to *see*, really, Jenn. I am meeting many gentlemen I like this Season. There is no reason to set my cap for any single one of them now."

Her sister was sounding far too pragmatic for her own good. Jenny laughed.

"Now what is it?" Maggie asked.

"I just realized I was fretting over you sounding practical, when you are saying exactly what I would wish you to say."

She would leave her sister to her own musings and let her find her way. No doubt, Maggie would decide on someone before the fall, and if she didn't, that would be fine, too.

"I CAN'T BELIEVE YOU'RE leaving before the Season's end." Maggie had a perplexed look upon her face as she spoke. Perhaps she hadn't noticed that only she was enjoying the events, along with their mother. Simon had been back for two months, and Jenny was showing enough that she truly should remain confined.

"I want to take long walks, and I can't do that here," Jenny explained.

"Most women only want to lie abed," Eleanor complained, not wanting her sister to leave either.

"Or perhaps they are given no choice," Jenny replied. "Besides, what difference does it make if I'm locked away here or back at Belton?"

Both her sister's faces fell, looking quite sorrowful indeed.

Maggie reached out and touched her arm. "It *does* make a difference. We love you, and your presence is always welcome, even if you are back here at home waiting to hear the details of what's happening with Lady Pomley or Lord Twiggins." Her eyes welled up. "However, I completely understand that is selfish of me. You should do what's best for you. If you feel the need for country air and walks in the field, then that's what you should have."

"Thank you." Jenny did appreciate her support, for it was exceedingly difficult to leave her family in London. Yet that was exactly what she, along with Simon, intended to do.

Eleanor sighed. "I suppose we must get used to being without you, in any case. When we get back to Sheffield, we'll be in our house and you'll be far away in your manor."

"You know you can visit anytime," Jenny assured her. "Besides, it's only a mile from door to door." They all laughed at Eleanor's melodramatic statement.

With Simon taking hold of her arm, Jenny didn't mind one more event of the Season. A more intimate affair than a coming-out ball, this dinner and dance would have only about sixty people, all friends of the hosts. Some, like she and Simon, were married, some were being paired up by the hostess who had been charged with a little matchmaking by the debutante's parents. Maggie would be there, too.

As the host and hostess were good friends of his father's, Simon wanted to attend and take his place in society as the new Earl of Lindsey. Moreover, before returning to Sheffield, he wanted to put to bed any lingering doubts about his competence.

"You are easily the most beautiful woman here," Simon whispered in her ear as they entered the magnificent dining hall, already festive and noisy as people searched for their place cards with the assistance of maids and manservants.

"I am easily the plumpest woman here. Henrietta has had to let this dress out to its utmost." Still, she smiled at her husband, so dapper in black and gray.

Once seated, the host called for quiet and introduced himself and his wife at the other end of the table. The guests were charged with enjoying themselves and "to not bore the others."

Everyone laughed. Jenny was relieved that at this affair, she had been allowed to sit beside Simon and not separated as was common at most events. The married couples were there simply to fill in and provide stability while the unmarried guests were paired up according to some whim of their hostess as to their suitability. Maggie was across from her, seated next to a young man whom Jenny had never seen before.

Picking up her lemonade, which Jenny found kept any queasiness at bay, although that rarely occurred anymore, she took a sip, glancing as she did down the long table. Among the thirty or more couples, her eyes registered Lord Cambrey, who was already deep in conversation with a fair-haired young woman.

She had been wrong on all counts. Cambrey didn't look to be upset or pining for her sister. Glancing across at Maggie, she seemed completely entranced by her partner for the evening.

More's the pity, Jenny thought. They had seemed a likely match.

Her eyes travelled farther and—Neddy! Staring rudely at her. For a moment, her heartbeat seemed to trot with anxiousness. What malice might her cousin get up to this evening? Then Simon laughed at something his neighbor said. At the same time, she felt his warm hand crawl into her lap and rest on her inner thigh. Her pulse sped up in a delightful way.

Her anxiety dissipated instantly. Ned didn't dare speak to her, not with her husband beside her.

As it turned out, her cousin was not bright enough to realize he shouldn't dare. When dinner was finished and the musicians were warming up, Simon left her side briefly to speak with their host in the gentleman's drawing room. Ned must have been awaiting his chance. For no sooner had Simon disappeared between a lady in a gorgeous blue dress and a man in an absurd green suit, than her cousin appeared in front of her.

"Lady Lindsey," he said.

"Ned," she returned, not even bothering for polite formality.

He blanched at her insolence, but Jenny found she didn't care in the least. Something about creating a baby made her less disposed to give a fig about incidental things such as her cousin.

"Your husband has returned."

"How very observant of you."

Ned's expression was dour. "I wanted to offer my belated congratulations on your marriage."

"Really?" She paused, for certainly there was something more.

"Yes, I can't blame you for going after the earl in any way you could," he glanced at her stomach, whose blossoming size could no longer be hidden by the folds of her gown.

That Ned even made mention of her condition, however obliquely, was beyond the pale, but she refused to get worked up. Jenny decided simply to walk away for, clearly, he was going to hurl more insults to soothe his own pride.

Attempting to pass him, she felt his fingers curl around her upper arm.

"Manners of a countess dictate you don't walk away in a huff. We are family, after all."

She tried to yank free of his grasp, but he held fast.

"You forgot we were family when you tried to humiliate me and embarrass my husband at the Chantel-Weiss's gathering."

"A word of advice," Ned said, ignoring her remark at the same time as he stroked his thumb up and down her arm, making her skin quiver with revulsion. "Don't let anger at ending up with Lord *Despair* cause you to grab any offer for a few minutes of happiness. For instance, one hears that Lady L was seen at the Serpentine with Lord A."

Struggling to free herself, she brought her heel down on his boot.

"Oof," Ned expelled a sound of pain but only gripped her harder. "You should comport yourself with a little more dignity."

"As should you! You have a sister to think of. Your actions might reflect badly on her chances when she comes out. Unhand me."

"The lady asked you to unhand her," came Simon's voice. "Yet you have not instantly obeyed her. How dangerously stupid of you!"

CHAPTER THIRTY-ONE

With great haste, Ned dropped his hand from her arm. Simon stepped close to her cousin, chest-to-chest, despite her husband being a good four inches taller. She watched Ned crane his neck to try to look Simon in the eyes and swallow nervously at facing the earl.

"What I cannot understand, Darrow," Simon continued, his voice low, "is why you were touching my wife in the first place. I should call out at dawn to settle this."

Jenny felt a rush of fear. She had no doubt Simon was the better shot and swordsmen, but accidents happened every year. She had no desire to become a widow.

Ned's face went white. "That's illegal, Lindsey, and you know it."

Simon tut-tutted. "Hiding behind a technicality? I could spread your cowardice around and you'd be laughed out of every club in London by midnight."

Ned looked to her for assistance, and she couldn't help rolling her eyes at his suddenly childish appearance. Still, she had no desire for blood to be shed, not over such ridiculous behavior. Better to use the opportunity to teach the man a lesson.

"Does my husband appear to be impaired, mentally or otherwise?"

Ned swallowed again, his nervous glance going between Simon and Jenny.

"No, no, of course not."

Jenny placed her hand through Simon's arm, tugging him back slightly and holding her to him. She felt his muscular body relax.

"Then I suggest instead of spreading rumors, you consider how your connection to the house of Devere might help both you and Maisie. As I said before, your actions might harm your sister's chances during her first Season. However, they also may help, as will the Darrows' new association with the Lindseys. Think on it. Instead of facing certain death at dawn, why don't you consider spreading the story of the return of your brave, intelligent, new cousin-in-law?"

Simon practically snorted, doubting such a truce could happen. Yet Ned looked thoughtful. After all, he had nothing to gain by his animosity and everything to lose.

There was a brief pause.

"Obviously, my dear cousin is absolutely correct. Lord Lindsey, my apologies for any perceived rudeness on my part. I wish you and your countess only the best."

With a deep bow, he disappeared.

Simon looked at her, his eyes wide, a small frown, even his mouth slightly open. "How in the hell did you do that?"

Jenny smiled at him. "I merely appealed to his practical side."

"I vow, wife, you should go to Parliament, not I, for you are a natural diplomat."

"Truthfully, I want to go home to Belton."

"And so we shall. First, however, I'm going to dance with my countess and show her off to everyone."

IT WAS OBVIOUS FROM their first night home things were going to be different.

Before anything else, the staff informed them of Lady Devere's departure to France along with Peter and Alice. Jenny experienced a pang of sadness. Even though the widow had not been any company at all, the children were lively and good fun. With more time together, she knew her fondness for them would have grown into love.

"I hope she will return to visit and bring the children," Jenny declared, looking quite morose.

"I hope she didn't take the silver and family jewels," Simon muttered, and then he went about trying to take his wife's mind off of their absence.

With the house empty, there was no one to mind when they retired early. Except Binkley, who was facing another night on his cot in case the new environment caused any relapse for his lordship.

Simon could see Jenny was exhausted by their voyage from London, and with great restraint, kept his hands off his wife, even when she tried to tempt him. Enfolding her in his arms, he dozed off almost immediately . . .

And awakened in his cell.

At first, he wanted to howl with the unfairness of his life. He had met the perfect woman and fallen in love. How in blue blazes had he ended up recaptured and back in Burma?

Pushing against the floor to bring himself to standing, he felt the soft dirt give beneath his palms. Pliable dirt. That wasn't right. He knew it should be hard as rock. He stood anyway, and quickly, for the longer he lay on the ground, the more chance the rats would begin to bite him. Except there weren't any.

Simon nearly laughed with relief. There were no vermin of any kind. The cell was as clean as any room at Belton. This wasn't real. He knew the imaginary Toby was somewhere in the dream, too, and that sobered him. However, he'd had the nightmare so many times, he knew when to avert his eyes to avoid seeing him at all. And then the jailer came, rattling his keys.

It's not my fault Toby died, nor can I help him now. There is no reason to try to kill the jailor.

And with that realization, Simon awakened, still lying close to his gently snoring wife, her back pressed against his arm.

Feeling blessed, he closed his eyes and drifted back into peaceful sleep.

AS THEY UNDRESSED FOR bed the following night, Simon nuzzled her neck before declaring, "You can start decorating the nursery as soon as you like."

Jenny bit her lip at his words. "That's bad luck, isn't it? Besides, we haven't picked out a room. Where will the nursery be?"

Taking her hands in his, he pulled her against him.

"Your old bedroom will be the nursery, with the child as close to us as a thin door, because you will no longer be needing it."

She couldn't contain the smile that erupted on her face, and his next words only made it widen.

"I'm hoping, dear wife, that we can dispense with Binkley at our feet. Shall we do so tonight?" He cradled her face in his hands.

Not hesitating a moment, Jenny nodded. "Yes, absolutely, I think we should."

They sealed their new arrangement with a kiss, after which he gestured toward the windows where the butler's cot was conspicuously absent. She clapped her hands in delight.

"It will be especially welcome not to have to constrain our lovemaking to merely once before we sleep," Simon said as he finished unbuttoning her dress and slid it from her shoulders, then he turned her in his arms.

"Sometimes, I awaken in the night and long to sink into you, only to realize Binkley is snoring in the corner of the room."

Jenny giggled, causing him to reach down and grab her buttocks with both hands, squeezing and kneading them with strong fingers.

"I can't pull you against me tightly anymore," he realized.

Jenny sighed softly. "My belly is becoming an impediment."

"Nonsense, it simply means we have to become more creative in our endeavors. Right now, we need to remove our clothing and quickly. I must have better access to that luscious body of yours."

She felt herself blush from head to toe but acquiesced, allowing him to remove her undergarments as hastily as possible. At this stage of her pregnancy, she was finding herself particularly heated and throbbing in all the right places.

Why, Simon barely had to look at her and she felt dampness between her thighs. Was that normal? Normal or not, her appetite for her husband was nearly insatiable. Jenny thanked her lucky stars Simon had been strong enough to leave her and get treatment. She was even more thankful he'd returned when he had.

"Why are you grinning like that?" he asked, pulling her onto the bed and immediately lowering his mouth to her ripe rosy nipple, not waiting for a reply.

"No more Binkley," she murmured, arching to meet his wicked tongue and teeth.

Raising his head, he looked at her.

"Your lips are parted like a wanton, your hair is flowing around you, you are stark naked, your body round and bountiful, and your eyes are glazed with passion. That is to say, you are a goddess, exactly how I want you. Yet you are thinking of Binkley?"

She laughed, unable to help her throaty tone, laced with desire.

"No, husband. I am *not* thinking of Binkley. For God's sake, touch me again. Touch me everywhere. But especially here."

She brushed the moisture-laden curls below her blossoming stomach. "Please," she added.

"With pleasure." Simon took her nipple into his mouth again while his hand displaced hers to stroke her already-swollen flesh.

Moaning, she closed her eyes, unable to think. She would spend fast and then do so again after he penetrated her, sometimes even more than twice. As he gently flicked her sensitive nub precisely where she pulsed the hardest, Jenny felt as if a dam burst within her.

"Yes," she cried, grasping at the sheets while her hips rose from the bed. "Yesss."

Her climax caused every muscle in her body to coil and then release. When her body seemed to melt back onto the coverlet, she let out a satisfied sound.

"I needed that."

"I hope you are not yet satisfied," Simon said, his tone a little gruff, "for I am rather in *need* myself."

Rolling to her side as she'd learned was most comfortable, she pressed back against Simon until he eased his yard into her heated passage.

"Are you comfortable?" he asked, still moving gently.

"I'm not complaining," she said. "Not to sound too pragmatic, but any way we can accomplish this is fine."

That caused him to chuckle and nearly unseat himself.

"You are priceless." Kissing her neck, he set to bringing them both to release.

"SOMEONE HAS TAKEN UP residence at the hall," Jenny exclaimed after bursting into the library where her dear husband sat working.

She had just returned from one of the rare walks on which Simon hadn't accompanied her, as Cam had sent papers from London with Parliamentary business. Simon would be leaving again shortly to listen to debates and to vote. She wasn't thrilled at the prospect but accepted it was her husband's duty. After all, this time next year, they would both remain in London for the duration of the Parliamentary session, and she counted her blessings he'd left London for her sake and that of their unborn child.

Standing quickly at her entrance, Simon scattered papers across the table.

"Don't rush about like that," he ordered. "Did you run all the way back here and dash up the stairs?"

"Perhaps," she allowed, taking a seat demurely on the sofa where she'd once read books to Maude's children. She missed them still. Soon, however, she would have her own child to whom she could read.

"Why are you smiling?" Simon asked, coming to sit beside her. "Is it because of the hall's occupant?"

"Oh, the hall! I'd already forgotten."

"Dear wife," Simon said, clasping her chin and making her look at him. "I must say that is happening more and more. The larger your stomach, I fear the smaller your brain." Then he laughed until she wrenched her chin free. And still he laughed, reclining on the sofa and closing his eyes as he did.

"It's not funny," she said, feeling quite annoyed with him. She knew her faculties weren't quite as sharp as prior to becoming *in the family way*, but he needn't rub it in as if she were no more than a brainless sheep.

He wiped at his eyes. "It is, though. I'm sorry to have been blunt, but you came in here all excited about Jonling Hall and then two seconds later you were sitting there with a faraway empty look upon your sweet face, all thoughts of it forgotten.

"Humph!" She crossed her arms and rested them on her bulging stomach. "I was only thinking of sitting in this library reading to our own children someday."

That sobered him.

"I cannot wait to see it. You will be a splendid mother. Speaking of which, we should find the best *accoucheur* in all of England and get him here at once."

"*Him?* What if I find a midwife? In fact, I know of one already. She is the wife of the baker whose accounts I used to balance."

"A baker's wife to deliver my child?"

She nearly laughed at her husband's shocked expression.

"I much prefer the notion of Emily to some strange man. Only think how awkward that will be, especially with you threatening him with bodily harm every time he so much as looks at me. Besides, Emily has had seven of her own children."

He appeared mollified but still asked, "And who delivered her seven, that's what I want to know?"

"As far as I know, she did it with no more help than that of her husband. Perhaps you would like to assist me?"

Simon glanced away. "I think Emily will do fine. Now tell me who moved in to the hall."

She couldn't contain her laughter at herself. "Well, I don't know. There was a carriage in the drive and smoke coming from the main chimney. I came straight home to tell you."

A frown appeared on her husband's handsome brow. "I think I will send word first, welcoming our new neighbor and inviting him—"

"Or her," Jenny reminded him.

"Or her to the manor for a light luncheon. We can hardly show up on their doorstep."

"No, you're right, of course." She still felt the mortification of that moment with Ned. "Yet it wouldn't be entirely out of line to leave a calling card and expect an immediate response, since it was your family's residence."

"True, but I'd rather have this stranger come here than blindly enter that house without any *reconnaissance*."

"You sound like a soldier."

He shrugged.

"Well, all right then," Jenny agreed. "Send Binkley with the invitation at once. I'm extremely curious."

He gave her such a loving smile, he took her breath away.

"Yes, wife. I will. Immediately at your command. And may I say you sound like a general?"

As it was, they didn't even have to wait a day to hear back, for an hour after Binkley delivered the message to the hall, a message came back inviting them to dine the next evening.

"Let me see it," Jenny begged, reaching for the missive Simon held.

He let her snatch it from him excitedly.

"A man's handwriting, to be sure," she surmised. "Not too fussy, rather willy-nilly, in fact. Still, quite legible. And signed as J. Turner."

Simon poured himself a drink.

"A very solid surname," Jenny said.

Her husband shrugged. "It means nothing to me."

"I guess we shall have to wait until tomorrow." Sometimes being patient was not easy, but Jenny had weathered the worst of impatience while in London waiting for Simon. She could certainly handle a few hours until she met this mysterious stranger.

"I wonder if we should refuse?"

Simon's words were like a bucket of cold water poured over her head. Like a child, she experienced the disappointment of a potential outing dashed unexpectedly.

"I know you'd rather this Mr. Turner came here, but I'm sure he can mean us no harm if he's invited us to dine with him."

"Yet a bit high-handed of this stranger to refuse our invitation in lieu of his own."

"Simon, please, may we go?"

He smiled at her and she knew they would.

"You have only to ask anything of me, dear wife, and you know I will grant it."

"That is why we suit so well together." And she dissolved into laughter at his expression of surrender.

CHAPTER THIRTY-TWO

Simon knew Jenny was excited to finally set foot inside Jonling Hall. For his part, though, it brought back crystal-clear memories of Toby and the many times they'd laughed and dined together. He had been like a brother, and for his sake, Simon had gone to Burma, not willing to let his cousin face the dangers alone. *Look how that had turned out!*

Shaking off the cobwebs of sadness, Simon helped Jenny down from their carriage, his tilbury suited perfectly for two. With her hand on his arm, they approached the front door. Clearly the servant had been told to watch for them, for it opened before they reached it.

Simon wished he didn't feel the prickle of unease, bringing his pregnant wife into this once-joyful place while facing down the unknown.

A friendly maid, not a serious butler, greeted them at the door. A sign this Turner, as Simon suspected, was not of the nobility.

"Good evening, my lord," she said curtsying to Simon, "and to you my lady." The maid dropped low for Jenny. "My master wishes you to attend him in the sitting room."

Simon found it hard to swallow past the lump in his throat. How terribly odd to have this strange young lady leading him through the house he knew as well as his own. Moreover, with a jolt of recognition, he realized Maude had left the furnishings. There was the mirror he'd seen Toby check his hair in the last time they'd left for dinner with Simon's father.

And here, as they entered the parlor, was the chair Simon had sprawled on while Toby told him a joke about two horses racing. He'd laughed until his eyes had watered, the way Jenny made him laugh now. Thank God he had Jenny.

Squeezing her hand, more to reassure himself than her, Simon stood in the center of the room as the maid left.

"We should sit," Jenny said.

Simon didn't move. His eyes were fixed on a landscape painting above the fire.

"It's all exactly as it ever was, before Toby's death, from even before Maude came."

Feeling her touch his shoulder gently, he looked down at her, but she was looking toward the door. Turning, Simon realized with a start their host had entered, quietly and without his having noticed.

"You!" Simon exclaimed.

The man came forward, his hands clasped behind his back, and Simon nearly pushed Jenny behind him to protect her.

"I am glad you accepted my invitation, Lord Lindsey," the man greeted with a deep bow. "And your lovely countess, I presume." He bowed to her as well.

"What is the meaning of this?" Simon demanded.

"I don't understand." Jenny turned to him with concern. "Simon, what's wrong?"

"This is the gambler I met at Crocky's," he told her, keeping his eyes on the man's face. "The one who has been playing for my uncle."

"Really!" She turned to the man openly assessing him. He loved her even more for her reaction. Neither fear, nor hysterics.

"It's true, my lady. However, there is more to the story, which is why I bought this house."

"Do tell." Simon didn't like games.

"I mean you and your wife no harm. And now we are neighbors. Will you dine with me?"

Simon nearly dismissed the notion out of hand. However, the man's manners were impeccable so far, and there was no overt threat from him despite the somewhat unsavoriness of his profession and the secretive way he had obtained Jonling Hall.

It was Jenny's quick acquiescing glance, however, that convinced him.

"Very well, Mr. Turner, formerly Mr. Carlyle. We shall dine."

In short order, they were seated at one end of the dining table with Jenny and Simon facing each other and their host at the head.

When they'd each been served a glass of wine and had hare soup in front of them, Simon could wait no longer.

"I do not wish to be rude, but why the subterfuge, why the various aliases? Are you Turner or Carlyle, for I don't like dining with strangers or liars."

Their host nodded. "I am a Turner. Carlyle is my middle name."

"Will you tell us the mystery of how you came to be here?" Jenny's voice and question were far less assertive than his own as befitting a well-mannered countess.

Hoping if he were honest, Turner would follow, Simon added, "In truth, you looked familiar to me in London, although I do not believe we've ever met. Am I wrong?"

"I believe you are seeing a familial resemblance. I am your cousin, the eldest son of James Devere."

Simon felt as if he'd known it all along. Still, the notion this man was Toby's half-brother, now living in his house, struck Simon a blow. Tamping down the instinct to deny the man's words or to feel angry toward him for being alive while Toby was dead, Simon asked the only question he could.

"Did Tobias know about you?"

"No."

"J. Turner," Jenny said. "Are you James, as well."

"Jameson," he said quietly. "My mother is a Turner, and the only way to give some recognition of my sire was for her to name me such."

Simon was still considering what Toby would have thought of having a bastard brother.

"I believe Tobias would have been happy to know you, or at least of you."

"Do you think?" their host asked. "I often wondered. I asked my father to let me meet my half-brother, but he denied me."

"Perhaps to spare Tobias's mother any embarrassment?" Simon considered, as they were acknowledging without saying the man was illegitimate.

"Perhaps. He was happy enough to use me for his gambling, and I tried to help him by keeping Crocky happy. You may not believe it, but the amount the Devere estates paid combined with the amount I won at the tables was about what my father owed."

"I see. And *my* father was aware of this?"

"I don't know. I know Tobias was instructed by your father to send those revenues to help out his brother."

"It seems everyone knew about this debt but me," Simon said, trying not to sound sour.

"You were not the Earl of Lindsey at the time, and Tobias only knew he was obeying the earl and helping out his father at the same time."

"What will your father do now?" Jenny asked, having stayed quiet.

Simon watched as this stranger turned to Jenny, and something in his profile looked so like Toby, it softened him toward Jameson Turner.

"My father will continue in the impoverished state he is in, I suppose, but at least the possibility of one of Crocky's men seeking him out and breaking his legs, or worse, has been removed. Thanks to you, Countess."

Jenny blushed prettily.

Simon steered the conversation back to the questions he still had. "You must have already contacted my uncle before I did, for he never even sent a return letter when I informed him of the cessation of his gambling funds."

"I did. Better I should bear the brunt of his annoyance than you."

Hmm. Considering where he now sat and with whom he dined, Simon wondered if he had a spy in his midst and to whom Jameson owed his allegiance.

"What about this house? I understand you bought it directly after my father died, right out from under Tobias."

"No," Jameson shook his head. "Not out from under him but to save it *for* him. Unfortunately, my half-brother had poured all his assets into helping our father, who is, I'm sorry to say, a bottomless drain. Money slips through his fingers like water."

"Yes, I have seen his residence at South Wingfield. The scarcity of funds is obvious."

Jameson nodded. "I heard my father suggested Lady Devere sell the hall while her husband was away. No doubt, he hoped she would give him the money from the sale."

"How would you have heard that, living in London?" Grudgingly, Simon was warming to the fellow.

"I have kept my eyes and ears upon my younger brother always, especially after our father got him involved in the matter with Mr. Keeble. While it was sanctioned by the earl, I didn't think it a good idea, knowing my father as I do. Despite what you think, I tried to contain the situation as best I could. In any case, I would have helped Tobias out when he returned."

He took a sip of wine and then added, "I am saddened he did not, for I had intended to go against my father's wishes and make myself known to my brother. In any case, I could save his house for him by buying it. At least it is still in the family."

"Lady Devere did have some money and was in contact with you," Simon surmised.

"Yes. I made sure she kept it all, for it was her fervent wish to return to France. I advised her to put the rest aside for her children."

"Why, that was quite generous of you," Jenny said. "I am sure it has not been easy to—"

However, as she broke off with a gasp and a strange look came upon her face, they would never hear what she was sure of.

Pushing back his chair, Simon was on his feet and around the table in an instant. "What's wrong?"

"I . . . I'm not sure. I felt—oh, there it is again." She placed her hands over her stomach.

His entire world narrowed down to one woman whose face looked pale and pinched.

"Are you in pain? Right now?"

She said neither yes or no. "I think I want to go home." Her words were a whisper.

Looking to his host, who was standing now, his hands gripping the back of his chair, Simon said, "We came in a tilbury."

The man's brow rose, and he headed for the door. "I'll get my carriage brought around front at once. It's a berlin, quite comfortable."

Just like Toby in his manner, Simon thought, as he pulled his wife's chair out. "Can you stand?"

"Yes, it's gone off a bit now. But, Simon," she began and clenched the hand he held out to her. "It's far too soon."

"I know, my love. I'll send for the baker's wife anyway. Don't worry."

TRUE TO HIS WORD, nearly as soon as Jenny was settled into their bed at home, Emily entered. Simon, who was sitting on the side of the bed having carried her from Jameson's carriage up the front steps and up the main staircase, was still breathing hard and looking rather fierce, no doubt with worry.

He jumped up at the midwife's arrival.

Immediately, the woman brought a calming presence with her as she approached Jenny's side and took her hand.

"What's happening here, young lady? Are you causing a fuss and worrying the earl?" Her tone was warm and caring. Then she glanced at Simon, taking in his demeanor. "My lord, would you mind removing yourself to the chair over there?"

At her husband's querying look, Jenny nodded, smiling as he stroked her forehead before taking the seat by the window.

"I felt a strange sensation I hadn't felt before."

The woman nodded. "May I touch you?"

"Yes, of course," Jenny said.

"Was it here?" she asked, resting a hand on Jenny's gown over her rounded belly. "Did it feel as if your stomach tightened and hardened?"

"Yes, exactly." Relieved Emily knew exactly what had happened, she nearly cried.

"Is she all right?" Simon asked, before Jenny could say more.

"I believe so," the midwife said. "This is not the start of labor. It's only false contractions that make your body ready for the real event. It can certainly be frightening at first. But it wasn't painful, was it?"

Jenny considered. "No, I don't think it truly hurt. It was uncomfortable and frightening. I was about to enjoy my soup," she added, realizing she was hungry. "And I'm sure I smelled roast woodcocks for our supper."

Hearing Simon laugh, she looked at him.

"I'm sorry to have spoiled our dinner with Mr. Turner. He seems like a nice man. Perhaps you should head back there and finish the meal."

"I'm not leaving you. That's final." Then he ordered the maid waiting patiently in the corner to go get some soup for her mistress.

"And bread," Jenny added. "And if we have some cold chicken, that would be lovely. But bring the soup first please. I'm famished."

"I, FOR ONE, AM pleased to have him as our neighbor," Jenny told him later that night when they were in bed. Yawning broadly, she closed her eyes.

"I'll reserve judgment for now," Simon told her, cradling her close with her back against his chest.

"Did you remember to send word that everything was fine?"

He nuzzled the top of her head. "I did. Stop worrying about a thing. Sleep well, my love."

In a few moments, holding his warm, relaxed wife, Simon felt the tug of sleep draw him down. It seemed as if almost instantly, Simon awakened in his cell in Burma. Instead of feeling an ounce of dread, however, he closed his eyes once more and said, "Enough."

When he opened them again, he was home.

EPILOGUE

"Y̶ou were right," Simon told her.

"Say that again, my lord."

"Why? Can't you hear me over the squalling baby?"

Jenny grinned. "Your son is lusty with life, *not* squalling. And I can hear you perfectly. I just want you to say it again."

"You. Were. Right."

"I accept your statement, but about what?"

"Emily. She is better than any *accoucheur* I could have hired."

In truth, the rather scary event of childbirth and afterbirth had gone quite smoothly if painfully. After months of fretting over it, knowing the many stories of both joy and tragedy, Jenny had been delivered of a beautiful boy.

"And she brought fresh clove buns." Reaching over to the basket of baked goods beside the bed, she helped herself to another as Maggie came back into the room. "I doubt any mid-husband, no matter how competent, would have thought to bring the baker's best goods."

Maggie helped herself to a bun as well. "I doubt an *accoucheur* would be married to a baker anyway," she said, spraying a few crumbs onto the counterpane. "By the way, the admiral has taken Emily home. She said she would stop by again tomorrow to help you with . . . *um* . . . ." Her eyes widened and she glanced at Simon.

"With what?" he asked.

She looked back at Jenny and gestured her head from the baby to her sister's chest. "With feeding the little one there. Emily said you didn't seem the type to have a wet nurse."

"Of course I won't. Why would I let my own milk go to waste?"

"So practical," remarked Simon, and they grinned at each other.

"Please sit, Mags. Where's Mummy?"

"She'll be back shortly," she promised, easing herself onto the edge of Simon and Jenny's bed. "She and Eleanor are still settling in."

"I'm glad you made it in time, but sorry you had to cut your Season short again."

Maggie shrugged and look unbothered. "No ball or duke is as important as you."

"You can still go back," Simon offered. "The townhouse awaits you."

"I appreciate that. However, I believe I am done for this year."

Jenny shot her husband a glance.

Maggie continued, "The Season is ending in a week or two. I see no reason to drag out the agony. There might have been an offer coming, but not one I would have accepted."

Reaching out, Jenny touched her sister's hand.

"No," Maggie said, "don't get all sympathetic on me. I'm perfectly fine. What a dear little boy. If only he wasn't bawling quite so loudly. It's hard to hear oneself think."

Laughing, Jenny looked at her husband. "Perhaps we should call him Lionel, for he roars like a lion."

"I like it," Simon agreed.

"Here let me hold him," Maggie said.

Jenny let her sister scoop him from her lap and stroll about the room with him, swaying him to and fro. He continued to yell.

"Hmm," Maggie considered. Then she slipped her smallest finger into the young heir's open mouth. He closed it firmly and there was silence.

"Dear God in Heaven!" Simon marveled.

"How did you know?" Jenny asked.

"I saw Mummy do it with Eleanor. You were busy at the time doing something useful, I'm sure. My goodness, he's got quite a grip."

"Let me try," Jenny said, popping the last of the sticky bun into her mouth and wiping her fingers on the coverlet.

Maggie returned the baby to his mother.

"If the finger works so well," Jenny considered, "I imagine the breast will work even better."

"Oh my," said Maggie because of the earl's presence.

Jenny wasn't deterred one bit. She was with the three people she loved most in the world. Cradling him in one arm, she lowered her shift, giving her son access to her left nipple.

"Ouch," she exclaimed at once.

Simon leaped from his chair in concern, then stopped, perhaps self-conscious to be standing beside his sister-in-law, both watching his wife who was half bare-breasted.

"Well," Maggie said. "I'll see about getting you some tea."

With that, she left the new parents to the wonder of their son.

"I could swear he has teeth," Jenny muttered.

Simon sat on the bed gazing down happily at the vignette of mother and son. "To think where I was a year ago, I could never have imagined this life with you."

"To think where I was a year ago, my lord, I could say the same."

"This is no dream?" he asked, reaching out and stroking her face.

She beamed at him. "Oh yes, my love, I think this is an exquisite dream, one from which we shall never awaken."

ABOUT THE AUTHOR

USA Today bestselling author Sydney Jane Baily writes historical romance set in Victorian England, late 19th-century America, the Middle Ages, the Georgian era, and the Regency period. She believes in happily-ever-after stories for an already-challenging world with engaging characters and attention to period detail.

Born and raised in California, she has traveled the world, spending a lot of exceedingly happy time in the U.K. where her extended family resides, eating fish and chips, drinking shandies, and snacking on Maltesers and Cadbury bars. Sydney currently lives in New England with her family—human, canine, and feline.

You can learn more about her books and contact her via her website at SydneyJaneBaily.com.

Printed in Great Britain
by Amazon